THE MAID OF
SHERWOOD
FOREST

A McQUIVEY'S COSTUME SHOP ROMANCE

THE MAID OF
SHERWOOD
*F*OREST

A McQuivey's Costume Shop Romance

PROPER ROMANCE

SIAN ANN BESSEY

SHADOW
MOUNTAIN
PUBLISHING

For Tyler Sommer,

who insisted that visiting Sherwood Forest
was a good idea—and then took me there.

Library of Congress Cataloging-in-Publication Data

Names: Bessey, Siân Ann, 1963– author
Title: The maid of Sherwood Forest / Sian Ann Bessey.
Description: Salt Lake City : Shadow Mountain Publishing, 2025. | Series: McQuivey's costume shop romance | Summary: "Mariah Clinton exits a changing room in London's McQuivey's Costume Shop to find herself in twelfth-century Nottingham. Forced to pose as a servant, she inadvertently draws the attention of the legendary Robin Hood with her archery skills. As danger mounts and love ignites, Mariah must choose between returning home or staying in a past where her heart now belongs"—Provided by publisher.
Identifiers: LCCN 2025018511 (print) | LCCN 2025018512 (ebook) | ISBN 9781639934676 trade paperback | ISBN 9781649334886 ebook
Subjects: BISAC: FICTION / Romance / Time Travel | FICTION / Fairy Tales, Folk Tales, Legends & Mythology | LCGFT: Fiction | Romance fiction | Time-travel fiction | Novels
Classification: LCC PS3552.E79495 M35 2025 (print) | LCC PS3552.E79495 (ebook) | DDC 813/.54—dc23/eng/20250523
LC record available at https://lccn.loc.gov/2025018511
LC ebook record available at https://lccn.loc.gov/2025018512

Printed in the United States of America
Publishers Printing

10   9   8   7   6   5   4   3   2   1

CHAPTER 1

London, Present Day

Mariah Clinton raised her bow and arrow, her eyes focused on the distant target. Under calm conditions, the bull's-eye would be almost impossible to miss, but this morning, the light breeze was playing havoc with everyone's scores at the London Archery Club's outdoor range.

Another gust of wind tugged gently at her long chestnut ponytail, and Mariah adjusted her stance fractionally. With her right hand, she pulled back the bowstring to its anchor point, held the arrow in place for three long seconds, and then set it free. The arrow took flight, sailing over the newly mowed grass to pierce the target's black center with a dull thud. She lowered the bow, her lips curving into a satisfied smile.

"Nicely done!"

Mariah swung around. "Hi, Patrick." The club's longtime manager stood behind her. "I didn't know you were here today."

"Ah, you know how it is." Patrick surveyed the busy archery range. "I'm pretty much a permanent fixture here these days."

Patrick's wife had died of an unexpected heart attack eight months earlier. Ever since then, he'd seemed to find it easier to be at the club, surrounded by familiar faces, than to stay in an empty house by himself.

"I understand," she said. "Dad did the same thing when Mum died. His archery mates—you included—were a lifeline for him then."

"That seems so long ago." Patrick's expression turned reflective. "But I seem to remember you were at his side holding his arrows every time he came."

Mariah laughed. "I made a pretty good assistant, didn't I?"

"The best." He cocked his head to one side. "How old were you then? Six? Seven?"

"Seven," she said. "Mum's cancer diagnosis gave us a little more warning than you had with Sandra, but it's never easy."

"No. Never. But you managed all right in the end?"

Mariah recognized his need for reassurance. "We did. It took time, but we muddled through. When other little girls went shopping with their mothers, I went to the archery club with my dad." She grinned. "It was a bit unconventional, but I ended up with the world's best hobby."

"There's not many here who shoot as well as you do."

She smiled. "I was taught by the best."

"That may be, but your dad would be the first to admit that your skill with the bow has surpassed his." Patrick's brows came together. "You really should've gone pro."

Mariah shook her head. This wasn't the first time they'd had this conversation. "I love archery, but I'm not up for a life on the circuit. Besides, I have my job at Ricardo's, and I love that too."

"How's that going?" Patrick asked.

"Great. Busy." Mariah could have added *exhausting* and *frustrating*, but she didn't want to give her father's old friend any more ammunition. "I was really lucky to get the sous-chef position with Chef Heston right out of culinary school."

He grunted. "If you ask me, that Heston fellow was lucky to get you. And if how little I see of you at the range these days is anything to go by, he's working you too hard."

She'd been wise not to tell him anything more about her work, especially since he was right about her long shifts. It had been months since she'd worked anything less than a seventy-hour week. "Well, the good news is I have all day Monday off," she said.

"That's perfect."

She looked at him blankly. Was something happening that day that she'd forgotten about. "Why?"

"Angela Lambert called this morning. She's in charge of the medieval reenactments at Warwick Castle this summer. Some flu bug has hit half her employees, and she's needing replacements for Monday."

"Do they want someone for the archery tournament?"

"Not anymore. I spoke to Mike Bamforth earlier. He said he'd go up for the day to fill that spot."

The spark of hope that had lit Mariah's chest fizzled. Mike was a decent archer. He'd hit the targets, at least.

"Let me guess," she said. "They wanted a man for that position."

"Afraid so. Something about not having armor that would fit a woman."

"Or not wanting a woman to make the other gallant knights look bad."

He conceded her point with a shrug. "There might be some truth to that too."

"I'm glad Mike was available."

"Me too. But they need a couple of women as well."

Mariah gave him a long-suffering look. "To play the damsels in distress?"

Patrick chuckled. "You're exactly the kind of fair maiden knights would fight over."

"I don't think so."

"Are you kidding? Any knight worthy of the title would throw himself on his sword for you."

Mariah rolled her eyes and reached for another arrow. "I'm not spending my first full day off in weeks walking around Warwick Castle in a long gown, pretending to swoon if Mike looks at me twice."

"It might get your foot in the door," Patrick said. "All it would take is someone in charge seeing you doing some target practice."

Mariah nocked the arrow and raised her bow. "Even if I had a chance to shoot, what good would it do? They don't have female archers in their reenactments."

"Change their minds," Patrick said. "It's not like you've never done something like that before." He looked at her expectantly. "Who was it who pestered me into allowing a nine-year-old into the teenagers' class?"

Mariah fought back a smile. It had taken her a month, but she'd finally worn Patrick down over the club's strict age-limit rule. "I'd only be at Warwick Castle one day. I can't do much pestering in that amount of time."

"Have your pitch ready before you go, and then wow them with your mad skills," Patrick said.

She dropped her shoulders, and with the arrow still trapped between her fingers, she lowered her bow. "You really want me to do this, don't you?"

"It would be good for you," he said. "It will get you out of the restaurant and the city for a bit." He paused. "Loneliness and I have become well acquainted over the last few months, and I recognize it in you."

"Patrick, I—"

He raised his hand to stop her. "I know you have friends in the restaurant and here at the club, but you shouldn't be spending all your time at those two places. Not when you're only twenty-three. With your dad remarried and moved away, there's an empty space in your life that needs to be filled."

"And you think I'm going to do that by going to Warwick Castle for one day?"

"Well, no. No exactly. But it's a step in the right direction, isn't it?"

Not really. But Mariah couldn't bring herself to tell him that. "If I do this, will you promise to not bother me again about how I spend my time?"

"I'll do my best."

"Patrick!"

"Hey, it's my job to step in for your dad when it's needed."

"No, it isn't," she said.

He ignored her. "If you can persuade someone at Warwick Castle that lady archers could be the next great attraction there, I'll send in a glowing letter of recommendation for you."

Mariah shook her head in bemusement. How Patrick thought she could fit performing at Warwick Castle into her already over-booked work schedule at Ricardo's, she had no idea, but she couldn't fault him for doing his part to open doors in the archery world for females.

"Fine," she said. "I'll fill in for one of the medieval ladies on Monday."

Patrick beamed. "Great. I'll call Angela to let her know you'll be there."

"Wait," Mariah said. "What about a costume?"

"Oh, that's right. Angela said to have you go to McQuivey's Costume Shop at Pickering Place to pick one up that's your size. If you take the receipt for the rental with you on Monday, Angela will reimburse you the cost."

Mariah narrowed her eyes. "Did you already tell her I'd do it?"

"No," Patrick said. "I told her I thought you *might* do it." And then, with a disconcertingly gratified look, he walked away.

———··✳··———

Two hours later, Mariah found herself following the narrow passageway that led past the old wine merchant's shop, Berry Bros. & Rudd, and into Pickering Place. The small public square was quiet, the sounds of the city muted behind the walls of the tall Georgian

buildings that surrounded the flagstone courtyard. A cat lay doz-
ing in the sun beside a flower planter that stood next to a wooden
bench. The cat looked up as Mariah approached, remaining wary
until Mariah started up the three steps that led to the door of the
building in the corner.

The only indication that the historic building was a costume
shop was the brass plaque hanging on the wall beside the front door
and the two mannequins in the window. Mariah glanced at the
clothing on display and smiled. A burgundy flapper dress complete
with beaded fringe and a WWII navy uniform sporting an impressive array of medals were a far cry from the type of clothing she
needed, but both pieces appeared to be in excellent condition. All
being well, McQuivey's selection of medieval costumes would be
equally impressive.

A bell rang somewhere in the back of the shop as Mariah stepped
inside.

"I'll be right there!" a female voice called, and moments later, a
diminutive older lady appeared around one of the racks of clothing.
Her snow-white hair was pulled up into a tidy bun and was a stark
contrast to the enormous pink flowers on her bright-green dress. The
pink theme continued in the plastic rims of her cat-eye glasses and
her lipstick. "Welcome to McQuivey's Costume Shop," she said with
a smile. "How may I help you?"

"I was told that I might find a medieval gown here," Mariah said.

"Of course. We have several. Did you have any particular style
in mind?"

Mariah eyed the clothing racks helplessly. Her lack of clothes-
shopping experience as a teenager came back to haunt her far more
often than she cared to admit. Facing a full rack of clothing was
almost as intimidating as offering Chef Heston a newly created dish.

"I'm open to your suggestions," she said. "Nothing too elaborate
or constrictive though. I'd like to have full use of my arms so that I
can use a bow and arrow if needed."

"Ah." The shop proprietress cocked her head to one side and studied Mariah more closely. "You are obviously a practical young lady with unusual skills."

Mariah smiled. "I think most people would consider my request very odd, but it's nice of you to view it in such a positive way."

"There's a time and place for all such things." The woman's hazel eyes sparkled. "That's one of the wonders of life."

"Well, I'll keep my fingers crossed that Monday is one of those days," Mariah said.

"Oh, I have no doubt it will be." The proprietress stepped toward a rack at her left. "Come, my dear. We must find you just the right outfit."

Mariah followed her. "Do you own this shop?"

"I do." She was already working her way down the rack, sliding coat hangers along the rod with well-practiced ease. "My late husband and I opened it almost five decades ago, and I've been matching people with costumes ever since." Her fingers paused, and she looked up. "My name's Marigold McQuivey. May I ask yours?"

"Mariah. Mariah Clinton."

Mrs. McQuivey appeared strangely pleased. "Lovely." Her attention returned to the clothing, and moments later, she withdrew a blue velvet gown. "What do you think of this?"

The square neck was lined with lace and a ribbon zigzagged down the back, cinching the fabric, much like a bodice. A narrow gold belt hung low at the waist and long sleeves opened into wide bell shapes, the tips of which almost brushed the floor.

"It's beautiful," Mariah said, "but it might be hard to—"

"I agree." Not waiting to hear more, Mrs. McQuivey slid the hanger back onto the rack. "It's a little too fancy for what you're after." Moments later, she pulled out another hanger. "Now then, this might be just the ticket. It comes from the same era but a different social class."

This costume appeared much more rustic. A white smock with three-quarter-length sleeves lay beneath a pale-green wool bodice and attached skirt.

"This is a kirtle," Mrs. McQuivey said, running her hand over the outer layer. "You'll see the upper part is tied in the front with thin leather strips. The long smock doubles as a blouse and a slip." She pulled a small bag off the top of the hanger. "This contains an apron, hose, and some leather shoes."

"You've thought of everything," Mariah said. "And it looks perfect. As long as everything fits."

"We shall find out soon enough." She draped the costume over her arm and started toward the back of the shop. "There's a changing room in the corner. After you've put everything on, you can come out and show me."

The changing-room door was painted dark green. The brass doorknob gleamed as though it had been recently polished and was etched with a miniature sun, moon, and stars. Mrs. McQuivey held the door open and allowed Mariah to step inside before handing her the clothing.

"Take your time, my dear," she said. "I have plenty to do. I'll come back and join you when you're ready."

"Thank you." Mariah hung the costume on one of the small hooks on the tiny room's whitewashed wall. "It shouldn't take me long."

Mrs. McQuivey offered her an encouraging smile and walked away.

Closing the changing room door, Mariah studied the costume more closely. It didn't have the elegance of the first gown, but in its own simple way, it was just as attractive. She smothered a smile. Her father had run a small fish-and-chip shop. A peasant's dress was right up her alley.

Mariah set her jeans and T-shirt on the bench above her shoes and handbag, then she donned the medieval clothing and looked at herself in the mirror. The costume fit perfectly. Even the shoes were the right size. She pondered her reflection for a moment. Tucking her late mother's silver sixpence pendant beneath the smock, she removed the elastic from around her ponytail and shook her head slightly. Her hair fell in a thick curtain halfway down her back. She paused. Loose hair seemed more in keeping with the costume, but perhaps a plait was more sensible.

It took only a few seconds to twist her hair into a long rope and attach the elastic to the bottom. Then she studied herself in the mirror again. At five feet eight inches, she was taller than many women, but her height came in handy when she was reaching for things in the kitchen or handling a longbow. She'd inherited her chestnut-colored hair, green eyes, and small nose from her mother, but her wide smile was just like her father's.

Running her hands down the crisp linen apron she'd tied around her waist, she turned in a slow circle. This was the right costume. She didn't need Mrs. McQuivey's approval, but she guessed the older lady would be disappointed if she didn't see Mariah wearing it. Reaching for the doorknob, Mariah opened the door and walked out of the changing room.

CHAPTER 2

Nottinghamshire, 1193

The costume shop was gone. Mariah was standing in a vast room with stone walls and a straw-covered wooden floor. Across from her, a fire burned in the largest fireplace she'd ever seen. A pig was roasting on a spit above the flames, and beside it, a caldron steamed. People—too many to count in her dazed state—filled the room, all dressed in medieval garb, all intent on their work.

Mariah took a stumbling step back, instantly hitting her head on the doorframe.

"Ah!" Her cry was instinctive, her fingers finding the tender spot behind her ear. What in the world was going on? And why did her head hurt so much?

"There ya are!" A loud female voice reached her over the clatter of pans and chopping of knives. "It's about time ya showed up."

Mariah stood motionless as a stout middle-aged woman left her place beside a large wooden table and marched across the room toward her. The woman was dressed very much like Mariah was, except that her apron was splattered with stains, her gray hair was covered by a white cloth, and she was wielding a wicked-looking knife.

"'Enry told me th' extra 'elp would be 'ere first thing this mornin'. Why it took ya so long t' get 'ere, I can't imagine."

"I . . . I'm sorry. I didn't know." This had to be a joke. Who on earth was Henry? And where was this place?

"Well, what's done is done." The older woman waved her cleaver in the air. "Yer 'ere now." She leaned forward, eyeing Mariah grimly. "D'ya know yer way around a kitchen?"

"Yes." The answer fell from her lips before she could recall it. There was no way helping at her father's chippy or working as a sous-chef at Ricardo's had prepared her for anything like this.

"I'm right glad t' 'ear it." The woman frowned. "I don' recognize ya from town. What's yer name?"

"Mariah Clinton."

"Marian o' Clifton, ya say? Well, that explains it." Her ire appeared to diminish slightly. "If ya've walked all the way from Clifton, ya must've started right early."

Mariah was suffering from a severe concussion. It was the only possible explanation for this madness. "It's Mariah," she said, unwilling to dwell on the fact that the vision before her had existed—at least in her mind—before she'd hit her head.

"I know. I 'eard ya the first time." The woman swung around. "Ellen, get over 'ere."

A slight servant girl with light-brown hair, who looked to be about fifteen or sixteen years old, hurried across the room to join them.

"Yes, M-Mistress Agatha."

"Marian 'ere can 'elp ya with the peas. I need 'em all shelled afore the church clock strikes the 'our, so there's t' be no idlin' yer time with chatter."

"Yes, M-Mistress Agatha," Ellen repeated. "Come, M-Marian."

Mariah shook her head slightly. "It's—" She broke off as the pain above her ear began to pulse. It wasn't worth it. She'd answer to Marian until this crazy concussion-induced vision disappeared.

"F-From Clifton, are you?" Despite Ellen's stutter, her speech was easier to follow.

"Actually, I'm from London."

Ellen's eyes widened. "London! Mercy, that's m-much farther than Clifton. What're you d-doin' all the way up here?"

"I have no idea," Mariah said, attempting to curb the panic welling within her. She desperately wanted to escape this nightmare but didn't know how.

Ellen opened her mouth as though to ask something else but must have thought better of it. Giving Mariah a puzzled look, she pointed to a large wicker basket on the floor beside two wooden bowls. "I've made a d-decent start, but M-Mistress Agatha's right. It's goin' to take a m-miracle to have them ready in time."

"In time for what?" Mariah asked, gratefully claiming the short, three-legged stool nearest the bowl full of shelled peas and resting her spinning head on her hand.

"Why, the sh-sheriff's evenin' meal, of course." Ellen dropped onto the other stool and reached for a handful of pods. "It's always a g-grand feast, but when he entertains visitors, it's even m-more of a to-do."

Mariah took a deep breath. A few more seconds. Surely that was all it would take for this hallucination—or whatever it was—to disappear.

Ellen gave her a concerned look. "Are you w-well, Marian?"

"I thought I was, but . . . " She winced. "I hit my head on the doorframe, and it seems to be affecting me more than normal."

Ellen tossed an empty pea pod into one of the bowls and glanced over her shoulder. "I'm r-right sorry about your head, but I fear that if you don't start w-workin', Mistress Agatha'll be after us both. She may be hard of hearin', but she p-pounces on a slackin' servant faster than a hawk c-catches a fleein' mouse."

Mariah reached for some pea pods and began mindlessly shelling the peas. The tiny green balls rolled through her fingers and into the bowl, much like her sanity appeared to be doing.

"Where's Mrs. McQuivey?" Mariah asked.

"Who?"

"Mrs. McQuivey. She owns the costume shop. She's short, with white hair and pink-framed glasses."

Ellen's expression hinted at mounting alarm.

"She's . . . she's supposed to be out here." Mariah was positive McQuivey was the older lady's surname. It had been on the sign beside the door; she remembered seeing it. And she *had* walked into McQuivey's Costume Shop. She was sure of it. But if she had, how had she walked out of the changing room and into this . . . this medieval kitchen?

"I know no one b-by that name," Ellen said. "Not here in the c-castle leastwise."

The castle. Mariah latched on to those words. That had to be it. All Patrick's talk of going to Warwick Castle earlier today was to blame for bringing this on. She spent so much of her time at Ricardo's kitchen that her befuddled mind must have simply combined the two.

"I'm not really in Warwick Castle's kitchen, am I?"

"'Course not," Ellen said. But before Mariah could claim any measure of relief from those comforting words, Ellen grabbed another fistful of pea pods and continued. "It would t-take days to get there from Nottingham."

Nottingham and a sheriff in a castle. Mariah gazed around the room filled with servants dressed just like her, her heart pounding uncomfortably in her chest. It wasn't real. It couldn't be. With trembling fingers, she reached for more pea pods. A concussion with memory loss? A convoluted dream twisting everything Patrick had told her? Either way, she had to wake herself up. And if this vision had been caused by the bang to her head, she might need to seek medical attention.

"I need you to wake me up, Ellen," Mariah said.

"But you are n-not asleep."

"I am. I have to be. Even if it doesn't look like it. How else could I suddenly be in this medieval reenactment?"

Ellen's brows came together. "What's a 'm-medieval reen-nact-ment'?"

Mariah pressed the heel of her hand to her forehead and closed her eyes. Fine. If Ellen didn't want to break with character, Mariah would play along. "Acting like people from the past."

"L-Like a histrio?"

What in the world was a *histrio*?

"Like, we're dressing up in these clothes and pretending to be medieval ladies," Mariah explained.

Ellen glanced at her well-used apron over her serviceable kirtle. "I'm no lady. An' I have no other clothes th-than these. Leastwise, n-none that are fit for workin' in the kitchen."

No other clothes? What was she talking about? Mariah glanced at the other young women in the large room. Each was intent on her work. Each appeared to be preparing a portion of a plentiful but rustic meal. And if the smells were any indication, the food was real.

A few unsettling doubts wiggled past her disbelief. When had she ever seen a reenactment actor wear an apron as stained as Mistress Agatha's? Or felt the same sense of urgency on a set that she'd only ever experienced in a restaurant kitchen preparing food for paying customers? How could she put an archaic word like *histrio* into the mouth of a person in her imagination if she didn't even know the word herself?

No. She was being ridiculous and needed to get a grip. There had to be a logical explanation. She must have heard the word *histrio* on the telly and subconsciously filed it away. It could have been on one of those documentaries her father used to watch when she was young. Yes. That had to be it. Ellen and everyone else around her was a figment of Mariah's overactive imagination.

She shelled a couple more peas, her thoughts flying in every direction as more misgivings took hold. When had anyone ever accused her of having an overactive imagination? Never. Mrs. Cotton, her fifth form English teacher, had consistently given her low scores on her creative writing papers because she'd claimed they "lacked imagination." Mariah had simply devoted what little creativity she did possess to experimenting in her chemistry classes—which had then led to her passion for creating new dishes. But for her to have come up with a dream this elaborate, this realistic . . . She swallowed, her throat suddenly dry. Time travel was impossible. There was no way she'd actually gone back in time . . . was there?

"Ellen, do you know who's on the throne right now?" she asked.

"Why, R-Richard the Lionheart." The teenager paused, fear suddenly filling her pale-blue eyes. "Have you heard s-somethin'? Is there fresh news f-from overseas about the king?"

This was ludicrous. But could she have conjured up such seemingly accurate details with a concussion? "Not . . . not that I know of."

Ellen placed a hand to her chest. "Oh. You had me r-right worried for a moment there."

Maybe Mariah didn't have a concussion after all. Maybe she was part of an elaborate hoax at McQuivey's Costume Shop.

"Because of what Prince John might do if King Richard dies?" she guessed.

Ellen glanced over her shoulder again and lowered her voice. "Since you're new here, I'd best w-warn you. It's not safe to t-talk of such things. 'Specially in th-the castle."

"Is Prince John here now?" Mariah could hardly believe what she was saying.

"Not at present. But I d-daresay he'll be back afore long." She sighed, and the sound seemed to carry a multitude of heavy emotions. "It's the B-Bishop of Hereford who's dinin' with the sheriff t-tonight."

Mariah strained to remember the characters in the last Robin Hood film she'd watched. Had there been a Bishop of Hereford? Was he a good guy or a bad guy? "I'm not familiar with the Bishop of Hereford."

"If you aim to s-stay in Nottingham, you'll come to know him s-soon enough," Ellen said, and then she pressed her lips together, obviously attempting to follow the counsel she'd so recently offered Mariah.

Mariah took the hint, mindlessly reaching for more peas while her thoughts spun like a Category 5 typhoon. Nottingham Castle at the end of the twelfth century! *Impossible. It isn't real. It can't be real.* The words circled her mind in a never-ending chant. But how did a person know if they were hallucinating? How did one break free from an alternate reality? Then again, what if she were simply being pranked and this were all a cruel joke? What did she need to do to have it come to an end? She didn't have any answers. And that scared her. A lot.

———·�֍·———

Sunlight was filtering through the leaves of the trees bordering the road that cut through Sherwood Forest, dappling the dusty thoroughfare with gently shifting shadows. Birds sang from the branches, and a steady buzzing came from the bees hovering above the purple clover on the ground below. Robin stood beneath the largest oak, his gaze on the bend in the road some fifty paces distant. All at once, a bird took flight. Two more followed, and Robin tensed. Had they sensed the approach of horses before the sound of hooves had reached him?

Little John had run into Much the Miller in town earlier that morning, and the fellow had been adamant that the Bishop of Hereford was to arrive at Nottingham Castle before sunset. Robin and his men had greeted the news with enthusiasm. It had been weeks since they'd been in a position to assist more than a handful of Nottingham's poorer citizens, and the lofty Bishop of Hereford never traveled without a purse weighed down with gold coins. Redistributing some of his ill-gotten wealth would give them all a great deal of pleasure.

A branch cracked somewhere to Robin's right, a sure sign that at least one of his men was moving closer. He turned his head, listening for something more. And then, at last, the steady cadence of hooves hitting the hardpacked ground reached his ears. Drawing an arrow from the quiver hanging at his belt, he nocked it on his bowstring. And as the first horses in the bishop's entourage rounded the bend, Robin stepped into the road.

A shout went out and the half dozen horses came to an abrupt halt. Vaguely aware that the men riding on either side of the bishop were armed, Robin kept his attention on the man who rode at the head of the group.

"Well met, Your Grace," he called. "May I be the first to welcome you back to Sherwood Forest."

"Who are you to stop our progress?" The anger in the bishop's voice was unmistakable. "Lower your bow and move aside, you scoundrel!"

"A scoundrel, you say?" Ignoring the bishop's injunction, Robin raised his bow a fraction higher, his target in sight. "Well, I daresay if you and I were gifted with truly clear vision, we would discover that scoundrels surround us on every side."

Beneath his purple velvet cap lined with jewels, the bishop's face turned an ugly shade of puce. "What are you waiting for?" he cried to the guard at his right. "Take him!"

With a zing of steel, the guard drew his sword.

Instantly, the bushes alongside the road trembled, and a dozen of Robin's men, all dressed in Lincoln green, stepped into the open, each armed with a bow or a staff. In unison, the bishop's remaining guards drew their swords and urged their mounts forward. Robin waited no longer; he released his arrow. Two heartbeats later, it pierced the small leather pouch hanging from the bishop's saddle. At the bishop's cry of indignation, the guards closest to him turned back. It was precisely the distraction Little John had been waiting for. Taking two long steps, he swung his staff, catching the nearest guard's blade and sending it clattering to the ground.

Robin nocked a second arrow. Little John, Will Scarlett, and Allan a Dale were already wielding their staffs against the other guards' blades, their comrades standing ready along the roadway with bowstrings drawn. Robin darted past a skittish horse and raised his bow again.

"Call down your guards, Your Grace!"

The Bishop of Hereford swiveled in his saddle, and upon seeing Robin standing a mere two paces from him with an arrow aimed at his chest, the excess color drained from the bishop's face.

"Enough!" At the bishop's hoarse shout, the clatter of clashing weapons and thudding hooves ceased. Robin did not turn to look. He had full confidence in his men's ability to keep the guards—and their blades—firmly within their sights until the convoy was out of the forest.

"There is no reason for us to delay you any further," Robin said. "If you would be so good as to untie the purse at your side and toss it to the man who so deftly disarmed your guard just now, you and your men can be on your way." Robin eyed the cleric's velvet robes, jewel-adorned hat, and gold chain upon his chest. "What think you, Little John? Is there anything more that the good bishop might offer to the people of Nottingham?"

His friend stepped closer, and leaning against his staff, he studied the stone-faced cleric. "I fear the Sheriff of Nottingham might not recognize the good bishop if he were to arrive without his costly robes and headwear, but someone so laudable as the Bishop of Hereford undoubtedly owns more than one gold chain; mayhap he could spare the one currently around his neck. The links are such that the chain might be broken down and shared amongst many."

"A worthy suggestion," Robin said. He held his aim steady. "Your pouch and gold chain, if you please, Your Grace."

With shaking fingers, the bishop tugged the leather pouch free of his saddle. Then, grasping Robin's first arrow with one hand, he yanked it out of the leather and threw it to the ground. A glimmer of gold shone through the newly formed hole in the sack. Little John moved forward to claim the pouch and then waited while the bishop lifted the heavy chain from around his neck.

"You shall pay for this thievery with your life, Robin Hood." The bishop spat the words. "And your men shall suffer the same fate."

Robin raised his eyebrows. "How remarkable! The Sheriff of Nottingham has told us the very same."

Giving him a venomous glare, the bishop set his jaw and turned his head away. "We ride for Nottingham Castle!" he ordered.

His guards returned to their positions beside and behind him. Keeping their arrows nocked, Robin and his men warily moved to stand along the grassy verge. The Bishop of Hereford gave his mount an impatient tap with the heel of his silk shoe, and then he and his entourage started forward, never once looking back.

CHAPTER 3

Over the years, Mariah had done more than her share of serving food. Between helping at her father's fish-and-chip shop in her youth, taking plating classes at culinary school, and working at Ricardo's, she'd thought she had plenty of catering experience. But this meal was stretching her supposed proficiency to its limit. There were no individual plates, only enormous platters and wooden trenchers. Cutlery was limited to vicious-looking daggers. Silver goblets had replaced glasses, and wine, mead, and ale were being served from silver pitchers rather than bottles. The only thing that was remotely familiar in the bustling medieval kitchen was the sense of urgency to deliver the food in a timely manner.

"Where are me servers?" Mistress Agatha barked. "Th' meat platters should 'ave been in th' dinin' 'all long ago."

"M-Make haste, Marian," Ellen whispered, ducking her head to avoid Mistress Agatha's frowning look and picking up a large wooden platter covered in roughly cut slabs of roast pork. "We must m-make amends for taking so long to shell the p-peas, or we shall both suffer the consequences."

Mariah did not ask what those supposed consequences might be. In this terrifying alternate reality, hanging from the gallows seemed a distinct possibility. She reached for a platter of roast duck and followed Ellen out of the kitchen.

The heat the kitchen's roaring fire produced was suddenly gone. In its place was a cold passageway filled with more echoes than people.

Sturdy wooden doors and an occasional smoldering torch were the only things that interrupted the long stretch of stone wall. Every door was closed and gave no hint of what lay beyond its threshold.

"Watch yourself on the s-stairs." Ellen's voice bounced eerily off the stone walls. "It's nigh impossible to s-see the steps with these p-platters in hand."

Mariah looked up to see an arched opening ahead. "How far do we have to go?"

"One flight of s-stairs is all. The sheriff always eats in the g-great hall when he has guests."

Mariah tightened her grip on the platter, a vision of falling down the unending stone steps of a spiral staircase filling her head. It would be a suitable ending for this nightmare. "I don't know if I can—"

"You must." Ellen had already disappeared around the tower's central column. "And there's no t-time to waste. There'll be others from the k-kitchen comin' after us."

The only thing worse than climbing a castle's spiral staircase with a large platter in one's hand would be doing so with others pushing past her on the narrow slivers of stone that constituted steps. Swallowing her fears, Mariah pressed herself against the damp outer wall and started up.

She almost lost her footing twice, and by the time she reached the upper floor, her legs were trembling, and her arms were shaking from the strain of holding the platter level.

"Thank heavens," she breathed, when she stepped out of the tower and into another hall.

"You'd best be s-savin' your breath," Ellen said, leading the way once more. "We'll be up and down lots m-more times yet."

Hurried footsteps coming up the staircase confirmed Ellen's earlier warning and offered Mariah no reason to disbelieve the latest one.

"If I'm not already having an out-of-body experience, this might actually kill me," she muttered.

Thankfully, Ellen must not have heard her because the young woman came to a halt beside an enormous set of double doors. "This

here's th-the great hall," she said. "We'll set the p-platters down afore
the sheriff and his g-guests. If there's ought to be t-taken away, we'll
gather that up. Then it's straight b-back to the kitchen for more."

Mariah nodded. In and out. She could do that.

Balancing the meat platter on one hand, Ellen pulled open the
door and slipped inside with Mariah right behind her. The crackle
and warmth of the fire burning in the fireplace was the first thing to
greet them. A long table stood in the center of the room, and a row of
finely dressed men and women sat on benches that were positioned
on either side of the table. The pungent aroma of wine mingled with
the lingering scent of roasted meats and the faintly dusty, sweet smell
of the straw that covered the wooden floor.

At the center of the table, a tall, thin man with dark hair and a
dark pointed beard was listening intently to the man at his side. The
second gentleman was dressed in purple velvet robes. Each of his
fingers bore a heavy gold ring, some of them containing jewels that
sparkled in the light coming from the candles on the table. He waved
one hand expressively, sending reflective beams dancing across the
ceiling even as his eyes glistened with anger.

"It will not do, my lord sheriff. Robin Hood and his men control
every inch of the road through Sherwood Forest. Had I not had the
foresight to wear gloves over my rings, he would have stolen everything of value on my person."

Mariah unconsciously slowed to a stop. They were talking about
Robin Hood—discussing him as though he were a person they knew
rather than a character in a popular legend. She shook her head
slightly. What was she thinking? It didn't matter what these men
said. None of this was real.

"Marian."

At Ellen's urgent whisper, Mariah stirred herself and hurried over
to the table.

The dark-haired man was speaking now. The gold threads wo-
ven through his black velvet tunic gave him a tiger-like appearance.

It was an impression that was redoubled by his snarled response. "How would *you* propose that we capture the villain, Your Grace? A warrant for his arrest has proven futile. Indeed, I defy you to find a yeoman or peasant—man, woman, or child—in Nottingham town who will utter a word against the outlaw."

The man who looked and acted more like royalty than a priest snorted. "Are you truly so dependent upon commoners to catch your man, Sheriff?"

Ellen set her platter before the two gentlemen. Neither paid her any attention. The others seated at the table were unnaturally quiet. Mariah placed her platter beside Ellen's. Still, no one spoke.

The sheriff twirled his knife, his expression unreadable. "I have men enough to capture him, but Robin Hood is as slippery as an eel."

"Then match his trickery with your own."

"How?"

The Bishop of Hereford's oily smile sent a shudder down Mariah's spine. "My dear sheriff, trickery is dependent upon secrecy."

"Just so." With a smirk, the sheriff raised his goblet. "To secrecy, trickery, and the capture of Robin Hood."

Immediately, those seated around the table reached for their goblets, breaking their silence with a cheer.

The Sheriff of Nottingham lowered his goblet to the table with a thud. "You, girl," he said, directing his attention to Ellen for the first time. "Fetch us more wine."

Ellen bobbed a curtsy. "Yes, Sheriff. R-Right away." She picked up the silver pitcher at his elbow and hurried to the other end of the table to claim another before moving quickly to the door.

Hoping to escape the room without notice, Mariah reached for a basket that had once held bread but now contained a partial crust and a few crumbs and followed her out.

Ellen was already in the tower when Mariah reached the top of the spiral staircase. Anxious to catch up with her, Mariah started down without giving any thought to the servants on their way up.

She'd barely rounded the first bend when she came face-to-face with a young man carrying a tray full of custard tarts.

"Watch yerself," he warned, steadying his load as Mariah gasped, pressing her back against the wall in an attempt to maintain her own balance. "Yer goin' t' 'ave t' take the narrow bit if I'm t' get past ya with this tray."

Mariah swallowed. The narrow part was the sliver of stone that connected the triangular-shaped stairs to the center column. The thought of standing there turned her knees to jelly, but the alternative—to go back up—was an even worse solution. The chances of her making it down without meeting anyone else was virtually nil. "Yes. All right."

Placing a clammy hand on the cool stone central pillar, she shuffled sideways until the tips of her toes were balanced on the narrow slice of the stair. *Don't look down. Don't look down.* The unspoken words echoed through her head.

"Can you pass me now?" she asked.

Balancing the tray at shoulder height, the youth shimmied sideways for two steps before straightening and increasing his pace up the remaining stairs. Mariah slid back to the wider part of the step.

More footsteps were echoing up the tower, drawing closer. She started down again, this time moving faster. The more steps she put behind her, the closer she'd be to the bottom when she had to cling to the inner post again. And the better her chances of talking to Ellen before her young friend started back with the full pitchers of wine.

Mariah ran into Ellen at the door leading into the kitchen. The girl was already on her way back, a pitcher full of wine in each hand.

"Wait," Mariah said. "Let me put this bread basket on the table, and I'll carry one of those jugs for you."

"You'll have to b-be quick. The sheriff's not known f-for his patience."

"I'm sure." Mariah ran into the kitchen, dropped the empty basket on the nearest table, and, before Mistress Agatha could give her another assignment, raced back to Ellen. "Give me one of them."

Carefully, Ellen transferred a heavy pitcher into Mariah's outstretched hands. "Do you have it?"

"Yes."

Ellen nodded and set off down the corridor at a brisk walk.

Holding the pitcher with both hands, Mariah attempted to keep pace. The dark-red liquid sloshed over the lip to land on her apron. "Did you have to fill these jugs so full?"

"If it s-saves us another trip, it'll be w-worth it."

Mariah couldn't argue with that. Not with the tower stairs looming ahead.

"The sheriff and bishop were talking about Robin Hood," Mariah said.

"Aye. He comes up in the sh-sheriff's conversations a lot." She lowered her voice. "As far as the sheriff is concerned, Robin Hood is like a bad rash that w-won't go away. Hearin' fresh news 'bout the men in Sherwood Forest always p-puts him in a foul mood."

This was completely ridiculous.

"Let me guess," Mariah said. "Because it shows him in a bad light."

"Shh." Ellen's whispered warning echoed off the walls, her expression showing no hint of amusement. "You saw how the p-people in the great hall acted. When you're in the c-castle, it's best to say nothin' at all than to say the wrong thing."

It seemed that Mariah's wisdom and sanity were integrally connected because over the last couple of hours, both were failing her.

Ignoring, Ellen's caution, she pressed the teenager further. Surely Ellen would crack at some point. "Have you seen him?" Mariah asked. "Robin Hood, I mean."

"Not me," Ellen said. "But I know p-plenty who have."

"And he really lives in Sherwood Forest?"

Ellen tossed her a perplexed look. "'Course he does. Where else would he be able to s-stay hidden all this t-time?"

Throughout her time in the kitchen, Mariah had held fast to the hope that with time, her confusion would pass and her normal world would be restored. Instead, the opposite seemed to be happening. A fresh wave of trepidation washed over her. It was simply not possible that she'd walked into the middle of a popular legend. But how was she to escape this madness? Should she run or play along? The gutting reality that she had nowhere to run to made the answer easy.

"So, Robin Hood is real?" she said. "A deposed nobleman actually lives in Sherwood Forest with a band of outlaws?"

"A nobleman?" Ellen gave a breathless laugh. "Well, that's one I ain't heard afore." She grinned. "I d-daresay Robin'd be right pleased to hear it though."

"But I thought Robin Hood's real name was Robert of Locksley and that he was the Earl of Huntington or something like that?"

"I don't know who you've been t-talkin' to. No one in these parts, that's fer certain. Afore he b-became an outlaw, Robin was a yeoman. Higher class than us servants, t' be sure, but a l-long way from bein' a nobleman."

The young man Mariah had encountered earlier met them on his way down the stairs. This time, he slid to the narrow side of the steps, and she continued her upward march with the wine slapping the side of the pitcher as she moved. Two more servants followed the other one, but Mariah barely noticed. Her thoughts were on all the films she'd watched featuring Robin Hood—stories of a wronged nobleman who'd been ousted from his lands by wicked Prince John and who had then devoted his life to taking from the rich to feed the poor. Why would Ellen debunk all those stories?

"Ellen, wait." They'd reached the top of the stairs, and Ellen was hurrying toward the large doors.

Ellen paused, but her expression was worried. "The sh-sheriff's goblet will be empty by now. We m-must hasten inside."

"I know." Mariah shifted her grip on the heavy pitcher's handle as she also attempted to keep a grip on all reason. "What about Little John and Friar Tuck? Do they live with Robin Hood?"

"So I believe." Ellen reached for the door. "Now, r-remember." Her voice dropped to a whisper. "No more talkin'. 'Specially 'bout the m-men of Sherwood Forest."

———— · ✳ · ————

"Four hundred pounds, Little John." Robin leaned back on his heels, gazing in disbelief at the piles of gold coins he'd counted out on the grass. "And that's without whatever we can procure for the good bishop's gold chain."

Little John muttered a curse beneath his breath. "The *good* bishop makes a mockery of his profession. He's a wolf in sheep's clothing."

"Why, Little John!" Friar Tuck crossed the clearing toward them, two bowls of steaming pottage in his hands. "It fills my heart with gladness to hear you quote from the Good Book."

Little John accepted the bowl Friar Tuck offered him with a wry grin. "And it fills my heart with gladness to know that you heard only my last few words."

Friar Tuck's bushy eyebrows came together. "Truly, Little John, you have much to learn with regard to when to make a full confession."

Robin chuckled and took the second bowl. "Rest easy, Friar Tuck, it was not so bad as all that. Little John was simply marveling that the Bishop of Hereford would carry such an excess of gold when so many of his flock are starving."

"Exactly right," Little John said, shoveling the pottage into his mouth with alacrity. "You see, my thoughts were solely upon sheep and flocks."

"And wolves." Friar Tuck slipped his hands into the wide sleeves of his brown cassock, a knowing expression in his eyes. "Have you determined how best to distribute the wealth to those in need?"

"I am still pondering the matter." Robin scooped up half the coins and slipped them into the repaired leather pouch. "These we shall retain for challenges that lie ahead that are yet unknown." Gathering the remaining coins, he poured them into a second pouch. "On the morrow, I shall take this sack with me to Nottingham. I see no reason to delay easing the burden of the poorer people in town."

"Do you desire company?" Little John asked. "Of your two dozen men, there's not one who would balk at the opportunity to share of this bounty."

Robin looked out over the shady glen. A large cauldron bubbled over a fire in the center of the clearing. Close to a dozen men surrounded it. Seated on animal hides upon the ground, they were eating and talking merrily. A few more men had chosen to take their meal beneath the trees, their backs up against the sturdy trunks, their comfortable silence a sure indication of their contentment. Their relaxed postures were a testament to the peace found in the forest. Every man had arrived broken and fearful, often escaping an unjust punishment. Here they'd been offered hope and had found purpose. It was a powerful combination—albeit not quite strong enough to grant them the freedom to leave this sanctuary with impunity.

"The men of Sherwood Forest have good and willing hearts," Robin said, "but I believe I shall make this journey alone. With the Bishop of Hereford in residence, the castle guards will be especially vigilant. One man dressed in Lincoln green may slip through the gates unnoticed; a band of men dressed thus would not be so fortunate."

"That may be true, but entering the town alone comes with its own set of risks," Friar Tuck said.

"Fear not, my friend," Robin said, setting his hand on the friar's shoulder. "I shall take great care."

Little John eyed him skeptically. "When it comes to interacting with those who would wish you ill, I cannot recall any particular incident during which you took great care."

Robin chuckled. "A compromise, then. You shall be in charge here, and if I have not returned by sundown, you may organize a rescue party."

"Does he truly think a statement like that will put our minds at ease?" Little John asked Friar Tuck.

Friar Tuck sighed. "It might be less worrying if we returned to talking of sheep and flocks."

"Aye," Little John said ruefully. "But if we did that, it would not be long before we were speaking of wolves again."

CHAPTER 4

Mariah lay on a pallet, staring up at the ceiling of the small room where all the female servants in the castle slept. The meager fire that had burned in the fireplace when she and Ellen had first entered the sleeping chamber had died long ago, and the thin wool blanket one of the other girls had offered her was not nearly enough to compensate for the lowering temperature. She turned her head. Ellen hadn't moved in some time. None of the girls had. Mariah didn't know what time they'd risen this morning, but if the heavy breathing and gentle snores now filling the room were any indication, it had been early.

Mariah was similarly exhausted, but sleep remained far away. Fear and confusion battled for dominance as the events of the day circled her mind in a never-ending loop. She'd woken in her small flat in London. It had appeared to be a perfectly normal Saturday in June. So how had she ended up here? Come to that, where exactly was *here*? If Ellen were to be believed, Mariah was in Nottingham Castle in the late twelfth century. It certainly looked and felt that way. But it couldn't possibly be. Could it?

Her thoughts settled on McQuivey's Costume Shop. Everything had been fine until she'd stepped out of the changing room. Had the white-haired lady with the twinkling hazel eyes known what was going to happen? What was it she'd said? Mariah put her hand to her forehead, trying to remember. *I'll come back and join you when you're ready?* Well, after spending the evening working in the kitchen,

facing her dread of heights on the tower stairs, serving the menacing Sheriff of Nottingham and creepy Bishop of Hereford, and then
washing dishes until it was dark, Mariah was long past ready. But
she'd seen absolutely no sign of Mrs. McQuivey.

Her fingers found the spot behind her ear where she'd hit the
doorframe. It was a little tender, but she'd not thought about it in
hours. Surely, if she were suffering from a concussion, she'd be in
more pain and would be suffering other symptoms. This experience
didn't feel like a dream either. Her back and feet ached, and her
fingers were raw from scrubbing pots and pans with sand. She'd always believed that dreams were pain-free. Then again, she'd always
believed time travel was made-up.

She took an unsteady breath. Somehow, she must return to her
normal life. Even if the unthinkable had actually happened and she'd
truly been transported to another time and place, there had to be
a way back. Did she have to walk through a door to return to the
changing room? A vision of the castle corridor outside the kitchen
flashed before her. She'd noticed all the doors when she'd been going
to and from the great hall. Had she arrived here by stepping out of
one of the ones near the kitchen? She turned her gaze to the other
side of the room. It was so dark, she could barely see the outline of
the bedchamber door, but if she was going to check on the other
doors, now was the time to do it.

Peeling back the blanket, Mariah groped along the side of the
pallet for her shoes. Other than her apron, which she'd rinsed in an
attempt to get the wine stains off and had left drying on a rack in the
kitchen, her shoes were the only articles of clothing she'd taken off.
Once she'd located them, she rose to her feet and tiptoed between
the sleeping girls until she reached the door. Stopping long enough
to put on her shoes, she lifted the latch and opened the door just
enough to slip out into the passageway.

A single torch burned near the entrance to the tower that led up
to the ground floor. Quickly, she moved toward it. The faint light

illuminated only the first few steps, so she placed her hand on the tower's cold, stone wall, feeling for each stair with her toes before climbing one step at a time. A slight diminishing of the darkness marked the entrance to the ground floor. Grateful that she didn't need to continue up to the great hall, she exited the tower. Another single torch lit her way down the corridor toward the kitchen.

The passageway was quiet. Eerily quiet after the clamor and chaos of a few hours earlier. Mariah's heart pounded. She approached the first door and reached for the round brass handle. She turned it, attempting to raise the latch. It was locked. Swallowing her disappointment, she hurried to the next one. It, too, was locked. On her fourth try, the latch lifted. Her breath caught, but she pushed the door open, the hinges creaking, the sound echoing down the hall.

She stood in the doorway, peering into a small, dark room. Barrels lined one wall, and above them, lumpy sacks lay on shelves. She sniffed. It smelled like apples. Stepping up to the closest barrel, she lowered her arm into it and touched the fruit immediately. The skins weren't as smooth as those on freshly picked fruit, but if they'd been in barrels for months, it would explain the warm, cidery smell permeating the room. This must be one of the food storage rooms.

She hurried out, closing the latch behind her and making for the next door. This one was opposite the kitchen door. If any of these doors led back to the costume shop's changing room, it was most likely this one. Her hand trembled slightly as she tried turning the brass ring. It shifted, and the latch lifted with a click. Pushing the door open, she stepped inside. In the faint torch light, she made out sacks piled three deep and stacked against the wall. The dirt floor was dusted with a white coating. She crouched, brushed her fingers against the powder, and then raised her hand to examine it more closely. Flour, more coarsely ground than she was used to, but she recognized it nonetheless. She rose, brushing her hands against each other to dust them off. This, too, was a storage room, but it was for flours and grains.

A lump rose in her throat. Locked doors and pantries. Even though it was what she should have expected, she was unprepared for the despair that washed over her as hope for an easy return to McQuivey's Costume Shop vanished. Fighting tears, she backed out of the room and closed the door. The solid click was followed by another one, and suddenly, heavy footsteps filled the corridor. Mariah swung around.

"Oy! Who goes there?" A guard materialized in the darkness.

With the thud of the guard's rapid steps and rustle of his chainmail, Mariah experienced a new level of fear. There could be no doubt that he'd seen her, and if she tried to run for it, she was more likely to get lost or injured by a fall than she was to escape. But if he captured her, what then? Would she be thrown straight into the dungeon?

Acting instinctively, she stepped away from the storage room and toward the kitchen.

"Halt!" The guard's raised sword glistened in the torchlight.

Mariah froze. "I'm unarmed."

"A woman!" His sword lowered a fraction. "Who are ya, and what are ya doing in the west wing at night?"

"I'm Marian o' Clifton," she said. If she didn't use the name Mistress Agatha had given her, no one would come to her rescue. "I . . . I just arrived at the castle today," she added, hoping he might go easier on her if he realized she was new. "I left my apron in the kitchen and even though it's late, I thought I'd better come back for it because Mistress Agatha wouldn't want me showing up tomorrow morning without one."

Given that Mistress Agatha was the one who'd told her to leave her apron there to dry, that was a stretch, but Mariah was willing to guess that a castle guard knew very little about the workings of the castle kitchen.

The guard's face was in shadow, but she sensed his hesitation. "Yer speech is right odd, even fer someone from Clifton."

Mariah winced. She knew better. Attending the St. George's Festival in Bedford over the years had given her an ear for the more common medieval expressions and words. She needed to make a better effort to fit in. Ellen had been unusually unfazed by Mariah's modern English. Given how much Mariah had been trying to take in today, that had been a godsend. Not everyone would be so understanding though. "Forgive me," she said. "I was startled."

"Rightly so. No one should be wandering the castle at this hour."

"I realize that now. It was foolish. But I did not want to displease Mistress Agatha so soon after arriving."

With a muttered grumble, he re-sheathed his sword. "Make haste, then. I have no time to waste."

Relief surged through her. The guard might not know anything about the kitchen, but it seemed he understood the desire to please superiors.

"I'm very grateful." She entered the kitchen. Thankfully, the coals from the fire were not completely out, and by their red glow, Mariah made her way around the large table to the rack set up in front of the fireplace. Her apron was just where she'd left it. And it was dry. "I have it," she said, waving it before her.

The white fabric must have been visible because the guard grunted his approval. "Now, get yerself back to the servants' quarters," he said.

With her apron in hand, Mariah left the kitchen and half walked, half ran down the shadowy corridor. She didn't even care that she had to navigate the tower in the dark again. The knowledge that she could have been taken somewhere far worse made her unexpectedly grateful for the familiar spiral staircase.

Thankfully, no footsteps followed her, and she met no one else before reaching the female servants' sleeping chamber. Pausing long enough to take a steadying breath, she carefully opened the door. One of the girls muttered something in her sleep. Mariah stood completely still. A rustle sounded from a nearby pallet, but the noise was over almost before it began. Closing the door behind her, Mariah took off her shoes and crept back to her primitive bed. She lay down and pulled the threadbare blanket up to her chin. A single tear rolled down her cheek, quickly followed by another. The stones beneath her pallet were hard, cold, and immovable. The girls and women asleep all around her were living, breathing people. She may not know how or why she was here, but as frightening and seemingly futile as her nighttime excursion had been, it had taught her one thing: If there was a way back to her former life, she didn't know how to find it.

———— · · ✳ · ·————

The early-morning sun was painting the horizon every shade of yellow and filling the day with promise. Robin smiled. The leather pouch filled with the Bishop of Hereford's ill-gotten gold hung from Robin's belt, the coins chinking gently as he walked the forest road that led to Nottingham. He had yet to determine exactly how he would appropriate the money; he knew only that the town's poorest citizens would end the day happier than they had started it. And that was all the more reason to smile.

He turned a bend in the road, and the distinctive rumble of cart wheels reached him. It was unlikely that a member of the upper classes was abroad this early, but regardless of Little John's teasing, Robin had not evaded capture this long without employing a healthy dose of caution. It was in his best interest to discover who was on the road ahead of him rather than simply stumble upon a foe.

Leaving the path, he entered the trees and wove through the underbrush at a steady jog, using the sound of the creaking wooden wheels to guide him. Before long, he caught sight of a man bent over a large handcart. The stranger's blue wool tunic was cinched at the waist with a narrow rope. His brown hood came to a long point and was attached to a short cape that covered his shoulders. His cart appeared to be heavily laden, but from this distance, it was impossible to identify its contents.

As Robin watched, the man gave a grunt and then paused his pushing long enough to run his sleeve across his forehead. The simple act was telling. He may have sufficient funds to own a heavily laden cart, but he was no nobleman. A gentleman of higher rank would have a horse or pony doing such onerous manual work.

Placing his trust in instinct, Robin stepped out from between the trees. "Good day to you, stranger."

The man looked up with a start. "And to you." He looked up and down the road, a hint of wariness entering his voice. "Do you travel this road alone?"

"I do," Robin said. "And it would appear that you do also."

"Aye, though I wish it were not so."

Robin raised an eyebrow. "Why is that? A morning so fair as this one all but begs to be enjoyed in solitude."

"I have no time for enjoying pleasant vistas." The stranger took up the handles of his cart and began to push once more.

Robin moved to walk beside him. "You are in a hurry to be elsewhere, then?"

"Aye. The market at Nottingham." One of the wheels encountered a rock and veered off course. With another grunt, the fellow heaved it back. "The best spots are claimed early, and this morning, I aim to have one."

"What are you selling?"

"The very best cuts of venison, lamb, and beef in the county," he said.

"You're a butcher."

"Aye. And my wife can dress a goose better than anyone," he added proudly. "There's half a dozen of them in the cart, and I guarantee you'll not find any better."

"I'm inclined to believe you," Robin said, the beginning of an idea forming in his mind. "But I fear you run the risk of being so tired by the time you reach the market that you shall want nothing more than to lay yourself upon the ground and sleep away the day."

"Would that such an option were mine. As it is, I must sell every last cut of meat by day's end if I am to return home with sufficient money to purchase more cattle."

Robin rubbed his tidily trimmed beard thoughtfully. "There may be a way to send you home rested and with a purse full of gold."

"If your plan can be accomplished without bringing the sheriff's men down upon me, you have my full attention."

Robin chuckled. "A wise stipulation, and in this instance, one that can be met without difficulty."

"Go on, then."

"Sell me your cart," Robin said. "The conveyance and everything within. I shall push it to market and you may return home to rest with a purse full of gold."

"How much gold?" the butcher asked cagily.

"One hundred and eighty pounds," Robin said. "Two hundred if you sell me your clothes as well."

The man came to an abrupt halt. "You wish to buy my old tunic for twenty pounds?"

"It appears to be well made and warm," Robin said.

"Well, it is that, but . . . " He paused, obviously attempting to think through Robin's astonishing offer. "Would you have me return home in nothing but my undergarments?"

"Not at all." Robin gestured to his own knee-length green tunic. "You shall have mine."

The butcher gaped, his ruddy cheeks reddening still further. "But you are paying me—" He snapped his mouth closed. The fellow might be an excellent butcher, but he obviously had much to learn about striking a profitable bargain. It was fortunate for him that Robin was far more interested in entering Nottingham disguised as a butcher with meat to sell than he was about haggling over the price.

"What say you?" Robin asked. Now that he had a plan for helping the good people of Nottingham, he was anxious to execute it. "Are we agreed?"

"If you have two hundred pounds upon your person," the butcher said, "you are welcome to all that I have."

Robin untied the leather purse from his belt and held it out. "You may count the coins if you wish."

The butcher took the purse, his eyes alighting at the distinctive clink of coins from within. Setting the bag on his open palm, he bounced it gently. "Any butcher of worth has a good grasp of weights and measures," he said. "You have paid me more than enough."

"Your tunic and hood, then, if you please," Robin said, already loosening his belt so as to divest himself of his outer garment.

Within minutes, the exchange had been made.

Appearing very pleased with his morning's transaction, the butcher attached the heavy purse to his new belt and offered Robin his hand. "My wife will scarcely believe her eyes when I arrive home so soon with a full purse and in so fine a tunic."

"I am glad for your good fortune and mine," Robin said. "And I would have you tell your wife that Robin Hood aims to find a worthy home for each of her finely dressed geese."

The butcher's eyes widened, and his gaze flew from Robin's face to the Lincoln green tunic he now wore. "Rob . . . Robin Hood, you say?"

Robin grinned. "Good day to you, sir." And before the fellow could verbalize another word, he seized the handcart's handles and began pushing it down the road.

CHAPTER 5

Mariah straightened and brushed away the wisp of hair that had escaped her plait with the back of her hand. Her fingers were covered in flour. So was her apron. She glanced at the sunlight tracing a line across the castle kitchen's flagstone floor. The band of light was much wider than it had been. And brighter. She stretched her aching back. With no clocks anywhere in the castle, it was difficult to know exactly what time Ellen had roused her or what time it was now. Her only clues were the distant chimes of church bells. She'd counted six soon after she'd entered the kitchen. A few minutes ago, there had been nine.

"Them are lovely, M-Marian. Real lovely." Coming up behind her, Ellen pointed to the eight venison pies lining the table.

"I hope Mistress Agatha thinks so." After she'd awoken from her extremely short night's sleep to find herself still in the castle, Mariah's emotions had run the gamut, from utter despair to dogged resolve. Her mind had been reeling all morning, considering and ultimately rejecting every possible idea for how she could have arrived here. And though her head screamed for answers for why she was the one who had been caught in this time trap and, even more importantly, whether or not her arrival here was reversible, she could not look beyond today. Anything more was too overwhelming. The only surety she could currently claim was that if she were to have any hope of surviving—of having somewhere to eat and sleep in this new world—she had to improve her performance in the kitchen. Yesterday's slow pea shelling and muddled food serving wasn't going to cut it.

Thankfully, her first assigned task this morning had been a somewhat familiar one. Her culinary school experience with making hot-water pastry hadn't gone as far as making venison pies, but she knew how to shape the pastry into a free-standing container strong enough to hold a filling. Unfortunately, with no recipe to follow, exactly how much meat each pie required remained a mystery.

"If ya've finished pluckin' the quail, ya'd best be startin' on the duck, Ellen," Mistress Agatha said, leaving her position beside the large pot hanging over the fire to approach the table where Mariah and Ellen stood.

Ellen gave an anxious nod, already moving back toward the far corner of the room. "Yes, M-Mistress Agatha. R-Right away."

Stepping aside so Mistress Agatha had a better view of her pies, Mariah clasped her floury hands together. "I made eight, just as you asked."

"Well, I've never seen pie tops sealed quite that way." The older lady studied Mariah's fluted pastry edges. "But they're right tidy, Marian. I'll say that much."

"Thank you," Mariah said, and when Mistress Agatha showed no sign of hearing her, she repeated herself more loudly. "Thank you!"

Mistress Agatha nodded. "Put them in th' oven and watch 'em close. The sheriff is most particular 'bout 'is pies."

Mariah glanced around the room. The smell of baking bread filled the kitchen, so there had to be an oven nearby. She just hadn't spotted it yet. "What temperature should I bake them at?"

"Aye," Mistress Agatha said. "They must be piping 'ot." Then she moved away, leaving Mariah none the wiser.

Another servant—Ellen had introduced her as Mildred when they'd been in the bedchamber—walked into the kitchen, carrying three hot loaves. Mariah looked back the way the girl had come. Was it possible that the oven wasn't in this room?

"Is the oven outside, Mildred?" she asked.

"Aye." Mildred set down the fresh bread. "Come with me. I'll show ya where it is."

Grateful for her help, Mariah loaded four pies onto a wide wooden paddle and followed Mildred outside.

"That there's the bake'ouse," Mildred said, pointing to a small stone structure in the center of the courtyard. It looked a little like a garden shed, but it was built of stone and had a thatched roof. A thin trickle of smoke escaped through the thatch.

Mildred led her inside. A fire burned brightly in a cavity on the opposite wall, and directly above it, a semicircular opening marked the entrance to the oven. Claiming a long stick with a wooden paddle at the end that had been leaning against the wall, Mildred bent down and fished out two more loaves through the opening.

"That's the last o' th' bread," she said. "So ya should be able t' fit all yer pies in at once."

"What about the temperature?"

"I added more wood right afore I took out th' loaves," Mildred said, "So it's plenty 'ot enough."

It appeared that the oven had two temperatures: hot and cold. Mariah hadn't needed to be told which one was currently in play. Heat radiated out of the opening in scorching waves. She caught her lower lip between her teeth, attempting to think through a rudimentary bake time. The pies needed to be in the oven long enough for the meat to cook through but not so long that the pastry became leathery. She would have been hard-pressed to achieve that goal in Chef Heston's state-of-the-art oven. To accomplish it in a fiery furnace in the wall seemed all but impossible.

With seemingly no other option available to her, Mariah used the wooden paddle to slide the pies into the rustic oven and then hurried back to collect the others. When she had them all lined up on the hot stone slab, she returned to the kitchen to clear up her work area. She hadn't done more than scrape the pastry bits off the tabletop when Mistress Agatha swooped down upon her again.

"Leave it," she ordered. "Stephen can take care o' this." She turned toward the scullery room. "Stephen!"

At the sound of his name, a young boy ran out, a rag in hand. "'Ere, Mistress Agatha."

The older woman gestured to the floury mess. "The table needs cleanin', lad."

With a vigorous nod, the boy set to work, but Mistress Agatha's attention had returned to Mariah.

"I want ya t' start on th' bread puddin'," she said. "Mildred can show ya where t' find yesterday's bread."

Following Stephen's example, Mariah nodded. Even if Mistress Agatha's hearing were better, Mariah was quite sure that asking for a recipe would get her nowhere. Frantically racking her brain for a list of basic ingredients and the baking methods used for bread pudding, she feigned a confidence she didn't feel and went in search of Mildred.

It wasn't long before Mariah was fully immersed in her new assignment, and she had no idea how much time she'd spent on it when Stephen flew into the kitchen.

"There's somethin' burnin' in th' bake'ouse," he cried.

Mariah dropped the spoon she'd been using to mix the eggs and milk and raced outside. The acrid smell of charred food reached her immediately. Lifting her skirt, she ran to the bakehouse and yanked open the door. A billow of black smoke met her. Coughing, she reached for the tool she had used to put the pies in the oven and drew the closest ones out. They were black. Her fingers on the long pole trembled. Swallowing the lump in her throat, she reached for the pies nearer the back. These looked more like large lumps of charcoal than anything edible.

"The pies!" Mistress Agatha had arrived, and if her indignant exclamation had not been indication enough, the look of fury on her face would have told Mariah all she needed to know. "They're ruined!"

"Forgive me. I was so caught up in making the bread pudding, I didn't think . . . " It was a terrible excuse, and Mariah knew it. To work in a professional kitchen, one had to be a master at multitasking.

"Well, I shall tell ya exactly what t' think now," Mistress Agatha said, her hands on her hips. "It's off t' the market with ya. An' all the way there, yer goin' to be thinkin' 'bout 'ow any money ya may 'ave earned in the next three weeks is goin' to buy two fresh cuts of venison. The moment ya 'ave procured the meat, yer to get back 'ere t' make fresh pies." She narrowed her eyes. "An' if ya don't think ya can do that, ya'll be back in Clifton by sundown. Is that understood?"

"Yes." Mariah clutched her apron. As awful as her current situation was, if she were evicted from the castle and the job in the kitchen that she'd miraculously procured, she'd be both homeless and penniless in the twelfth century. And in her current state of disorientation, it was impossible to see how she'd ever survive that predicament. "I can do it."

"Well, what are ya waiting fer?"

"The market that sells venison," she said loudly. "Where is it exactly?"

Mistress Agatha gave a frustrated grunt. "Ellen!" Moments later, Ellen appeared in the courtyard. "Go with Marian." Mistress Agatha pointed at Mariah. "'Elp 'er find th' butcher at th' market. An' then come straight back 'ere t' finish yer work."

"Yes, M-Mistress Agatha," Ellen said. Her gaze landed on the burnt pies, and she winced. "C-Come, Marian."

⁂

Robin had not enjoyed himself so well in a very long time. The guards at the gate had scarcely given him a second glance when he'd entered the town. After all, a butcher with his head bowed over his heavy cart was a common enough sight on market day. And having met with no other hindrance, Robin had quickly claimed one of the better locations in the square to sell his wares.

Once his meat was on display, he'd clapped two cleavers together and called out his asking prices.

"For all wealthy noblemen and priests, I shall sell three penny-worth of meat for sixpence," Robin cried. "Aldermen may purchase the same cuts for thrupence. To those ragged children sent to the market by their mothers, I shall sell three penny-worth of meat for a penny, and to all bonny lasses at the market today, the price is naught but a kiss."

At first, the other merchants in the vicinity had reacted with blatant stares and head shakes, but word that the new butcher at the market was selling his meat for ridiculous prices had spread rapidly. And with an ever-growing line of people around his cart, some of Robin's neighbors had begun joining in the merriment.

"Come, Mistress Ursula," the tanner whose cart stood beside Robin's beckoned a bent old lady forward. "Are you willing to give this knave a kiss on the cheek in exchange for a plucked goose?"

"Does he consider me to be a bonny lass?" the aged woman asked.

"What say you, butcher?" the tanner asked. "Is Mistress Ursula not the bonniest of all the lasses who have approached your stall this fine morn?"

"Why, yes, indeed," Robin said. "I have rarely seen the like."

The poor widow cackled with laughter, her faded blue eyes shining. "You are a worthy jester, sir, but I shall take a goose for my kiss."

"Done," Robin said, bending low so she could press a kiss to his cheek before wrapping one of the plucked geese in a hemp sack and handing it to her.

She rewarded him with an almost toothless smile. "Bless you, sir. I shall eat better this night than I have in over a year."

Robin met her smile with his own. "I am glad to hear it."

"If ya please, sir."

Robin swiveled to see a young lad of six or seven years leaning over his cart. His tunic was two sizes larger than his thin frame warranted, and his feet were bare. He held a single penny out to Robin. "Me mam would be most grateful fer a piece o' meat."

"How many are there in your home, lad?" Robin asked.

"Six, if ya count th' baby," the boy replied.

"Well then, I believe two cuts of venison for a penny might be just the thing."

The child's eyes widened, filled with new hope. "If ya say so, sir."

With a chuckle, Robin cut two generous slabs of meat from a leg of venison, wrapped them, and handed them over. "A penny, if you please, young man."

The boy handed over the single coin and was gone before Robin could add it to the purse at his belt.

The next person in line was a servant girl of about fifteen or sixteen years. Her fair hair was pulled back in a linen cap, and she was accompanied by a young lady with green eyes, a long chestnut-colored plait tied with a pale-green ribbon, and an anxious expression.

"Ask 'im," the servant girl urged. "We need t-two pieces of venison. One kiss from each of us is heaps b-better than losin' your pay for th-three weeks."

"But it's absurd."

"It is that, miss." The tanner joined their conversation, leaning close, as though imparting a secret. "But if this 'ere butcher's daft enough to sell his meat fer a kiss, who are you and me to argue."

"Two cuts o' venison for two kisses," Robin said. He'd repeated the phrase multiple times already. Why the request suddenly made him feel unaccountably self-conscious, he could not say.

"I'll t-take one," the younger of the two said, rising onto her toes and brushing Robin's cheek with a soft kiss.

"Duly purchased," Robin said, handing her a wrapped piece of meat.

The girl smiled shyly before turning to her companion. "Do it," she whispered. "M-Mistress Agatha is waitin' on us."

The young lady took a deep breath and stepped forward. "A second rump roast of venison, if you please," she said.

The fresh hint of pink in her cheeks only served to further enhance her beautiful face, and maintaining his focus on the job at hand became inexplicably difficult. Robin cleared his throat. A rump roast? He was unfamiliar with that designation of meat. Was that what he'd given the other girl? "Please, make your selection," he said, gesturing toward the meat on his cart.

He caught the young lady's slight grimace as the movement sent a swarm of flies airborne, but she pointed to one of the larger pieces of meat. "Some of that would be marvelous."

Robin nodded, using the butcher's cleaver to cut off a goodly portion and then wrapping it for her much as he had done for every other customer. Unfortunately for Robin, the tanner had seemingly become tired of watching the same routine play out.

"Now then," the fellow called to the crowd. "The good butcher 'as just given away one of 'is largest cuts of meat. I say this comely young lady owes 'im something more than a fleeting peck on the cheek. What say ye?"

The crowd cheered its approval.

"A dance thrice around the cart," someone shouted.

"A song," called another.

"Nay," a fellow in the back yelled. "It must be a true kiss upon the lips."

At the third suggestion, the crowd cheered louder.

"A true kiss! A true kiss!" The chant was quickly picked up by all.

The tanner turned to Robin and grinned. "Better that the people demand it now than when you were serving Mistress Ursula," he said.

Given what Robin had been about all morning, the tanner's teasing was hardly surprising. So, too, was the crowd's high-spirited involvement. But Robin found himself unreasonably irritated by the fellow's meddling—an emotion that surged to even greater heights when he saw the raw panic in the young lady's eyes. She extended the sack he'd just given her toward him, as if returning it would silence the crowd. Robin knew better.

Even though none would hear him over the chanting, he ignored the proffered meat and lowered his voice. "I fear they will not take kindly to you rejecting me or my venison."

She glanced over her shoulder and must have reached the same conclusion because in one brisk movement, she handed the venison to her companion. "One brief kiss. That is all."

Robin raised an eyebrow. He was beginning to wonder if he should take offense at her seeming aversion for the task ahead. "Is the thought of kissing me truly so abhorrent?"

"I . . . I don't even know you."

The girl had stumbled on some of her words, but there was something more unusual about her speech. "You are not from these parts."

She shook her head, and in that moment, he was struck by an unexpected insight. It was not simply panic that shone from her eyes. She bore the same look as many of his men when they first arrived in Sherwood Forest. It spoke of being overwhelmed, displaced, and fearful of the future. Frustration that the tanner had increased her discomfort further ate at Robin, but he could not undo that damage. He could only ease her through it as quickly and painlessly as possible.

He glanced at the tanner, who gave him an anxious look. In the few minutes he'd taken to talk to the young lady, the crowd's mood had begun to shift from jubilant to belligerent.

"Ya'd best be getting on with it," the tanner said. "All this noise will 'ave the castle guards 'ere in no time."

The fellow was right, and Robin would very much like to prevent such a meeting. With newfound urgency, he turned back to the young woman. "I had not thought that crafting so frivolous a payment for my meat would cause you such difficulty, but if we act swiftly, I believe one fleeting kiss will ensure your safe removal from this tumult."

He reached for her hand. She tensed but did not pull away. Her skin was soft. Uncommonly soft. And he was struck by an overwhelming desire to run his thumb across her knuckles. Shaking off the impulse, he drew her closer. "The moment I release you," he continued, "circle my stall and use the alley to make good your escape."

Her nod told him that she understood, and he waited no longer. Releasing her, he cupped her face in his hands, lowered his head, and pressed his lips to hers. The spark was instant. It lit his chest as the feel of her skin beneath his fingertips filled him with spine-tingling awareness—of her, of their proximity, of the rarity of this moment. He could not define any part of it; he only knew that he ached for more.

The crowd roared its approval, the sound penetrating Robin's befuddled mind and causing some semblance of intelligence to return. A brief kiss. He had given her his word that this would be a brief kiss. He drew back, and her eyelids fluttered open. For two heartbeats, he held her gaze. Then she blinked, and the surrounding commotion returned in a rush.

"Go," he said. "Straightway."

She staggered back a pace.

Her companion grabbed her sleeve and tugged. "Come, Marian. M-Make haste." She pulled her around the burley yeoman standing at the corner of the cart, and with one last bewildered glance at Robin, the young lady named Marian disappeared from his sight.

CHAPTER 6

Mariah stumbled after Ellen, her head spinning. A stranger had kissed her. A tall, broad-shouldered stranger with dark-brown hair, a tidily trimmed beard, and stunning blue eyes. If this new reality was to be believed, he was a twelfth-century butcher, and the kiss had been nothing more than a lark. A gimmick designed to draw shoppers to his stall.

Then why had it felt so . . . so . . . She drew a ragged breath. She didn't even know how to describe her feelings. Her lips were still tingling, her heart still pounding. She hadn't kissed anyone since she'd dated Trevor Sackville two years ago. And his kisses had never caused her to lose every thought in her head.

"Guards!" Ellen's warning cut through muddled thinking. "Keep your head d-down and act like everythin's n-normal."

Normal? Mariah could hardly remember what normal felt like, but she tucked her chin a little lower.

"Why don't we want the guards to see us?" she whispered.

"'Cause as often as n-not, the guards and trouble go t-together."

The marching feet were heading toward the butcher's cart.

Mariah hazarded a glance over her shoulder. The crowd behind them was dispersing rapidly.

"Everyone's leaving."

"Aye. That's usually the way of it." Ellen followed Mariah's gaze and then released a hissing breath. "The sh-sheriff's with them."

One of the guards moved slightly to the left, exposing the man walking at his side. If the Sheriff of Nottingham's haughty posture and confident stride had been insufficient to set him apart from others in the marketplace, his elegant clothing would have done the job. This morning, his dark velvet tunic was trimmed with red ribbon, and a gold medallion hung around his neck.

"What's he doing here?" Mariah was quite sure the sheriff didn't stoop to buying his own groceries.

"I c-cannot say," Ellen said. "But his p-presence never omens well." She veered off the main square and into a dimly lit narrow alley. "Come. If we take this l-lane, we'll reach the castle without risk of meetin' any m-more of the sheriff's men. And it's best that we r-return to the castle afore anything else happens."

Mariah considered asking what kind of things might happen but then thought better of it. If this morning's debacle with the burning pies had taught her anything, it was that she couldn't afford to lose her concentration again. For the next few hours, she needed to expel all thoughts of the marketplace—and the blue-eyed butcher she'd kissed—and direct her attention completely on making up for her mistake in the kitchen.

———— · ✸ · ————

Robin hadn't needed to hear the tanner's muttered curse to know that trouble was coming. And if the speed at which the crowd was dispersing was any indication, the threat was significant. Keeping his ears attuned for any indications of the danger, he tugged the front of his brown hood a little lower over his eyes and moved to stand behind the cart.

The clipped steps of castle guards drawing closer was his first clue to the newcomers' identities; the tensing of the tanner's shoulders was his second.

"Who comes?" Robin asked.

"The sheriff and his men."

"How many men?" Raising his head to count guards would not be in his best interest at this point.

"Five. Nay, six," the tanner said while making a show of reorganizing the satchels hanging from the hooks on his cart. "An' they're headin' directly this way."

With the sheriff, that was seven. Seven against one was poor odds. Robin had faced worse, but not without his bow and arrows. If he were wearing his usual Lincoln green, the sheriff would know him immediately. But the despicable lawman would not be expecting him to be within the walls of Nottingham town dressed as a butcher. Robin whooshed another swarm of flies off the last remaining plucked goose hanging from the cart. He would attempt subterfuge. If that did not work, he may be forced to resort to a foot race with the guards.

"You there!" The sheriff and his men came to a halt before his cart.

"My lord sheriff," Robin said, bowing his head lower.

"What have you been about to cause such commotion in the market?"

"Nothing more than outselling my competition, Sheriff," Robin said.

The sheriff eyed Robin suspiciously. "Word is you are giving away your wares."

"Not so," Robin said. "Each piece of meat has its price, but I would rather earn a penny for a leg of lamb than return home with it unsold because no one could afford to pay me sixpence."

Silently, the sheriff studied the remaining meat on the cart. "Are you so wealthy that you have no need of the additional coins?"

"Is not wealth a matter of perspective? My brothers and I are free to roam numerous acres whenever we please, and there are over five hundred horned beasts grazing the land. But I doubt another would consider us wealthy since we cannot sell a single one, and I must resort to butchering to line our purses with coins."

A calculating look entered the sheriff's dark eyes. "Over five hundred beasts, you say?"

"Aye. All healthy and strong."

"And yet no one has come forward wishing to purchase any of them?"

"It grieves me to admit to it," Robin said. "Particularly when we could so readily make use of the money."

The sheriff folded his arms, his eyes narrowing. "How much are you asking for your cattle?"

"Well, they are worth at least five hundred pounds."

"A shame," the sheriff said. "That is too much for me." He paused as though considering the situation further. "But a fellow who is so desperate for coins that he would sell his meat for a penny must needs be willing to accept additional help, no matter the sum. I can give you three hundred pounds for them all, and it shall be in the gold and silver you desire."

Fiddling with the small purse at his belt, Robin made a great show of supposedly deliberating this insulting offer. "So many cattle are worth far more," he said. "But my brothers and I do need the money."

"Bring me the cattle, and you shall have the money straightway."

At this, Robin straightened his shoulders. "Nay, Sheriff. For such a small payment, I shall not deliver the beasts to the castle. But if you will travel the road that leads from town as far as its entrance into Sherwood Forest, I shall meet you there at dawn on the morrow."

The sheriff's frown was fleeting. He was likely unused to bartering for that which he desired, but he was unwilling to relinquish so advantageous a trade. "My clerk shall draw up a paper that will bind you to the sale," he said. "You shall not have a single coin without my receiving the beasts in return."

"Fair enough," Robin said.

The sheriff's smirk told of the smug pleasure he took in swindling a yeoman out of his inheritance. "Your name, good fellow?"

"Robert," Robin said. "Robert o' Locksley."

"Very well, Robert o' Locksley," the sheriff said, signaling to his guards. "We shall meet again at sunrise."

Robin bowed, and by the time he raised his head, the sheriff and his men were halfway across the square.

"Are you quite mad?" The tanner did nothing to hide his incredulity. "Three hundred pounds for five hundred head of cattle is scarcely short of robbery."

"Agreed," Robin said. "But who am I to turn down the Sheriff of Nottingham?"

The tanner gave him a troubled look. "No man embraces a night or two in the dungeon, but I did not take you for one who would fall for the sheriff's deceit so easily."

Reaching for his cleaver, Robin bit back a grin. "Mayhap you are not so mistaken as you think."

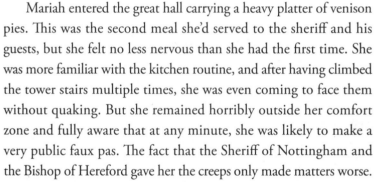

Mariah entered the great hall carrying a heavy platter of venison pies. This was the second meal she'd served to the sheriff and his guests, but she felt no less nervous than she had the first time. She was more familiar with the kitchen routine, and after having climbed the tower stairs multiple times, she was even coming to face them without quaking. But she remained horribly outside her comfort zone and fully aware that at any minute, she was likely to make a very public faux pas. The fact that the Sheriff of Nottingham and the Bishop of Hereford gave her the creeps only made matters worse.

Moving toward the center of the table, she carefully lowered the platter to an empty spot between two pitchers of ale. These pies were her second attempt, and after she'd put them in the bakehouse oven, she'd gone out to check on them after every second piece of bread she'd broken into the bread pudding dish. No one could accuse her of negligence this time. The pastry was golden and as evenly baked as it could be in such a primitive oven, but she had no idea what the filling was like. And that was terrifying.

On the other end of the table, Ellen deposited her platter of roast duck and picked up an empty bread basket. Mariah followed her example, reaching for the one closest to her.

"I hear you struck quite a bargain with a butcher at the market today, Sheriff." The Bishop of Hereford set a drumstick on his trencher and licked the grease off his fingers.

Mariah's fingers tightened around the basket. Was he talking about the butcher who'd given her and Ellen cuts of meat for a kiss? A kiss that she hadn't been able to stop thinking about since it had happened.

The sheriff's self-satisfied expression was instant. "Indeed. I discovered him quite by accident beside the tanner's stall, and I have rarely enjoyed so satisfying a morning at the market."

"Am I to assume that you robbed the poor fellow?"

The sheriff's smile showed his discolored teeth. "Not yet, but it will happen soon enough."

Mariah walked the length of the table, mindlessly checking the quantity of ale remaining in each of the pitchers. She had gone from wanting to leave the room before anyone cut into one of her pies to looking for excuses to stay. What had the odious sheriff done to the butcher?

"I am twice intrigued," the bishop said. "Please, enlighten me."

The sheriff grinned. "The simpleton has five hundred head of cattle and yet is selling his meat for pennies to fill his purse. I simply offered to purchase his cattle so that he would not want for gold and silver any longer."

"I see." The bishop dipped a piece of bread in the meat drippings in his trencher and raised it to his mouth. "And given your gratified countenance, am I to conclude that he accepted a preposterously low price for his cattle?"

"To a country yeoman, three hundred pounds is no paltry amount."

The bishop's eyes widened. "If the fellow agreed to that price without coercion, he is more fool than butcher."

Mariah didn't know anything about the butcher, but the clear blue eyes that had met hers at the conclusion of their kiss had not been those of a fool. He'd also exhibited above-average intelligence in his ability to read the volatile crowd's mood swings. Surely he'd recognized the sheriff's efforts to cheat him for exactly that.

As though ascertaining her thoughts, the sheriff snorted. "Oh, he is a fool, all right. He has agreed to meet me on the road that leads out of Sherwood Forest at dawn to exchange his five hundred head of cattle for a purse of coins."

A ripple of laughter ran along the table. Mariah snatched up a half-full pitcher, indignation that the butcher was being mocked in such a humiliating way gnawing at her. No one deserved to be ridiculed so publicly, particularly someone who had given food to those who could not afford it and had treated her with respect.

"I am surprised you agreed to meet the fellow so early," the bishop said. "I would not have thought you left your bed before dawn."

"Losing a few hours' sleep for so valuable a prize is worth the sacrifice." The sheriff shrugged, a sly look on his face. "Besides, I shall not stay long enough to wait for the fellow to count the coins and express disappointment or outrage if there are only two hundred pounds' worth. I shall place my men in charge of the cattle, which will leave me free to return to my bedchamber if I so desire."

Mariah glanced at the guests surrounding the table. Three of the men appeared amused at the sheriff's confession; the others were focused on their food. Did no one feel outraged by what he was planning? Not only had the detestable man offered the butcher far less than his cattle were worth, but he was also planning to swindle him further by not paying him the full amount.

"I shall look forward to hearing all about it upon your return," the Bishop of Hereford said. "Unlike you, I have no desire to rise before the sun."

Even though all the servants did. The discouraging certainty that those who served these men were forced to awaken so long before them heightened Mariah's frustration over the sheriff's ability to make his own rules.

Not wanting to hear more, she started toward the door Ellen had just exited. Mariah was exhausted, but she and the rest of the kitchen help had all the cleanup to do before their day was over. And tomorrow's chores would undoubtedly start just as early as they had today.

Her footsteps slowed as a new thought took hold. Unless something miraculous occurred in the next few hours, she would awaken tomorrow morning in the castle. And it would be before the Sheriff of Nottingham arose. Was it possible that she could reach the rendezvous spot at Sherwood Forest in time to warn the butcher of the sheriff's plans to swindle him further? She vacillated. It was a crazy idea. She was as likely to get lost on the unfamiliar roads as to be helpful. Besides, if she wasn't back in time to start her morning chores, she ran the risk of angering Mistress Agatha again.

She shook her head helplessly. Had she actually reached the point at which she'd come to accept that this medieval existence was her future? She didn't want to relinquish all hope of escaping it, but living in a state of constant confusion, doubt, and fear was as draining as it was disheartening. Perhaps if she did something more than simply stumble through her assigned daily chores, it would help lift the despair that clung to her.

Memories of the butcher's kiss and her traitorous body's instant response to it infiltrated her perplexed thoughts. The butcher had upheld his end of the bargain. He'd given her a large cut of meat for no monetary payment and had helped facilitate her escape from the crowd at the market. Returning one good deed with another was simply the right thing to do.

With fresh purpose, she closed the door behind her and hurried to the tower. Ellen would know where the main road from Nottingham town met Sherwood Forest—and how long it would take to get there on foot.

CHAPTER 7

Somewhere outside, an owl hooted. As far as Mariah was concerned, it was a sure sign that morning had not yet arrived. Unfortunately, Ellen didn't seem to feel the same way. She'd woken Mariah even earlier than she had the day before and was now leading her through a maze of stone passageways toward a lesser-used outer door.

Forcing her tired body to move more quickly, Mariah attempted to keep up with her friend. Their footsteps were little more than a whispered echo, but an occasional thud or scrape that reached them from nearby rooms and corridors kept both young women listening for the heavy tread of a castle guard's feet.

They reached another corner, and Ellen paused. "This is it." She spoke softly. "The d-door to the inner c-courtyard is around this bend. R-Remember, once you're past the bakehouse, you'll see the ent-trance to the outer courtyard. S-Straight ahead after that, and you'll reach the g-gates."

"And you still think I can get out without being stopped?" Mariah asked. The terror of being caught by a castle guard the night before still lingered. As much as she wanted to help the butcher, she had no desire to end up in the dungeon for her efforts.

"Aye. There'll be p-plenty of activity at the gates by now."

Given that the sun had yet to fully rise, that was hard to believe, but up until now, Ellen had not led her astray.

Ellen hurried forward again, and Mariah followed. Taking ahold of the metal ring on the thick wooden door, Ellen eased the latch upward. It made a loud grating noise. Mariah held her breath.

When no other sound followed, Ellen cracked the door open and peered out through the narrow gap. "It's clear," she said. "If anyone s-sees you, just hold your head up and act like you've been sent by M-Mistress Agatha. There's not many who's willin' to risk p-puttin' Mistress Agatha in a foul mood."

Mariah managed an anxious smile. It seemed that no matter the century, people were reluctant to upset the person who fed them. "Let's hope I don't do exactly that," she said.

Ellen glanced at the sky and then shook her head. "If you hasten, I r-reckon you've time to get to the m-meetin' place and back afore Mistress Agatha is d-dishin' out orders. And if she asks for you, I'll t-tell her you're in the cheese r-room. That excuse won't l-last long, mind, so you can't be dilly-dallyin'. You're g-goin' to have to give the butcher your message and then l-leave straightway."

"I will," Mariah said, a new wave of nervousness causing her stomach to clench. "And thank you. I couldn't have done this without your help."

Last night, when Mariah had expressed her desire to outwit the sheriff, Ellen had immediately offered to guide Mariah out of the castle. Ellen had drawn a rudimentary map with her finger in the flour on the floor of the grain storage room, showing Mariah how the road leading away from the castle would take her directly through the town gates and into the forest. It appeared that in the twelfth century, Sherwood Forest completely surrounded Nottingham—which explained the Bishop of Hereford's frustration over Robin Hood's control of the road. If Ellen was right, Mariah would have less than a mile to walk to reach the sheriff and butcher's rendezvous point.

"After what that b-butcher did yesterday, givin' meat to them that haven't eaten any in w-weeks, I'm right glad to do my part."

Her eyes sparkled in the half-light. "Though, I will say, it must have b-been quite a kiss to cause you to take such r-risk."

Warmth flooded Mariah's cheeks. "This has nothing to do with that ridiculous kiss and everything to do with preventing a generous man from being cheated."

"As you say." Ellen's teeth glistened in the darkness, and Mariah knew that her young friend was smiling. "Though why he hides them b-blue eyes of his beneath that b-brown hood is beyond me."

"I must go," Mariah said, now as eager to cut this conversation short as she was to put her reckless assignment behind her.

Ellen must have sensed her need to concentrate on the task at hand because her smile disappeared as quickly as it had come. "Once you're through the gates, turn l-left," she said, repeating the instructions she'd given Mariah earlier. "After that, the road'll lead you right to the edge of the f-forest."

Mariah slipped through the door. Ellen closed it behind her, and as the latch dropped into place, Mariah was struck by how quickly she'd come to rely on Ellen. In this medieval world where Mariah knew and understood so little, Ellen had become her anchor. Standing in the inner courtyard, completely alone, she felt overwhelmed by the path ahead—both out of the castle and into the future. Last night, foiling the Sheriff of Nottingham's despicable plan had seemed completely doable. Now, it seemed even more foolish than the butcher's decision to sell his cattle to the odious man. Who was she to step into this era and think that she could singlehandedly make a difference? She could barely make a pie.

Drawing the thin blanket she'd taken from her pallet more closely around her shoulders, she took a steadying breath. It was now or never. The darkness was lifting, and she didn't have time for indecision. A dog barked, a door creaked, and then came the clop of hooves. Mariah took off running. If horses were being led out of the stables, the sheriff and his men were expected soon.

She reached the outer courtyard in seconds. The torches that must have been burning all night at the castle gate still flickered, shedding additional light on an old man leading a mule-drawn cart into the castle. Mariah moved closer to the wall, relying on the shadows to hide her as she watched two guards approach the new arrival, one from either side of the gate.

One of the guards spoke. The old man answered and gestured toward the cart. Both guards stepped closer, one of them lifting the covering. Mariah was too far away to identify the cargo, but she was grateful for whatever it was. With all three men's attention diverted from the entrance, she picked up her pace, slipped past them, and walked out of the castle with her eyes fixed on the dirt road ahead.

There was now enough light that she could make out the grass verge and the dark ribbon of water at the base of the hill. Following the road to the left, she continued down the slope. Behind her, the castle walls loomed gray and forbidding, but up ahead the pale-gray skies that heralded daybreak silhouetted a sea of trees.

Mariah stumbled to a halt. Sherwood Forest. It had to be. For a brief moment, the doubts she'd been harboring lifted. A forest this large, this magnificent, could not possibly be a product of her imagination. It was so much bigger and more impressive than the woodlands in twenty-first century Nottinghamshire that grew miles away from the City of Nottingham. Her breath hitched at the thought. Was this truly her new reality? She was like a boat adrift without moorings. And she barely knew how to operate the rudder. Her only guide was instinct and her innate sense of right and wrong.

She chanced a glance over her shoulder. The road behind her remained devoid of travelers, but she had a sinking feeling it wouldn't stay that way for long. The sheriff and his men must be close behind her by now. Raising the hem of her long skirts, she started running downhill toward the trees.

* * ✳ * ·

Robin stood beside the largest oak at the edge of the forest, his eyes on the road leading to the castle. The sheriff would come, Robin was sure of it. The man had yet to control the glint of greed that lit his dark eyes when he saw or spoke of something he wished to claim as his own. And the butcher's fictitious cattle fell firmly into that category.

Five hundred head for three hundred pounds. Robin snorted. The corrupt official must think Robin every kind of fool for accepting such an offer. Of course, such thinking would not last much longer.

Movement—one flitting shadow rather than men on horseback—caught his attention on the hillside. He strained to identify it. Deer rarely ventured so close to the castle walls, but whatever or whoever it was was moving rapidly. He caught the flutter of something in the slight breeze. Mayhap a cloak or skirt. He frowned. Was this a diversion conceived by the Sheriff of Nottingham? It was uncommonly early for a servant to be without the castle walls, particularly a solitary female.

Robin watched a moment more before slipping into the forest's undergrowth. Situating himself behind a tall hydrangea bush, he kept his ears open and his eyes on the narrow road. It wasn't long before he heard the sound of hurried feet, and moments later, a woman came into view. A thin gray blanket covered her head and shoulders, making her impossible to identify, but the simple clothing showing beneath her makeshift cloak suggested that she was a servant, and the speed at which she'd traversed the hill spoke of her youth.

She came to a halt opposite the oak tree and turned in a slow circle, as though searching for something.

"Butcher?" Her voice was hesitant. She cleared her throat and tried again, this time more loudly. "Butcher?"

Robin tensed. He was currently dressed as a butcher, and to the best of his knowledge, there was no other butcher in Sherwood Forest. He knew for a certainty that none of his men had left that profession to join his band. The Sheriff of Nottingham was expecting to meet a butcher at this spot, but why would he send a young lady in his stead?

"What business do you have with a butcher?" he called.

She started, swinging around to face the dense foliage between them. "Who are you?"

"A friend of the butcher's," he said.

Her fingers tightened around the blanket at her neck. "I have come to warn him." Her gaze darted from one bush to another. "There's not much time. The Sheriff of Nottingham and his men will be here any minute."

"How do I know you are not sent from the sheriff to trick the butcher?"

She stiffened. "Because I would refuse to do that."

It was a ridiculous response. He had yet to find a servant who did not live in fear of the sheriff, but he could not fault her boldness. "Forgive me if I find that difficult to believe."

"You don't have to believe me." She turned to look back the way she'd come. Atop the hill, four mounted horses were exiting the castle gates. She gasped and swung around. "We're running out of time." She took a half step back. "Tell the butcher that the young lady he kissed at the marketplace came to warn him that the sheriff intends to trick him into selling his cattle for even less than the insultingly low price they agreed upon."

Robin froze. Countless ladies had brushed his cheek with their lips to earn a piece of meat the day before, but he had kissed only one. "Marian." The name escaped in a whisper, just as it had throughout the night when the memory of the simmering connection he'd experienced with the unknown young lady had kept him tossing and turning beneath his canopy of leaves.

Who was this woman who had so fully captured his imagination in one brief encounter? Her manner of speech indicated that she was not from these parts. Her uncertainty in the marketplace supported that notion. And yet, she was bold enough to seek him out in the forest before full daylight.

He stepped out from behind the bush. "Why would you risk so much for a man you have met but once?"

She stumbled back a few paces more. "You're here!"

"Aye. And I must ask your forgiveness for not showing myself sooner. With the blanket covering your head, I did not know you." Though Robin knew he should prepare himself for the sheriff's imminent arrival, he kept his eyes on her. "Why are you here?"

"I—" She swallowed. "I heard the sheriff talking of his plan to swindle you, and I couldn't ignore it. No one deserves to be treated like that, least of all someone who was so generous with others at the market."

"You came here solely to warn me of the sheriff's scheme?"

"Yes. There will be far less than the paltry amount you agreed upon in the purse he gives you."

"How much less?"

"He bragged about acquiring five hundred head of cattle for two hundred pounds," she said.

Robin barely caught the curse before it crossed his lips. The depth of the sheriff's greed was unfathomable. And the sheriff must truly have thought the butcher a simpleton. Either that, or desperate beyond measure.

"I thank you for the forewarning," he said. "It was most courageous of you to come."

The pounding of horses' hooves was louder now.

She took another step back. "I think the word you're looking for is *crazy*," she said, a hint of panic lacing her voice. "I must go. And you should too."

Robin had no notion what the word *crazy* meant, but he surmised it was a negative trait. "I stand by my word choice," he said. "Now, leave this place. As quickly as you can."

"But what about you?"

He shrugged. "I gave the sheriff my word that I would meet him here at sunrise, and so I shall."

"He's going to try to pull the wool over your eyes," she insisted. "And if you call him out on it, his men will step in."

Her vocabulary was all but impossible to understand, but her mounting anxiety was obvious.

"I am far more concerned about your safe return to the castle than I am about facing the Sheriff of Nottingham and his men," he said.

"Butcher!" The sheriff's voice reached them through the trees.

"He's here!" she gasped.

Robin pointed to a small break in the bushes beside the large oak. "Take that path," he said. "It will take you away from the forest road initially, but ere long, it bends to join the main thoroughfare leading to the town."

She crossed to the spot directly, the blanket slipping from her head and exposing her silken chestnut hair as she ran.

When she'd reached the safety of the ancient tree, she turned. "Please," she whispered. "Do not let him cheat you." And then, before he could muster a response, she was gone.

Battling an unaccountable desire to chase after her, Robin turned to face the men approaching him on horseback.

"Fear not, Maid Marian," he said softly. "In this instance, at least, the Sheriff of Nottingham has met his match."

CHAPTER 8

R obert of Locksley." The Sheriff of Nottingham reined his mount to a halt. "As you see, I have come at our appointed time. And yet, there is no herd of cattle to be seen."

"As you say, my good sheriff," Robin said, bowing low. "But I can attest that the beasts are here. We have only to venture a little farther into the forest to see them."

"Nonsense." The sheriff's voice rang with irritation. "You were to bring them with you."

"Not so. I agreed to meet you here, but there was no mention of the animals. Truly, the herd is so large, the beasts would assuredly scatter if they were this close to the open road."

The sheriff issued a displeased grunt. He could not argue against Robin's point, but neither did he make any effort to agree. "Our destination had best be a short distance from here."

Robin smiled. "I cannot say for certain—animals are prone to wander, after all—but I feel confident that we shall see them soon enough." He moved to stand beside the sheriff's horse. "Shall we go?"

The sheriff eyed the narrow road through the trees warily. "This place harbors thieves and scoundrels who have no respect for the law. To leave your cattle in the forest unguarded is folly."

"Oh, my brothers are nearby," Robin said. "I daresay we shall encounter one or another of them as we journey."

He started forward, and the sheriff seemingly decided that if he were to acquire the cattle he wanted so badly, he had no choice but to follow. And so, they made their way deeper into the forest, with Robin walking alongside the sheriff's mount and the sheriff's three men riding behind. No one spoke. All around them, branches cracked, and leaves trembled in the light breeze.

The sheriff's gaze darted nervously from one tree to another. "This is quite far enough, butcher," he said.

"I think I hear them, my lord sheriff. Did you not hear the grunt just then?"

"Why would I be listening for a grunt? We are here for cattle, not forest animals."

Robin came to a sudden halt. "Well, this is an unfortunate misunderstanding," he said.

"There should be no misunderstanding," the sheriff growled. "We had a good-faith agreement."

"Aye. Three hundred pounds for five hundred beasts." Robin set his hands upon his hips. "Have you upheld your side of the bargain?"

"Who are you to question my integrity?" For a man caught in his deception, the sheriff was making an admirable show of appearing affronted.

"The very same fellow who knows full well that you intend to cheat me out of one hundred pounds," Robin said.

The sheriff released a hissing breath. "You are playing a dangerous game, Robert of Locksley."

"This is no game, Sheriff, and I am in no danger here."

The words were no sooner spoken than a rhythmic rumble began, setting the ground vibrating beneath his feet. The horses nickered nervously, but Robin grinned. If one of his men had set the deer running in so timely a fashion, he would have to thank the fellow.

He gestured farther down the path. "Behold a portion of my herd."

An elegant stag broke free of the vegetation, leading a dozen dun-colored does across the road. They thundered by without pause, disappearing between the trees again with a thundering of hooves.

The sheriff's jaw tightened, and his eyes flashed with anger. "You are no more a penniless butcher than am I, Robert of Locksley. You may have brought me down here on a fool's errand, but you will be the one who shall wish it never happened." He snapped his gloved thumb and finger, but before the sheriff could issue an order to his men, Robin raised the horn hanging from his belt to his lips and blew three short blasts.

"Seize him!" the sheriff shouted.

The nearest guard had scarcely moved when the bushes on either side of the men quivered, and Little John, Allan a Dale, and Will Scarlett stepped onto the path.

"Greetings, gentlemen," Little John said cheerily, strolling toward the sheriff as though unaware that Allan a Dale and Will Scarlett had immediately drawn their bows, or that each of the sheriff's guards had his hand upon the hilt of his sword. "Robin Hood told us that we might expect guests to eat with us this fine morning. May I say, you are most welcome."

Awareness of Robin's true identity lit the sheriff's features. "Curse you, Robin Hood!" In one swift movement, he swung his mount around. But Allan a Dale anticipated his attempt to escape and stepped into the center of the path, his bow and arrow ready.

"I had not taken you for a man who would refuse to share a meal with neighbors, Sheriff," Robin said.

"You are no more my neighbor than are the worms beneath my feet," the sheriff retorted.

"Far be it for me to disagree with so distinguished a gentleman," Friar Tuck said, stepping out from between the trees with his customarily late timing, "but the Good Book makes it abundantly clear that all God's children are neighbors, one to another."

"I thank you for your words of reassurance, Friar Tuck," Little John said. "Although I would venture that there are worse creatures in this world than the humble earthworm. A wolf who devotes his life to attacking others out of self-indulgence must surely be considered of lesser value."

Friar Tuck nodded solemnly. "Wise words, Little John. For on more than one occasion, God has warned His children to beware of wolves."

"Enough!" the sheriff roared. "Your moment of entertainment is passed. Detain us any longer and the entirety of the castle guards shall sweep down upon you and remove you to the castle dungeon."

His threat held no sway. Not only was it wholly unlikely that the captain of the guards was aware of the sheriff's destination this early in the morning, but also if sending the entire garrison into the forest was a sure way of capturing Robin Hood and his men, the sheriff would have employed the tactic long ago.

"I fear your guests have no interest in sharing our meal, Robin," Friar Tuck said, slipping his hands into the wide sleeves of his brown robe and appearing suitably crestfallen. "And I have used the very best ingredients for the pottage."

"The sheriff is an uncommonly busy man, Friar Tuck," Robin said. "It should not surprise us that he cannot spare an hour to eat with us. But given that you have spared no expense on this meal, I am quite certain he would be willing to repay you the cost of your ingredients."

"Well now." Friar Tuck gave every appearance of perking up. "That is something."

"How much must you recoup, Friar?" Little John asked.

"Fifty pounds should cover it," Friar Tuck said.

The sheriff spluttered a furious oath. "Are you quite mad? Fifty pounds for a bowl of pottage?"

"You are a worthy minister, Friar Tuck," Robin said, ignoring the sheriff's outburst, "but a man of numbers you are not. There are four men here. If the sheriff's bowl of pottage is worth fifty pounds, four bowls require a payment of two hundred."

"By the saints, Robin." Drawing on his flair for the dramatic, Friar Tuck smacked the side of his bald pate. "You have the right of it yet again. Two hundred pounds it must be."

Whereas the sheriff had been indignant moments ago, he was now rendered voiceless. His mouth opened, but when no sound emerged, he snapped it shut again.

Robin was quite content to speak first. "How fortuitous that you filled your purse with that exact amount, Sheriff." He pulled his knife from the scabbard at his belt and pointed it at the purse's leather straps hanging from the sheriff's saddle. "As you appear to have no further interest in purchasing my beasts, donating the insulting sum you intended to pay me to the good friar would seem to be a fair compromise."

"That is preposterous!" the sheriff bellowed.

"No more so than offering two hundred pounds for five hundred head of cattle," Robin said.

"Guards!" The sheriff waved his arm feverishly. "Take him!"

Instantly, his men urged their mounts forward. But Allan a Dale was faster. The sheriff's guards had moved fewer than five paces when his arrow landed on the ground immediately before the lead horse. The animal reared, his rider battling to regain control as the other horses came to a staggering halt.

"I should warn you," Robin said calmly. "Allan has already nocked another arrow, and methinks it unlikely that he means for the next one to be a warning." In truth, though Allan a Dale's skill with a bow had aided the men of Sherwood more than once when they were in need of fresh venison, he had never used it to injure a man. The sheriff and his men did not know that, of course, and Robin was not of a mind to enlighten them. He stepped up to the sheriff's horse. "Shall I cut your purse free, or would you rather untie it?"

The sheriff's haughty snort may have fooled his guards, but Robin had caught the fear mingling with fury in his eyes. And when the unprincipled lawman raised his prominent chin and looked away,

Robin leaned forward and severed the purse's leather straps. The heavy pouch fell into his waiting hand with a clink of coins.

Robin raised it. "I thank you, Sheriff. As does Friar Tuck and the many poor parishioners in Nottingham who shall benefit from an unexpected coin or two."

"If any remain after I have recouped the cost of my fine pottage, that is," Friar Tuck added.

"Of course." Robin fought to keep the grin from his face. Friar Tuck's pottage was not known for being tasty, and it was unfailingly lacking in costly or memorable ingredients.

"Speaking of which," Little John said, "I am ready to eat, and if the sheriff is so busy as to refuse to join us, he had best be on his way."

"Well said, Little John." Robin moved to stand beside his friend. "It was a pleasure doing business with you, my lord sheriff. I hope you will join us at a later date."

The Sheriff of Nottingham shot him a hate-filled glare. "Mark my words, Robin Hood," he said. "You shall pay dearly for this." And then he wheeled his horse around and started back the way he had come at a gallop.

As one, the guards swung their mounts around to follow after him. Robin and his men watched them go until they turned the bend and disappeared from sight. Only then did Allan a Dale and Will Scarlett lower their bows.

"Masterfully done, men," Robin said, attaching the sheriff's leather pouch to his belt. "Although, I am not sure who deserves the greater credit: Allan for his skill with the bow or Friar Tuck for his thespian abilities."

"Do not discount your role in this, Robin." Little John raised his staff across his shoulder. "You can be sure that the honorable Sheriff of Nottingham will not. And for all his airs of indifference, he left here in as foul a mood as I've ever seen him." He offered Robin a warning look. "And that does not bode well for you."

"I daresay it would be most discouraging to embark upon an outing during which one means to cheat a fellow of his entire livelihood only to lose one's purse and return home with nothing," Robin said.

"To lose face in front of his guards was an additional blow," Allan a Dale said.

"Little John is correct, Robin." Will Scarlett joined them, his bow across his back once more. "You had best stay clear of Nottingham for a period. The sheriff will be all the more anxious for your head after this. Two hundred pounds is no paltry loss."

"No, indeed," Robin said. "And yet it was two-thirds of what he offered Robert of Locksley, the butcher."

Lines appeared on Little John's forehead. "How did you come to know precisely what was in his purse?"

"A rather remarkable young lady named Marian told me."

"Marian?" Little John said. "Where did you happen upon her?"

"In the forest. And at the market before that."

Little John's frown deepened. "Is she new to the castle or the town?"

"That, I cannot tell you." Robin started for the gap between the trees, his thoughts on the mysterious and startlingly beautiful woman who had risked so much for the butcher. "But—the Sheriff of Nottingham's desire for revenge notwithstanding—it is something I intend to find out."

———— · * ⁕ · ————

Mariah hurried up the last portion of the hill leading to the castle gates. Already, the morning sun was bathing the stone walls with pale-yellow light, and a straggling line of men and women were filtering in past the guards standing sentinel on either side of the entrance. The sheriff and his men had galloped past her a short time earlier. What that meant for the butcher, she didn't know. Neither could she devote any more time to thinking about it. Her focus had to be on how she could explain her horribly late arrival to Mistress Agatha.

Lowering the portion of the blanket that covered her head to her shoulders, she approached the nearest guard.

"What business do ya 'ave at the castle?" he asked.

"I work in the kitchen," she said.

He eyed her suspiciously. "I know all them that work with Mistress Agatha."

"I just got here a couple of days ago." Had it truly only been that long? Her life in modern-day London seemed like a distant memory. "I haven't met many people yet."

He grunted. "It's plain t' see that yer not from around 'ere."

Concerned, Mariah glanced down at her clothing. She'd thought the costume from Mrs. McQuivey's shop blended in well with the clothing of the other servants at the castle.

"Where d' ya hail from t' be talkin' like that?"

It was her speech. Again. Mentally kicking herself for not being more careful, she managed a weak smile. "London."

"That would do it."

He stood aside, and Mariah offered a silent sigh of relief.

"I thank you," she said.

He nodded. That expression, at least, was something he recognized.

Battling her desire to run, she started across the outer courtyard at a brisk pace. She had passed the stables and was almost to the inner courtyard when she heard a familiar voice.

"Marian!"

Swiveling, she spotted Ellen coming from what looked to be a low-walled well. She carried a full pail of water in each hand.

Mariah rushed toward her. "What are you doing here?"

"G-Gettin' water," she said. "And prayin' with every b-breath in me body that y-you'd return straightway."

"Is Mistress Agatha upset?"

"Aye. But n-not 'cos you were gone. Stephen knocked over the b-bucket of ashes right after M-Mildred finished clearin' the f-fireplace. It were a t-terrible mess. M-Mistress Agatha were fit to be t-tied." She raised one of the pails of water. "That's why I'm f-fetchin' more water."

As sorry as Mariah was that Stephen was in trouble for what had surely been an accident, she couldn't help but be grateful that his mishap had saved the cook from dwelling on her absence.

"Give me one of the buckets," Mariah said, reaching for the nearest one. "We'll go back together."

Ellen relinquished a pail. "If we go past the b-bake'ouse, you can leave your blanket in a c-corner there and f-fetch it at the end of the day."

"Good idea." Mariah had almost forgotten she still had the extra covering across her shoulders. "Honestly, what would I do without you?"

Ellen smiled shyly. "I'm happy to have a friend."

As they started toward the inner courtyard together, Mariah pondered Ellen's immediate acceptance of her. "You offered me friendship from the moment we met," she said. "Even though I obviously know so little and talk so differently than anyone else in the castle."

"You're from L-London. I'd expect you to sound different." Ellen watched the water sloshing in her pail. "Besides, not once have you m-mentioned my c-clumsy speech."

"Your stutter? But that's completely out of your control."

Ellen attempted a weak smile. "That's how it feels to me. But others d-don't see it that way. Most say me b-bodily humors are out of balance and want nothin' to do with me. Th-Then there's them that feel it th-their place to hit me f-face whenever the sky's overcast."

"They hit you?" Mariah did nothing to hide the horror in her voice.

"It's to strengthen me tongue, so they s-say."

"How could they possibly think such a thing?"

She studied Mariah curiously. "Do they n-not do somethin' similar in L-London?"

"Not in the London I know," Mariah said vehemently.

"I'm right glad to hear it," Ellen said. "It don't happen s-so much now that I'm at th-the castle. People here have b-become accustomed to it." She shrugged. "At least no one has th-threatened to cut me tongue for a while. I r-reckon that would hurt m-much worse."

"Not only would cutting your tongue be completely inhumane, but it also wouldn't help anything. It might even make your stutter worse."

"That's what me b-brother said as well." This time her smile reached her eyes. "Will w-wouldn't let anyone with a knife anywhere n-near me. Ever."

"I already like your brother Will," Mariah said with feeling.

Ellen laughed, and it cleared the sadness from her eyes. "I reckon you'd get along r-right well."

"Does he live in Nottingham?"

"N-Not anymore." She cleared her throat. "Now, tell me, d-did you find the b-butcher in time to warn him?"

"I did. Barely."

Ellen leaned closer and lowered her voice. "The sh-sheriff. Did you see him as well?"

"He and his men rode past me not long ago." They'd reached the bakehouse. Mariah set down her bucket, quickly removed the blanket from her shoulders, and rolled it into a small wad. Two guards marched past. One of them eyed her curiously before continuing toward the gate. "As soon as I've hidden this in the bakehouse, I'll tell you all about it," she said.

Ellen eyed the short distance to the kitchen. "I'd l-like that, but you'd b-best be quick. It won't do to d-displease Mistress Agatha any further today."

Mariah didn't need to be told twice. In a matter of seconds, she'd entered the small structure, tucked her blanket behind a barrel, and raced back to reclaim her bucket.

"The truth is, I may never know what happened in the forest after I left," she said as they hurried across the short distance to the kitchen. "But I'm glad I warned the butcher of what the sheriff had planned."

"It was r-right brave of you." Ellen slowed her feet to steady the sloshing water and darted an inquisitive glance Mariah's way. "I daresay he remembered you w-well enough."

Mariah's cheeks warmed. "He did. But only after I told him who I was."

Ellen snorted. "He must be daft. How could he forget a k-kiss such as the one you shared in the market? It were easy to see you all but b-bowled him over."

"Hush!" They'd reached the door, and Mariah's cheeks were now flaming. "If I'm to get away with such a late arrival, we must be fully focused on our work."

It had been the right thing to say. Ever anxious to please the cook, Ellen steadied the bucket in her hand and made directly for the blackened patch on the kitchen floor.

"Make haste," Mistress Agatha barked. "Both of you. There's more t' be done in this kitchen than cleanin' th' floor."

Mariah dropped to her knees beside Ellen and reached for a rag. Somehow, she'd escaped censure for her late arrival. Now she needed to do whatever it took to stay in Mistress Agatha's good books.

CHAPTER 9

Robin was playing a dangerous game. To loiter at the market and outside the castle gates for ten consecutive days was pure foolishness. Especially when the Sheriff of Nottingham was undoubtedly spending those same days pacing his chambers, raging over the way Robin Hood had tricked him out of his purse. Admittedly, Robin had been wise enough to shed his Lincoln green tunic in favor of a dull-brown farmer's tunic before leaving Sherwood Forest, but the risk of being taken in for questioning by one of the more vigilant castle guards remained.

"I am beginning to believe that this Maid Marian of yours is someone you dreamed up on a particularly restless night," Little John grumbled. They'd been standing beneath the eaves of the blacksmith's shop for nigh on two hours. And they'd done the exact same for three hours the day before. "Not one of your men has set eyes on her."

"She is real." Though Robin had no tangible proof, conviction filled his voice. He could see Marian's beautiful face in his mind's eye as clearly as if she were standing before him now. "I may know nothing more about her, but I can assure you of that."

"Have you considered that she was simply visiting a distant family member and is now gone from Nottingham?"

"Aye." In truth, it had been a daily reoccurring and discouraging thought. "It is entirely possible. Though I cannot shake the belief that the details she shared regarding the sheriff's plans could only have come from someone living within the castle." He frowned. He could not continue keeping watch like this indefinitely. Neither could he ask it of his men. Mayhap it was time he accepted the unfortunate realization that he might never see the elusive young lady again. "One hour more, my friend," he said. "Then we shall return to Sherwood and turn our attention to other matters."

Little John gave an approving grunt. "Well now, there may be a modicum of wisdom remaining in that handsome head of yours after all."

An old man ambled past, leading a donkey. Both walked with an uneven gait, their advancing years obvious. Two young ladies followed behind, and Robin tensed. They wore the serviceable clothing of castle servants and each carried a basket.

"Do not be too sure of that," he muttered.

"Of what exactly?" Little John asked. "Your wisdom or your comeliness?"

"Both." Robin stepped out from the safety of the shadowed wall. Unless an obliging merchant rolled his cart between Robin and the nearest stalls in the next few moments, he would be in full view of the castle guard positioned at the well. Tugging the brim of his farmer's hat lower over his brow, he approached the young ladies with a measured pace.

The women were conversing, but their voices remained indistinct. One of them said something, and the other raised her head to laugh, giving Robin his first look at her face. Dark eyebrows above dark eyes. Frustrated, he turned his attention to the other one. A shawl covered her head. He moved closer and caught sight of a flaxen-colored plait beneath the woolen fabric.

Disappointment stabbed his chest.

"Is either of them known to you?" Little John had joined him.

"Nay." A prickling sense that he was being watched overshadowed his regret, and instinct told him this was not the time to draw any further attention to himself, the young ladies, or his search.

Without turning his head, he lowered his voice. "How fares the young guard at the well? Is he maintaining the same bored expression he has worn since we arrived?"

Little John redirected his attention over Robin's shoulder. His jaw clenched. "He is moving this way, and there is purpose in his steps."

It was time to leave.

"I shall go left," Robin said. "You go right. We shall meet again in Sherwood."

"Wait!" Little John set a hand on Robin's arm. "His attention has been diverted. Something is happening at the guildhall."

All around them, the shouts of bartering merchants and chatter of shoppers had dimmed. Some were moving toward the imposing building at the center of the square; others remained where they were, watching the activity curiously. Robin and Little John wove their way between a couple of stalls before entering the safety of the growing crowd.

"What do you see?" Robin asked.

Little John strained his neck to one side. "'Tis the town crier," he said. "He's making his way to the upper step of the guildhall, a scroll in hand."

"A notice from the castle, no doubt," Robin said.

"Aye." Little John leaned back on his heels and folded his arms. "But is the author the honorable Sheriff of Nottingham or Prince John himself?"

It did not escape Robin's notice that Little John had failed to suggest King Richard. The monarch's captivity in Austria had continued for so long that even his most ardent supporters had begun to lose hope that he would ever return to England.

"It hardly matters," Robin said. "What e'er the message, if it originates in the castle, we can be certain it does not omen well for commoners."

The clang of a handbell filled the square.

"Oyez! Oyez!" the town crier called.

The low hum of chatter ceased.

"Let it be known," the crier continued, "that by order of the honorable Sheriff of Nottingham, in ten days hence, on the twenty-first day of this month, a grand archery tournament shall be held at Nottingham Castle."

Like a gust of wind, an excited murmur traveled through the gathering.

The town crier raised his scroll a fraction and cleared his throat. "Contestants are to congregate beside the dais on the north meadow at noon on said day. The tournament winner shall be rewarded with a purse of gold coins and the title of Best Archer in All of Nottinghamshire." He lowered the scroll and uttered the expected closing sentiment, "And thus it is written. God save the king."

The crowd's excited whispers rose in volume and were interrupted by a handful of cheers.

Robin released a hissing breath. "There has to be more to this unforeseen contest. The sheriff never willingly gives of his ill-gotten gains—least of all to an archer who will likely be wholly unconnected to him."

"Indeed." Little John eyed Robin critically. "Although, if you cannot instantly see through his trickery, I worry that your clear-headedness has truly forsaken you."

Robin scowled. "If the deception is so obvious, pray, enlighten me."

"It's a snare," Little John said. "To catch Robin Hood."

Robin stared at him. "You believe this is how the sheriff aims to catch his man?"

"Why not? Over the last few months, his every effort to seize the outlaw—be it by offering a reward to the captor or sending castle guards to search him out—has failed. Mayhap he has finally learned that he is more likely to catch a bear with honey than with a pack of hounds."

"A bear?"

Little John chuckled. "A fox? A man more wily than he. Whatever you prefer. The sheriff knows full well that Robin Hood is likely

the best archer in Nottinghamshire and that the poor sap cannot resist the opportunity to redistribute a purse filled with the nobleman's
gold to others."

"The poor sap?" Robin glared at Little John. His friend was taking full advantage of the fact that Robin's men were under strict orders to never address him as Robin Hood in public. "You are taking
considerable liberties with these unfortunate labels. I daresay liken-
ing the swift-footed Robin Hood to a lumbering bear was preferable
to calling him a poor sap."

"Well," Little John said, raising an eyebrow in challenge and giving no appearance of relinquishing his position, "that depends upon
whether he is fool enough to fall into the sheriff's trap."

"*If* it is a trap." Two could play at being stubborn.

"What else could it be?"

"An opportunity to gain favor with the townspeople by offering
a day of entertainment."

Little John snorted. "Have you ever known a time when the
Sheriff of Nottingham concerned himself over gaining favor with his
people?"

Truthfully, no. But Robin was reluctant to give up so easily. "Mayhap he intends to bring in a renowned archer from elsewhere so that
he might pit the fellow's skills against those of the castle guards."

"And then give him a full purse for his efforts?" Little John shook
his head. "I think not."

Robin was spared from having to generate another weak reason
by the pounding of a hammer. The town crier was nailing the proc-
lamation to the door of the guildhall. Two gentlemen waited for him
to complete the assignment before stepping forward to study the
parchment. But as most of Nottingham's residents were illiterate, the
crowd was rapidly dispersing. Shoppers, merchants, and guards were
returning to their work, which meant it was past time for Robin and
Little John to remove themselves from view.

"We shall discuss the tournament further when we are away from here," Robin said. "And when our friends may participate in the conversation."

Little John accepted his words with a nod. "Do you wish to separate?"

Robin spotted the guard. The fellow had reached the place where Robin and Little John had been standing only minutes before and was surveying the marketplace with newfound intensity.

"I believe that creating two diverging targets might currently work for our good," Robin said, already retreating into the shadows of the nearby cobbler's shop.

"Agreed," Little John said, scouring the direct route across the square before stepping around a cart. "If you keep your wits about you, old bear, I shall see you forthwith in the forest."

Robin's retort died on his lips. At this juncture, words would avail him little. It would be better to simply show Little John who it was that most closely resembled a lumbering beast. With one last glance at the distant parchment fluttering against the wooden door, Robin darted into the nearest alley and started for the town gates at a steady jog.

———··✦··———

Mariah stood over the enormous fire in the castle kitchen and stirred another pinch of parsley into the liquid bubbling in the large pot. After the incident with the blackened venison pies, she'd managed to avoid burning anything else, but attempting to keep sauces from scorching in pans hanging over open flames was almost as difficult as preventing them from developing lumps. Not for the first time, she wished for the French whisk she'd regularly used at Ricardo's—along with a dial for controlling the cooking temperature.

She sighed. Two weeks and nothing had changed. Well, almost nothing. She had developed calluses on her hands from carrying so many buckets of water from the well, and she had learned to sleep on her pallet. Not because it had become any more comfortable but because her work in the castle kitchen had taken her to a whole new level of exhaustion.

Now that Mariah had proven herself capable, Mistress Agatha had assigned more and more of the cooking to her. It was both terrifying and exhilarating. Terrifying because despite what the cook thought, Mariah's experience with medieval ingredients and dishes was almost nonexistent. Exhilarating because she'd been able to take some of the basic principles she'd learned in culinary school and apply them in completely new ways. Never before had she used breadcrumbs to thicken sauces, but her experiment had worked beautifully two nights ago, and she intended to try it again this evening.

The hours she'd spent kneading bread and stirring sauces and soups had given her ample time to think, but she was no closer to understanding what had happened to her now than she had been when she'd first walked out of Mrs. McQuivey's changing room and into the castle kitchen. But reflecting on her former life filled her with an aching sadness. Not because of the people she missed but because of how few people would likely miss her. Patrick at the archery club had been right. She'd allowed her life to become so dominated by her work at the restaurant that she had lost whatever close connections she'd once enjoyed.

Swallowing the lump in her throat, she gave the pot another stir. Chef Heston was undoubtedly furious at her nonappearance in his kitchen. If she ever made it back to the London she knew, the chances that she'd still have a job with him were nil. Would anyone else miss her? It was possible that her father had begun wondering why she hadn't called him back, if she'd missed any phone calls, but she doubted he'd traveled all the way from his retirement home in Portugal to look for her yet. As for Patrick, he was probably still anxiously awaiting a report from Warwick Castle. She shook her head slightly. How had she gone from subbing for a stand-in at one castle to living medieval life to its fullest in another?

She'd returned to the market three times since her first visit. Each time, she'd secretly hoped to see the butcher again. And even though she'd tried to ignore the nervous anticipation that had spiked when she'd neared the spot where he'd had his cart, it was impossible to overlook her disappointment when she'd realized that another vendor had been in his place.

Mariah wished she could have spoken to the butcher one more time. To know that he'd escaped the sheriff's trap, to learn his name, to have him look at her again the way he had right after they'd kissed.

She smothered a groan. She was a mess. Just because the butcher was unsettlingly handsome and had exhibited the kind of gallantry she'd rarely seen in a twenty-first-century Londoner, there was no reason for her to keep thinking about him. Especially since he'd probably forgotten all about her by now.

"'Ow's th' sauce, Marian?" Mistress Agatha's voice cut into Mariah's solitary observations.

Mariah lifted the long-handled wooden spoon so the cook could gauge the sauce's thickness. "I believe it is close," she said.

Mistress Agatha took the spoon from her and tasted the liquid pooled at the end. It was probable that she hadn't heard Mariah clearly, because she made a noncommittal noise. "It's almost ready," she said. "Ya'ave blended th' 'erbs well enough, but it needs a pinch more salt."

Mariah bobbed a curtsy. "Yes, Mistress Agatha."

The cook moved away, and Mariah reached for the small bowl of salt on a nearby shelf. She didn't think the sauce needed more, but perhaps medieval dishes were saltier than twenty-first-century ones. It probably helped that everyone was blissfully unaware of the correlation between salt intake and high blood pressure.

Two of the scullery maids entered the kitchen, hauling buckets of water and chattering excitedly.

"Make 'aste, girls," Mistress Agatha said. "We 'ave no time fer idle prattle."

The girls clamped their mouths closed, but there was no hiding the enthusiasm in their eyes as they hurried toward the scullery room. It was not the look one usually associated with the anticipation of scrubbing pots. Puzzled, Mariah watched them go, and then she added some salt to the pot.

Moments later, Ellen entered the kitchen. She was also carrying water, but as usual, she was alone. After Ellen had shared some of the challenges she'd experienced because of her stutter, Mariah had paid more attention to her friend's interactions in the castle. It hadn't taken long to realize that the other servants tended to avoid Ellen. Their behavior was so horribly unfair that Mariah had struggled to suppress her frustration, particularly when a couple of the serving girls had repeatedly ignored Ellen in the servants' bedchamber. Mariah had wanted to call them out on it, but instinct had told her that she was not yet in a position to do it. If she remained here much longer, however, she wouldn't keep silent. In the meantime, she'd happily show everyone in the castle how much she appreciated Ellen's friendship.

"D-Did you hear the n-news?" Ellen lifted her pail of water to fill a waiting pot near the fireplace.

"I don't know." Mariah tried to think of anything unusual that had happened since they'd risen this morning. Stephen knocking over a bowl of eggs in the pantry couldn't possibly count. He was always knocking things over. "Have I?"

Ellen giggled. "If you d-do not know, then you have not heard it."

Now that Mariah was doing more of the cooking, she helped plate the food in the kitchen but rarely served it to the sheriff and his guests. She was happy to avoid climbing the tower stairs with heavy platters and kowtowing to the unpleasant dignitaries visiting the even more unpleasant sheriff, but the change had prevented her from eavesdropping on their dinner conversations.

"You'd better tell me, then." Mariah paused. "Does it have anything to do with the butcher?"

As soon as the words were out, Mariah wished them unsaid. It was bad enough that her thoughts had instantly gone to the nameless man who seemed to have claimed a permanent place in her heart and mind; Ellen did not need further ammunition for teasing her about him. Mariah had already admitted to thinking about the butcher occasionally but had attributed it to her curiosity over what had happened in Sherwood Forest after she'd left. The sheriff's storming rage over an encounter with Robin Hood that same day had completely overshadowed his interaction with the butcher, and there'd been no further mention of him in the castle.

Ellen gave her an uncomfortably knowing look. "N-Not unless the b-butcher considers himself an excellent ar-rcher."

"An archer?" Mariah's heart rate quickened. "Your news has to do with archery?"

"It does." Ellen's eyes shone. "There's to be a g-grand archery tournament at the c-castle. And word is, the w-winner will go home with a purse full of g-gold. Everyone at the castle will be p-permitted to attend."

"To attend, or participate?"

"B-Both," she said. "I d-daresay there'll be several g-guards who fancy their chances and enter the c-competition."

"What about me?" Mariah pressed. "Could I enter?"

Ellen stared at her. "'Course not. You're a maiden."

Mariah attempted to tamp down her irritation. It shouldn't surprise her that the limitations at Warwick Castle's reenactment stemmed from actual medieval customs, though that knowledge didn't lessen her frustration. "But I can handle a bow quite well."

If Ellen was surprised, she didn't show it. Perhaps after a fortnight full of Mariah's oddities, she'd become numb to them. "No m-matter how well you shoot," Ellen said, "it d-don't change the fact that you're a m-maiden."

It was such a ridiculous reason. If Mariah could outshoot a castle guard, what did it matter that she was female? She gave the sauce an extra vigorous stir. It slopped over the lip of the large pot and landed in the fire with a hiss.

"Ellen, is th' water ready fer th' carrots?" Mistress Agatha's voice carried from the other side of the kitchen, abruptly ending their conversation.

"Aye, M-Mistress Agatha," Ellen said. Then she scurried away to fetch the missing vegetables, leaving Mariah alone with her thoughts once more.

CHAPTER 10

No matter how much Mariah wanted to test her skills—or prove her worth—against medieval archers, her only hope for being admitted into the tournament was to pose as a man.

After a restless night filled with all sorts of outlandish ideas for how she might trick the castle officials into allowing her to participate, she'd come up with nothing better. Entering the tournament disguised as a man was the most straightforward solution—albeit no less daring than anything else she'd considered and then rejected. But it was completely dependent upon her finding male clothing, a bow, and arrows.

"Ellen." Keeping her voice low, Mariah reached across to the neighboring pallet and gently shook her friend's shoulder.

Ellen stirred. "It c-cannot be morn so s-soon. I d-do not believe it," she muttered.

"Not yet, but I think it's close," Mariah whispered.

Ellen groaned. "Then go back to s-sleep."

"I will, but I need to ask you something first."

Ellen's pallet shifted, and when she spoke again, her voice was clearer. "What are you n-needin'?"

"You are such a good friend."

"I thought the s-same of you till you woke me."

Mariah sighed. "No. I am your crazy, lost, and trying-to-find-her-way friend."

There was a moment of silence. "What is the m-meanin' of *crazy?*"

"Mad. Foolish."

"I confess, you do have those t-tendencies," Ellen said.

Mariah smiled into the darkness. How could she not love Ellen's honesty? "I know, and I'm sorry." She paused. "I'm not usually this bad; it's just that I'm—"

"L-Lost an' tryin' to find your way?" Ellen provided.

"Yes. Exactly."

Nearby, another pallet shifted, and someone moaned. Mariah dropped her voice even lower. "Do you know of anyone who could lend me some male clothing, a bow, and some arrows?"

Another moment of silence. Ellen was not stupid; she obviously knew exactly where this was leading. "Do not . . . M-Marian, you must not g-go full crazy on me," she said. "You can g-go to the archery tournament and w-watch, but you have to put all thoughts of c-competing aside."

"Why?"

"'Cause if you were f-found out, you'd likely end up in th-the dungeon."

The chilling thought gave Mariah pause. She knew enough about the brutal punishments meted out during the medieval era to know that Ellen probably wasn't exaggerating. Was the thrill of competing against Nottingham's top archers sufficient to warrant such a risk? Then again, if she kept her male disguise in place throughout the tournament and award ceremony, none of the other archers need ever know that they'd been beaten by a woman.

The mere thought of competing in a medieval tournament caused her adrenaline to spike. How many years had she wished to participate in archery contests at medieval reenactments only to be turned away because she was female? It would be poetic justice to defeat men who actually lived in this time period and used a bow on a daily basis.

She stifled a sigh. The opportunity to prove herself might be reason enough for her, but it would not be enough for Ellen. There had to be another stronger motivation for her friend to look past the fearsome risks.

"What if I were to win?" Mariah whispered. "Think of what winning those gold coins might mean. How they could help your family."

"What does me f-family have to do with this?"

Only a day ago, Ellen had admitted that after her father's death two years ago, her mother and younger siblings had been turned out of their house and had been forced to take refuge with her uncle's large family in order to survive.

"You told me about your mother's struggles to provide for the younger children," Mariah said. "After all you've done to help me, I'd love to give back to them."

"You'd d-do that?"

"Of course," Mariah said, meaning every word. She had no idea what a purse of gold coins would buy, but surely even a portion of the winnings would make a significant difference to a family with almost nothing.

"But the r-risk . . . "

"I'm willing to take the risk, Ellen."

"It's t-too much," she whispered.

Mariah closed her eyes. If she never returned to future London, she would go mad doing nothing more than slaving away in the castle kitchen. As much as she enjoyed cooking, there had to be more to her life than that. She loved archery, and if this surreal experience had taught her anything, it was that she needed to give far more time to the things in life that brought her joy and to her relationships with others. Entering the competition may enable her to do both those things—as long as she could reassure Ellen of her ability to come through it unscathed.

"If you can find me a bow and some arrows in the next couple of days, I would have time to practice," she said. "I promise that if

I discover that my skill with a new bow is insufficient to win, I'll abandon the idea of entering the tournament."

"Truly? You g-give me your word on that?"

"Yes."

Ellen's pallet rustled. "I'll send a m-message to me older brother on the m-morrow. He's the only one I know who m-might have an extra bow."

Relief mingled with excitement. "That would be fantastic."

"I c-cannot say if he'll be willin' to help you, mind."

"I understand, but I'm grateful to you for trying." She paused, thinking back on an earlier conversation. "I thought you told me your older brother left town."

"He did," Ellen said. "But he v-visits every once in a while."

Mariah's friend was offering her an extremely slim chance of attaining her wish, but it was more than she'd had an hour ago. "Thank you, Ellen. I'm sorry I woke you."

"As am I," Ellen replied. And then she laughed softly. "In case you w-were unsure, methinks you are correct about bein' c-crazy."

Mariah smiled into the darkness. "I know."

"Is it truly worth the risk, Robin?" Friar Tuck's question was an echo of the very question Robin had been asking himself for two full days.

He had yet to settle on a firm answer, so he responded with a question of his own. "How high do you place my chances of winning the purse?"

"High," the friar said.

"And how high do you consider his chances of being caught?" Little John countered from his position beneath the oak tree and beside the friar and Will Scarlett.

"Equally high," Friar Tuck said.

Robin released a frustrated breath, walked six paces across the leafy glade, pivoted, and then retraced his steps. It was the same path he'd been marching for the last ten minutes. "If the sheriff has orchestrated this tournament to capture me, he likely believes that I will enter with no thought of entrapment. He may expect me to appear in costume but would have no reason to believe that my men would be standing by, alert for any untoward movement by his guards."

"That may be true," Little John conceded, "but you are placing a great deal of trust in your Merry Men."

For the first time since the discussion had begun, Robin grinned. "And why should I not? They are loyal to a fault and will not let me down."

"Unless they are prevented from acting by an overabundance of armed castle guards," Will said. "We can do little to assist you if we are being held at knife or arrow point ourselves."

Robin's grin disappeared as quickly as it had come. "I refuse to place my men in peril over this."

"Then stay away," Little John said. "Allow the sheriff his tournament, and let him soak in his disappointment when Robin Hood does not appear."

Robin paced his short circuit once more. Was it pride urging him to throw caution to the wind and enter the tournament? Or was it the belief that he could not let down the townspeople who would attend expecting to see him perform? Mayhap that thought was misguided and was ultimately ruled by pride also.

He ran his fingers through his hair, wishing he could sift through his turbulent thoughts so easily. The winning purse would feed his men and many of the destitute in Nottingham for months. But if he were captured, he would likely lose his life and be of no assistance to anyone ever again.

"I fear that this conundrum has no answer that will please everyone," he said. "And so, I shall continue to ponder my choices with the hope that I shall finally settle upon the answer that is best for most people."

"You should settle on the answer that feels best to your heart," Friar Tuck said. "That is the most reliable guide."

Robin offered him a small smile. "Wise words, Friar."

"I have been told on numerous occasions that much of what I choose to share with others falls into that category," Friar Tuck said, heaving himself to his feet. "Here is another example: It is long past time that we ate."

Little John chuckled as he and Will also rose from their seats on the ground.

"Truly, Friar Tuck, your pearls of wisdom confound us on a daily basis," Little John said.

"Just so." Friar Tuck started toward the fire with a deceptively open expression. "Follow me, Little John, and I shall offer you more of the same as you scrub out the large cooking pot."

Little John's face instantly fell, and Robin's laughter joined Will's.

"Wily and wise," Robin said. "It is a rare but powerful combination in a man of the cloth. You'd best heed his every word, Little John."

With a long-suffering look directed at Robin, Little John followed after Friar Tuck.

"Will!" Allan a Dale entered the grove. "I am glad to find you here."

Will greeted him with raised eyebrows. "I hope you have not been looking long. I had no notion you were seeking me."

Allan shook his head. "Not long at all. I am just come from the White Stag." He turned to Robin. "Mistress Talitha wished to be remembered most particularly to the gallant and brave Robin Hood."

"Very good of her," Robin said, ignoring the grin on Will's face. Mistress Talitha was almost old enough to be his mother, and Robin endured her uncomfortable overtures only because her inn, located just inside the town gates, served as the perfect location for the transfer of timely information from the castle or messages of dire need from the town's inhabitants. "Did she have any other communication of note?"

"Aye," Allan said. "An urgent message for Will."

Will's brow furrowed. "For me? Who is it from?"

"Your sister Ellen."

Worry now entered Will's eyes. "What does she have to say?"

Allan raised his cap slightly and scratched his head. "It's an odd request, to be sure. She has a friend who wishes to participate in the upcoming archery tournament, and to that end, she wishes to know if you could supply said friend with a full set of men's clothing, a bow, and some arrows."

Will stared at him dazedly, and Robin fully understood his confusion.

"Is her friend truly so indigent that he requires a full set of clothing?" Robin asked.

Allan shrugged. "That, I cannot say. I am merely the messenger."

"By all the heavens, Ellen," Will muttered. "Who have you become entangled with?"

Robin set his hand on Will's shoulder. "It may not be so bad as you think. I seem to remember you telling me that your sister is a level-headed maiden."

"I had thought so. But it has been some months since I have spoken with her. A great deal can change in a young woman's life during the course of so many weeks." Will ran his hand across his face. "Would that I could simply walk into the castle and speak with her."

"Not the most prudent thing to do when one is an outlaw," Allan said grimly.

Will's jaw clenched. Even though the men of Sherwood were a jolly group, they each bore the burden of an excessively harsh sentence—most often due to action taken to feed their family members. They rarely spoke of the unfairness of their situation, preferring to dwell on their camaraderie and unlikely opportunity to help others. But occasionally, when a loved one was in need, the enforced separation was hard to bear.

"No matter the amount of time that has passed since you last saw her, it is doubtful that your sister's core disposition has changed,"

Robin said. "It could be that she is simply offering assistance to one in need. Much like her brother does."

Will released an uneasy breath. "Be that as it may, I have no spare bow to offer the fellow."

"Do you have an extra tunic and hose?"

"Aye. The tunic has a hole in one elbow, and the hose is well worn," Will said, "but they're both still serviceable."

"Well then, you have all that is needed," Robin said. "I have a bow and a quiver of arrows her friend may have."

"Truly, Robin, you do not need to—"

Robin raised his hand to halt Will's argument. "As you said of your own offerings, they are worn but still serviceable. I daresay someone within our band can donate a hat and pair of shoes that fit the same description."

"Regrettably, I have no clothing to offer," Allan said, "but I volunteer to take the items to Mistress Talitha. As I left, she assured me that she would see to it that any form of response was delivered to your sister forthwith."

"Your service is appreciated, Allan," Robin said. He turned to Will. "Set your mind at ease, my friend. You know full well that I applaud anyone who is willing to ask for assistance for another with no thought of themselves. For that reason alone, Ellen deserves our aid." He smiled. "Besides, do you not think that any fellow who wishes to compete in an archery tournament is—by the very nature of his request—worthy of Robin Hood's consideration?"

The concern that had tightened Will's shoulders lessened a fraction, and a flicker of amusement lit his eyes. "Most certainly," he said. "But have you taken a moment to consider that you could be aiding the very person who will snatch the tournament's purse of gold out from under your nose?"

Robin's smile widened. "There may be more truth to that statement than I wish to admit. But if that be the way of things, then more fool me."

CHAPTER 11

Mariah led Ellen out of the servants' chambers, closing the door behind them. Torches lit the passageway still, but with the pearl gray of early morning filtering in through the cracks in the shutters, someone would come to snuff out the flames very soon.

Pressing a hand to her stomach, Mariah willed away the nervous butterflies. "You don't need to come with me, Ellen," she whispered. "I can meet you at the field later."

"My d-decision is already made." Ellen took her hand and began towing her toward the stairs. "And if you are t-truly going to g-go through with your m-madcap scheme, we have n-no time to waste."

Ellen was right, and though Mariah had felt obligated to offer her friend an out, she couldn't help but be grateful that Ellen had chosen to ignore it. Tucking the bundle of clothing more securely beneath her other arm, Mariah increased her pace. They needed to reach the bakehouse before anyone else this morning.

Every day for the past week, Mariah had risen before the other servants, leaving the castle under the wary eyes of the night watchmen and returning when the morning guards had taken their place. She'd told the watchmen that she was on an errand to forage the nearby woods. At that hour, they undoubtedly assumed she was collecting the mushrooms that popped up overnight. She didn't bother correcting the possible belief. It was just as well that they didn't know her foraging actually involved reclaiming the bow and arrows she'd hidden in a thicket not far from the castle wall.

Hardly daring to hope that Ellen's brother would provide the things she'd requested, Mariah had been elated when her friend had approached her in the pantry to tell her that a bow, quiver full of arrows, and bundle of clothes had been delivered. Thankfully, the courier had been wise enough to leave the items in a grove of trees outside the castle gates and had simply sent a message to Ellen informing her of where to find them. It would have been almost impossible to explain why a female kitchen servant was toting a weapon through the inner courtyard.

They had slipped out together that first day, and upon locating the delivery, they'd determined to hide the clothing beneath their blankets in the servants' bedchamber but leave the bow and arrows outside the castle. That was where Mariah would need to practice anyway. And practice she had. Every morning since then, from the moment the sun had risen enough for her to see her target until the cockerel had called her to her work in the kitchen. The loss of precious sleep had made the remainder of her workdays challenging, but the familiar feel of a well-balanced longbow in her hands and the thrill of having her arrows hit their targets had made up for it.

It had taken three days to adjust to the weight of the hand-hewn yew longbow and the draw of the sinew bowstring. The arrows, which she guessed were made of ash rather than the fiberglass she was used to, had goose-feather fletchings and metal, triangular broadhead tips. She'd been forced to alter her stance and grip several times in her attempts to adapt to the unfamiliar shafts, but four days ago, she'd experienced a breakthrough. Since then, she had pierced the tree trunks she'd used as targets with remarkable accuracy, and she now took comfort in the knowledge that whoever had crafted the well-used bow and the wooden arrows in the worn leather quiver was an exceptionally skilled craftsman.

"Wait," Ellen whispered. They had reached the door that led to the inner courtyard. "Allow m-me to ensure that th-there is no one about." She eased the door open a couple of inches and peered through the gap. "Very well. It's c-clear."

She pulled the door wide, and they stepped outside. The air hung heavy, painting the slumbering world with dew. A white cat curled up beside the door raised its head to watch them pass and then quickly lowered it again. It seemed that two servants crossing the courtyard in the predawn half-light were insufficiently intriguing to rouse him completely.

Their soft leather shoes brushed the cobblestones with a gentle whisper. One of the three birds resting on the bakehouse roof fluttered its wings as Mariah and Ellen approached, but none took to the sky—even when Ellen opened the door.

Mariah stepped inside and set her bundle on top of a sack of flour. Her fingers fumbled as she worked to undo the knot in the rope that tied it.

"L-Let me," Ellen said, reaching for the rope. "I shall h-hand you the clothing once y-you have shed your kirtle."

Shifting her attention to the ties at her bodice, Mariah worked to loosen them enough to draw the kirtle over her head. "What of my smock?" she asked.

Ellen shook her head. "You w-will need something shorter." She drew a rough linen shirt from the bundle. "Here. Exch-change it for this."

Mariah put on the shirt. The sleeves fell below her wrists, the fabric rough against her skin. "I'll have to roll up the sleeves," she said.

"I believe you sh-shall need to do the same with th-the hose," Ellen said, raising the dauntingly long tubular pieces of clothing.

"They will never stay up," Mariah said. "I'll have to use my own hose."

Ellen frowned. "They w-will appear most odd."

"At least my legs will be covered. And if the tunic is anywhere near as big as the hose, it will cover a good portion of them."

Setting aside the hose, Ellen reached for the tunic. It was made of brown wool and appeared enormous.

"How tall is your brother?" Mariah asked, threading her head through the opening. It was a question she should have asked ten days ago.

"T-Taller than most."

Mariah suppressed a moan as the top of the tunic settled on her shoulders and the rest dropped below her knees. "I may be the strangest-looking archer at the tournament today," she said.

Catching her lower lip between her teeth, Ellen held out the shoes. They were twice as wide as anything Mariah had ever put on her feet.

"Oh no. I'd be waddling around like a duck in those," Mariah said, her heart sinking. "And that's only if I were able to keep them on my feet." She took a deep breath. "I'll wear my own shoes, along with the hose. The most important thing is that I have a tunic and the bow and arrows."

"And a h-hood," Ellen said, drawing the last item out from the bundle. "This w-will enable you t-to hide your hair."

Relief coursed through Mariah. An oversized hood was the best possible option for covering her hair and face. Pulling it over her head, she tucked her single plait down her back and settled the fabric across her shoulders before looking up at Ellen. "What do you think?"

"That you are qu-quite mad," she said, tugging the rope free of the bundle and threading it around Mariah's narrow waist. "B-But with the hood up, I c-cannot see your features well. If we are f-fortunate, people will see only a g-gangly stranger wearing his father's stained tunic with a h-hole in the sleeve and a r-rope to cinch it tight."

"Exactly," Mariah said, rolling her kirtle and smock into a tight wad and adding it to the shoes and hose on the flour sack. "Do you think these will be safe if we leave them here?"

Ellen nodded. "There w-will be very few servants about today. If we hide the b-bundle in the back, n-no one will see it."

Mariah scrambled around the sacks and wedged the clothing between the last sack and the wall. Her kirtle would be covered in dust and flour, but since she worked in the kitchen, that could be easily explained away.

"We m-must hasten," Ellen said, already at the door. "The sun is rising."

Mariah joined her, and together they exited the bakehouse and crossed the inner courtyard at a brisk walk. The castle was coming to life. A man's voice came from somewhere near the stables. It was followed by a dog's bark and the bang of a door.

The light was brightening. Mariah looked upward. A few wispy clouds trailed across the pale-blue sky. Unless the wind picked up, it was a perfect day for an archery competition.

A surge of adrenaline pumped through her veins, heightening her anticipation and nervousness. She was entering a tournament filled with medieval archers—men whose very livelihoods depended upon their skill with a bow. It would undoubtedly be her toughest competition yet, particularly as she'd be performing with someone else's bow. But she was ready. She wanted to prove herself—even if she and Ellen were the only ones who ever knew what she'd accomplished.

"L-Lower your head," Ellen murmured. "We are approaching th-the gate."

It was a timely reminder. If she were to escape discovery, she would need to keep her chin down from now on. She slowed her steps slightly, allowing Ellen to take the lead as a guard came into view.

"We are off to the t-tournament," Ellen said, preempting the guard's question.

"Aye. The first of many headed there this morning," he grumbled.

"I am g-glad to hear that we are ahead of most," Ellen said cheerfully. "It bodes well for securing a good v-vantage point."

"Ya'll be with all th' other commoners," the guard warned. "There's no special treatment fer th' castle servants." He glanced at Mariah. "'Specially them that dress like they 'ave no 'ome."

"I understand," Ellen said. "Good d-day to you."

Mariah offered the guard a mute nod of acknowledgment and followed Ellen through the open gate. The less Mariah spoke, the better—and the sooner she'd reach the thicket and the hidden bow and quiver of arrows.

———— · ✳ · ————

"It seems t' me that there's a castle guard posted every twenty paces all the way around the field," Little John muttered.

Robin didn't refute the observation. He'd already come to the same conclusion. The townspeople had formed a broad band of enthusiastic spectators who lined the roped-off target area in the center of the field. Their excitement was a stark contrast to the somber expressions of the men keeping watch over the proceedings. "It was wise that our band divided and will filter into the crowd in twos and threes."

"It would have been wiser if we had not come at all," Little John said.

Ignoring Little John's ill-tempered response, Robin surveyed the scene carefully. He could not tell how many of his men felt as Little John did—few were as open with their opinions—but he thought it likely that the majority were glad for a chance to join in the festivities.

"The men would have wished to mingle amongst the throng and eat roasted chestnuts and honeycomb regardless of whether I chose to enter the contest."

"Aye. But they would not have had to divide their attention between eating their fill and observing the guards," Little John said. "One of these armed men could seize you at any moment."

"No one will know me." Robin ran his hand across his smooth chin. It had been years since he'd been clean-shaven. He'd scarcely recognized himself in the small looking glass they kept in the cave at their camp. "The sheriff and his men will be looking for a bearded man wearing Lincoln green, not a fresh-faced apprentice carpenter come straight from his employer's shop."

Little John heaved a defeated sigh. "Your sawdust-covered blue tunic may deflect suspicion for a time, but when you outmatch the other archers, you will undoubtedly draw undesirable attention."

It was true, but when the time had finally come to choose whether he should shoot or stay away, Robin had been unable to resist the allure of the grand prize. Every one of the gold coins in the sheriff's purse could be put to good use.

"I shall remain watchful throughout the competition," Robin said. "And the moment the winnings are in my hands, I shall be gone from here."

"*If* you win."

"Ah!" Robin placed a hand to his heart. "Have you truly so little faith in my abilities?"

For the first time since they'd entered the field, Little John chuckled. "I am betting on the nameless fellow wearing my old shoes."

"If he fits those shoes, he will be a formidable foe indeed."

"Aye. And so, you'd best make no mistakes." He pointed toward a small gathering of men toting bows. "Add your name to the list of competitors, Colin the Carpenter. I believe I shall offer my services tasting the various honeycomb." He waggled his eyebrows. "Few can differentiate between lavender and clover honey as well as I. It takes a most discerning palate."

Grateful that Little John's sour mood had been lessened by the prospect of sweet honey, Robin raised his bow in farewell and started toward the rapidly growing cluster of contestants.

Despite his altered appearance, he kept his head tilted away from the watchful guards and joined the straggling line of archers. The tournament appeared to have attracted a wide assortment of challengers. They varied greatly in age, from a stooped and gray-haired fellow to a gangly youth with even less facial hair than Robin. There were at least three castle guards in the throng, and though most of the others looked to be tradesmen or country gentlemen, there were also two gentlemen whose colorful finery spoke of their positions as knights. Robin bit back a smile. The sheriff would be most gratified by their appearance.

"Name?" An impatient clerk sat at a table, his quill poised over a scrap of parchment.

"Colin," Robin said.

"Colin." The clerk frowned. "That is all?"

"Colin the Carpenter," Robin said. It was sufficient.

The clerk grunted and made a mark on the parchment "Very well. You will shoot in the third group." He waved his quill toward the starting position. "Find your place over there."

Robin moved aside, and the gangly youth stepped up to the table behind him.

"Name?" the clerk asked again.

"Michael." The fellow's voice cracked slightly. He cleared his throat. "Michael o' London."

London. Robin turned back in astonishment. Surely the lad had not journeyed all this way alone. He doubted even the knights had traveled so far. Robin moved to join a small cluster of archers, purposely keeping himself out of the nearest guard's line of vision while he studied the young fellow at the table more closely. The lad's head was lowered, his hood hiding his face from view, his shoulders barely wide enough to hold up the oversized tunic.

A hole in one of the tunic's elbows caught Robin's attention. His eyes narrowed. Will had mentioned that there was a hole in the elbow of the tunic he gave away. Robin's gaze dropped to the lad's feet. The dainty shoes were not Little John's. Of that Robin was certain. They were so narrow that they could pass as a woman's shoe.

The young man straightened slightly, and as he did so, the leather quiver hanging from his rope belt came into view. Robin released a tight breath. He may not have been fully sure of the tunic, but he would know that quiver anywhere. It had hung on his own belt for years.

A horn sounded. All around, those in the field ceased their chatter to bow and curtsy. Dragging his gaze from the youth at the table, Robin turned toward the incoming dignitaries and executed a bow of his own. He had no desire to bend his knee to the loathsome sheriff, but the expected sign of respect enabled him to avert his face as the Sheriff of Nottingham and his retinue made their way onto the canopied wooden dais that had been erected in front of the archery range.

The horn sounded again, this time loud and long. Robin raised his head a fraction. On the dais, all were seated except the sheriff. He stood in front of his regal-looking chair, seemingly awaiting the attention of all in attendance. Complete silence blanketed the field.

"Let the tournament begin!" the sheriff called.

The crowd cheered, and the archers at Robin's side immediately made to join those already at the starting position. Determined to remain with the group, Robin followed. He glanced over his shoulder once. Michael o' London was gone from the table. Pushing aside his disappointment that the mysterious youth was now nowhere in sight, Robin increased his pace. His curiosity over Ellen's friend would have to wait until after he had made it through the first round of the competition.

CHAPTER 12

Mariah flexed her fingers. They ached. She was missing the finger tab and thumb ring she usually wore when she was shooting. Some of the other archers in her group were also without them. Unfortunately, almost all of those without the additional equipment had now been eliminated, which suggested that even in medieval times, serious archers found them beneficial.

She rolled her shoulders, waiting for the castle guard behind her to take his shots. The tournament was a series of roving marks, which meant that the archers shot at one target only to then shoot at a second one from the position of the first and then at a third target from the position of the second. Each archer was allowed five arrows. Those who missed the target were eliminated. Her group had started with ten archers and was now down to four. Once this round was over, they would combine with those who had moved on from the other two groups.

Up until now, she'd been spared speaking more than an occasional word or two. She attempted to use a lower pitch, but most of the time her voice broke, and she ended up having to cough to cover it up. Thankfully, no one had shown undue interest in her. Perhaps her ill-fitting, odd clothing was enough to discourage anyone who might have otherwise been tempted to strike up an acquaintance with his competitor. It was an unanticipated silver lining for walking around in a giant potato sack.

The man shooting now, a castle guard, released his last arrow, and it landed in the center of the distant target with a solid thump. The crowd cheered, and with a grin, the guard marched toward the target to reclaim his arrows. A horn blew somewhere near the dais, and an official—not the sheriff this time—stood.

"There will be a ten-minute intermission for the relocation of the roving marks," he called. "Those archers who remain in the tournament are required to be in position at the starting point when the horn sounds next."

At the conclusion of his announcement, there was a sudden surge of movement. Guards hurrying across the field to move the targets, archers joining family and friends in the crowds, and children chasing each other with high-pitched squeals of delight. An unexpected wave of loneliness washed over Mariah. Her father hadn't attended many of her recent archery tournaments. In fairness, she hadn't entered many since starting work at the restaurant, but there'd always been someone in the crowd rooting for her, even if it had only been Patrick.

She swallowed. How—why—had this journey to the past happened to her? Was it simply to teach her that she did need other people in her life after all? She had all but given up on ever returning to her previous life, but the thought of what lay ahead in this new world, of facing everything on her own, scared her more than she could say.

Turning away from the happy families and friends, she glanced at the dais. The dozen or so men and women sitting comfortably in the shade were not so exuberant in their interactions as those standing behind the ropes, but they seemed to be in good spirits. Except perhaps the sheriff himself. He was staring at a distant group of archers, his eyes narrowed and with an expression of such loathing on his face, it caused a trickle of unease to skitter up Mariah's spine. Who was he looking at?

Unable to fully contain her curiosity, she started walking, angling her way around another group of archers to have a better view. She hadn't gone very far when she heard a familiar voice.

"Michael! M-Michael!"

It took a couple of seconds to register that Ellen was calling to her. Over the last few weeks, she'd become so used to being called Marian that she had started to think of herself by that name. But *Michael* was something she and Ellen had come up with as they'd entered the field. It was close enough to Mariah and Marian that it had seemed a sensible choice—in a world where absolutely nothing was sensible.

Mariah looked to her left to see Ellen standing at the rope, waving to her. The simple gesture lifted Mariah's lonely heart. She smiled and redirected her course.

"You were r-right!" Ellen stuttered when Mariah reached her. "You are marvelous with a b-bow. My brother was impressed. And r-rightly so."

"Your brother? He's here?"

Ellen nodded, her smiled broadening. "He f-found me. It was the v-very best surprise."

"Where is he now?" Mariah asked, torn between her desire to meet Ellen's brother so that she could thank him for his generosity and her fear of anyone else discovering her identity.

"He left." The light in her eyes dimmed a little. "He thinks it's b-best that he not be seen with m-me. 'Specially w-with me workin' at the c-castle now."

Mariah's mind raced. There was something she was missing here. Something important. "Why would being with your brother influence your job at the castle?"

Ellen's gaze dropped. "Will's n-not well liked by the sheriff."

"Ellen, I haven't been here long, but I can already say with certainty that if your brother *were* well liked by the sheriff, I'd be much more worried about him."

A small smile broke through Ellen's anxious expression. "Will w-would take to you straightway. I w-wish you could have met."

"I do too," Mariah said. "You told me he's gone from Nottingham. Where does he live now?"

Ellen hesitated, and when she replied, her voice was low. "In the f-forest."

In the forest. Disliked by the sheriff. Mariah swallowed. Ellen had told her that Robin Hood, Little John, and Friar Tuck truly existed, but with all that Mariah had been adjusting to over the last three weeks, it had been easier to push aside information that did not impact her directly. Was her new reality about to come face-to-face with a story she'd known since childhood?

She wrapped her fingers around the bow at her shoulder to hide their trembling. "Your brother, does he go by Will Scarlet?"

Ellen's head shot up, her eyes wide. "How do you know that n-name?"

"I heard it mentioned as the name of someone who lives with Robin Hood in Sherwood Forest."

"Hush!" Ellen pressed her fingers over Mariah's mouth. "Do not mention that n-name. Not with all the g-guards about."

Mariah stared at Ellen, her heart pounding uncomfortably as her friend lowered her hand. "Do you think he's here?"

"I cannot s-say for certain, but—" She looked right and left as though needing to reassure herself that no one else was listening. "In times past, where'ere one of the m-men of Sherwood Forest is f-found, there's sure to be others not f-far distant."

And Will was here.

Taking an unsteady breath, Mariah scanned the crowd. But she didn't know what or who she was looking for. Men in green tunics? A portly friar? She gave herself a mental shake. If Robin Hood were around and he was as wily as the stories suggested, it was probable that no one but his men would ever know he'd been here.

The blast of a horn brought Mariah out of her musings with a jolt. "The tournament," she gasped. "I have to go."

Ellen stepped back. "Yes. M-Make haste."

Grateful that she was not flopping around in the oversized shoes, Mariah placed one hand on her hood to secure it to her head and took off running.

———— · ✳ · ————

Robin could scarcely contain his surprise. Not only was Michael o' London one of the eight remaining challengers in the archery tournament, but the lad's arrow had also just hit its mark from a distance of almost fifty paces. Robin had watched him set up the shot. His form was impressive. Notwithstanding the lack of a thumb ring, finger tab, or arm bracer, he knew just when to release the bowstring, and his aim was sure. Robin shook his head slightly. The young man's arms were so slender, it was a miracle he could draw the bowstring back far enough to give the arrow flight, let alone successfully find the target.

"Nicely done, lad," Robin said.

Michael mumbled his thanks but did not meet Robin's eyes. Was the fellow uncommonly withdrawn or simply ill-disposed?

Robin could not tell, but with two archers set to take their turns before him, Robin made another attempt at engaging Michael. "Which deserves the credit for your success this day," he asked. "Your fine-looking bow or your well-made arrows?"

"Neither." The lad's voice seemed stilted. "I would say many years of practice."

"Many years? I would hardly have thought you old enough to claim more than four or five."

"Then you would be wrong." He walked away, leaving Robin staring after him in perplexity.

"Colin the Carpenter!" The official called him forward.

Temporarily pushing all thoughts of Michael o' London aside, Robin took his place. Withdrawing an arrow from his quiver, he raised his bow and nocked the arrow. The sun was warm and the air still. Robin set his sights on his mark, drew back the bowstring, and released. The solid thud of the arrow hitting the target was followed by a loud cheer. Robin nocked a second arrow. This one needed to hit one finger width farther left. He adjusted his stance a fraction and released. Another thump and another cheer. Allowing himself a small smile, Robin reached for his third arrow. Already, he knew that he would be through to the final round—with a castle guard named Cedric and Michael o' London.

Those who had failed to hit the latest mark conceded defeat and trailed away. Cedric, his head held high and a confident grin upon his face, led the way to the last target and the setting of their next matchup. Michael followed, but in stark contrast, he kept his head down. Robin did the same, studiously turning away from those seated on the dais.

"Good luck, Michael o' London!" someone in the crowd called out.

Obviously startled, the lad looked that way and immediately stumbled over an uneven tuft of grass. Robin shot his arm out, catching Michael's elbow and breaking his fall. Michael swiveled, his hood sliding back a couple of inches to expose chestnut hair and startling green eyes.

Robin's grip tightened. "Marian!" He took a deep breath, hoping it would clear his head. But the green eyes remained, staring at him in stunned horror.

"You are no carpenter," she said. "You are the butcher."

"Are you injured?" Robin's thoughts were whirling so fast he could barely think. Dear heaven, he was not sure which was worse: discovering that Marian was participating in the archery tournament or having her so quickly see through his disguise.

"No," she said. "I'm fine."

Her unusual inflection was gone, and now that he heard her natural voice, he knew her.

"What are you doing here?" he asked.

"Competing," she said. "Just as you are."

Robin released her arm. They needed to catch up to Cedric before anyone came over to discover what was delaying them.

"Walk," he said. "Rapidly enough that we are making progress but no faster. I must speak with you." He rubbed his hand across the back of his neck, unsure where to begin. In all his fanciful dreams, the opportunity to talk with Marian again had never felt so distressing. "You should not be here."

"I know the tournament is meant for men, but as you can see, I can hold my own."

"You misunderstand," he said. "At this stage in the competition, there is not a soul in attendance who does not admire your skill with a bow." He longed to ask her how she had become so accomplished, but this was not the time nor the place. "But that will mean nothing if the Sheriff of Nottingham discovers your identity."

"Why?"

Her green eyes appeared so guileless. Could she truly not know the danger she was in?

"Because your presence here will be seen as making a mockery of the sheriff's tournament." They were dangerously close to the target, and Cedric was waiting. "He will not take it well."

She paled slightly. "How do you know that?"

"I have witnessed the sheriff in a rage. There is no accounting for what he might do." He paused. As much as he wished it otherwise, for her own safety, he had to convey the seriousness of her situation. "The dungeon is likely. As is a hanging."

She stumbled a second time, and though she righted herself, she appeared shaken. "For entering a tournament?"

They had reached the target and their next shooting point; there was no time for further discussion.

"Miss the mark," he urged. "If you walk away now, with your true identity unknown, you will leave in safety."

Something flashed in her eyes. He thought it was shock, but as soon as she started speaking, he revised his opinion.

"You want me to purposely lose?" She clenched and unclenched her fists. "Are you truly so threatened by my skill that you need me to do that in order for you to win?"

"Not at all." How was it possible that she could look beautiful while seething? And what manner of disease would cause him to entertain that notion at such a perilous time?

"Cedric o' Nottingham," the official called.

The crowd roared, and the guard took his position. Robin had avoided looking at the dais the entire competition, but now he hazarded a glance that way. The sheriff was leaning forward in his seat, his posture tense, his unwavering focus on the final three challengers.

Swiftly, Robin turned back to Marian. The thud of Cedric's first arrow entering the target reached them, and the crowd's cheer rose in volume. "I beg of you, Marian," he said. "Misdirect an arrow. Your very life may depend upon it."

———— · ✴ · ————

The crowd's collective groan drowned out Cedric's curse. His third arrow had missed the target, which meant he'd opened the window for Mariah or the butcher to beat him. The butcher. Whether he was sporting a beard or clean-shaven, she'd have recognized his startling blue eyes anywhere. Mariah attempted to shake off her bewilderment. He couldn't possibly mean what he'd said about the danger she'd be in if she won. He must be desperate for the gold. If, despite her warning, he'd allowed the sheriff to swindle him, it was no wonder he was trying to reclaim funds. But why dress as a carpenter?

The official called her forward, and she took her position. Nocking her first arrow, she lifted her bow and steadied her stance. The crowd had grown quiet. Fury at the butcher's demand simmered in her chest, causing her limbs to tremble. She took a steadying breath, focusing on the distant target's dark center as she drew the bowstring back. She held it in place for the count of three and then released the arrow. It sailed across the field, straight and true, and when it hit the mark, the crowd erupted in cheers.

Refusing to look at the butcher, Mariah reached for her next arrow. She had held back her tempestuous thoughts and swirling questions for the amount of time it had taken to launch one arrow. She had to do it only twice more. Then she could ask him why he was hiding his true identity from everyone. Nocking her arrow, she stifled a groan. For all she knew, despite the fact that he'd had a cart full of meat at the market, he may not even be a butcher.

She drew back the bowstring, battling the maelstrom within her. She'd admired his generosity, been grateful for his help, and had reflected on his kiss more times than she cared to admit, but the fact remained: She didn't know who he really was. He could be Robin Hood, for all she knew.

Suddenly, the random puzzle pieces spinning in her head fell together to form a staggeringly clear picture: his giving meat to the poor, his meeting the sheriff in Sherwood Forest, his skill with a bow, his disguise. Ellen had mentioned that with Will attending the tournament, it was likely that Robin Hood was here too. Why—after all the Robin Hood films she'd seen—had Mariah not immediately assumed that he was participating in the contest? She'd been so consumed with keeping her own identity a secret, she'd not given any thought to the identities of her competitors.

Her fingers trembled. Forcing herself to take two deep breaths, she relied on instinct to take over. The fletching brushed her cheek. She aimed and released. Not waiting to see where the arrow landed, she swung around. Cedric had already disappeared. Only one man remained. In three short steps, she found herself standing immediately before him.

"What is your name?" she asked.

The shouts of the enthusiastic crowd all but drowned her voice, but he must have heard enough to know what she asked.

A fine line appeared along his forehead. "Colin."

"Your real name," she pressed.

His eyes met hers, and still, he hesitated.

"Michael o' London!" The official was calling her back to take her last shot.

"Please," she begged. "I must know."

His gaze darted from her face to the distant target and then back. "My friends call me Robin," he said. "And though I have given you no reason to believe a single word I utter, I would have you know that at present, my greatest concern is for your well-being."

Robin. Mariah backed up a pace, willing her racing heart to slow. *She was competing in an archery competition against Robin Hood.* Of all the preposterous things she'd experienced over the last three weeks, this had to be the most unbelievable.

She took her position in front of the target again, this time noting the location of her second arrow. It had penetrated the very center of the target, within a quarter inch of the first one. Two bull's-eyes. She swallowed. Could she pull herself together enough to do it again? Should she? The Robin Hood of legends was trustworthy. The man she'd met at the market had seemed honorable. So much so that she'd risked her job to warn him about the sheriff's plan. Heat flooded her face. She must have appeared such a fool for advising him against doing business with the sheriff.

Someone in the crowd whistled. Another person copied. They were becoming impatient. Raising her bow and arrow, Mariah prepared to shoot. She eyed the distant target. With no capricious breeze to contend with, all she had to do was control her nervous energy, and she'd hit the mark. Robin would be forced to shoot better—and that would be hard to do. She could have the distinction of having outshot Robin Hood, but what good would that do her if he were right about what awaited her if she won? Her head told her his concern was ridiculous; her heart begged her to listen.

In the time it took her to readjust the weight on her anchor leg, she'd made her decision. Blocking out the noise from the crowd, she aimed and shot. The moment the arrow left her hand, she knew it had gone wide. She lowered her bow, her chest aching for what she'd thrown away. The crowd's disappointed cry was almost as loud as their earlier roar of approval.

"They wanted you to win." Robin had come up behind her. "It is the highest of compliments, and yet their adulation would have sealed your fate. You would have been forced to remove your hood and show yourself to the sheriff and the crowd." His smile was strained. "I will shoot to win in order to protect you, but it should not have happened thus. When the tournament is ended and the field has cleared of onlookers, the purse of gold coins is yours."

Stunned speechless, Mariah watched as Robin stood where she had been seconds before. He waited only until her arrows had been removed from the target before raising his bow. Then, with swift, fluid motions, he launched three arrows in rapid succession. They landed in a tight cluster right on the mark. The crowd erupted in cheers. Horns blew. And suddenly, they were surrounded by a tight circle of guards.

Robin swiveled, nocking another arrow as he moved. "Go," he cried, pointing his bow toward one of the guards. The man stopped in his tracks, creating a temporary gap in the wall of armed men. "Now. Whilst you yet can."

Mariah stumbled backward, and over the sound of her pounding heart, she heard the Sheriff of Nottingham's thunderous voice coming from the dais.

"Seize the pretender!"

CHAPTER 13

Four heartbeats. That was all the time Robin was given between issuing his warning to Marian and feeling the prick of steel at his spine. But it was enough. Like a lithe nymph, Marian darted between the incoming guards, escaping the blockade in the nick of time.

"Lower yer weapon." The guard standing behind Robin leaned forward, his foul-smelling breath poisoning the air as he pressed his blade more firmly against Robin's back.

Silently berating himself for his dull-wittedness, Robin complied. His shock at discovering Marian participating in the tournament followed by his overarching concern for her safety had caused him to lose his focus. He should have been sensitive to the guards' movements, particularly as the tournament had come to an end. None of his men were close enough to the center of the field to prevent the wall of guards from forming. He alone—with a fleet-footed escape—could have prevented this trap from closing. He clenched his jaw. If the sheriff did not finish him off this time, Little John would likely take care of the job himself.

A second guard stepped forward, tearing Robin's bow from his fingers and drawing a rope from his belt. He handed the bow to another guard before pulling Robin's arms back and wrapping the rope around his wrists. Tying the cord in a hasty knot, he cinched it tight, pulling the rough fibers across Robin's skin with callous abandon.

Unwilling to give the fellow the satisfaction of a reaction, Robin clamped his lips together and kept his eyes forward. Beyond the guard's shoulders, he could see those who'd come to watch the tournament. The excitement that had filled the field only minutes before had been replaced by apprehension. A steady stream of people was hurrying toward the exit, likely wanting to escape lest the sheriff order his guards to widen their net. Others—the curious and the indignant, Robin guessed—were lingering, watching and waiting for what was to come next. He hoped his men were bent on making their own getaway, but he had an uncomfortable feeling that despite the threat his arrest would pose to their safety, most of them were in the latter group.

He scanned the faces, catching sight of a round-faced friar standing beside a tall, broad-shouldered fellow sporting a telling scowl. They were perilously close to the dais. Willing them to seek a safer spot, Robin turned his attention to the sheriff. The man was standing before his chair, watching the proceedings on the field with his arms folded, gloating.

The guard who had tied Robin's wrists drew a knife from his scabbard, and in one purposeful stroke, he sliced the belt off Robin's waist. Robin's knife and quiver fell to the ground.

"Ya won't be needin' those where yer goin'," he said, sweeping the items off the ground and nodding to the man at Robin's back. "Take 'im t' the cart."

Another firm jab in the back was enough to pierce Robin's skin. He felt the slow trickle of blood run down his spine as two more guards took positions on either side of him. They each grasped an arm, and as the wall of guards parted, they hauled him across the field and toward a cart waiting beside the dais.

Like a hawk eyeing its prey, the Sheriff of Nottingham stood on the wooden platform, watching their approach. The guards forced Robin to stop opposite the smirking nobleman.

"Remove his hat," the sheriff commanded. The guard at Robin's right whipped the felt hat from his head, and the sheriff's lips curled contemptuously. "Did you truly believe I would be duped by your paltry disguise, Robin Hood?"

Robin remained silent.

"And what of your men?" The sheriff gestured toward the thinning crowd. "Have any lingered long enough to see their leader wheeled off to the dungeon, I wonder? Mayhap they are so loyal they would rather join you there than continue their lawless pursuits in Sherwood Forest without their heroic leader." He sneered. "I am told that once the gallows are erected, it is as easy to hang half a dozen criminals as one."

So the dungeon and gallows were to be his lot. It was hardly surprising. Nevertheless, Robin had always hoped to avoid a stay in the castle dungeons. He had heard rumors. None were confirmed, as he had yet to meet anyone who had spent time there and lived to tell about the experience. But the tales were gruesome.

"Do I detect a hint of fear?" The sheriff set his hands on the railing and leaned forward, studying Robin with narrowed eyes. "Which do you dread most, Robin Hood? The rat-infested dungeon or a rope around your neck?"

"In truth, I believe your howling of displeasure when I am safely back in Sherwood Forest will be far more terrible than the prospect of either of those things," Robin said.

The sheriff's venomous glare paired perfectly with his hissing breath. "Take him away," he said with chilling vehemence. "And watch him around the clock."

The two guards tightened their grip on Robin's arms and hauled him onto the back of the cart. Robin's left hip hit the vehicle's wooden bed with a thump. He grunted. He would have a purple bruise by morning. Unfortunately, it was likely to be the first of many.

"Over there," one of the guards ordered, waving his sword in the general direction of the cart's far right corner.

Robin pushed himself backward until his shoulders found the spot where two of the cart's sides met. Three guards climbed in after him, each taking one of the remaining corners. Two more armed men took watchful positions on either side of the driver.

"To the castle," someone called, and the cart wheels began to roll over the uneven grass.

Ignoring the burning of his wrists and the throbbing of his hip, Robin braced his feet against the wooden slats and scoured the faces of the people lining their path. Most of the men looked grim; a few of the women were crying softly. Children clung to their mothers' skirts, surely not understanding what had happened to cloud the previously joyful day but aware of their mothers' distress regardless.

There was no sign of Friar Tuck or Little John. Where they had gone after he'd spotted them near the dais, Robin could not say. He prayed they had located all his men and were now well away from the sheriff and his guards.

Seemingly of their own volition, his thoughts then turned to Marian. Other than learning that she was yet in Nottingham and boasted astonishing skill with a bow, he knew nothing more about her than he had before. Where was she now? Had she escaped without anyone questioning her?

They had reached the gate that opened onto the road leading to the castle. The cart slowed as the horse veered right, pulling the cart wheels off the grassy pasture and onto the hardpacked dirt. The cart rolled over a deep rut, leaning heavily to the right before straightening again. Robin steadied himself even as his sense of dread inched higher. Already, the castle walls towered above him; he would be within the seemingly impenetrable bastion in no time.

A familiar zing sliced through the air above his head. One breath later, an arrowhead penetrated the center of the wooden cart, a pale-green ribbon fluttering below its fletching. Panicked, the guards shouted at the man at the reins, urging him to drive faster. Robin swiveled, his heart pounding. The arrow had come from his left, but where was the archer? Shuddering, the cart listed wildly as it picked up speed and barreled toward the open castle gates. The faces blurred, but Robin did not need to see Marian to know that she was there. He doubted that any of his men could hit a moving target with such accuracy, and he knew only one person who had worn a pale-green ribbon at the end of her plait.

His captors may be afraid for their lives, but Robin knew better. Marian's arrow had landed exactly where she had intended. She must have waited for a clear shot and realized that disarming all the guards before the cart entered the castle was impossible. Unable to facilitate an escape, she had done the next best thing; she had sent a message.

The guard sitting across from Robin gave another shout, this time directed at a guard manning the castle gate up ahead. Immediately, the rattle of chains began. With a creak of timber and judder of wheels, the cart sped through the entrance beneath the rapidly lowering portcullis.

A servant crossing the outer courtyard darted aside as the driver pulled back on the reins to slow the horse. Behind them, the portcullis's metal teeth hit the cobblestones with a resounding clang. It was an ominous sound, but Robin paid it no mind. Instead, he thought of Marian and Little John, of Friar Tuck, Will, and Allan. And the flicker of hope that had entered the cart with a ribboned arrow glowed a little brighter.

———— · * ✳ · · ————

Mariah leaned against the tree trunk, willing her racing heart to calm. Shooting that arrow had been a huge risk—not only to those sitting in the cart but to herself. If any of the guards had spotted her standing at the edge of the thicket with her bow in hand, she would have been headed to the dungeon along with Robin. She groaned. What a mess she'd made of things. Ellen had tried to warn her against entering the tournament, but she hadn't listened. She'd almost ignored Robin's admonition too. And if she had, she'd probably be the one going to the dungeon, and Robin Hood would still be free.

She hung her head. Why were such lessons so hard to learn? In her line of work, she'd repeatedly seen pride overrule wisdom among Europe's top chefs. The consequences had usually been a poor review from a disgruntled food critic or the loss of a Michelin star rating. If—as seemed ever more likely—she were to remain in medieval Nottingham, it was time she realized that a grievous error in judgment in the twelfth century could mean losing one's life.

"Marian!"

She looked up. Ellen was running toward her, and at her side was a tall, dark-haired man whose nose and eyes were so similar to Ellen's that he had to be related.

"It was you, w-wasn't it?" Ellen panted. "When I saw th-the arrow land in the cart, I knew it h-had to be you."

"I—" Mariah broke off. How did she begin to explain her actions? They made no sense, even to her. "It should have been me. I should have been the one being hauled off to the dungeon, not Robin Hood. He saved me, and—" Clenching her fists, she looked at Ellen's companion. "If you are who I think you are, you must gather Robin's men. My arrow may have given him hope that he's not alone, but that's not enough. We have to free him."

His eyes widened. "Ellen, would you care to explain why a young lady is wearing my old tunic and appears to know far more about me than she should?"

Ellen clasped her hands together anxiously. "This is my f-friend, Marian. She wanted to p-participate in the tournament, and well, you saw for yourself how s-skilled she is with the bow."

"Marian." He repeated the name as though it meant something to him. "And you truly believed that if she dressed as a man and used Robin Hood's bow, all would be well?"

She'd been using Robin Hood's bow! Mariah stared at the long, smooth yew bow in her hand, barely registering Ellen's stuttered reply.

"Sh-She was so anxious to do it. And she said she'd give some of the p-prize money to Mother."

"I did," Mariah interjected. "And I would have, had I won and the sheriff had had the decency to award me the purse." She moved to stand beside her friend. "You must not blame Ellen for any of this. It was all my doing, and I'm the one who must make up for what has happened."

"By freeing Robin Hood?" Will raised a cynical eyebrow.

"Yes." A whispered memory of her recent self-reflection on the ills of pride echoed through her head. "But I cannot do it without help."

"Of that I am certain," Will said grimly. He turned to eye the tall castle walls. "In truth, I am not sure that it can be done at all."

"We have to try. Surely Little John and Friar Tuck will have some ideas."

"Ellen." Will glared at his sister. "I had not thought you so loose with your tongue."

Color tinged Ellen's cheeks. "I have said n-nothing. Marian s-spoke those names when she first arrived."

"I have known of you for a long time," Mariah said.

Will folded his arms, his expression wary. "The outlaws of Sherwood Forest are known by name in London?"

"Yes," she said. "And how did you know I came from London?"

"I assumed as much since you took upon yourself the name Michael o' London. The name Marian is all Robin knows of you, but as he has mentioned you repeatedly these past weeks, it is also known to every one of his men."

It was Mariah's turn to flush. Had Robin brought up her name because he'd been humored by her naivete when she'd come to the forest to warn him of the sheriff's plans, or had the memory of their initial meeting and their unsettling kiss in the marketplace lingered with him as much as it had with her?

"If R-Robin has spoken of Marian, you should know that she can b-be trusted," Ellen said.

Will eyed the castle walls grimly. "What I know is that Robin has never been in more dire straits."

Guilt gnawed at Mariah. "Let us help him escape. Ellen and I have better access to the castle than any of the men of Sherwood Forest."

He eyed her silently for a moment, as though weighing two sides of a significant internal battle. "Do I have your word that you will not betray Robin Hood or any of his men to the Sheriff of Nottingham, Prince John, or any who associate with them?"

"Of course."

"Say it," he pressed.

"I give you my word," Mariah said.

"And you, Ellen."

"B-But I already—"

"Say it," he said. "Given what we are about to undertake, it bears repeating."

"I g-give you my word," Ellen said.

He nodded, and with that outward sign of acceptance, his guard fell away. "I must locate Little John straightway," he said. "And you must return to the castle."

"But—" Mariah began.

He raised his hand to stop her. "You will be doing more for Robin by resuming your positions there than any of his men can presently accomplish. If we are to have any hope of mounting a rescue, we must know exactly what the sheriff has planned, where Robin is being held, and how he will be transported to the gallows. Where will the hanging take place, and when? How many guards will be in attendance, and where will they be located?"

"We work in the k-kitchen," Ellen said. "How are w-we ever to learn such things?"

"After what happened at the tournament this day, there will be talk," Will said. "A great deal of talk—especially amongst the servants. If you listen well, you shall acquire more information than you can imagine."

"How are we to share it with you?" Mariah asked.

"When your work in the kitchen is complete, come to the White Stag Inn. Ellen knows where it is. Little John and I will meet you there." He looked around to check his surroundings. Now that they had formulated a plan of sorts, he was anxious to be on his way. "The White Stag," he repeated. "At nightfall." And then he was gone, walking toward the road at a brisk pace.

Mariah hid the bow and quiver in its former hiding spot in the thicket, and when Will disappeared around the bend, she and Ellen headed in the opposite direction, toward the castle. They passed a handful of people but exchanged no more conversation until they were within a few yards of the menacing portcullis.

An old man pushing a handcart full of cabbages approached the guards ahead of them, and Ellen's feet slowed. "Can we m-manage what Will has asked of us?" she whispered.

"We must," Mariah said. "Robin's life and the welfare of countless others depend upon it."

Ellen shot her a tremulous smile. "You sound like one of Robin Hood's men."

"Good," Mariah said, tugging her hood a little lower over her eyes. "Because regardless of how we are dressed, for the rest of the day, that's precisely what we are."

Ellen chewed her lower lip. "J-Just like Will."

"Yes," Mariah said. "But with access to the castle."

A fresh look of determination crossed Ellen's face. "When we r-reach the inner courtyard, I will k-keep watch whilst you recover your kirtle. And then I shall d-discover what Stephen has heard about the sh-sheriff's new prisoner from the other servant boys."

Mariah nodded her agreement. Questioning Stephen was a good place to start.

CHAPTER 14

The dungeon was worse than Robin had imagined. The putrid stench had assailed him the moment he had begun descending the stairs, and once he had reached the underbelly of the castle, it had been so nauseating that he'd retched. Since then, he had studiously worked to breathe through his mouth. But the foul smell lingered, clinging to his clothes and hair.

The guards had thrown him into a dark cave of a room. With no window and no other source of light, he'd been unable to gauge its size until he'd paced across it. Five steps one way, three steps the other. His only cohabitants were rats. And though he could not tell exactly how many shared his living space, the constant patter of small feet crossing the dirt floor suggested that there were several.

At first, having seen no one but the guards who'd deposited him in his cell, he'd wondered if he might be the sheriff's only prisoner. But more recently, he'd heard distant moans that told of agony and bone-weary exhaustion. There were others languishing in this foul place, though who they were or how long they had suffered, he could not tell. He only prayed that his own sojourn would be short.

A guard approached, bringing with him a flickering torch. Robin covered his eyes against its brightness. It seemed that this was to be his lot: an hour or two of abandonment followed by a brief visit from a guard. Why they felt the need to check on him, he could not say.

With his arms still bound, no weapon, and no light, even he could not fathom a way out of this nightmare.

"Robin Hood." It was a new guard; the voice was unfamiliar and rang with contempt. "After all this time, yer finally where ya belong."

Robin did not deign to reply. No matter what they had done, no humans belonged in this foul underground cistern.

"Do ya 'ear me?" The guard took hold of one of the bars that held Robin captive and shook it. It barely moved. "What do ya 'ave t' say fer yerself?" At Robin's continued silence, he snorted and leaned forward to sneer through the bars. "Not such a cocksure villain now, are ya?"

"If you are in search of a cocksure villain," Robin said, his voice echoing eerily through the cavernous dungeon, "I believe you will find him in the sheriff's chambers."

The guard retreated a step, as though unprepared for so firm a response. Then uttering a coarse curse, he raised the torch aloft again. "One day more, Robin Hood. That's all ya can claim. The gallows are goin' up as we speak."

And then he walked away, taking the light and his disdain with him.

Robin waited until the echo of footsteps faded to nothing, then he leaned back against the cold, damp wall. So he was to be hanged on the morrow. As relieved as he was to know that he would see daylight again so soon, he recognized what this meant for his chance of escape. It would be all but impossible for his men to manage a rescue in so short a space of time. Word of the sheriff's plans would likely not reach them until the hanging was over.

The thought was sobering and brought with it a flood of emotions: gratitude for his life of freedom and friendships in the forest, satisfaction for the aid he and his men had rendered to others whose lot had been much harder, sorrow for the family connections he had lost when the sheriff had pronounced him an outlaw, and regret for those things he had hoped for that he would never know. He took another breath through his mouth and closed his eyes.

Less than a month ago, the return of King Richard would have topped his hoped-for list, closely followed by a royal pardon for him and his men. More recently, however, he'd experienced a new longing—one that involved a mysterious maiden named Marian. A vision of her beautiful face mingled with the memory of an arrow bearing a pale-green ribbon sailing into the cart with deadly accuracy.

He leaned his head back, staring up at the blackness. He ached to know Marian better, to discover her likes and dislikes, to show her the forest he loved so well, to learn her background and how she had come to shoot so well. Their fateful kiss in the marketplace had awakened something within him—something he did not yet fully understand. But acknowledging that she was lost to him filled him with profound sadness. He trusted that their final interaction had shown her that he cared for her welfare. And during these last few hours, he would grant himself license to believe that her arrow—the one bearing her ribbon—was a sign that she cared for his welfare also.

———— · · ✦ · · ————

Darkness was falling rapidly. Mariah slipped her arm through Ellen's, relying on her friend to guide them through the narrow, winding roads of Nottingham. Now that the sun was disappearing, the warm temperatures they'd experienced earlier were dropping. Mariah readjusted the blanket around her shoulders so it covered her neck, grateful that she and Ellen had taken the time to claim another layer before slipping out of the castle. She had no idea how long they would be at the White Stag Inn, but it would undoubtedly be darker and colder when they made their way back up the hill.

Leaving the castle had been remarkably easy. Ellen had told the guard at the gate that they were going to visit family members and would be returning in an hour or two. The look he had given them suggested that he questioned whether the visit was to a brother or a boyfriend, but as long as he did not guess the real reason for their trip, Mariah didn't care.

"Are we getting close?" Mariah kept her voice low, though no one was in sight.

"Aye," Ellen replied, raising her free arm to point down the road. "The inn is j-just around y-yonder bend."

"Have you gone there often?"

"A few t-times," she admitted. "The last was when I sent a m-message to Will, askin' for the clothes and b-bow."

So the inn operated as a communication hub for the outlaws when they needed to pass information to someone in town or vice versa. It stood to reason that Will had suggested they meet here. If the men of Sherwood Forest trusted the proprietor with their messages, they undoubtedly trusted him with their identities too.

They turned the corner, and a small building standing alone came into view. A torch flickered in the sconce beside the thick wooden door. It illuminated a small portion of the white walls and dark timbers near the entrance but could not penetrate the shadows on either side. Mariah slowed her steps, causing Ellen to do the same.

"Where are we to meet Will?" Mariah asked.

"I've never m-met him 'ere afore," Ellen admitted. "So I c-can't rightly say."

"Ellen." The man's voice was barely above a whisper, but both women heard it and moved toward the far corner of the building.

"Will?" Ellen asked.

"Aye. And a friend." Will stepped out of the shadows. The man beside him was a head taller and half again as wide.

Ellen bobbed a curtsy. Mariah followed suit.

"Marian," Will said, keeping his voice low. "This 'ere's Little John."

She had guessed as much by his size. "I'm pleased to meet you," she said, although *stunned* might be a more accurate word.

"I could say the same." His voice was deep. "Even though Robin swore you were real, after our efforts to seek you out failed for a full fortnight, I had begun to doubt it."

Mariah strained to see his expression. Was he joking? "He was looking for me?"

"Like a man possessed," he grumbled. "I discouraged him from entering the tournament—told him it was a trap—but it did take his mind off you. Until this afternoon."

Mariah's heart fell. "Forgive me. I did not know that allowing him to win would lead to his capture."

"You allowed him to win?" Little John was obviously skeptical.

"Marian's skill with the bow is noteworthy," Will said. "I have seen her hit a moving target from over forty rods."

"Robin told me my life would be in peril if the sheriff discovered I was a woman," she explained. "He gave no indication that once his identity was known, he ran the same danger."

"He did not fully believe it." Little John sighed. "I daresay he is ruing that oversight at present."

"Were you able to discover his whereabouts?" Will asked.

"He's in the d-dungeon, as we thought," Ellen said. "Three g-guards watch the d-door that leads to the cells. I t-took them their evening m-meal. There was n-nothing for any prisoner."

"They will not waste food on a prisoner," Little John said. "Particularly one who the sheriff undoubtedly intends to put to death straightway."

Mariah battled her horror. "The spit-boy told us he heard that the hanging would occur at noon on the morrow," she said, repeating the wording Stephen had used.

"Noon on the morrow." Little John winced. "That gives us very little time to plan a rescue."

"I have seen the gallows," Will said. "The sheriff wasted no time on having the scaffold erected in the town square."

"So everyone in town can watch." Mariah was going to be sick.

"It must n-not happen." Ellen looked from Will to Little John. "There m-must needs be something that can b-be done to free him."

Little John ran his hand over his face, his concern obvious. "With Robin under such heavy guard, our best chance of saving him is at the hanging."

"But that means that if we fail, there is no second chance," Mariah said.

"Aye," Little John said. "And so, we must plan accordingly." He took a step toward the inn's front door. "Come, there are others you must meet. We shall share some mead and discuss what can be done."

The inn's public room was not overly large. The ceiling was low and traversed by dark wooden beams. A small fire burned in the large fireplace. Candles flickered on the tables, casting dancing shadows over the faces of those seated at them. The sweet aroma of mead mingled with straw and sweat.

Most of the room's occupants were men. A few sat alone, staring morosely into their cups. Others sat in small clusters, the rumble of their conversations interspersed by an occasional shout or guffaw. The ones sitting nearest the door looked up as the newcomers entered. They each acknowledged Little John and Will with barely discernible nods, although whether they were signaling that it was safe to enter the inn or simply offering them a courteous mark of recognition, Mariah couldn't tell.

Little John led them around the edge of the room to a table in the far corner. Two men sat at it, one short and dressed in brown robes, the other tall and lanky with thick, straw-colored hair. The robed man stood as Mariah and Ellen reached them.

Keeping his voice low, Will made the introductions. "Friar Tuck, this is my sister Ellen and her friend Marian."

"I bid you welcome." Friar Tuck offered Marian a sad smile. "Would that we were meeting under happier circumstances." He gestured toward the young man who was leaning to his right, a look of intense concentration on his face. "You must forgive Allan for not standing to greet you. We have been listening in on a rather fascinating discussion occurring at the next table, and he is anxious not to miss anything of great import."

Little John's eyebrows rose. "Would our mutual friend benefit from intelligence gained from said conversation?"

"I believe that is a distinct possibility," Friar Tuck said, making room for Will and Ellen next to him. "But you'd best be seated and judge for yourself."

Little John and Mariah quickly slid onto the bench beside Allan. Allan glanced at them briefly, placed a finger to his lips, and inclined his head toward the table immediately behind them. Not daring to turn around and look, Mariah strained to hear the male voices over the other noises in the room.

"A sittin' duck, that's what I was. An' I will be again." The man speaking stopped to take a long, slurping drink. "Not that anyone cares, mind. Least of all the sheriff."

"Nah. Yer thinkin's all wrong. Ya'll be an 'ero," a second man said. "The one brave enough t' drive Robin Hood t' his death."

"What good'll that do me if I'm dead along with 'im."

"It's not goin' t' 'appen. There'll be guards all around ya in the cart," the second man said.

"No amount o' guards is goin' t' stop an arrow comin' straight fer the driver. That arrow t'day came outa nowhere. Missed me ear by a whisker." The first man took another drink. "It 'ad to be one of 'is men who shot it. Why else would there be a green ribbon hangin' off it?"

Mariah didn't move a muscle. The man was talking about the arrow she'd shot into the cart. He must have been the driver.

The man moaned. "Haulin' wood. A month ago, that's all I was doin'. Mindin' me own business with me old 'orse an' cart. An' now look at me." He sounded as though he might sob, but instead, he took another drink and then slammed the cup back onto the table.

"More ale over 'ere." The second man's shout caught the attention of the young woman circling the room with a tray of wooden cups. She started toward their table.

"The fellow is well into his cups already," Little John murmured, leaning over the table so that Friar Tuck and Will could hear. "And more than a little afeared of the task before him on the morrow." He smiled. It was the first smile Mariah had seen, and she caught a glimpse of the mischief he was known for in legends. "I am inclined to assist the poor sap."

"Most noble," Friar Tuck said. "Though I doubt that is your primary motive."

Little John's smile widened. "The concerns he vocalized cause me to wonder how many guards are similarly anxious over their roles in Robin's demise. It might behoove us to ensure that those charged with watching the gallows have sufficient ale to shore up their courage."

He meant to get them drunk.

"I daresay Mistress Talitha would be willing to sell us a barrel of her most potent ale," Will said.

"Aye," Little John said. "But the guards are unlikely to accept a drink from us." He looked from Mariah to Ellen. "Can you be at the square by dawn?"

"Wait!" Will cut in. "If Ellen is seen assisting Robin Hood's men, she will lose her position at the castle. I imagine the same is true for Marian."

Ellen's smile was strained, but the determination in her eyes was unmistakable. "It is well, W-Will."

"But you may not—"

She covered his hand with hers. "Marian and I d-discussed this earlier. We may not dress like the M-Merry Men—" She shot an apologetic look at Mariah. "At least, not often. B-But we brought you the information y-you sought because we wish to support R-Robin and his band. We do not intend t-to abandon him or you now."

"Exactly," Mariah said, her heart swelling at Ellen's show of bravery. "What do you need us to do?"

The concern had yet to leave Will's face, but Little John eyed Mariah speculatively. "Is it true? Can you hit a moving target with an arrow?"

Unease skittered up her spine. "I have practiced that skill in the past."

"Can you do it whilst you are also in motion?"

Mariah hesitated. To be without sure footing made hitting a target infinitely more difficult. "What did you have in mind?"

He ran his fingers through his hair, all trace of his earlier good nature now buried in a frown. "I have conceived a plan. Our recent insight into the mindset of the driver behind us has confirmed its validity. The risk to those involved is staggering, and yet, as hard as I have tried, I cannot seem to generate a better—or safer—notion." He glanced at Friar Tuck and Will. "And to the best of my knowledge, neither have my friends here." Both men shook their heads solemnly, and Little John turned back to Mariah. "Its success rides heavily upon your skill with the bow."

Mariah's unease was now full-fledged dread. Fighting back the negative emotions, she thought of Robin—of the glimpses she'd already seen of his generosity, selflessness, and bravery. He hardly knew her, yet he would attempt the impossible for her. She knew that as surely as she knew that no matter what happened tomorrow, her life would never be the same.

"Tell me your plan," she said. "If I can manage the feat, I will do it."

CHAPTER 15

Robin had no way of measuring time, but it seemed as though he had been trapped in this pit of desolation for weeks. In truth, it was more likely that it had been several hours. His body ached with fatigue, though his head refused to relinquish its tenuous hold on reality. The guards checked on him at regular intervals, most often raising their burning torches high enough to see that he remained within the cell from down the corridor and then leaving straightway. The few who were seemingly immune to the rancid conditions in the dungeon lingered a sufficient amount of time to shake the bars and toss a taunt in Robin's direction. Robin had neither the desire nor the energy to respond.

His first clue that this routine had altered was the echo of multiple heavy steps on the stairs. He rose to his feet, waiting for the first flicker of light to appear in the passageway. Shadows confirming the arrival of more than one person danced across the stone wall moments before four guards appeared within the circle of a torch's flame.

"Time t' meet yer maker, Robin Hood." The guard who spoke had been the most deriding during his earlier visits, and Robin braced himself for an unpleasant exit. "Stand where we can see ya."

Robin moved closer to the bars, grateful that he had not been here long enough to become badly weakened.

"Let me see yer hands," the guard said.

Robin turned so that his roped and chaffed wrists were visible.

The guard gave a satisfied grunt, and Robin turned back around in time to see him take a large key ring from his belt, slide a key into the lock, and turn it. The bolt slid back with a click.

"Stay where ya are," the guard warned, signaling for two of the other men to enter the cell.

The two guards walked in and immediately took positions on either side of Robin.

"They're armed," the first guard growled. "We all are. So ya'll do exactly as yer told." Without waiting for a response, he raised his sword and pointed back the way he had come. "Out!"

With two guards walking ahead of him and two at his rear, Robin made the slow march down the narrow passageway and up the stairs that led out of the dungeon. The darkness began to fade, and the damp air that had weighed down his lungs with its cloying odor lightened. For the first time since he'd been incarcerated, Robin took a deep breath.

The guard in the front opened a door. Sunlight—piercingly bright—streamed into the stairwell. Robin gasped, stumbling to a halt as he instinctively turned his head into his upper arm to protect his eyes.

"Move!" The guard immediately behind him shoved him forward.

With half-open eyes, Robin faltered up the remaining steps and into a large room. He blinked, desperate for his vision to adjust before facing the direct sunlight outside. Four chairs were positioned around a table in the corner. On the table, knucklebones sat beside an unlit lantern and a trencher filled with the remains of a meal. It appeared that the men had made themselves comfortable while they'd kept watch over him.

Another guard stood at the outer door. "The cart's ready," he said. "We're t' set 'im inside straightway."

With an acknowledging nod, the nearest guard seized Robin's arm and propelled him across the room and through the door. Instantly, Robin was encircled by half a dozen guards wielding swords.

In the far recesses of his mind, Robin acknowledged that the escort was excessive for a solitary, unarmed prisoner whose hands were bound together, but such a notion could hardly compete with his overwhelming gladness at feeling the warmth of the sun on his face and seeing brilliant colors after hours of blackness.

Once outside, they marched him through the inner courtyard. A handful of servants stopped what they were about and hastened out of the men's path only to stand and quietly watch Robin and his escorts pass by. Shouts and the clatter of hooves coming from the direction of the stables filled the otherwise unnaturally quiet inner courtyard. Robin kept his face forward and his expression placid. If this was to be his final journey, he would have it be an honorable one.

A cart and horse stood waiting in the outer courtyard. Ahead of it, half a dozen mounted horses nickered and shifted nervously. Robin gave the company a brief glance. The sheriff, dressed in black velvet with red trim, watched Robin's approach with a hardened, calculating expression. Select members of his retinue made up the remainder of the riders.

Straightening his shoulders, Robin approached the rear of the cart. At first glance, it appeared to be the same vehicle that had brought him to the castle from the tournament. As before, the driver sat on the riding bench between two guards. Two more guards stood waiting in the bed of the cart. They came to attention as Robin's escort came to a halt.

"Get in!" One of the guards pushed him to the cart's edge.

Robin eyed the platform. His aching hip was a relentless reminder of what had happened the last time he'd been forced to climb in while bound, but any request for assistance would assuredly make matters worse.

As though responding to that very thought, the guard at Robin's right thrust him roughly against the cart. "He said get in!"

The wooden boards pressed against Robin's empty abdomen. Gritting his teeth against the discomfort, he leaned his upper torso against the cart's bed and heaved his legs up and over its edge. The moment he'd cleared the ground, two guards followed, purposely kicking his arms and legs as they stepped over him. Robin waited until they'd taken their seats in the four corners of the cart, then he rolled over and pulled himself into a sitting position.

The men who had delivered him but appeared to be going no farther backed away, and a rider approached. The guards in the cart scrambled to their feet; Robin did not.

"Good day to you, Robin Hood." The sheriff's voice was laced with irony. "How providential that you have chosen to join us on our ride to the town square."

Robin raised his head to meet the sheriff's eyes. "Indeed, Sheriff. This is a most fortuitous meeting. I imagine you are here to deliver the purse of gold you promised to the winner of the archery tournament."

The sheriff snorted. "Unless you aim to bribe the devil, you will have no need of three hundred pounds of gold at your final destination."

"Regardless, the gesture would confirm your reputation as a man of your word." Robin inclined his head. "And should I truly have no need of the purse by day's end, I daresay you could reclaim it with impunity."

The sheriff's jaw tightened, but he loosened the ties of the purse at his belt and tossed the small bag at Robin. "One hour is all I can grant you, I fear," he said. "I gave my word to rid Nottinghamshire of Robin Hood long before I offered so hefty a prize for the archery tournament. The one, for the sake of fair-mindedness, must supplant the other."

"For the sake of fair-mindedness," Robin repeated, twisting his torso so that he might grasp the purse with his swollen fingers.

With a glower, the sheriff swung his horse around to take his place at the head of the company.

As one, the guards lowered themselves into sitting positions once again, placing themselves strategically against the sides of the cart and leaving Robin in its unprotected center. Such stratagems made no difference to Robin. Unless his fortune reversed itself very soon, he was to die this day. How the event occurred hardly mattered. But if the guards were worried for their own safety, so much the better.

He tightened his grip on the small leather pouch. As tempting as pilfering the bulging purse might be to some of the less upright guards, Robin considered it unlikely that any would act upon that inclination. If they were as sure of his demise as the sheriff appeared to be, they would be reluctant to steal from it, as the sheriff would undoubtedly count every coin upon its return. And though Robin thought it unlikely that the devil would take a bribe, there was a slim possibility that a jaded hangman may consider it.

A horn sounded. The sheriff started forward, his small entourage in tow. The driver slapped his reins, and the sturdy cart horse took its first labored steps. A cat that had been sunning itself near the well took off in a blur of movement, and the courtyard was suddenly filled with the clatter of hooves, the creak of cart wheels, and the grind of the portcullis rising to let them through.

———— · ✸ · ————

Mariah filled a third cup with ale from the barrel Mistress Talitha had had delivered to the bakery across from the gallows in the town square. Friar Tuck had suggested the location, and Mariah couldn't fault it. Bertram the Baker had grudgingly allowed the barrel to be placed in his back room. He probably didn't appreciate Mariah and Ellen going back and forth through his shop to replenish cups, but the White Stag Inn supplied Bertram with fresh yeast, and refusing Mistress Talitha's request would have been poor business practice. Besides, bakery customers were all but nonexistent today anyway.

The barrel was hidden from the growing crowd's view and from the guards patrolling the gallows, but it was close enough that Mariah and Ellen could refill cups quickly. They had arrived just as the sun had broken over the rooftops and had not stopped serving drinks since.

The day was sunny and hot, and the guards were tired and excessively thirsty. It was precisely the kind of conditions Little John had hoped for.

"The guard stationed on the far r-right corner is taking a walk with Friar T-Tuck," Ellen whispered as she passed by on her way back to the barrel.

Mariah glanced across the square. Friar Tuck had his arm around a guard and was leading him slowly toward the nearby church. The guard tottered. Friar Tuck steadied him and drew him toward the arched entrance. By Mariah's count, that was the seventh guard to take refuge in the church to sleep off his drunkenness. That left three. And those who remained at their posts were in such poor shape that they had not even noticed their numbers were so badly depleted. The first phase of Little John's outlandish scheme appeared to be going as planned; Mariah could only pray that the remaining portions would fall into place so well.

Her stomach did a slow roll, and she set her tray on a nearby step. Extreme nervousness and lack of sleep were a poor beginning for someone who needed a steady hand.

Flexing her tired fingers, she studied the newly erected structure before her. The wooden scaffold held a commanding presence in the square. Oblong and raised off the ground, there was a ladder of sorts that led up to the platform. In the center of the platform, a post and beam had been attached in an upside-down *L* shape. A looped rope hung from the beam. Immediately beneath the rope was a trap door operated by a lever on the far side of the post. It was simple and was undoubtedly effective. Mariah could not look at it without horror clawing at her throat.

She lowered her head and took a few deep breaths. The last thing she should do was draw attention to herself. Turning her back to the scaffold and the crowd, she allowed her gaze to pass over the buildings that lined the square. Robin's men were out there somewhere. Dispersed among the buildings, hidden behind doorframes, and standing at open windows, they were awaiting the arrival of their leader and the signal to raise their bows.

Across from her, Friar Tuck slipped out of the church, closing the door quietly behind him. A murmur rippled through those gathered in the square. Mariah tensed. People began turning, straining to see past those standing behind them.

"They're c-coming!" Ellen arrived at her side as the sound of hooves hitting the cobblestones reached them. "Make haste, Marian. You m-must be ready when the cart c-comes."

Abandoning her tray, Mariah ran back to the bakery. Bertram must have sensed a change in the crowd's behavior because he'd left his position behind the counter and was standing at the doorway.

"I beg your pardon," Mariah said, sliding past him.

"You shall miss the hanging if you go back there now," Bertram warned.

Desperately wishing she could, Mariah pinned a smile to her face. "I will not be long."

Hurrying into the back room, she pushed her arm into the gap between the barrel and the wall and withdrew her borrowed bow. Repeating the procedure, she pulled out the quiver as well. With trembling fingers, she untied her apron and slid the leather loop on the top of the quiver through one of the ties before knotting the apron firmly around her waist again. It wasn't ideal, but it would do the job.

Slipping the bow over her shoulder, she returned to the shop. The clatter of hooves was louder now. Shouts and jeers came from the crowd, though whether they were directed at Robin Hood or those who held him captive, she could not say. Moving quietly so as not to draw Bertram's attention, she stepped closer to the window. The sheriff appeared, entering the square on horseback, his back ramrod stiff, his chin high.

He led a small entourage to the guildhall. The building faced the scaffold and would give those who sat on the ornately carved wooden chairs lining the top step a clear view of the proceedings.

One by one, the riders dismounted, and three or four young boys ran forward to lead their horses away, presumably to the stable behind the nearby blacksmith's shop.

Most of the dignitaries immediately climbed the stairs and took their seats, but the sheriff paused on the lowest step and scanned his surrounds with a wary eye. Mariah held her breath. Would he spot an archer? Or worse, the lack of guards in the vicinity? The guards who were still on their feet were within plain sight. Mariah offered a silent prayer that they would remain upright long enough to appease the sheriff's concerns.

The rhythmic clunk of cart wheels rumbling over cobblestones drew the sheriff's attention back to the route he had just traversed. Climbing the steps, he took his seat and watched intently as a horse-drawn cart pulled into the square. A strained hush fell over the crowd. Every sound seemed magnified—the horse's heavy hooves, a door closing, a man clearing his throat, someone sobbing. Her heart in her throat, Mariah shifted a few inches to better view the lumbering vehicle.

At first, all she could see was guards. Two sat on the bench on either side of the driver, and several rode in the back. She attempted to count the ones in the back. Three, no four. Four. She released a tense breath. Four plus the two at the front. Even though the ale's effect had cut the number of viable guards in half, that still left six whom Robin's men would need to distract.

The cart slowed, but before it had come to a complete stop, the guards began piling out. Mariah watched as they created a semicircular wall around the back of the cart. The last guard in the cart reached down and hauled the man who had been sitting at its center to his feet. The crowd gave a collective gasp, and Mariah swallowed the lump in her throat. It was Robin. His hat and belt were gone. His hair hung limp, and his previously clean-shaven chin was covered with stubble. Brown smudges streaked his cheek and clothing, but Mariah was too far away to tell if they were bloodstains or dirt.

A guard gave Robin a rough shove, pushing him to the end of the cart. Seconds later, Robin was dragged off and disappeared behind the barricade of armed men. The last guard jumped down and joined his companions, leaving the driver sitting alone with an empty cart.

"Forward!" One of the men shouted the terse command, and with two guards leading out, two at the rear, and one on either side of their prisoner, they began a steady march toward the scaffold.

When they reached the wooden ladder that led to the platform, four of the guards pulled away and moved to stand along the front of the scaffold. With drawn swords, the other two forced Robin up the ladder. Only when he reached the top did Mariah move her gaze from Robin long enough to see another man standing with folded arms beside the gallows. Dressed in black from his shoes to the hood covering his head, he exuded menace. And he was her signal to move.

She was through the bakery's door before Bertram knew she was there. Making use of the shops' overhanging roofs to stay in the shadows, she hurried toward the waiting cart. The eyes of everyone in the square were fixed on the gallows. She bumped into a few people, but they barely acknowledged her. And if any of them noticed what she carried, they were too preoccupied to point it out.

Up ahead, the cart horse snorted. She was close. Footsteps on the ladder marked the descent of the two guards who'd walked Robin to the gallows. Her time was running out. She squeezed past a large man and his wife and suddenly found herself at the back of the cart. Reaching for the edge of the closest plank, she hauled herself up. Her kirtle caught beneath her legs. She tugged at the fabric, wrenching it free and scrabbling forward. Slivers of wood dug into the palms of her hands, but she ignored them.

The driver turned his head. Relief flooded her. She had climbed on board not knowing if Little John had been successful in persuading the cart's owner to relinquish this task to him.

"I was startin' to worry," he said. "You'd best brace yourself. We have no more time."

He cracked the reins. The horse took a step, and the cart rocked. Mariah reached for the side of the vehicle and pulled herself up. Staying on her knees, she slid the bow off her shoulder and reached for an arrow. The cart was picking up speed, and she was being tossed to and fro.

"I can't do it," Mariah cried. "Not moving like this."

"Hang on." Little John steered the horse directly toward the platform.

Several people in the crowd shouted. A woman screamed.

From the direction of the guildhall, the sheriff's voice rose above them all. "Guards! Stop that cart!"

The guards rushed forward, their swords drawn. A drunk guard tripped and fell. Two others stumbled over him. And then a volley of arrows appeared in the air, raining down directly on the floundering guards. Cries filled the air as the onlookers ran to take cover.

"Hangman!" There was a new level of desperation in the sheriff's roar. "Do your work!"

Little John pulled the cart up against the platform and heaved back on the reins. "Now, Marian!" he yelled. "The fiend is placing the noose around Robin's neck."

Mariah didn't stop to think. She couldn't—not about the still-rocking cart or the chaos going on around her or what would happen if she missed. The hangman moved away from Robin's side to reach for the lever that would open the trapdoor beneath Robin's feet. As though watching from a distance, Mariah nocked her arrow, aimed, and shot. Two seconds later, the hangman screamed and staggered back a few paces, clutching his thigh.

"Jump, Robin!" Mariah cried.

"The rope!" With a frustrated shout, Little John slid to the edge of his seat, but before he could launch himself onto the platform to free Robin's neck from the noose, there was a flurry of movement at the top of the ladder, and Ellen appeared, racing across the platform toward Robin. Arriving at his side, she drew a small knife from the leather bag at her waist and seized his wrists.

"Marian!" Little John yelled over the clamor. "The hangman!"

The man in black had pulled Mariah's arrow from his leg. He took a couple of unsteady steps toward the lever, reached for it, stumbled, and missed. He swiped at it again. But before he could fully grasp the bar, Mariah's second arrow entered his upper arm.

CHAPTER 16

At the hangman's furious bellow, the servant girl standing behind Robin severed the last fiber restraining Robin's wrists. His hands were free. In one swift movement, he reached for the rope around his neck and pulled it up and over his head.

"We cannot use the stairs," the young woman gasped.

One of the guards had broken free from the barrage of arrows pinning the sheriff and his men in place and had almost reached the top of the ladder.

"The cart," Robin yelled. "Run."

The servant girl took off toward the waiting cart, and Robin hazarded a glance toward the ladder. The guard had reached the platform and was advancing with slow, deliberate steps, a lethal blade in his hand. He showed no interest in the fleeing maiden; he wanted Robin. Robin hesitated one heartbeat more. He heard a thud as the young woman dropped into the cart. She was safe. It was past time for him to follow. Keeping his eyes on the advancing guard, he took one step and heard a click.

The wood beneath his feet shifted, and instinct sent Robin leaping sideways. The trapdoor flew open beneath him. He teetered, one foot on the edge of the platform and one in the air. Throwing his weight forward, he landed hard on his knees. More vibration, this time on the solid portion of the platform. He looked up. The guard had abandoned his cautious approach and was running toward him.

Silently praying that the injured hangman had exerted all his energy on shifting the lever, Robin did not take the time to check that adversary's whereabouts. He had only one chance for escape, and he intended to take it. Springing to his feet, he raced across the short distance to the edge of the scaffold and vaulted into the cart.

The vehicle was already moving when he landed. He dropped low, tumbling into one of the cart's sides as it pulled away from the platform. A clatter sounded behind him. Had the guard also made the leap? He swung around. Already, the cart was picking up speed. A bow bounced across the cart as a man dressed in Lincoln green pulled himself on board. The pounding in Robin's chest eased a fraction. It was Will Scarlett.

Over the shouts and screams surrounding them, Little John's voice reached him from the driver's seat. "Good of you to join us at last, Robin. And you, Will."

Will ignored him. "The men have very few arrows remaining. You'd best exit the square with haste. They cannot hold the guards off much longer."

Clicking his tongue loudly, Little John slapped the reins. "Make way!" he shouted.

Like the fork in a river, the crowd ahead of them parted, and the cart barreled through. A few brave souls cheered, but their jubilation was short-lived.

"Guards!" the sheriff shouted. Robin could no longer see those who had been left impotent on the steps of the guildhall, but the sheriff's rage was palpable. "Arrest any who assist the outlaws!"

The torrent of arrows coming from the surrounding buildings slowed to a few, and if the clatter of steel was any indication, Robin's opponent's men were on the move. The local people must have also sensed the change. In twos and threes, they were quietly but swiftly disappearing into shops and down nearby alleys.

"We are losing our cover in more ways than one," Robin called up to Little John.

"I see that." If Little John's tense shoulders were any indication, he was concentrating fully on directing the shuddering cart out of the center of town at the greatest possible speed—preferably without breaking a wheel or all the occupants' teeth.

Suddenly, the clatter of the cart horse's hooves on the cobblestones became thuds. They had reached the hardpacked dirt road. The vehicle tilted sharply to the left. Everything and everyone slid that direction. Bracing himself against the cart's side, Robin repositioned himself, and for the first time, he had a good view of the cart's other occupants. The wheels rolled over a deep rut. The servant girl who had cut him free gave a startled cry and clung to the wooden slats, her expression fearful. Next to her, clutching his old bow and watching him with wide eyes was Marian.

"Are you—" she began.

With a shudder, the cart listed again, this time to the right, cutting Marian's question short and causing Robin to dig his heels into a groove on a nearby plank to prevent himself from falling.

"Cart tracks are not meant to be crossed at this speed," Will muttered. His complexion had taken on a greenish hue.

"Neither are cobblestones," Robin said. "But we have those behind us."

Will nodded and turned to look over his shoulder. Now that they were on the road, they were traveling even faster than before. The square—with its attendant crowd, scaffold, guards, and dignitaries—was lost from view.

"We're comin' up on the town gates," Little John called. "In case you were wonderin', I won't be stoppin'. An' it might be a good thing to keep your heads down."

"How many guards?" Will asked.

"Two," Little John replied. "An' they're startin' to look worried."

"Weapons?" Robin asked.

"Swords but no bows," Little John said with satisfaction. "Just like the ones at the square."

"Ha," Will said. "They won't be making that mistake again."

There was no doubt someone would pay for such an oversight, and Robin pitied any member of the castle guard who was called before the Sheriff of Nottingham this day. It would not go well for him.

"Make way!" Little John called. But unlike the onlookers in the square, the guards did not move. "Make way!" he repeated.

They held firm for a few moments more, and then, when it became obvious that Little John had no intention of slowing, let alone coming to a halt, they each dove for cover in the bushes that lined the road, and the cart clattered through the open gate.

"Now, on to Sherwood Forest!" Little John cried.

Closing his eyes, Robin released a tense breath. He could scarcely believe it, but for the first time since he'd entered the castle dungeons, he allowed the tiny grain of hope he'd harbored earlier to sprout.

"Are you all right?"

Robin opened his eyes. It was Marian. And it was likely the question she had intended to ask earlier. Her word choice was unusual, but he understood her meaning. He nodded. His fingers were swollen, his wrists badly cut. He had bruises and scrapes on his knees, hips, and torso. But he was alive. And he owed that—in overwhelmingly great measure—to the two maidens in the cart. "I am well enough," he said. "Thanks to you, your friend, and my faithful men."

"Marian's friend is my sister Ellen," Will said. "They work together at the castle kitchen."

"'Tis true," Ellen said quietly. "Though after t-today's events, I doubt we sh-shall be allowed to return."

Robin's heart sank. They had sacrificed their livelihoods and their good names for him. "Forgive me." He went to clench his fists only to tighten his grip on the sheriff's purse. He had been holding it so long, he had all but forgotten it was in his hand. His muddled thoughts spun. Mayhap he could offset their loss with some of the gold. "Were you happy at the castle?"

Ellen shrugged. "I was treated fairly."

"And you, Marian?"

"I have not been there long," she said, "but it . . . it was a roof over my head." She wrapped her arms around herself, and he caught the shake in her hands.

His concern rose. "Is something else amiss?"

She shook her head. "It's . . . it's nothing."

Vaguely aware that the cart was slowing, Robin kept his attention on Marian. She was pale—not the sickly color Will was exhibiting that would likely fade as soon as he left this conveyance but the ghostly appearance of someone with a more serious condition.

Ellen must have thought the same because she inched closer to her friend. "Marian?"

"I shot a man." Marian choked out the words. "In all the years I've used a bow, I've never . . . " She swallowed. "I've never injured anyone."

Robin's stomach clenched. He knew this emotion. He had experienced it himself.

"This is it!" Oblivious to Marian's grief-filled words, Little John brought the cart to a stop. "I told Elric I would leave his horse and cart at the entrance to Sherwood Forest. We walk from here." When no one responded, he turned in his seat. "Did you hear?"

"Aye," Will said, gathering his bow and sliding off the back of the cart. "Robin?"

"Go," he said. "Both of you. And take Ellen with you. I will follow with Marian."

Little John raised his eyebrows, but when he looked to Marian, his questioning look became one of alarm. "If she is unwell, I will walk back a short distance to stand guard until she is able to continue."

"No," Marian said. "P-P-Please go. All of you."

Her trembling had reached her mouth. A look of understanding flashed in Little John's eyes. He glanced at Robin, who gave him a terse nod. Little John recognized this response as well as Robin did.

"Right then." Little John jumped down from the seat, tied the horse's reins around a tree branch, and went to stand beside Will. "We shall see you at camp, Marian."

"Yes." Tears glistened in her eyes. "I just need a little t-time."

Ellen had yet to move. "You cannot s-stay here alone," she said. "I will r-remain with you."

"Go with your brother," Marian begged. "I shall see you shortly."

Robin met Ellen's stricken expression with a feigned calm one. "It will be well, Ellen. She shall not be alone for long."

Reluctantly, Ellen slid to the end of the cart and jumped off. Ignoring the pain in his knees and wrists, Robin followed.

"I th-thank you," Marian managed, and then she lowered her head to her chest.

"The hangman's injuries are her first," Little John said softly.

"Aye," Robin whispered. "I shall give her a moment to grieve, but no matter her request, she shall not—cannot—be alone for long."

"You will stay with her?" Ellen asked, appearing close to tears herself.

"I shall." He managed a weak smile. "Go now, with Will and Little John, and mayhap you can assist in starting a meal. Marian will need sustenance when this initial period of shock and mourning is past."

"I shall be g-glad of something to do," Ellen said.

Rest sounded far more appealing to Robin, but he was grateful for her willingness. "May I ask one thing more of you also, Little John?" He handed him the sheriff's pouch. "If you would take this to the cave for safekeeping, I would be much obliged."

"Ah, yes, the tournament prize." Little John grinned. "I was most impressed by that masterful piece of persuasion."

"If I had known you were seated so close, listening to every word, I would have given it to you before I left the cart the first time."

"Truly? How many cart drivers do you know with such a strapping physique?"

Robin glared at him. "I had a few other things on my mind at the time. Although I would be fascinated to know why you thought it necessary for me to go all the way to the gallows when we could have made our escape without me having to set foot on the scaffold."

"With all those guards in the cart with us?" Little John said. "I think not." He waggled his eyebrows. "Besides, who are we to rob the Sheriff of Nottingham of his much-anticipated moment of triumph? Alas, for the sake of all the poor in Nottinghamshire, a moment is all we could offer him. I trust he appreciated it."

"Aye." Robin's head was beginning to throb. He owed heartfelt expressions of thanks to countless people for facilitating his escape, but now was not the time. "Later, when we are all safely gathered around the campfire, I wish to hear how your plan came about."

"It shall be done," Little John said. His gaze darted to Marian's huddled form, and all humor in his eyes evaporated. "Tell her she was magnificent."

"I shall," Robin said heavily. "I only pray that she will believe me."

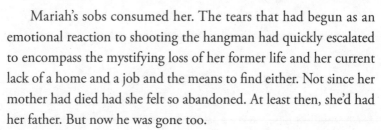

Mariah's sobs consumed her. The tears that had begun as an emotional reaction to shooting the hangman had quickly escalated to encompass the mystifying loss of her former life and her current lack of a home and a job and the means to find either. Not since her mother had died had she felt so abandoned. At least then, she'd had her father. But now he was gone too.

"Why am I always so alone?" Her voice broke on the whispered words.

"Not this time, Marian."

With a gasp, she raised her head. She hadn't realized she'd spoken the painful words aloud. "Robin!"

He was sitting on the end of the cart, watching her with such concern it made her throat ache all the more.

"Have you been there all along?"

"I have."

She brushed her hands across her wet cheeks. She could only imagine how swollen and red her eyes were. "I thought . . . I thought everyone had left."

"I sent the others on." His smile seemed a little forced. "You needed someone here to show you the way."

"Yes." She cleared her throat. "I should have thought of that." Embarrassment met her misery. "Forgive me. After all you've been through, you must be dying to reach your camp. You should not have had to wait for me to—" She stopped. How was she supposed to describe this female weep-fest to a twelfth-century, unnervingly masculine leader of a band of outlaws? "It's just that I—" Her shoulders dropped. It would be impossible to explain something she didn't understand herself.

"Marian."

She wanted to look away but couldn't bring herself to do it. Reluctantly, she met his eyes. They shone with compassion.

"After what you were called upon to do today," he said, "I would have been concerned if you had not reacted thus. I desperately wish that you had not been asked to shoot the hangman, but by doing so, you saved my life."

"But I may have ended his." She thought she had cried herself dry, but tears welled up in her eyes again. "It's the twelfth century. He could die of his wounds."

His brows came together. "It is indeed the twelfth century, but you hit his upper leg and arm, is that not correct?"

"Yes."

"Then they are flesh wounds, and if he is given good care, he may well live to end many more lives."

The irony of Robin's words was not lost on her. "You think I'm foolish for grieving for a man who administers torture to others."

"You are not foolish. And that is not the true cause of your grief."

She stared at him. "How can you say that? You barely know me."

"That may be, but I have felt the same anguish of soul."

"You shoot things all the time!"

He winced. "You are correct. I shoot *things*—targets at tournaments, wild game when my men are hungry, the ground at the feet of those threatening my life and the lives of my men—but I have only once shot a man. And my reaction to that experience was much like yours."

Mariah's indignation fizzled. Who was she to judge this man when almost all she knew of him came from legends? Only an hour or so ago, she had witnessed his men pin down the sheriff and his men with an impressive volley of arrows. As far as she could tell, none had been aimed directly at an opponent. If a guard had been injured, it was likely because he had run into an arrow meant for the ground at his feet.

"Was it . . . was it self-defense?"

He looked away, and for a few seconds, the only sounds were the song of a nearby bird, the buzz of an insect, and the whisper of the slight breeze through the trees. She waited. And when he turned back to her, there was sorrow in his eyes.

"Do you know how I came to be Robin Hood of Sherwood Forest?"

Mariah's thoughts turned to the films she'd seen. Had any of them chronicled Robin Hood's beginnings—other than the ones that portrayed him as a deposed nobleman, which were obviously untrue? "I don't."

"Then it is probably best that you hear it." He extended his hand to her. "If you are feeling strong enough, allow me to take you somewhere where we might converse more comfortably."

And more privately. The words went unsaid, but it was a good reminder. Notwithstanding the risk of discovery, Robin had waited with her on a public road and beside a cart that could be claimed by its owner at any moment. It was time to leave.

With Robin's old bow in one hand and a wad of her kirtle in the other, she scooted to the end of the cart. "You should take this," she said, handing him the bow. "Will told me it was yours."

He slipped it over his shoulder. "I thank you. I have not seen my newer one since the tournament, and I confess, it feels strange to be without one."

"I would give you the quiver, too, but you are missing your belt."

"If you wish to be rid of the arrows, I will carry it," he said.

Mariah caught her lower lip between her teeth. Perhaps he really did understand how she was feeling. The very thought of nocking an arrow and aiming at a target now made her stomach roil.

She untied her apron and slid the quiver free. "Here," she said, offering it to him.

He took it in his right hand and offered her his left again. She tied her apron back on, took his hand, and slid off the cart.

"Oh!" She stumbled, her legs stiffer than she'd anticipated.

"Take whatever time you need," Robin said. "Little John had us tossing around like turnips in that cart."

"He did, didn't he?" She summoned a smile. "But he got us away safely."

"Aye." He studied the tall trees that surrounded them. "My return to the forest is entirely due to the bravery of people like Little John and you." His gaze dropped to her face. "Little John wished me to tell you that your contribution in the town square was marvelous, and I wish you to know that I am forever in your debt."

Given her current state, Mariah doubted she would ever consider her part in today's events marvelous. She was equally uncomfortable with the thought of Robin being beholden to her. "If it's all the same to you," she said, "I would much rather have your friendship than your obligation."

He smiled, and his eyes filled with warmth. "It would be my honor, Maid Marian."

Mariah's heart stuttered. *Maid Marian.* Maid Marian was Robin's one true love. Despite all attempts to keep them apart, Maid Marian had remained faithful to him. According to some versions of the story, they'd even been married.

She was Mariah Clinton, and even though she was coming to admire Robin more than any other man she'd known, and the memory of the kiss they'd shared invaded her thoughts every night, it was vital that Robin Hood not get Mariah muddled up with the woman he was supposed to be with.

"We need to talk, Robin," she said.

He nodded. "Come." Without relinquishing her hand, he led her across the road to a narrow break in the trees. "The grove I have in mind is not far and boasts a small stream. I believe it will serve our purpose well."

CHAPTER 17

Robin crouched at the bank of the stream and washed his hands in the cool, clear water. He was filthy, and the pungent smell of the dungeons lingered on his clothing, but he would have to wait to bathe fully until after he had Marian situated safely at camp.

Marian. He glanced at her kneeling beside him. Having rinsed her tear-stained cheeks, she was now trailing her fingers through the water, a contemplative expression on her face. He smothered a groan. What was it about this woman that drew him so completely? Her beauty was undeniable, as was her skill with a bow. But it was more than that. He sensed a depth to her that he ached to discover. He had searched for her in vain for a fortnight, and now that he'd found her, he wished to know everything about her. Almost as much as he wished to kiss her again.

He looked away. His intense desire to gather her in his arms when she had been sobbing in the cart had been uncomfortably telling. Only the knowledge that she'd needed that time to fully release her emotions had kept him from her. Although, if her well-being was truly his priority, the fact that he smelled like a cesspool should have played a larger role in his decision. He frowned at the grime on his tunic, his thoughts inevitably settling on the more significant blemishes that were harder to see.

He rarely recounted his early days in Sherwood. Indeed, Friar Tuck and Little John were the only ones who knew the whole of his experience. It would be easier and far more pleasant to keep those memories from Marian, especially as her view of him would undoubtedly suffer from the telling. But he could not desire to know her heart better if he was unwilling to expose his own, and he sensed that sharing his personal struggle would lessen her current feeling of isolation and may even speed her recovery. For that reason alone, it was a risk worth taking.

"It's beautiful here." Marian had risen and was drying her hands on her apron as she looked around.

"I have always thought so." Not wanting to touch his dirty tunic, he shook the water droplets off his fingers and came to his feet. "I came upon this glade quite by accident a few years ago. It has become one of my favorite spots."

"I can see why." She rotated in a slow circle, taking in the cheerful stream that cut through the natural clearing, the soft grass mingled with clover underfoot, and the leafy trees—both ancient and new—that protected the area. She pointed to a large, lichen-covered rock. "That looks like a small table."

"Or a large stool," he said. "I call it my pondering rock."

She laughed, and his heart lifted. "I assume you sit on it, then."

"I do." He walked across the grass to the rock. "Try it for yourself. There is plenty of room for two." He waited until she was seated and then sat beside her. "What do you think?"

"It's lovely. I believe I could sit here all day and simply listen to the wind in the trees and the bees in the clover."

He shifted uncomfortably, his dread of what he had promised to divulge mounting. "I fear listening to me is a poor substitute for that."

"Not at all." She turned to face him, and to his surprise, he saw a similar emotion in her eyes. "But if you're willing, after you've told me your story, I would like to share something also."

"Of course." He was committed, and there was no benefit in prolonging the agony any longer. Leaning forward, he rested his arms on his knees. "My tale takes place many years ago. I was but eighteen years of age and had walked from the village of Locksley, where I was born and raised, to participate in an archery contest in Nottingham."

"You participated in those contests even then?" Marian asked.

"That was to be my first major tournament," he said. "I had enjoyed uncommon success in local competitions and rather fancied my chances at the one in Nottingham." He sighed. "I was far too sure of myself for my own good, but the ignorance of youth blinded me to my pride.

"On the outskirts of Sherwood Forest, I came upon a dozen foresters who were partaking of their midday meal. Ale was flowing freely between them, and several were well into their cups. One called to me, asking where I was headed. When I responded that I was off to win the archery tournament in town, they howled with laughter, calling me an infant with a one-penny bow and farthing shafts."

Even now, the memory of their taunting and all it had led to caused his chest to ache.

"Unfortunately," he continued, "pride was not the only weakness of my youth. It was accompanied by a quick and ready temper. And with a few derisive words, that ill-disposed forester had ignited both.

"Giving no thought to the consequences of my actions, I boasted that my arrows could pierce the center of any target. The fellow responded by throwing down a wager. Twenty coins if I could hit the noblest hart in the herd that was standing at the edge of the glade where the foresters had chosen to take their meal. His companions laughed heartily at the seemingly impossible task, which only served to fuel my indignation further. I took my bow from my shoulder, nocked an arrow, and let it fly. The herd scattered, but they left without the most noble hart. It lay motionless on the grass.

"The foresters flew into a rage, shouting that I had killed one of the king's deer and must needs be punished." He sighed. "Even then, I did not see what my hot-headedness had cost me. I knew only that

I had shown myself worthy of competing and had won twenty coins to boot."

"Did you claim your reward?" Mariah asked.

"No. Even as a foolish youth, I could tell that my departure was overdue." He paused, wishing more than ever that he could conclude his story there. But the worst was yet to come. "Whether he was most influenced by the vast quantities of ale he'd consumed or his humiliation at losing his wager to a stripling, I shall never know, but the forester who challenged me chose to send me on my way with a warning. His arrow flew within inches of my head."

Marian gasped.

"It was close," he admitted. "And I have often wondered if he would have hit his mark if his hands had been more steady."

"He meant to kill you?" Her eyes were wide.

"I shall never know. Anger seized me, and I swung around to take a similar shot. I aimed for the ground at his feet, but in his drunken state, he staggered directly into my arrow's path."

Thanks to Friar Tuck's counsel and insights, reflecting on the incident no longer produced the horrific guilt that had torn at Robin's heart, lungs, and throat for so many years, but the emptiness and deep sorrow Robin had felt that long time ago remained.

Her face paled. "Did he die?"

"Instantly."

"What—" She swallowed. "What did you do?"

"I ran," he admitted. "Some would consider it cowardly; others would see it as self-preservation. Whatever label you choose to place upon the act, I was gone from view before the remaining foresters could gather their wits."

"So, you truly are an outlaw." Her voice was low.

He gave her a puzzled look. Though his sordid past was known by few, he had never made a secret of his ignominious status. "I live in Sherwood Forest surrounded by men wanted by the sheriff and the Crown. Why would you have thought any differently?"

"I . . . I don't know. I heard about all the good you do for those in need. I suppose I thought the sheriff might be mean-spirited enough to paint you in a poor light because he wished to put a stop to the assistance you offer to those he taxes so cruelly."

"There is a two-hundred-pound bounty upon my head for poaching the king's deer," he said. "The sheriff desires that money for himself. Furthermore, the forester I shot was his kin, so along with the allure of a substantial reward and his hatred of my meddling in the affairs of those living in Nottingham, he sees my hanging as an appropriate punishment and a personal retribution."

"But the shooting was an accident. It could just have easily been you who was killed."

"That is true," he said, overwhelmingly grateful that she had not immediately fled from him. "Those first few days in the forest will forever remain the worst of my life. Like you, I was completely overcome by what I had done. Since then, I have striven to make peace with God and to make amends in whatever small ways I can."

For a moment, silence fell between them. A bird fluttered by, and Robin forced himself to meet her eyes. He saw sorrow there. But despite his greatest fears, it did not appear as though she had immediately turned to revulsion and judgment.

"I had no idea," she whispered. "No wonder you understood what I was going through in the cart. But . . . but unlike me, you had no one with you."

"I was completely alone," he said. "And tortured. I had killed a man. The life I had known previously was over, and I knew without a shadow of doubt that if I were granted the opportunity to make another life for myself, I had to make it more meaningful. Not only for me but for others too."

"How did you manage that on your own?"

"Thankfully, I was not alone overly long. Others joined me here. The foresters spotted some of them poaching food to feed their starving families. Those unfortunates took refuge in the forest to escape

excessively harsh penalties. Others were turned out of their inheri-
tances or despoiled by a great baron, rich abbot, or powerful squire.
A few, such as Friar Tuck, were simply wandering through the forest,
saw a need, and chose to stay." Robin managed a wry smile. "For all
his eccentricities, Friar Tuck has been a godsend. One by one, he
has ministered to the men of Sherwood, helping us see worth in our
battered souls and the value of moving forward with hope and faith
for a better future."

"He did that for you?"

"Aye. He took a broken youth who had committed a terrible—
albeit unintentional—wrong and guided him through the necessary
penance."

"Is that why you give to the poor?"

"My men have pledged to take that which has been wrung from
the poor by oppressive men and return it to those who have suffered
unjust taxes, land rents, or wrongful fines." He shrugged. "It is not so
brave an act as you may think. We are outlaws already, so we have less
than most to lose when we waylay tyrants traveling the forest roads."

"You can still be hanged."

It was a poignant reminder of all that had happened that day,
including her part in it.

"I am truly sorry that by taking so grave a risk, I caused you to
assume such a heavy burden."

"If you had not urged me to lose the archery competition, I
probably would have been the one at the gallows." She offered him a
sad smile. "It is hard to imagine that anyone would have attempted
to rescue an unknown woman foolish enough to enter an archery
competition dressed as a young man, so I owe my life to you as much
or more than you owe yours to me."

"I would have come for you," Robin said with surety.

"That is noble of you, but it would have been the wrong thing
to do."

He searched her face, attempting to make sense of her response.
"Why?"

"Because I am not who you think I am." Her hands were clasped so tightly that her knuckles were white. "Now that you have shared your background story, I need to tell you mine. It is going to sound so absurd you will think I am fabricating it." She took a deep breath. "I am not. There is nothing I can do that will provide you with indisputable proof, but I give you my word that everything I am about to tell you is the truth."

She was trembling again. He reached out and covered her clasped hands with his. "Whatever it is, it cannot possibly be more shocking than the account I shared."

"I think it might be," she said, staring down at his hand on hers. "But in a completely different way."

"Tell me."

She paused as though girding her courage. "My name is Mariah Clinton," she said. "I was born in London during the twenty-first century and have lived there my whole life, except for the two years I spent in Paris at culinary school."

Robin stared at her, mentally sifting through her unanticipated and staggering claims.

"I don't know how it happened or why," she continued. "One minute, I was in the changing room of a costume shop in London in the twenty-first century, putting on a medieval kirtle, and the next minute, I was in the castle kitchen in Nottingham in 1194."

"You just appeared in the castle kitchen from another time and place? From a century in the far-distant future?" He attempted to keep the skepticism out of his voice. She had been more understanding than he deserved when he'd told her about the foresters. He owed her an open mind. At least for a short time.

"I walked through a door," she said.

"Then why did you not walk back through it?"

"I . . . I couldn't find it."

It was a ridiculous response. And yet, if he was to believe that she had come from the future, there was no reason to question a disappearing door. He released her hand and watched the river gurgle downstream. "If your name is Mariah, why do you go by Marian?"

"Mistress Agatha, in the castle kitchen, is hard of hearing. When I said Mariah Clinton, she heard Marian o' Clifton and then introduced me to others with that name."

"Am I to call you Mariah, then?"

She shook her head. "That name belongs to my twenty-first-century life. No one here knows me by Mariah, and I have come to think of myself as Marian."

"I am glad," he said. "For I have come to think of you as Marian also." It was a poor effort at jest, and though she gave him a weak smile, he wished he'd managed a more sensible response. Currently, however, there was nothing sensible about this conversation. Not knowing what else to say, he applied the most obvious request. "Tell me about the twenty-first century."

"It is loud and fast and full of innovations designed to improve life."

"Such as?" he prompted.

She hesitated, as though struggling to conceive of one. Was this his first sign that her assertion was nothing more than a tall tale?

"So much has changed that I'm not sure what you will be able to grasp," she said, interrupting his disbelieving thoughts. "There are vehicles that run on petrol—which is a fuel found deep underground—there are medical advances that have increased life expectancy by decades, there are ways of communicating instantly with people on the other side of the world, and we have harnessed a power called electricity that runs innumerable inventions, including light."

"Forgive me, Marian." He ran his hand across the back of his neck. "This all sounds—"

"Completely unbelievable," she finished for him. "I know. And I am living it."

"How?" he asked. "If our world is so very different from yours, how are you able to cope so well?"

"I hardly think I am." Her shoulders drooped. "We have seen each other only a few times, and yet you have witnessed my ineptitude more than once. I entered an archery tournament without thinking through the consequences of ignoring social norms, I risked my position at the castle to warn you of the sheriff's plans when you knew them all along, and I did not know how to ask for a piece of meat even though I have worked in a kitchen for years." She sighed. "If it hadn't been for Ellen, I would have been sunk weeks ago. She has tutored me in so many areas."

"Have you told her this same story?" he asked.

"I've told no one else. I didn't want 'lunatic' added to my list of oddities. I have tried adjusting my language to better fit in." She gave him a helpless look. "Ellen thinks my unusual vocabulary is simply a product of being a Londoner and likely blames my general incompetence on the same thing."

"Incompetence?" Robin raised an eyebrow. "What else have you struggled with?"

"On my first full day in the kitchen, I burned the sheriff's venison pies because I didn't know how to use the oven."

Robin laughed. "I should have liked to see that."

"It was awful. Mistress Agatha was furious."

He sobered. "Have you suffered much?"

"Not physically—other than sleeping on the hard pallets in the servants' chambers and the lack of plumbing."

"Plumbing?"

"In the future, water goes in and out of homes through pipes. And the temperature is controlled by a lever called a tap."

The very thought that one could adjust the temperature and movement of water in such ways was outrageous. And yet, for Marian to have conceived of such ideas herself seemed equally far-fetched.

He pondered her earlier response. "If not physically, then how else have you suffered?"

"It's not important," she said.

"Marian." He waited until she met his eyes. "You gave me your word that you would tell the truth." Her chin quivered, and he was instantly reminded of her plaintive cry in the cart. "Are you feeling the loss of loved ones?"

A single tear rolled down her cheek, and she brushed at it impatiently. "I have been gone from my home for weeks, but I honestly don't know if anyone has really missed me."

"What of your family?"

"I have no siblings. My mother died when I was young, and though my father and I have always been close, he remarried and moved overseas a couple of years ago. We don't see each other often anymore."

"I am certain he has been shocked and saddened by your departure," Robin said, realizing as he did so that he was talking as though he believed her story.

She wiped away another tear. "If I am never to return, I suppose I should be grateful that he has someone else in his life now."

Robin knew the pain a permanent separation from family members caused all too well. His exile to Sherwood Forest had sent him on a similar heartrending journey. "Friar Tuck taught me that there is no shame in grieving for the loss of meaningful relationships—no matter how the loss occurs. During my early years as an outcast, he took it upon himself to repeatedly remind me that Jesus wept over the death of His loved ones."

Marian offered Robin a watery smile. "Thank you. You have been incredibly kind, regardless of whether you believe me."

Did he believe her? He wanted to, but nothing about her tale was even vaguely sensible. The very thought that she had come here across centuries of time was laughable, yet she was obviously convinced that she spoke the truth.

"If you have told no one else of your unlikely background, why did you choose to tell me?"

A hint of color touched her cheeks. "I needed you to know that my name is not really Marian."

"But I thought you had chosen to continue using that name."

"I did. And I shall, so long as I'm here." She took a deep breath. "But you must not confuse me with the other Marian."

He drew his brows together. "I know of only one other Marian. She lived in Locksley and was known for her skill with a spinning wheel. She was elderly when I was young. After all this time, she is likely dead."

"Are you sure?"

Was that panic he saw in her eyes?

"There must be another one," she insisted.

"I assure you, there is not."

"That can't be right," she whispered more to herself than to him.

Robin's misgivings increased. Had shooting the hangman affected her in uncommon ways? Or was she truly severely addled and had merely hidden it from him before now? That would explain her story of arriving from the future. But it would not explain his instant connection with her or her ability to execute Little John's escape plan so exactly.

"Forgive me," he said. "But are you quite well?"

Her look of apprehension remained. "To be honest, I'm not sure."

"Come," he said, rising to his feet. "We have both given the other a great deal to think on, but methinks the time has come to relocate to my camp. There you shall be reunited with Ellen and meet some remarkably noble outlaws. I daresay those two things will do much to ail your flagging spirits."

CHAPTER 18

Mariah followed Robin out of the glade, her thoughts whirling so fast it was all she could do to put one foot in front of the other. If Robin's startling and heart-wrenching account of his arrival in Sherwood Forest had not been enough to cause her to rethink all she'd thought she knew of him, his assertion that he knew no one by the name of Marian had been enough to tip the balance. Mariah placed her hand to her muddled head. Had the legends that had formed the basis of all the movies about Robin Hood been manipulated by Hollywood to please modern audiences? Weeks ago, Ellen had scoffed at Mariah's belief that Robin was a displaced nobleman, and now it seemed that Maid Marian—who, by all the accounts Mariah knew, was Robin's one true love—did not exist.

Mariah stumbled over a root, instinctively reaching for a nearby tree trunk to catch herself. Robin had been right. They both needed a while to think. But this journey on foot through the forest was not the time. She needed to get a grip—to calm her mind even as she steadied her legs—and focus on arriving at Robin's camp without twisting her ankle.

"Forgive me." Robin must have heard the slight gasp she'd made when she'd lost her footing because he had stopped. "Is our pace too swift?"

"Not at all." She pushed away from the tree to join him. "I simply need to pay more attention to where I'm going."

"The forest is as vast as it is dense. For those who are unfamiliar with it, navigating a path through the trees can be difficult."

"I'm sure." Mariah gazed around her. Tall trees blocked out much of the sky. They were surrounded by verdant vegetation with seemingly no landmarks in sight. "How *do* you find your way?"

He shrugged. "Most often, I follow my nose."

"That's not terribly helpful."

He chuckled. It was the first time his expression had lightened since she'd mentioned the burnt pies.

"Stand completely still," he said, "and breathe deeply through your nose."

Puzzled, she did as he asked, and for the first time, she caught a faint aroma that had nothing to do with forest life. "What is it?" She turned her head and sniffed again. "It smells like beef stew."

"You are not far wrong. That is Friar Tuck's pottage, and when I smell it on the air, I know I am close."

"So, we're almost there?" An unexpected wave of excitement washed over her. She was about to see the place Robin Hood called home.

He cocked his head to one side, studying her curiously. "That truly pleases you."

"Yes." How could she explain her feelings when he didn't fully believe her background? "I . . . I've heard stories about Robin Hood and his camp in Sherwood Forest since I was very young. Those stories have fueled my imagination for as long as I can remember." She shrugged uncertainly. "I think my love of archery made me especially fond of them."

Lines appeared on his forehead. "I am a displaced yeoman wanted by the Crown. I have no claim on fame or fortune. Why would such tales exist centuries from now?"

"Your devotion to caring for the poor and needy by redistributing wealth claimed by those who have excess made you a hero."

He ran his fingers through his hair and then abruptly stopped as though he only now remembered the filth of the dungeon that clung to him. "I am far too flawed to be considered a hero. Ask any one of my men. Little John, in particular, would be happy to set you right on that score. Though after our recent conversation, I daresay you can attest to it yourself."

Mariah had not had enough time to process all that Robin had shared, but she'd witnessed enough of his current life to contradict him. "Since arriving here, I've come to realize that some parts of those twenty-first-century legends are not completely accurate. But the accounts of your bravery in facing your enemies to ease the suffering of others are true."

"Ah," Robin said, clearly uncomfortable with the direction of this conversation. "It is truly a shame that Little John is not with us. In between his bouts of laughter, he would inform you that my so-called bravery is more often than not sheer foolishness."

"He might say that," Mariah conceded, "but the foolishness that pushed you to enter the sheriff's archery contest likely saved my life."

"It also placed you in an unwarranted position afterward. And for that, I feel only deep regret."

Mariah had no desire to think back on her part in today's rescue or risk having her mental anguish and physical trembling return. There were sufficient difficulties ahead without resurrecting those. She chose to change the subject completely. "Do you think Friar Tuck's pottage is ready to eat?"

"Undoubtedly."

Given Robin's earlier discomfort, Mariah guessed that he was more than willing to follow her into a discussion about food. She was proven right when he started walking again.

"It goes against Friar Tuck's core beliefs to have an empty pot on the fire," he continued. "He makes it his responsibility to keep us all fed."

Mariah smiled. As a sous-chef, she could understand that mentality. "I hope he has saved some for latecomers."

"As do I," Robin said with feeling.

As no food had been delivered to the dungeon, Mariah guessed that he hadn't eaten anything in well over twenty-four hours. She wasn't much better off.

"Since we're both anxious to eat, perhaps we should make haste."

Ellen's commonly used expression rolled easily off Mariah's tongue, and as expected, Robin accepted it without question. Picking up his pace, he guided her through a narrow gap in the trees, and moments later, they stepped into a wide, circular clearing.

The large area was carpeted by plush, mossy grass. At least a dozen men were in plain sight. Some were standing, laughing, and talking with one another; a few were seated beneath the trees. Most held wooden bowls, and if the smiles were any indication, the success of Robin's rescue coupled with Friar Tuck's pottage had made the band of men very happy.

"Marian!" Mariah turned her head to see Ellen hurrying toward her. "Are you r-recovered?"

"I am much improved," she said, touched to see the worry in her friend's eyes. "Thank you for your concern."

"But of c-course. We have all been anxious over your w-well-being."

As if to validate Ellen's words, Little John and Will came up behind her.

"We are glad to see you come," Will said.

"Aye." Little John spared Robin a meaningful look, and whatever passed between them must have pleased him because his expression became all the more jovial. "Robin is known to be distracted by pleasant groves and streams in these woods. Truth be told, it is somewhat of a miracle that you have arrived before nightfall."

Robin glowered at him. "We were not so long as all that."

"It was long enough that your portion of pottage was at risk," Will said with a laugh. "But you will be glad to know that Friar Tuck stood firm despite Little John's pleadings for a third helping."

"I have a larger frame to fill than anyone else," Little John grumbled. "And the bowls are pitifully small."

"Most are satisfied with filling their bellies and do not aim to fill their entire frames," Robin said, the humor in his eyes belying his serious tone.

"More fool them," Little John said. "They should be taught the principle of food storage."

Robin gave up his effort to curb his laughter, and after all they'd gone through the last twenty-four hours, Marian could not help but feel her own spirits rise to see the men so relaxed and happy to be back in Sherwood Forest.

"I shall be sure to commend Friar Tuck for his watch care over the pot," Robin said, "but if you will excuse us, Marian and I are more than ready to eat."

"Very well," Little John said, "though I must say the young lady is even more stalwart than I had supposed if she is willing to spend one moment longer in your presence given your malodorous state of being."

Robin turned to Mariah, his expression stricken. "Forgive me. I did not think. I shall take you to Friar Tuck and will return when I am clean."

Mariah shook her head. "You rinsed your hands and face in the stream. If you have gone without food for as long as I think you have, you should eat something right away." She gave Little John a knowing look. "Besides, I don't know Little John or Friar Tuck well, but it seems to me that it's entirely possible that your friend here might successfully persuade Friar Tuck that his second leg needs filling while you are gone."

This time, Little John roared with laughter. "Stalwart and as bright as a gold coin," he said. "A rare combination, to be sure."

"She is also greatly in need of nourishment," Robin said, setting his hand on Mariah's elbow and steering her to the far side of the clearing, where a fire burned in a large pit, and a cauldron hung over a metal frame above the flames.

"I shall r-ready your bowls," Ellen said, running ahead of them.

"Though not welcome, Little John's reminder bears consideration," Robin said softly, dropping his hand and increasing the space between them as they walked. "You have been very good not to complain of the smell of the dungeon that I brought with me, but I shall spare you that discomfort while we eat by sitting some distance away."

His intent was both practical and thoughtful, so it was completely ridiculous that it also filled her with regret. The distress of the last few hours had obviously taken its toll on her equilibrium. She was very used to being alone. And even if the other men ignored Mariah, Ellen would probably stay nearby.

"I thank you," she said. Reason was still there, buried beneath a blanket of lingering uncertainty, grief, and fear. She simply needed to rely on it more.

He gave a slight smile. But before they could exchange anything more, they were at the fire pit, Friar Tuck plying them with food and Robin responding to the well-wishes of the men gathered around the simmering pot.

Mariah took her wooden bowl and spoon from Friar Tuck with grateful hands. Moving away from the male conversation, she made for a spot beneath a nearby oak tree. Carefully, she lowered herself to the ground and took her first taste of the pottage. It was hot, but despite its appetizing smell, it was surprisingly tasteless. She stirred the thick liquid and then took another bite, analyzing the ingredients as they hit her tongue: carrots, suede, and cabbage. Barley, cooked until it was soft and swollen, and a few mushrooms. As far as she could tell, there were no seasonings or salt.

"It tastes d-different from the pottage Mistress Agatha m-makes, does it not?" Ellen dropped down beside her.

"Very different."

It was a study in contrasts. Mistress Agatha relied almost exclusively on salt, and on more than one occasion, Mariah had had to force the briny mixture down because she'd known it would be a very long time before she would eat again.

Ellen smiled. "I am right g-glad that you are f-feeling well enough to eat."

"I was starving."

Ellen's smile widened. "You are fully r-recovered, then."

Fully recovered? Mariah would not go that far. Quite apart from Robin's revelations and the quandary she found herself in from his skeptical response to her backstory, disturbing memories of her part in today's rescue would undoubtedly return to plague her at night. "The terrible trembling is gone," she said equivocally. "And that is a big relief."

"That is a very g-good thing." Ellen drew her knees into her chest and tucked her arms around them. "This c-camp. I've n-never seen the like, have you?"

"Not at all." All the medieval reenactments Mariah had participated in had been held in castles or open fields. This sanctuary in the forest, with its leafy protection and atmosphere of unity and friendship, was extraordinary.

"I hope R-Robin Hood will allow us t-to stay," Ellen said.

Mariah gave her a disconcerted look. She'd been so consumed with the events of the day that she'd not given any thought to what would come next. But she should have. Neither she nor Ellen would be welcome back at the castle. They'd probably be incarcerated if they as much as set foot through the gates. Ellen's mother may be in no position to support her, but at least Ellen had family to turn to for a roof over her head. Mariah had no one. She tightened her grip on the wooden spoon. What was to become of her?

"Well now, Marian. How do you find the pottage?"

Startled, Marian looked up to see Friar Tuck approaching.

"It is wonderfully filling," she said, sticking to the truth. "And I enjoyed the variety of vegetables."

He looked sufficiently pleased, and it gave Mariah courage to pose a question. "Have you ever considered adding sage or thyme to the pot?"

"Bless my soul." Friar Tuck gave her a startled look. "A worthy suggestion indeed. I fear I am guilty of giving all my attention to such plants' healing properties and fully neglecting their ability to flavor food."

"Do you have access to herbs like that?"

"Surely, surely," the kindly man said. "As I told Robin years ago, I am too slow to travel far for a handful of parsley, no matter how badly one of our men may complain over an ailing stomach." He chuckled. "He took pity on me, good man that he is, and dug me a garden not far from the cave entrance."

"The cave entrance?"

"Aye." He wrinkled his brow. "I daresay you have yet to see that place."

"As far as your camp goes, I've seen nothing more than this clearing."

"We enjoy this gathering spot when the weather is fine," he said. "But as you well know, the weather is a fickle thing, and no matter the canopy of leaves, the rain and cold eventually find their way in. That is when we retreat to the cave."

Mariah took her last bite and rose to her feet. Ellen scrambled up beside her.

"Would you show us?" Mariah asked.

Ellen nodded enthusiastically. "If you please, F-Friar. I should very much like to see your g-garden and the cave."

"With pleasure," he said. "But I must not overstep. It may be that Robin wishes—" He turned his head to seek out Robin Hood, but there was no sign of him. "Well, I had thought he was nearby."

"If he has finished his food, he has likely gone to wash away the last of the dungeon from his skin," Mariah said.

"Just so. And given his condition, he may be scrubbing for some time." Friar Tuck slid his arms into his wide sleeves. "Well, mayhap I should take upon myself the task of being a guide to our humble dwelling place."

"Please do," Mariah said.

He smiled. "Come. One of the men will mind the fire and the pot. We shall go straightway."

CHAPTER 19

Mariah and Ellen followed Friar Tuck along a narrow path that cut through the trees surrounding the clearing. Unlike the path Mariah had taken with Robin, this one seemed fairly well traveled. It currently appeared as a dusty brown ribbon meandering through the greenery, but she thought it likely that a good rainstorm would quickly turn the hardpacked dirt into mud.

"Do the men sleep in the clearing when the weather is good?" she asked.

"Often enough." The path veered to the right, and Friar Tuck's pace slowed. "Albeit, some of them have learned the hard way that clear skies cannot always be trusted. Many a fellow has sought shelter in the cave in the early hours of the morning." He gave a displeased grunt. "They tend to drip rainwater over those of us who are more sensible."

Mariah fought back a smile. It would be difficult to find one's way through the forest and a darkened cave on a cloud-covered night. Under those conditions, escaping the elements probably included stumbling over those already lying on the cave floor.

"The cave must be quite c-close, then," Ellen said.

"Aye." Friar Tuck stopped and pointed. "There it is."

Up ahead, the trees parted to expose a craggy hill. Vegetation grew in the crevices, pitting the rocky surface. Thin scraggly trees, short shrubs, and grass mottled the reddish sandstone with various shades of green. Half a dozen wide, uneven stone steps began at the forest floor and ended at a gaping cavity halfway up the rock face.

"Oh!" Ellen stared. "It's a r-real cave."

Friar Tuck chuckled. "The few outside our band who have come here have never seen the like. It's a remarkable sight from this spot, to be sure, but once you are within . . . well, you shall see."

Without bothering to clarify further, he started toward the cave again. Mariah and Ellen followed, but they had not gone far when Mariah heard a loud clucking. Puzzled, she looked around. The familiar sound seemed completely out of place in the middle of the forest.

"Was that a chicken?" she asked.

The clucking came again, and this time, Friar Tuck stopped. "By all the saints, if that bothersome fox has had the impudence to return after I chased it all the way to the river last week, I shall have strong words to say to it."

"So, it w-was a chicken?" Ellen said.

"More than one of them, I wager," the friar said grimly. "If you will forgive me, I had best see what has disturbed them."

Turning off the main path, he took a smaller trail that appeared to circle around the right side of the hill. Tossing Ellen a mystified look, Mariah hurried after him.

The clucking continued, intensifying in volume as they drew closer to the craggy hill, and then suddenly, the vegetation cleared, and they entered an area cordoned off by a rudimentary wooden fence. On one side of the enclosure, about a dozen chickens stood huddled in a corner. Across from the chickens, and separated by another low fence, were three goats.

"Be gone, you vexing creature!" Friar Tuck waved his arms, and his wide sleeves flapped.

Mariah caught a flash of dark-orange fur as the animal darted under a bush beside the chicken run and disappeared.

"I shall have to inform Robin," Friar Tuck said with a frown. "The hens will cease their laying if they are repeatedly traumatized by that nuisance of a fox."

The chickens released a few more anxious clucks, and then with a flurry of feathers and significant head bobbing, they inched out of their huddle.

"All is well, ladies," Friar Tuck said, leaning over the fence and speaking to the chickens. "You are safe to resume your normal activities."

Mariah smiled. She was coming to like the unorthodox friar very much. During their earlier conversation, Robin had hinted at how much Friar Tuck had helped him. It seemed that the cleric's assistance ran the gamut, from spiritual comfort to physical nourishment. Living among lively outlaws could hardly compare to living in a pious monastery, but if his treatment of the chickens was any indication, he was motivated by kindness.

She stepped up beside him and watched a single white chicken separate herself from the brown ones and trot over to the stone trough filled with seed.

"Good day, Lady Kluck," Mariah said.

"I beg your pardon." Friar Tuck turned to face her.

Mariah shook her head. Any kind of explanation would be more trouble than it was worth. "Do the chickens have names?"

"The men refuse to name them, for fear of becoming overly attached." He leaned a little closer and dropped his voice. "When they no longer lay, they end up in my pot."

"Oh dear."

"Aye." He sighed. "It's a sad truth for all of them, but I confess, I truly hope the little brown one in the corner continues laying for some time. A hazel nut fell upon her head when she was but a tiny chick, and she has never been very steady on her legs since. I confess, when I am tending to them alone, I am prone to call her Hazel and have become quite fond of her."

As though awaiting the end of Friar Tuck's account to demonstrate her unsteady gait, little Hazel chose that moment to stagger over to the feeding trough.

"Hazel is a perfect name," Mariah said. "And the white one should be called Lady Kluck."

The friar chortled. "Lady Kluck. You have discerned her temperament well. That one does tend to keep the others in order."

"Well," Mariah said, feeling ridiculously pleased. "It was meant to be. There really should be a Lady Kluck living in Sherwood Forest."

"What of the g-goats?" Ellen asked. "Do they have names?"

"Aye." He pointed to the brown-and-white one nearest the fence. "That one is beech, the black one is oak, and the white one is ash."

It was Mariah's turn to laugh. "They sound like they were named by foresters."

"I believe those appellations were Little John's doing," Friar Tuck said dryly. "What he lacks in creativity, he makes up for in brute strength."

"I think it's marvelous that you have your own chickens and goats," Mariah said.

"Aye." Friar Tuck nodded. "The forest provides us with berries, mushrooms, and meat. The chickens and goats give us eggs and milk. We must rely on the local people for grain and fresh produce, but naught can be done about that. The trees prevent enough sunshine from reaching the ground to grow more than my herbs."

"An herb garden is a wonderful thing." Mariah did nothing to hide her enthusiasm.

"An infirmary garden is what I call it," Friar Tuck said. Now that the chickens were calm, he moved away from their enclosure and pointed to a little plot of ground on the other side of the goats.

Mariah stepped closer to the tangle of plants. "Thyme, sage, rosemary, parsley, and mint," she said, easily identifying the closest ones.

"The thyme is especially helpful in easing sore throats and coughs," Friar Tuck said. "A poultice of sage eases most insect bites, and I use the comfrey most often for wounds."

"Several of these would be wonderful in your pottage," Mariah said.

"Marian is a m-marvelous cook," Ellen piped up. "Mistress Agatha had her m-makin' all sort of foods f-for the sheriff."

"Is that so?" Friar Tuck said.

"I do enjoy being in the kitchen," Mariah said.

"Mayhap M-Marian and I can help you, Friar." Ellen's hands were tightly clasped, her expression earnest. "After today, w-we will not be welcomed back to the c-castle. But Marian can c-cook, and I grew up milkin' a g-goat and gatherin' eggs." Her cheeks had turned pink. "I'm willin' to work for a p-place to rest my head at night, and I daresay M-Marian is as well."

Friar Tuck looked from Ellen to Marian. "Do you feel similarly, Maid Marian?"

Mariah wasn't sure that she would ever get used to that title, but she nodded. "If Robin will allow it, I would very much like to stay."

It was an unlikely scenario. Robin had not believed her background story; Mariah could hardly blame him. But if he thought her account was a lie, then her earnestness would paint her as a lunatic. He wouldn't want a lunatic in his camp. He may not even want females in his camp.

Friar Tuck knew nothing of this, however, and he appeared to be contemplating Ellen's suggestion. "When I chose to stay in Sherwood Forest, I had thought I would devote my efforts to the welfare of my companions' souls. Two days of eating nothing but a few berries and stale bread caused me to quickly reassess, and I made my first pot of pottage." He shrugged. "I came to learn that well-fed men are far better listeners than those who are hungry."

"I'm certain your pottage was well-received by all," Marian said.

"Well, I am no cook, and there are some who would say that by spending so much of my time preparing victuals, I am failing in my ecclesiastical calling. But I saw a need and filled it to the best of my ability." He studied Mariah thoughtfully. "You may be an answer to an unuttered prayer, my dear. In truth, if we consider the events of earlier today, I should likely say you are the answer to *numerous* unuttered prayers." He nodded as though agreeing with his own conclusion. "I shall bring up this matter with Robin. I have no doubt he shall know what to do."

————·· ✳ ··————

Robin was at a loss. He had washed the dungeon grime from his body, hair, and clothing, but no amount of scrubbing could clear away the confusion in his heart and mind. Marian. The very thought of her caused his heart to trip. Her startling green eyes that had sparkled with humor and glistened with tears. Watching her sobbing in the cart had almost been his undoing. What she had done today was more than any young lady in all of England should have had to do. At least, in the England he knew. His heart rate dropped to a dull thud.

Her assertion that she had come from the future was a blatant falsehood. It had to be. So why did he continue to revisit the notion? Was it simply because he so desperately wished she had told him the truth? Or was it because there was a tiny grain of doubt boldly attempting to take root in his mind? Her contention was preposterous. Yet there were a few aspects of her story—her seeming unawareness of the most basic of social protocols, her stilted speech, her blatant errors in the castle kitchen . . . He groaned and ran his fingers through his wet hair. She used a bow with the confidence of a renowned knight. Surely someone who was so skilled in one facet of her life would not so fully ignore other even more vital areas.

With no real thought for his direction, he took the path that led from the river to the cave. Clean and dressed in his Lincoln green tunic once more, he felt more like himself. In outward appearance, at least. He'd been tempted to burn the foul clothing he'd worn in the castle, but his sense of frugality had prevailed. Lye soap and fast-running river water had done much to restore the blue fabric to its former condition, but Robin was not keen to don the tunic again in the near future. He would hang it out to dry on the bushes near the cave's entrance along with his other clothing. If the rain held off, they would be dry by morning and could be put away until another member of his band required a disguise.

Nearing the cave, he located a scrub oak with branches strong enough to support the wet fabric. Once he'd finished this task, he would return to the clearing. And to Marian. It was imperative that he put aside his inner turmoil and draw upon basic common sense to devise some means of seeing her delivered someplace away from the castle, where she could safely live and work.

Voices reached him. Setting his hose atop a bilberry bush, he slowly scoured the area. There was no sign of movement anywhere. The stone steps leading to the cave's entrance were clear, but as he turned to face them, the voices came again. From higher up, within the cave itself. And unless he completely missed the mark, at least one of them was female.

He crossed the short distance to the base of the steps in a few long strides. Moments later, he was at the top. He tilted his head slightly to listen. Two female voices? They had to belong to Marian and Ellen. He hesitated a fraction longer, and then he heard a distinctive chuckle. Friar Tuck.

"Friar Tuck!" Marian was speaking. "This place. It's . . . it's absolutely incredible."

She liked it. Robin's chest swelled with something that felt disturbingly like pride. It had taken years to make the cave and its adjoining chambers what it now was. And though it could not compete with castle chambers or even a manor's well-furnished rooms, it was comfortable and provided the shelter he and his men required.

He stepped through the entrance, blinking as his eyes adjusted the dimmer light. Friar Tuck had lit a candle, and shadows were dancing across the rock walls.

"I am pleased that you approve of our humble abode," Robin said.

Ellen gasped in surprise at his sudden appearance, but Robin kept his gaze on Marian. She swung around, her startled eyes warming when she saw him.

"When Friar Tuck told me you found sanctuary in a cave during inclement weather, this was not at all what I pictured," she said.

"Have you seen the whole of it, then?" he asked.

Friar Tuck answered for her. "We have yet to leave the large cave." His eyes crinkled. He appeared to be experiencing vast enjoyment in Marian's undisguised pleasure.

"There is more?" Marian asked, her eyes widening.

Robin grinned. "What you see here is our sleeping quarters. Each of the twenty-eight pallets was made from young saplings so as to allow for movement. They are covered in animal hide or fur. Some of the men cover themselves with wool blankets they brought with them when they first arrived; others make use of blankets purchased in town or of additional furs."

"And the furniture?" she asked.

"Thankfully, Thomas, a longtime member of our band, is a skilled woodworker, and he took it upon himself to train others. He deserves all the credit for the table and chairs. His students made the more rudimentary benches." He gestured toward the rock wall. "The cave naturally provided us with shallow shelves. They are sufficient for a few personal items and a candle or lantern, but for larger items, we needed additional space."

She spun in a slow circle. "Where?"

Friar Tuck chortled again. "You'd best show her, Robin. I shall sit here upon one of Thomas's finest pieces to await your return."

Robin gave his old friend a questioning look. Outside his trusted band of men, few had entered this cave. None had gone beyond the cavern where they now stood.

Friar Tuck gave him an almost indiscernible nod. It seemed that the good man trusted these two young ladies. Of course, he had not heard Marian's fabricated tale.

"Very well." No harm would come from them seeing more. Ellen was Will's sister and had repeatedly proved her loyalty. And no matter how confused Marian's mind might be about her past, she had risked her all for him. "Come this way."

Lighting a second candle from Friar Tuck's candle's flame, Robin led Marian and Ellen past the rows of pallets to the back of the cave and lifted his light to expose another opening. "Beware the low ceiling," he warned as he stooped and entered the small passage.

Not more than ten paces later, the path opened into another cave. Significantly smaller than the first, this one housed an assortment of barrels. The larger ones contained mead; the shorter ones held root vegetables. Sacks of barley and oats leaned against the walls. There were reed baskets filled with lye soap and others bearing candles. Firewood lay stacked in a tidy pile in one corner—a vital source of dry fuel when rain soaked the forest for weeks.

"No wonder you have survived in the forest so well," Marian said.

The awe in her voice prompted Robin to lead her to yet another opening. This one led directly into the smallest cave of them all. It housed a stash of arrows and two chests.

"The smaller chest contains the coins we collect to distribute to others," he explained. "The other contains miscellaneous pieces of clothing that occasionally assist us in our work."

"As when you w-wish to appear in town wearing the g-garb of a carpenter," Ellen guessed.

"Aye. Or when someone joins our band and is in need of clothing that enables him to remain hidden in the forest."

"Lincoln green would be an improvement over red or blue," Marian said.

Robin smiled. "Just so."

"It was good of you to show us all this," Marian said. "Neither Ellen nor I will speak of what we have seen here to anyone outside your band."

"No, indeed," Ellen agreed.

"You have my thanks." He hadn't asked for the reassurance, but somehow, Marian had guessed that he desired it. "I confess, I had not expected to find you here. It seems that you earned Friar Tuck's full trust in no time at all."

"But unfortunately, not yours." Marian spoke the words softly, but the hurt in her eyes pierced him.

He flexed his fingers, battling his instinctive desire to offer comfort and support by taking her hand. It would not do. Over the last couple of days, the intangible connection he'd experienced when he'd kissed her in the marketplace all those weeks ago had strengthened. If he did not maintain some distance, all hope of rational thought would be gone. And until he had reconciled her implausible past with her current situation, his need to think clearly was paramount.

"We should return to Friar Tuck," he said. "I daresay you are ready to see daylight once more."

"Yes." The slight drop of Marian's shoulders belied her affirmative response. "We can leave now."

Frustrated over his stumbling efforts to redirect the conversation onto a safer course, Robin led them back to the large cave in silence.

"Ah, there you are!" Friar Tuck's head bobbed up from his chest as they entered. "Had you been gone much longer, I would have been tempted to take a nap."

Robin gave him a knowing look. "I wager you managed one regardless."

Friar Tuck tutted. "No respect. Did you hear that, Maid Marian and Maid Ellen?" He rose to his feet and released an exaggerated sigh. "I garner pitifully little deference at this camp."

Robin eyed him suspiciously while Ellen smothered a giggle. She had taken the wily cleric's measure quickly enough but likely did not know that Friar Tuck regularly employed this tactic when he wished to make an unpopular request.

"Forgive me, Friar," Robin said, prepared to give Friar Tuck the opening he sought. "I meant no disrespect. How may I make amends?"

"Well, since you asked, there is something I would speak to you about." Friar Tuck set his candle on the nearest rock ledge and blew out the flame. "Mayhap we can converse privately as we walk back to the clearing together."

Robin raised his eyebrows. Friar Tuck was known for being forthright, but to summarily dismiss their guests was unlike him. Before Robin could make an alternate suggestion, however, Marian spoke.

"It was good of you to bring us here, Friar Tuck, but we will not impose upon your time or Robin's any longer. Ellen and I shall leave straightway so that you may talk."

"You are sure?" Robin asked. It was absurd that he felt cheated by having her leave before he was ready.

"Yes." Marian started toward the entrance and the light beyond. "The path is easy to follow, so we shall find our way without difficulty."

"We shall join you again shortly," Friar Tuck said.

Marian offered him a small smile and disappeared from sight.

"Many thanks, Friar Tuck," Ellen said, bobbing a curtsy before hastening after Marian.

Resigned to having been left behind, Robin returned his attention to Friar Tuck. "Very well, my oft unjustly treated and devout friend, what is of such import that you could not wait until Marian and Ellen are gone from Sherwood to discuss it?"

"They are," Friar Tuck said. "Other than your recent lapse in judgment that ended in your being carted off to the dungeon, you are not known for being a half-wit. But I would count you the greatest fool in Nottinghamshire and beyond if you allow those two maidens to leave Sherwood Forest."

Robin stared at him. "I beg your pardon?"

"Which portion do you wish me to repeat? The *recent lapse in judgment* part or the *greatest fool in Nottinghamshire and beyond* part?"

"The words that came after those two statements would seem to be of most significance," Robin said, glaring at him.

"I am glad you agree, though we might should give some thoughtful consideration to your more rash choices over—"

"Enough!" Robin raised his hand to halt the pending lecture. "Before you dwell any further upon my foolhardiness, might I suggest that you look inward. To suggest that Maid Marian and Maid Ellen should abide in Sherwood Forest places your own wisdom firmly in question."

"Why?"

Was it not obvious? "You know full well that the forest is no place for a young woman to call home."

"So, you consider the dungeon a more hospitable environment?" Friar Tuck asked. "For, after their actions at the town square today, that is surely where they will be taken the moment they set foot in Nottingham."

"I had not thought to take them to Nottingham."

Friar Tuck folded his arms. "Then, pray tell, where are they to go?"

Robin ran his fingers through his still-damp hair. He had no response. He had hoped one of his men might know of a place in a nearby village—a manor house or farm—that would take on two new servants. "I intend to take recommendations from amongst our men."

"Well, *I* recommend that they stay, and given the choice, I daresay most others will agree with me." Friar Tuck raised his arms much as he did when praising God. "Robin, Maid Marian can cook! Can you imagine? Food that tastes of something other than turnips and barley? And young Ellen confessed to being a proficient milkmaid. I could spend my morning in prayer rather than in subduing unruly goats who want nothing whatsoever to do with me."

For a fleeting moment, Robin allowed the dream of a well-seasoned venison pie to enter his thoughts, and then he pushed it away. "I appreciate a tasty meal as much as the next man," he said. "But our personal convenience should not dictate Marian's and Ellen's future well-being."

"I foresee an arrangement that would be mutually beneficial to all parties," Friar Tuck said. "They are protected from the evils of designing men, and we are blessed by their practical skills."

Robin looked away, desire, hope, fear, and uncertainty churning within him. Only this morning, had his men approved, he would have seized the opportunity to have Marian with him in Sherwood. But now he was left feeling unsure—of her, of his feelings, and of the path he should take.

Friar Tuck cleared his throat. "May I say that for a man who spent hours—days even— seeking out the elusive Maid Marian, your reluctance to approve this notion is somewhat startling."

"You do not understand the whole of it, Friar."

"Then enlighten me."

Could he? Marian had said she'd told no one else of her supposed background. She had entrusted him with her secret. Would relaying her story to the cleric be breaking that confidence? He knew the answer. "It is not my tale to tell. Nevertheless, should the time come that you need to know, I shall share more with you."

"Very well." Friar Tuck's expression had turned compassionate. "Then, in the meantime, I would simply remind you that God is a being of goodness and light and that those who emulate such qualities are not as easily found as He—or we—would desire."

"Do you believe Marian upholds those virtues?"

He shrugged. "I scarcely know the young woman, but during your rescue, she displayed no small measure of bravery and selflessness. Since then, she has exhibited a tender heart and a willingness to make time for a humble man of the cloth. Those things are rarely far removed from genuine goodness."

The friar had said nothing that Robin could refute, and Robin had long since learned that when Friar Tuck's counsel took the form of a personal sermon, he had best take heed. He sighed. Mayhap it was time to listen to the whisperings of his heart over the clamoring of his mind and place his trust in his devout friend's guidance once more.

"Come with me to speak with Little John," Robin said. "If he shares your opinion and sees no reason why the men would be against two women joining our band, I shall broach the subject with Marian and Ellen."

CHAPTER 20

Mariah sat alone beneath one of the beech trees that edged the clearing. Across from her, men were talking in small clusters beneath the wide limbs of the giant oak. Ellen was there, standing beside her brother Will, smiling at something one of the men was saying. Robin and Friar Tuck had arrived not long ago, and Friar Tuck had immediately begun stirring something in the large pot hanging over the fire. If the smell was anything to go by, their evening meal would be exactly the same as their midday meal.

Robin was in deep discussion with Little John. Mariah was too far away to hear what they were saying, but the subject was serious enough to cause Little John's habitual smile to slip into something that resembled a thoughtful pondering. It was possible they were discussing what to do with her and Ellen. Especially if they had been the subject of Friar Tuck's earlier conversation with Robin.

She drew her knees up and wrapped her arms around them. She could not think of what her future might hold beyond this moment. It was too frightening. And solitary. She looked away—up to where the tips of the trees touched the sky. The bright sunlight of the day was fading to the softer light of early evening. If she and Ellen were to leave the forest, it would happen soon.

She thought about her father. How had he reacted to her un-expected disappearance? Mariah guessed he'd be worried enough to contact the authorities to file a missing person report. But unless

Mrs. McQuivey had one of the policemen try on a medieval costume in her changing room, there would be no trail for anyone to follow. Maybe, if her father visited the costume shop, Mrs. McQuivey would reassure him that Mariah had been well and happy when she'd been there.

It felt like the events of that day in London had occurred an eternity ago. Somehow, she had survived weeks in medieval England, and if she focused on learning new skills and adapting to her environment, maybe she would eventually come to a level of comfort that would enable her to find happiness here. As long as she wasn't alone. Tears stung her eyes. She desperately didn't want to be alone anymore.

"Marian?"

With a start, Mariah swung her head around. Robin had crossed the grass from where he'd been talking to Little John and was standing above her.

"Robin!" She scrambled to her feet. "I didn't see you coming."

"Forgive me for startling you." He searched her face, and a small line creased his brow. "Are you unhappy?"

Mariah brushed the moisture off her right eyelashes. "Yes. No. I . . . I was just thinking of home."

"Of London?"

She nodded. "Of my father, of London, of the twenty-first century."

His frown deepened. "Marian, the impossibility of—" He broke off and shook his head slightly. "Forgive me. That must needs be a conversation for another time."

Mariah caught her lower lip between her teeth. She'd rarely felt so helpless. When she had shared her experience with Robin, she'd hoped he would sense her sincerity and that that would be enough to cause him to at least give her the benefit of the doubt.

He cleared his throat. "I have just come from speaking with Ellen," he said. "She expressed a desire to remain in Sherwood Forest rather than relocate somewhere more far-distant. I came to ask if you would consider the same. At least for the foreseeable future."

She stared at him in shock. "You . . . you want me to stay?"

"I do."

"But you think I'm lying to you or, worse, that I'm not right in the head."

He raised an eyebrow. "Which of those is truly worse, do you think?"

"I don't know, and it doesn't matter. Neither of them is correct." Her voice caught, and she fought to gain control of it. "I'm sorry. It's just that I so badly want you to believe me."

The look in his eyes softened. "If it is of any comfort to you, I wish to believe you too."

"Maybe one day," she said sadly.

"Then you will stay?"

She really wanted to. His offer had lifted her heavy heart and had given her new hope. But something—a modicum of pride perhaps—held her back. "Are you asking for yourself or for Friar Tuck?"

He met her eyes. "I confess, Friar Tuck is more than ready to relinquish his cooking duties to you, if you are willing to accept them. And I have no doubt my men would all appreciate an improvement in their diets. But that is not why I asked." He released a tense breath. "I neglected to put forth the suggestion earlier because I did not want to place my own desires above your well-being. It was only after Friar Tuck helped me realize that remaining in the forest would offer you greater protection than you are likely to find elsewhere that I allowed myself to truly entertain the notion."

Like a healing balm, Robin's caring words eased the ache his lack of confidence in her integrity had caused, and she felt her guard lower a little. "I secretly hoped Ellen and I would be able to stay but didn't think it would be possible."

He smiled, and it was as though a weight lifted off his shoulders. "Then I am twice glad that I asked."

"I am very grateful," she said. "And I am more than willing to take on the cooking—although I cannot promise that I will not burn something as I learn to work with unfamiliar methods of heating food."

"What have you used in the past?" he asked.

"An oven with a temperature control," she said, not bothering to also mention a timer and oven light.

He looked thoughtful. "It may be possible to craft an oven."

"Really?" It would involve a great deal of trial and error on Mariah's part to get the temperatures right, but to have the means of baking bread or pies would be a game changer.

Robin chuckled at her enthusiastic response. "We have river rocks and mud aplenty. I do not imagine it would be overly difficult to construct one, but I shall make inquiries amongst the men to see if there is someone with oven-building experience."

"Thank you."

"I believe I am the one who should be thanking you." He paused. "Though mayhap I should reserve my thanks until I have tasted the results of your culinary efforts."

"Oh, believe me, my burnt pies are better than any burnt pies you have had in the past," Mariah said. "Blacker, sootier, and harder on the teeth than the shiniest lump of coal."

Robin laughed, and Mariah's pulse tripped. Reluctantly, she acknowledged what she'd only guessed to be true at the archery tournament: dressed in his signature Lincoln green tunic, the real Robin Hood had more power over her heart rate than Errol Flynn, Kevin Costner, or any of the other big-name actors who'd played his part on the big screen.

It was a disconcerting revelation, and in an attempt to regain her composure, she looked away.

Robin must have misinterpreted her movement because he retreated a step. "I shall leave you to your solitude now and will see that two sleeping pallets are prepared for you and Ellen in a corner of the cave. As soon as we have acquired some fabric, we shall erect a curtain to give you whatever privacy we can."

"That is very kind," Mariah said. "And truthfully, I was glad of the interruption."

The strumming of a stringed instrument reached them, and Robin gestured toward the men now sitting beneath the oak tree. "In that case, would you care to join us? I believe it fair to assume that after the events of this day, none of us has sufficient vigor remaining for a competitive game, but an evening spent listening to Allan a Dale sing might be just the thing."

"I have heard that he has a wonderful voice," she said.

He offered her his arm. "Come, and you shall hear for yourself."

She set her hand on his sleeve, her thoughts spinning. She was to stay in Sherwood Forest, and Robin Hood had just asked if she would like to listen to Allan a Dale sing. It was the stuff dreams were made of, yet her journey here had taken a significant physical and emotional toll. This was her new life. And it was incredibly hard. But for the first time since she'd arrived at Nottingham Castle, Mariah wondered if she would feel any regret if she were to wake up lying on her comfortable bed in her London flat and discover that everything she'd thought was real had been nothing more than a trance.

———· ✴ ·———

Robin forced his eyes open. The first light of morning was filtering in through the cave's entrance. On the pallet beside him, Little John was snoring. Someone lying several pallets away echoed the sound. David o' Doncaster, most likely. David was the only one of the Merry Men whose snores could rival Little John's in volume.

Robin shifted and stifled a groan. His body ached. The bruises he'd gained during his visit to the castle dungeon would be paining him for days to come. But his lot could have been worse. So much worse. He set his arm across his eyes, mentally reliving his journey in the back of the cart to the town square, his walk across the scaffold, the noose around his neck, and the zing of Marian's arrow as it had sailed past him to hit the hangman's thigh. After that, everything had happened so fast it was hard to separate the individual incidents, but the overwhelming feeling of gratitude that had washed over him as Little John had driven the cart out of the town had yet to fade. He was alive, and he was free.

Inevitably, his thoughts shifted to Marian. Never had he experienced so many conflicting emotions as he had during the hours he'd spent with her. But as he had hoped, their time together last evening under the oak tree, listening to Allan sing, had brought a welcome calm to the tumultuous day. He lowered his arm and turned his head to peer through the half-light. Marian and Ellen were sleeping on the other side of the cave. Two of his men had volunteered to remain outside in the clearing so the young women had a more comfortable place to rest until they made extra pallets.

Robin squinted, straining to better see into the shadowy corner. One of the maidens stirred, and he caught the pale blue of Ellen's sleeve as she pulled the blanket higher. The other pallet—the one that should have held Marian—was empty. He jerked into a sitting position. His back muscles screamed in protest, but he paid them no heed. His attention was fully on the second pallet. He had not been mistaken. Marian was gone. A quick scan of the cave confirmed that every other pallet was occupied. His stomach clenched. Marian had left the cave and gone into the unfamiliar forest alone.

Tossing back his blanket, Robin grasped his shoes. The moment they were secured, he rose, seized the bow and quiver leaning against the cave wall at the head of his pallet, and made for the cave entrance. By the time he reached the bottom of the stone steps, he had the bow across his shoulder and the quiver attached to his belt. He studied the dusty path. Too many had passed this way to single out Marian's footprints. How was he to choose which direction she had taken?

He took one step toward the clearing and then vacillated. He would try the river first. If there was no sign of her at the water's edge, he would go to the clearing and rouse the men sleeping there to ask for their assistance in finding her. His decision made, he started along the trail at a steady jog.

The chickens were awake, and their clucking increased in volume as Robin rounded the corner. The white one sped across the enclosure in a flurry of feathers, and one of the goats bleated its disapproval. Robin gave the indignant goat a brief glance. If Marian had passed this way, she had not lingered with the animals. The path curved slightly, and suddenly—almost before it began—his search was over. He staggered to a stop. Marian's back was to him. She was on her knees, leaning over the plants in Friar Tuck's infirmary garden. Like a shimmering curtain, her long hair lay loose across her back, and she was digging in the dirt with a fist-sized, flat, pointed rock.

Relief flooded him. "Marian!"

With a gasp, she swung around. "Oh! You scared me!"

"Forgive me," he said. "Though I wager your fear was not nearly so great as mine when I awoke to find you gone."

She sighed. "I couldn't sleep." She flicked a few strands of hair from her shoulder. It was the first time Robin had seen her hair out of its usual single plait, and he was finding it hard to concentrate on anything else.

"So you elected to dig?" He could think of at least a dozen activities that he would have chosen over this one.

"To weed," she corrected with a smile. "My best hope of improving the way meals taste is to make use of Friar Tuck's herbs."

He squatted down beside her. "You believe that using these herbs will make a difference?"

"I'm sure of it," she said. "But I need them to thrive so that if I take some to add to a soup or stew, I won't be leaving Friar Tuck without what he needs for treating your men's ailments."

"Hmm." Sliding the bow off his back, he set it on the ground and picked up a short, sturdy stick lying nearby. "Since I am also awake and this is such a worthy endeavor, I believe it would be in the best interest of my stomach to assist you."

Marian laughed. "I will not turn down any offer of weeding help."

"I am glad to hear it." He pointed at the nearest plant. "Should this one stay or go?"

"Stay," she said. "That one is chives, and it's one of my favorite herbs."

"Very well." Robin began digging out the small-leafed plants growing around the chives' base.

Seemingly assured that he was attacking the correct vegetation, Marian leaned over another plant that had soft, delicate leaves and began turning over the top layer of soil with her rock. A bee buzzed over the purple flowers on the chive plant. Robin ignored it. Behind him, one of the chickens clucked loudly again.

"Lady Kluck must be laying an especially big egg," Marian said. "She has been very vocal this morning."

"Lady Kluck?" Robin stopped his digging. "Did you name one of the chickens?"

"Yes," she said. "The white one. Friar Tuck told me that you prefer not to name them in case one of them ends up in a pot, but I asked if he'd make an exception with the white one." She was still bent over her work, but she turned to face him. "It's the name of a rather marvelous plump, white chicken that appears in one of my favorite Robin Hood stories."

She was speaking of her supposed future life again. "If Friar Tuck has agreed upon the name Lady Kluck, who am I to argue." He had no wish to spoil the amity they'd been enjoying by revisiting her claims, so he pointed to a silver disk hanging from a narrow chain around her neck. As he'd not seen it before, he assumed it had slid free from beneath her smock. "Is that a coin?"

Marian dipped her chin to see. "Yes." Brushing the dirt off her hand, she reached for it. "It belonged to my mother. It's a—" She gasped, and her head shot up. Her widened eyes met his. "It's a sixpence!" Dropping the stone in her other hand, she fumbled for the clasp at the back of her neck. "Why on earth did I not think of this earlier?"

"Marian, stop," Robin said, slightly alarmed by her unexpected change in mood. "You do not need to remove it for my sake."

"Yes. Yes, I do!" She drew the chain off her neck and placed the disk in her hand. "Can you read Latin, Robin?"

"A little," he admitted. "Friar Tuck has taught me enough to read portions of the Bible."

"And numbers?"

He nodded. He could not fathom why Marian was suddenly so excited or so intent upon knowing his level of literacy.

"Can you read this?" She thrust her hand forward with the silver disk face up on her palm.

He took the disk from her. It was perfectly round. Flawless grooves ran along its edges. At its center, there was an impression of a woman's head. A row of raised dots decorated the disk's circumference and between that and the woman's head were the words *Dei Gratia Regina Elizabeth II*. Hesitantly, he translated the Latin. "By the Grace of God Queen Elizabeth the Second."

"Yes. Now turn it over and read the number."

He flipped the disk. "One, nine, six, two." He frowned. "What does it mean? And what is this medallion?"

"It's not a medallion," she said. "It's a coin. As I said before, it's a sixpence. It was legal tender in this country until 1980, but this one was minted in 1962. My mother had it made into a necklace, and after she died, my father gave it to me." She pointed to the impression of the woman's head. "That is Queen Elizabeth II. She was the reigning monarch in England when this coin was made."

Robin swallowed against his suddenly dry throat. The coin was unlike anything he'd seen before—and he had seen countless coins. It was entirely uniform in thickness, shape, and inscription. And the date . . . if the numbers truly meant what Marian said they meant . . . He looked up to meet her eyes. They shone with unshed tears.

"You brought this with you," he said slowly. "From the future."

She nodded.

Was it possible? He flipped the coin over. There was nothing on either side that signified it had originated in England. Could it have come from another country? Latin was spoken universally across the Holy Roman Empire. Who was to say that this coin had not originated in the kingdoms of France or Sicily? He studied the numbers again. 1962. It was currently 1193. If this number truly denoted the year the coin had been made, it made no difference which country it had come from. It had been created over seven hundred years in the future.

Over seven hundred years! How was one to grasp so vast a quantity of time? He released a ragged breath. He had wanted proof, and she had literally handed it to him. This unlikely verification did not make her claims any easier to understand, but it clearly pointed to her having spoken the truth.

"Forgive me," he said, his mind yet struggling to comprehend the ramifications of what this truly meant. "Your story was . . . is . . . so inconceivable . . . so incomprehensible . . ." His words trailed off as guilt seared his chest. "You accepted my distressing past without question, and yet I allowed my doubts to overshadow the struggle and isolation you have surely experienced because of yours."

"Mine is far more difficult to assimilate," she said. "Even for me." Her expression remained anxious. "Do you believe me now?"

"How can I not?" He turned the coin in his hand once more, marveling at what he held. "Everything about it is so exact."

"Centuries from now, coins are made on devices that can roll and cut the metal into perfectly even sizes."

"And the imprinting?" Robin asked.

"Also done by a contrivance built for that purpose alone."

"Remarkable." He stared at the image of Queen Elizabeth II. What manner of monarch was she? Did she leave her country to embark upon a crusade? Or go to battle abroad with no assurance that she would ever return? Once the questions began formulating in his mind, there was no holding them back. They spun in dizzying circles around his head, and he knew it would take weeks to ask them all. But there was one—one question—that burned above all others. "Tell me," he said, scarcely daring to hope. "Will King Richard return to England?"

"He will," she said. "I wish I could remember exactly when it will happen, but I can assure you that he will come back. And Prince John will be forced to answer for the discontent he has sown in England during his brother's absence."

Relief, pure and sweet, flowed through Robin, and he could not contain his grin. "I imagine you have untold wondrous stories to share, but for now, that single piece of information is all I need to know."

"Your many efforts to ease the suffering of others will be worth it," she said. "And will be remembered."

He shook his head sadly and held out the necklace for her. "And yet, it will not undo the great wrong I have done."

She took it from him, put it back on, and tucked it under her clothing once more. "What happened to the forester was unintentional, Robin, and even I can tell that your penitence over his death is real. You told me that Friar Tuck has helped you take that burden to God, and I can't help but think that if all the people through the centuries who have shared legends of Robin Hood could put aside that part of your story, then maybe God is willing to too."

"And King Richard? Given that my men and I have taken up residence in his forest and have repeatedly poached his deer, it is entirely possible that he will see no reason to forgive my past deeds."

"It is equally likely that he will recognize the loyalty and valiancy you've shown during his absence," she said.

"That is a pleasant, albeit unrealistic, thought." He offered her a grateful smile. "Though I confess, I prefer your prediction to mine."

Behind them, a chicken issued a loud and prolonged string of clucks.

"There. You see?" Marian asked, her lips quirking upward. "Lady Kluck agrees with me wholeheartedly, which must mean that I am correct."

"You are sure that was Lady Kluck?" he asked.

"Absolutely. Which of the other chickens would be so presumptuous as to interject her opinion so forcibly?"

Despite his personal misgivings, he could not help but feel that Marian was intent on holding firm to a more hopeful future. Faced with such optimism, it was impossible to hold back his grin. "You are right," he said. "It must have been Lady Kluck. I shall have to discuss her bold conduct with Friar Tuck."

Marian laughed, and Robin waved his stick in the general direction of another plant. "Until the good cleric awakens, however, mayhap you would be willing to identify another herb that needs a portion of my attention while I direct the rest of it to listening to your experience in the costume shop once more."

"The parsley," she said, picking up her rock and pointing to a dark-green plant with curly leaves. "And where would you like me to begin?"

"When you first entered the establishment," he said. There would be time enough to discover more about Marian's previous life after he had reevaluated the miraculous means by which she had arrived here.

CHAPTER 21

Mariah emptied a pailful of mud beside a rapidly growing circle of river rocks that marked the foundation of a medieval oven. Had it only been last night that she'd mentioned her wish for an oven to Robin? He must have polled his men immediately after they'd arisen, because David o' Doncaster had approached her soon afterward to ask where she would like the oven to be located. Ever since then, half a dozen men, including Robin, Little John, and David, had been hauling rocks from the river while she and Ellen had been gathering pailfuls of mud from the river banks.

Robin appeared around the bend in the path, his arms wrapped around two large rocks. "David and Little John will be here shortly," he said. "They have the rock that we shall use as the baking slab." He set down his load and studied their existing work critically. "We may need to add some smaller rocks to the left side to level it."

"Should we do that ahead of setting the slab?" Mariah asked.

Before Robin could respond, Little John's disgruntled voice reached them. "Remind me once more why we were assigned to carry this weight?"

"We drew the short sticks." David was panting.

"We were tricked, more like."

The two men staggered clear of the path, carrying a large, flat stone between them. Sweat ran down their faces.

"Make way!" David gasped.

Mariah stepped backward and bumped into Robin. She stumbled, and his hand shot out to steady her.

"I'm sorry," she said.

"I am to blame; I was poorly situated." The warmth of his hand had penetrated her linen sleeve and was now spreading up her arm. "We should both move. There is no telling when Little John's strength will give out."

Little John shimmied around the low stone wall and glared at him. "More aid and less talk would be much appreciated."

"Of course," Robin said. "How thoughtless of me." He tilted his head as though gauging the distance between the men and the rocks. "You have another four or five paces."

Little John muttered something unintelligible and then promptly ignored Robin. "To your left, David," he grunted. "Then we set this beastly rock down once and for all."

David positioned himself on the opposite side of the oven's foundation. "Now?" he asked through clenched teeth.

"Now," Little John repeated.

They released the slab. It landed with a solid thud. Some of the smaller rocks below shifted, but thankfully, they settled again.

"That is the last time I shall touch that rock," Little John vowed, placing his hands on his back and slowly stretching.

"Aye." David was mopping his brow with his sleeve. "Let us pray it does the job adequately."

"Marian," Robin said, "in case you were yet unsure, it appears that the leveling of the slab will occur after it has been laid."

"And it shall be done by none other than Robin Hood himself," Little John said.

"Likely with one hand behind his back," Allan a Dale added, arriving alongside Ellen and two other men, who were each bearing rocks or a pail of mud.

Little John scowled at Allan. "If any nonsense of that kind appears in one of your ballads, Allan, I shall interrupt your singing with my own. My voice will pain the ears of everyone within hearing, but blame for their extreme discomfort shall fall entirely upon you."

Robin snorted, and suddenly, everyone was laughing.

Even Little John mustered a grudging smile. "You mark my words," he said, wagging a finger at Allan. "If Little John's remarkable strength and skill with the quarterstaff is not the subject of your next ballad, I shall be most put out."

The laughter redoubled.

Mariah waited for it to subside before expressing her thanks. "I'm very grateful to each of you for helping with this project. Little John and David, I believe that with the delivery of this large rock, you have earned the rights to the first loaf of bread that comes from this oven."

Little John slapped David on the back. "You hear that, David? I say we go for more rocks to secure our positions."

With the sounds of their good-natured teasing following after them, the men started back toward the river. Robin was the last to go.

"Out of interest," he said. His tone was serious, but Mariah caught the humor shining in his eyes. "Should I mention to Little John that the first loaf of bread out of the oven may resemble charcoal?"

"No," she laughed. "Any charcoal loaves will remain a secret between me and the goats—if the goats deign to eat them, that is."

"Understood," he said, and then with a wink that was so subtle Mariah wondered if she'd imagined it, he followed after his men.

She watched him go, her heart feeling inexplicably fragile while simultaneously overflowing with emotion. She had never experienced anything like the camaraderie that existed within this band of men.

"It's l-like bein' in a family full of big b-brothers, is it not?" Ellen said.

"Is this what a big family feels like?" Mariah reached for her empty bucket. "I never had any brothers or sisters."

"I daresay that's a l-lot of what you're feelin'," Ellen said. "Leastwise, w-with most of them." A knowing smile tugged at her lips. "I d-do not suppose that applies to R-Robin though."

Mariah willed the warmth threatening to flood her cheeks to stay away. Ellen could not possibly know that the pressure of Robin's fingers on Mariah's elbow still lingered or that Mariah's heart had responded to his wink before her head had fully registered it.

"I don't suppose many females feel that way about Robin Hood," Mariah said, and then before Ellen could pursue the subject any further, she continued. "Where's Will? How did he escape this manual labor?"

"Robin s-sent him into town on a special errand," Ellen said.

Mariah frowned. "Isn't that dangerous so soon after what happened there?"

"I d-daresay." Ellen did her best to hide her worry, but Mariah caught it in her eyes. "But safer for Will to go than f-for Robin." She shrugged. "He gave me his w-word that he would go to the b-bowyer and nowhere else."

The bowyer? Even if Robin wished to replace the bow he'd lost at the tournament, why would he feel any urgency to do it straightway since he had the bow she'd returned to him? She didn't know enough to have an answer.

"Will knows his way around town and the forest," Mariah said. "I'm sure he'll be back very soon."

Ellen nodded. "And then he can t-take charge of my pail."

"As a true older brother should," Mariah teased.

"Aye." The concern had yet to completely leave Ellen's eyes, but she managed a smile. "On certain d-days, older brothers can b-be useful."

——— · * ✹ * · ———

The loud crack of one quarterstaff hitting another brought a cheer from Robin's men. Moments later, Godfrey o' Mansfield lay on the ground, pinned down by the end of Little John's pole.

"Take that, you young upstart!" Little John yelled, and the men sitting around the clearing roared with laughter.

Robin chuckled, grateful to see them enjoying the evening's entertainment so well. Godfrey had been trying to best Little John in a quarterstaff battle for weeks. Unfortunately for him, it appeared that once again, his grand aspirations were not to be realized.

"Who shall be next?" Little John asked, holding his staff above his head and turning in a slow circle to view his audience. "I am ready."

Seated at Robin's left, Marian leaned a little closer. "Does Little John ever tire of this? That is the third man he has beaten, and he barely seems winded."

"Little John is a master with the quarterstaff," Robin said. "Every person living in Sherwood knows it and respects him for his skill. But knowing how rarely he is bested simply adds to the younger men's desire to try."

She shuddered. "They need their heads examined."

Robin had spent the day attempting to come to terms with the proof Marian had offered him of her origin. Its ludicrousness continued to haunt him, but he could not explain away the coin at her neck. And when she occasionally slipped from using current vernacular to using unfamiliar expressions, such as 'needing their heads examined,' it became that much easier to believe her story.

"I daresay you are correct," he said, guessing at her meaning. "They likely still have lumps on their heads from their last attempts."

"Robin!" Little John had completed his circuit and was now facing him. "What say you? Are you prepared to take your chances?"

"Not this night, Little John," Robin said. "My body has bruises enough from its sojourn in the castle dungeon. I would rather not add any more."

"Ah!" Little John waggled his eyebrows. "Methinks our fearless leader is afraid."

"Take him, Robin," Allan called. "You are the only one who can humble the fellow."

Robin felt Marian's eyes upon him. The knowledge that she would be watching might be sufficient to push him to victory. But at what price? Rising this morning had been difficult. It would be all but impossible on the morrow if he added to his injuries tonight.

"I am willing to take you on, Little John, but a quarterstaff is an unduly merciless weapon for my current state." He returned his friend's challenging look. "Conversely, an archery contest would offer no risk of bruises to either of us."

All around, the men cheered.

"Think on it, Little John," David called. "If Robin is so wounded as he maintains, you may taste victory at last."

Little John scowled at the obvious reference to his previous inability to best Robin with a bow. "Mayhap you should be the one to go up against Robin, David," he said. "You have yet to perform this evening."

"I say it should be Marian," another voice called.

At his side, Marian stiffened.

"Aye!" a second and then a third man shouted. "Let it be Marian who goes against Robin."

Robin glanced at her. The terror in her eyes told him all he needed to know. He had never asked why she'd slept so poorly, but if his experience with the forester was any indication, her head had yet to relinquish the images of her arrows in the hangman's limbs. And though he knew how important it was to move past that, now—in front of all these men—was not the time.

He shifted slightly, using his shoulder to block her from view for most of the onlookers. Already, she had gone from relaxed to shaking.

"I . . . I cannot take up a bow." She swallowed. "Please don't make me . . ." She swallowed again. "I cannot explain it, but I—"

"You do not need to explain, Marian," he interrupted gently. "I understand." He reached for her trembling hand. It was cold. With a muttered curse at his lack of foresight, he wrapped his fingers more firmly around hers. After her reaction in the cart, he had guessed she would have difficulty taking up a bow again. This was not the way to undo that fear.

"Marian versus Robin!" The calls for their participation were increasing.

"I wish to return to the cave," she begged. "Please, Robin."

Tears were welling in her eyes, and Robin felt as though his heart were being shredded. This was his fault. He was the one who had suggested an archery contest.

"Of course," he said. Somehow, he must remedy this. "But you cannot go alone."

"I shall g-go with her." Ellen spoke up from her position on the other side of Marian. "And so can Will."

The men who were calling out requests from the other side of the clearing evidently had no notion of what was holding up Robin's response, but Will must have ascertained it. Rising from his position beside his sister, he gave Robin an understanding nod. He had been with them at the cart and obviously needed no further explanation.

"Allow me to escort Marian and Ellen to the cave," Will said. "Marian's pottage outdid Friar Tuck's efforts by so wide a margin that the men will accept any allowance she wishes to make. Tell them she is overly tired this evening. It will explain why she may need some additional assistance."

Will was right. And it was a good thing one of them was yet able to think clearly. Robin desperately wished he could be the one to walk her to the cave, to stay with her until her trembling subsided and sleep came, but the only way he could guarantee that Marian was given the privacy she needed was for him to stay in the clearing and keep the men entertained.

"I am most grateful, Will," he said. Gently, he squeezed Marian's hand. "I will keep the men here whilst Will and Ellen see you safely to your pallet."

She nodded.

He rose and drew her to her feet. "Go now," he said. "I shall come as soon as I am able."

"Is something amiss?" Little John had joined them, all trace of his previous amusement and bravado now gone.

"Marian is overly tired," Robin said, reluctantly relinquishing her hand so that Ellen could place her arm around Marian.

Little John took one look at Marian's face and then winced. He recognized the symptoms. "Forgive me, Marian," he said. "I did not think."

"Neither did I," Robin said grimly, uncomfortably aware that the rowdy calls for the next competition had fallen silent. "She needs time to clear her head."

"And she shall have it." Little John swung around and raised his voice. "It is decided, gentlemen. Robin and I shall shoot for the opportunity to be the first to taste Maid Marian's next meal. She and Maid Ellen are retiring for the night, but I would wager that their decision omens well for the excellence of our victuals on the morrow."

If the men suspected there was more to Marian's sudden departure than fatigue, they were sensible enough to refrain from comment.

"A cheer for Maid Marian and the best meal we've eaten in months!" David o' Doncaster shouted.

"Go ahead and cheer," Friar Tuck called out in response. "I shall nobly choose to turn the other cheek and not be offended."

Laughter mingled with the men's cheers, and by the time the noise subsided, Robin had taken up his bow, and Will, Ellen, and Marian had disappeared from sight.

CHAPTER 22

Mariah tiptoed toward the cave's entrance. If she was going to make a habit of waking up too early, she was also going to have to go to bed earlier. Last night, even though it had been comforting to have Ellen and Will nearby, it had taken Mariah a long time to fall asleep. Mental images of her part in Robin's rescue refused to leave, but eventually, she had stilled her breathing enough to make Ellen believe she had been resting comfortably. Her friend had lain on the pallet beside her, and it hadn't been long before Ellen's breathing had been deeper than Mariah's.

Despite the Merry Men's attempts at a quiet entry into the cave, Mariah had been aware of their arrival. Someone had come to the far side of the cave to check on her. She'd heard the soft footsteps stop beside her pallet and a gentle hand had lifted her blanket a little higher. Not wanting to speak to anyone, she'd kept her eyes closed, but if her heart's instant response to the brush of his fingers across her skin was any indication, her visitor had been Robin.

She took an unsteady breath. The more time she spent coming to know the real Robin, the more she wanted to be with him. And that was terrifying. She didn't belong in his world. Showing him her mother's necklace had helped, but it was possible that he would never fully accept her past; it was certain that he would never fully understand it. And that would create an untraversable chasm between them. She fought back the heartache that thought produced and forced her eyes to remain focused on the pale morning light at the cave's entrance rather than glancing toward his pallet.

One of the men mumbled something in his sleep, and Little John gave a responding snore. Mariah smiled into the darkness. It was remarkable how quickly she had become fond of these men. If Ellen was right and the relationship Robin's men shared was like that of siblings, then Mariah had really missed out in the past. But maybe her future—her new future—would include those bonds in a completely unique and rather wonderful way.

She stepped outside. There was a slight nip to the early-morning air, but a brief look upward confirmed that the sky was clear of clouds. All being well, the day would warm up quickly. She hurried down the steps and then stumbled to a halt as Robin stepped onto the path before her.

"Robin!" she gasped. "What are you doing here?"

"Waiting for you to come." His response should not have had so much power over her pulse. "I had hoped you would rise early as you did yesterday."

She was suddenly glad that she hadn't slept in. "Are we the only ones up?"

"We are," he said. "And I wondered if you would be willing to take a walk with me while it is yet quiet."

"Of course."

He smiled and pointed to the trail that led away from the chickens, the goats, the herb garden, and the half-completed oven. "This way."

The path was too narrow to walk side by side, so she followed him, content to listen to the birds and the rustle of leaves rather than maintain a conversation. Before long, the gurgle of running water joined the other forest sounds, and they entered a familiar grove.

"You've brought me back to the pondering rock," she said.

"It seemed a good place to converse freely and privately."

Memory of their last discussion here assailed her. It had not been an easy exchange for either of them.

"What would you like to talk about?" she asked.

"Firstly," he said, "I wish to know how you are faring."

"I'm fine."

He raised an eyebrow. "Fine?"

She tried again. "I am well." When he continued to regard her silently, she knew he would wait until she offered him more. He seemed to truly understand her struggle, and as much as she hoped that everyone else would forget her hasty exit from the clearing the night before, it was extremely unlikely. "I am grateful to you and Little John for distracting the men when I was incapable of using the bow. Ellen and Will were very kind, and after a little time at the cave, the worst of the shaking subsided." She met his eyes. If she was to verbalize her real fear, this was the time, and Robin was the audience. "But my reaction scared me. What if I never get over this? If the tremors return every time I so much as think about picking up a bow?"

His expression was a mixture of compassion and sympathy. "It is a credit to your tender feelings that you are affected so greatly, but I would have you know that I have seen similar reactions before. With time, the worst of it will pass, but to reclaim your confidence, you will need to be brave enough to take the bow in your hand and shoot an arrow."

Mariah shook her head. She wasn't sure that she had what it took to be any braver than she'd already been. "Maybe one day."

"Not one day," he said. "*This* day."

Mariah shook her head more vehemently and took a step back. "No."

"Trust me, Marian." He reached for her hand, clasping it firmly and drawing her toward him. "The longer you wait, the harder it will be to overcome your uncertainties. By facing your fears straightway, you prevent them from growing any larger."

"I cannot—" Her trembling had begun again.

"You can. I am sure of it. And you shall not do it alone. I shall be beside you."

He slid the bow lying across his shoulder free, and she swallowed against the lump in her throat. "Not the same bow, Robin."

"I agree." He raised the highly polished yew so that she could see it more clearly. "This is not my old bow. It is a different one. It is yours."

"Mine? I don't have one here."

"From this moment forward, you do." He ran his fingers across the smooth wood, angling it so that she could see the finely engraved *M* at its upper tip. "I had the bowyer initial the bow so that you would recognize it amongst the many others at camp."

She stared at him. This was the errand that had taken Will to town. "You bought me a bow?"

"Aye." For the first time since they'd entered the grove, he looked uncomfortable. "I feared that you would struggle to take up mine, and someone who shoots so well should not be without one."

A handmade longbow of this quality would cost a fortune in the twenty-first century.

"It's too much," she said.

"Marian." He waited until she met his eyes again. "You saved my life. To purchase you a bow is hardly commensurate with that."

"But I can't . . . " She blinked back her tears. Maybe he didn't understand her PTSD after all.

His grip on her hand tightened. "I have been told that the most courageous of knights know moments of trepidation. You have already proven to be as fearless as the noblest of the king's men."

"I was pretending."

His lips twitched as though he were holding back a smile. "Then I shall add consummate acting skills to your ever-growing list of accomplishments."

She released a tense breath. It looked like he was going to have to see her collapse on the floor like a spineless jellyfish before he took her seriously.

"Examine it," he said, releasing her hand and offering her the bow. "The bowyer's craftsmanship is highly commendable."

Mariah could tell. And a bow that had been created from a unique piece of wood rather than fiberglass poured into a mold was matchless. She lifted her hand to touch it. Her fingers trembled slightly, but there was something unexpectedly comforting about the smooth wood.

"How does the weight compare to bows you have used in the past?" Robin asked.

"It's a little heavier," Mariah said, realizing that Robin had tricked her into holding the bow so that she might gauge its weight. "It's more like yours." She ran her finger over the *M* etched into the polished wood. "Before coming here, I'd only ever used a fiberglass bow. Fiberglass is a man-made product that is very durable but nowhere near as beautiful as this polished yew."

Curiosity flitted across his face, and Mariah guessed he would have far more questions about bows of the future, but for now, his attention was on the one in her hands.

"I have discovered that every bow has its own strengths and weaknesses," he said. "And I believe it is up to us as archers to discover those qualities and work with them." He smiled. "I daresay your bow will be glad for a slow and gentle introduction."

"You talk about the bow as though it's a person," she said.

He chuckled. "As I have oft been accused of treating mine as though it is my best friend, there may be more truth to that observation than I am willing to admit."

Mariah studied the bow in her hand. Would she ever feel so attached to it as Robin was to his? During particularly successful archery competitions, she'd felt at one with her bow, but she couldn't help but think that there was a greater connection to an instrument that had been handcrafted. "It's beautiful," she said.

"I look forward to seeing you use it." He drew an arrow out of the quiver at his belt and offered it to her.

"Now?" Panic clenched her throat. "But I'm not ready."

"Your first shot will be the hardest," Robin said. "But I will be beside you, and it matters not where the arrow hits." He gestured to the empty grove. "You can harm no one here."

He was right. Deep down, Mariah recognized it. After a fall, riders were urged to remount their horses as soon as possible. Gymnasts did the same with their equipment.

"My hands will shake."

"I would expect nothing less," he said.

She took the arrow. It felt familiar, and she found unexpected reassurance in that. Surely she could manage to shoot one arrow in the safety of the forest. Her trauma was real, but her love of archery ran deep. Archery was part of who she was, and despite her overwhelming distress, she recognized that she would lose something vital if she did not make the effort to reclaim it. She could not allow fear to rob her of such an intrinsic part of her life. Setting her feet in a familiar stance, she attempted to nock the arrow. Her trembling fingers fumbled.

"I don't think . . ." She took a breath. "Robin, my fingers will not . . ."

He stepped behind her, placing his right arm alongside hers. His hand cupped hers, his fingers warm as they guided hers into position. "The arrow is nocked," he said. "My arm is simply there to steady yours. When you are ready, draw the string back and release."

Draw the string back and release. Mariah repeated the words two more times before setting her sights on the ash tree on the other side of the grove. Robin's chest pressed against her back, his left arm circling her waist. As she pulled on the string, his right arm moved in unison with hers. She released a breath. Her emotions were as taut as the bowstring, but in his embrace, she felt safe and inexplicably cherished.

"Now," she whispered.

She let go of the bow string, and the arrow sailed across the mossy ground to land in the ash tree's trunk with a thump.

"Nicely done!" Robin remained behind her, but Mariah heard the smile in his voice.

"I probably shouldn't admit that I was aiming for the knot above the one I hit," she said.

He laughed, and she felt the vibration in his chest against her back.

"It is enough that your arrow reached the tree." Keeping his arm at her waist, he stepped around her so that they were facing each other. "I am truly impressed, Marian. Given the circumstances, that was no small feat."

He was so close that she could see the flecks of green in his blue eyes. Eyes that were currently gazing at her with a look that made the simple act of breathing seem even more difficult than using a bow.

"I . . . I could not have done it without your assistance."

"I believe you could. It may have taken a few days longer to subdue your anxiety, but your dauntless courage would eventually have risen to the fore."

Mariah's thoughts flew from her hasty departure from the clearing the night before to her burning desire to flee this grove when Robin had suggested that she nock an arrow. "If you think I have dauntless courage, you do not know me well."

"Ah, so does your inclination to ignore the bravery you have exhibited since arriving in a completely new century mean that I should add 'humble' or 'conveniently forgetful' to your list of virtues?"

Her cheeks warmed. If Mariah did not escape Robin's gaze soon, she would need a brown paper bag to restore her breathing—and that commodity was in short supply in twelfth-century Sherwood Forest. "I choose 'convenient forgetfulness,'" she said. "Then I can use it whenever I burn meals."

"I fear Friar Tuck may have already used that excuse after omitting key ingredients in his even-more-tasteless-than-usual pottage." He shrugged with feigned regret. "So as ungentlemanly as it is for me to refuse your request, 'humble' it must be. And 'beautiful.' We must not overlook that one."

Her cheeks were undoubtedly flaming by now. "You are being ridiculous."

The corner of Robin's mouth ticked upward, and she received the distinct impression that he was enjoying himself immensely. "I am simply stating things as I observe them."

"No. You are teasing me."

The humor left his eyes immediately. "It is the truth, Marian."

She looked away, struggling to understand her warring feelings. How could she thrill at having Robin's arm around her and hearing him say such wonderful things while simultaneously being terrified of the direction her heart was urging her to go?

"Marian?" Robin's voice was low. "The number of days we have spent together may be few, but I feel as though I have known you for a lifetime. I have shared more of myself with you than almost any other person, and I was under the impression that you have done the same." He placed his finger beneath her chin and gently guided it until she was facing him again. "Is that correct?"

"Yes." She could not deny it.

"Well then, it may be that we have need of one another."

"You are Robin Hood," she said. "The townspeople love you, and you are surrounded by men who look up to you. Why would you need me?"

"I am more fortunate than I deserve, but leadership can be a lonely endeavor."

A vision of the clearing filled with men who seemed more like brothers than acquaintances flashed before Mariah's eyes. Had she missed something in their interaction with Robin? "Are you lonely?"

"If you had asked me that a month ago, I would have said no. Now, I am less sure."

"What has changed?"

There was vulnerability in his smile. "You came to the market. And for the first time, I was given a glimpse of what I was missing."

Mariah's heart was pounding so hard that she was quite sure he could feel it. None of the Robin Hood stories went like this. "But I'm a girl from the twenty-first century who arrived in Nottingham Castle with absolutely no idea what she is doing here."

"And I am an outlaw in Sherwood Forest who has no claim on a future at all."

There was a level of sorrow in his declaration that she'd never heard before. Acting instinctively, she reached up and touched his cheek. "You have a future, Robin. A wonderful one."

He turned his head to kiss her palm. Her hand tingled, and a new heightened awareness buzzed between them. Slowly, she lowered her arm.

"You are teaching me to believe in things that have previously seemed impossible or fully unattainable," he said.

"But they are real and true," she whispered.

He leaned closer until his face hovered above hers. "So I am coming to understand."

The air stilled between them, and then his lips were on hers, one arm drawing her closer as his other hand lifted to cup the back of her head.

All conscious thought fled. The bow dropped from her hand onto the mossy ground with a light thud as she returned his desire with her own. She reached upward, threading her arms around his neck and holding on as her whole world spun.

Somewhere beyond the barrier of trees, a man's voice reached her. Another replied, and Robin pulled away.

"Forgive me," he said, his voice husky. "I had no intention . . ." He ran his fingers through his hair. "I wish you to know that this was not . . ." He seemed to be struggling to complete his sentences. "Forgive me," he repeated. "You must know that my sole intention this morning was to aid you in the first steps of your journey to reclaiming your love of archery. Not . . . not this."

Mariah shook her head dazedly. Why was he apologizing? Surely he'd been as emotionally invested . . . as filled with wonder by that earth-shattering kiss as she had been. Did he just not know how to express his feelings? But if that were the case, why would he apologize? Was *she* sorry it had occurred? She stumbled back a couple of steps, uncertainty searing her fragile heart. Who was she kidding? He was Robin Hood, and she was Mariah Clinton. It was not her place to be kissing him at all. Whether he regretted it or not, she could not take the place of his Maid Marian in this medieval world.

"Thank you for your help with the bow and arrow," she said. "But it sounds like your men are rising, so I'd better return to the clearing to make breakfast."

His brows came together. She wasn't sure what he'd expected her to say, but apparently, she had surprised him.

He bent down to pick up the new bow. "I shall guide you back."

"There's no need." Mariah was already moving toward the gap in the trees. "I remember the way."

"Marian."

Despite her reluctance, there was something in his voice that made her pause. She half turned. "Yes?"

"You did well today." He raised the bow in his hand. "I shall place this beside your pallet, along with a quiver of arrows. Whenever you wish to try shooting again, I would be happy to assist you."

"Thank you again."

Another archery session with Robin wouldn't happen. As much as she appreciated his friendship and generosity, she could not risk another encounter like this. Not if the ache in her chest was any indication of her true feelings for him. Her priority from now on must be to avoid one-on-one time with Robin at all costs. She could not be responsible for putting his relationship with the real Maid Marian in jeopardy.

Raising her hand in farewell, she hurried away. Loneliness was better than heartbreak.

CHAPTER 23

R obin stood statuesque beside the alder tree, his bow ready. The dun-colored rabbit had darted beneath the bramble bush before Robin had had time to nock his arrow. But once the animal believed the human threat had passed, it would come out into the open once more. Robin had only to wait.

He'd promised Marian that he would provide meat for this evening's pottage. And he meant to do it, even if she had barely acknowledged his offer. He frowned at the memory of their stilted conversation outside the cave. It was the only interaction they'd had since returning from the grove, but she'd been far more interested in going with Friar Tuck to collect the chicken's eggs than she had been in talking to him. He could not understand what had happened between them. One minute, she'd been responding to his kiss as though her heart were in tune with his, and the next moment, she'd been fleeing the grove as though her life depended upon her escape.

In retrospect, he should not have placed his arm around her when she'd been in need of a steady hand. That had been his first error; the second had been stepping closer when he should have stepped away.

He stifled a sigh. Never before had he experienced the intensity of emotions that she aroused in him. She filled his thoughts. His pulse quickened at the very sight of her. Little John and Friar Tuck notwithstanding, there was no one else he'd rather be with. He wanted to talk to her, learn from her, shoot with her, protect her, laugh with her. And kiss her. Fool that he was, he desperately wished to kiss her again.

His vision blurred as he relived their short time together in the grove. Marian's courage and compassion had both impressed and touched him, but the kiss they'd shared had rocked him to his very core. And it had taken every drop of self-discipline he possessed to release her when Little John's voice had reached him. The men's voices had brought his senses back in a rush. Caught up in the moment, he had allowed his feelings to override caution. The moment he'd pulled away from her, he'd known he should not have been so forward. Not when Marian had yet to recover her equilibrium and when her emotions had been so fragile. He winced at the memory of her stunned expression. He'd apologized, but it had not seemed to help.

The bramble bush trembled, and Robin forced his attention back to the present. The rabbit's nose appeared. It twitched, sniffing the air. Robin stood completely still. Two hops out of the bush. That was all he needed from the creature. At this distance, he could not miss.

From somewhere at his left, a horn sounded. The bramble bush leaves rustled, and the rabbit disappeared. Robin hardly noticed. He'd already lowered his bow. Little John's warning meant that there was something of far greater import to worry about. Dropping his arrow into his quiver, he shouldered his bow and took off at a run.

The call had come from somewhere near the wide bend in the road leading to Nottingham, and when Robin came within sight of the oak trees that lined the thoroughfare, he slowed his steps and approached more cautiously. A twig snapped at his left. He swung around and was reaching for the knife at his belt when Will Scarlett appeared through the trees. Lowering his hand, Robin waited for his friend to approach.

"You heard Little John's horn?" Robin asked.

"Aye." Will glanced toward the road. "Someone of note must be approaching."

"Or someone who wishes us ill."

Will gave him a wry look. "Most often, they are one and the same."

It was true, more's the pity. And it was why they would need to approach the road carefully.

"Ready your bow," Robin said, already nocking an arrow. "We shall move in together."

They had almost reached the stand of trees lining the thorough-fare when Little John stepped out from behind a thick hawthorn bush.

"You took your time," he muttered. "The unfamiliar knight is almost upon us."

"Who is the unfamiliar knight?" Will asked.

Little John gave him a long-suffering look. "If I knew that, I would not have titled the fellow *unfamiliar*."

"How large is his retinue?" Robin asked.

"He has none."

Robin's eyes narrowed. "No one rides with him?"

"He is entirely alone."

"And yet, you believe he is a knight?" Robin said.

"He wears a hauberk beneath his surcoat and carries a sword and shield."

A rider wearing the distinctive garb of a knight without the cus-tomary escort was mysterious indeed.

"I hear horse hooves," Will warned.

Robin nodded. "Come. It is time that we introduced ourselves to our new visitor."

The men cut through the vegetation and took their positions side by side, with their legs apart, facing the bend in the road. The steady drum of the horse's hooves was unmistakable now.

"Prepare yourselves," Little John muttered.

Moments later, a dapple-gray mare appeared, and on her back was the most dejected-looking knight Robin had ever set eyes upon. No matter the bright-red and -gold stripes upon his white surcoat or the fearsome lion upon his shield, the fellow's head was bowed. His chin lay against his chest, and his shoulders were slumped as though they bore the weight of the world.

"Good day, Sir Knight," Robin called.

The man's head rose, and he eyed Robin and his companions with more curiosity than fear. "For myself, it is the very worst of days," he said, "but I would offer you each a good day regardless."

As far as Robin could ascertain, the only weapon in the knight's keeping was the sword hanging at his belt. And since the gentleman had made no move to unsheathe it, Robin determined to approach without nocking an arrow. "Your name, good sir, if you please."

"Sir Richard of the Lea," the knight said. "And who might you be?"

"I am known in these parts as Robin Hood," Robin said. "And the fine gentlemen who accompany me are Little John and Will Scarlet."

Sir Richard gave an acknowledging nod. "Your fame precedes you, Robin Hood, but if you mean to rob me, I fear you shall be sorely disappointed, for my purse holds no more than five shillings, and I own not a groat more."

Robin eyed him thoughtfully. "Are you willing to pledge upon your knightly honor that you speak the truth?"

"Aye." He untied the small purse at his belt. "You may see the contents of my purse yourself."

Robin had no need. The knight's humble demeanor bore witness to his honesty. It was unfortunate that Sir Richard was unable to contribute of his means to the poor of Nottingham, but Robin was beginning to wonder if the gentleman might be in need of assistance himself.

"Where are you off to?" Robin asked, ignoring the knight's proffered purse.

"I must be at the Bishop of Hereford's palace by week's end."

Robin raised his eyebrows. The Bishop of Hereford was an all-too-frequent and distinctly unpleasant visitor at Nottingham Castle, but the journey between his palace and the castle was no small undertaking.

"That is a long distance to travel alone."

"Aye. Would that it were not so, but I find myself both penniless and without retainers, so I have no recourse but to put my trust in God and in the good people I might meet along the way."

Out of the corner of his eye, Robin caught the puzzled look that passed between Little John and Will. They were obviously as perplexed by this knight's situation as Robin was.

"Might I be so bold as to ask how a knighted gentleman came to be in such unfortunate circumstances?" Robin asked.

"You may, but the telling will likely take more time than you wish to offer me."

"I, for one, should like to hear your tale," Little John said, extending his arm toward the empty road. "As you see, we have no alternative entertainment at present."

If Little John had assumed that his mild jest would elicit a smile from the gentleman, he was to be disappointed. The knight's response was a heavy sigh.

"Very well," he said. "I have but one son. Though only twenty and four winters old, he has won his spurs as a knight. Three years hence, a jousting tournament was held in Chester. My wife and I traveled there with our son. It was a proud day, for Henry unseated every knight he jousted. Then it came time for him to go against Sir Walter of Lancaster. Their lances connected, and Henry's split. He remained atop his mount, but a portion of the shaft pierced Sir Walter's visor." Sir Richard sighed again. "Sir Walter died before his squire could unlace his helmet, and the knight's kinsmen stirred up things against my son so that to save him from prison, I was forced to pay a ransom of six hundred pounds in gold.

"All might yet have gone well, but I was tricked into pawning my inheritance for money to pay the doctors of law who were set upon destroying my son's future. I have only five days more to pay back what I owe, or I lose my home and lands."

"Where is your son now?" Robin asked.

"I cannot say for certain," Sir Richard replied. "He left for Palestine to fight for the cross and holy sepulcher beside King Richard. Sir Walter's kinsmen's lingering hatred meant that there was no place in England where he could peaceably dwell."

"And your kinsmen?" Will asked, speaking up for the first time. "Do you not have family and friends to come to your aid at this time of need?"

"When I was rich, I had friends aplenty, but since I have become poor and beset with powerful enemies, those supposed friends are lost to me. As to kinsmen, they are few in number. One has expressed a willingness to take in my dear wife when she loses her own home. As for me, I shall travel to Palestine to join my son and liege."

"As glad as I am to hear that your wife will be cared for, the resolution you describe is scarcely a happy one," Little John said.

"No, indeed." The knight's shoulders slumped even lower. "To lose my lands is a bitter thing, but to have failed the woman I love above all others is far worse."

Robin's sojourn in the castle dungeon had given him fresh understanding of the anguish and sorrow that was borne of utter helplessness. And he recognized those feelings in Sir Richard's dispirited bearing. "Tell me, Sir Richard," he said, "what more do you owe to the Bishop of Hereford to pay off your debt?"

"Four hundred pounds."

"A pox take that black-hearted cleric," Little John exclaimed. "A noble estate forfeit for four hundred pounds!"

"It shall not happen," Robin said.

Sir Richard's smile was halfhearted. "Though I appreciate the sentiment, I have traveled across England in search of a means of extricating myself from this trap with no success. My time has run out, and there is no other way forward."

Robin made eye contact with Little John and gave a subtle nod.

Little John's answering grin was immediate. "Do not abandon hope just yet, Sir Richard," he said, moving to stand beside the knight's horse. "There are many who have thought themselves friendless but who have found an unforeseen ally in Robin Hood."

"Aye." Will took his place on the horse's other side. "And most recently, that friendship includes sharing in a well-cooked meal."

Sir Richard looked from one man to the other, his brow furrowed. "Forgive me. I do not understand."

Robin pointed to the trail all but hidden by a nearby hazel tree. "Go with my men, Sir Richard," he said. "They will lead you to a place in the forest where you may enjoy nourishment and rest. I have a previous assignment that I must attend to, but when I have what I need, I shall join you there. And then we shall discuss the way in which you shall pay your dues to the Bishop of Hereford."

"But I—" Sir Richard halted and began again. "How can you—"

"I would suggest that you save your questions for the campfire," Little John said when the knight's words failed him a second time. "There will be time aplenty for that when all the men of Sherwood are gathered together."

"*All* the men of Sherwood?" His uneasy gaze moved from Little John to Robin. "How many more are there?"

Robin chuckled. "Sufficient that you shall no longer feel alone." He slid his bow off his shoulder and raised it in farewell. "I must be about my business, but I shall join you anon."

———·· ✳ ·· ———

Mariah sat beside Ellen beneath the large oak tree. The rumble of conversation around the clearing had lowered to a minimum as the men's attention had turned to their evening meal.

"I b-believe the men approve of y-your rabbit stew," Ellen whispered. "They'll be linin' up for more s-soon enough."

She'd barely finished speaking when Allan a Dale rose to his feet and started toward the large pot hanging over the fire.

"I'm glad Friar Tuck offered to take care of serving seconds," Mariah said. "I have a horrible feeling we're going to run out."

"Well, when it's g-gone, it's gone." Ellen's practical nature was a blessing. "The m-men will accept that easily enough."

"I hope so."

Three more men had joined Allan at the fire pit, and Mariah couldn't help but feel a tiny portion of pride amid an overwhelming measure of relief. Chef Heston may not have approved of the meal, but given what she had to work with, Mariah was pleased with the results. A hearty stew filled with chunks of carrots, parsnips, turnips, and rabbit meat, seasoned with fresh herbs from Friar Tuck's garden. It was a change from Friar Tuck's pottage, at least. And perhaps, after David o' Doncaster declared the oven ready for use, she would also be able to add bread to some of their meals.

"What d-do you think Robin and his g-guest are speaking of so earnestly?" Ellen asked.

"I don't know." Mariah had been making a concerted effort not to look in their direction. She'd spoken to Robin only once since he'd left to hunt rabbits this morning, and that had been when he'd brought the game to her this afternoon. She'd offered him an awkward thank-you. His puzzled expression and lingering presence at the fire had suggested that he'd hoped to say something more, but to her relief, Friar Tuck had hurried over to take charge of the rabbits and had also taken over the conversation.

It had been Will who'd come to tell the two women that there would be a guest for dinner. Sir Richard of the Lea had been accompanied by Little John or Robin Hood ever since he'd entered the clearing. Although whether that was out of an abundance of caution on the men's part or because they had much to discuss, Mariah couldn't tell. Either way, it had made her life easier. With she and Robin equally busy, there was less chance of them running into each other.

"M-Mayhap you could ask h-him more about the knight," Ellen said.

"I don't see why Robin would feel the need to tell me." A pang of sadness entered her heart. Only yesterday, she might have agreed with Ellen. But not anymore. Robin's obvious regret after they'd kissed must serve as a firm reminder that she didn't really belong in his life.

"Well, he seems intent upon t-tellin' you somethin'," Ellen said.

Mariah swiveled. Robin was crossing the clearing. He had changed from his Lincoln green tunic into the clothing he'd worn while posing as a butcher in the marketplace, and he was walking toward her with undisguised purpose.

"I b-believe I shall see if Friar T-Tuck is in need of assistance," Ellen said, coming to her feet in one swift movement.

"No," Mariah said. "Please don't go."

Ellen gave her a puzzled look. "Robin is c-clearly coming to speak with you, so methinks it b-best that I do."

"You don't know that for sure." Mariah scrambled to her feet and brushed the bits of moss off her skirt.

"Good evening, Marian. Maid Ellen."

Mariah had not acted fast enough. Robin had reached them.

"Good evening, Robin," Ellen said. "I am just on m-my way to help Friar T-Tuck."

Robin glanced at the growing line of men waiting for another serving of stew. "I have no doubt he will be glad of your assistance."

"Aye. I should g-go." And then, without another look in Mariah's direction, Ellen made her escape.

With her heart pounding uncomfortably, Mariah forced herself to meet Robin's eyes. "Good evening, Robin. I hope you enjoyed the stew."

"It was the best I have ever tasted," he said. "And I would wager every man in this clearing would say the same."

She held back the smile clamoring for release. "I'm glad. The addition of the meat you provided made all the difference."

"I am quite sure the superior flavor was due to far more than the meat," he said. "But I am pleased that I was able to contribute to the meal."

This stilted conversation was becoming more and more uncomfortable. Desperate to end it, Mariah gestured toward the visiting knight. "I should let you get back to your guest."

Confusion clouded Robin's eyes, but he took a step back. "I came to tell you that I am leaving."

Mariah's stomach dropped. After how hard she'd tried to avoid Robin today, she should be glad for this news. But she couldn't seem to muster up a single drop of happiness or relief. "Where are you going?"

"To Hereford," he said. "Sir Richard of the Lea has unfinished business with the Bishop of Hereford. Little John and I will accompany him there to see that he is treated fairly."

Barring a return to Nottingham Castle, this was the worst possible destination.

"But the Bishop of Hereford is as likely to put you in chains as the Sheriff of Nottingham is."

"It will not happen." When she said nothing, he continued. "I have learned my lesson, Marian. This time, I shall not drop my guard." His smile was slight, but it was there. "With no female archers in the vicinity, methinks that will be an easier task than it was during the tournament in Nottingham."

Warmth filled her cheeks, but before she could figure out how to respond, Little John joined them.

"I have collected the sheriff's gold and our blankets from the cave," he told Robin. "Sir Richard is awaiting us."

"Very well."

"You're leaving now?" Mariah asked. "But it's almost dark."

"Sir Richard has a horse," Robin said, "but Little John and I must travel on foot. If we are to arrive in Hereford by the appointed hour, there is no time to delay."

Mariah experienced a wave of dread. It shouldn't matter that Robin was leaving. But it did. A lot. "How . . . how long will you be gone?"

"Ten days if our interaction with those at the bishop's palace goes as planned and the weather is kind," Robin said. "A fortnight if not."

"I hope all goes well." Clasping her hands together, Mariah assumed a falsely placid expression. "Travel safely."

Little John's brows came together, and his gaze darted from her to Robin and back. "Right then," he said, clearing his throat. "We should be away."

"Aye." Robin gave her one last long look, then stepped back. "Farewell, Marian."

"Farewell, Robin," she replied. "And you, Little John."

Little John made to follow after Robin and then paused. "Two weeks hence," he said, "if you could ask one of the worthless Merry Men staying behind to catch a couple more rabbits, I'd be right glad of another meal like the one you served this evening."

Mariah wanted to cry, but somehow, she managed a smile. "I will do my best," she said.

"That's good enough fer me," Little John said, and then he was gone, walking swiftly across the grass to join Robin and the knight who was now on horseback.

CHAPTER 24

Robin approached the arched stone entrance leading to the bishop's palace with no small amount of relief. He was quite sure his companions felt similarly. The journey from Sherwood Forest had been long and arduous, with minimal victuals and very little rest.

Remarkably, notwithstanding his noble status, Sir Richard had willingly endured three uncomfortable nights bedded down on the ground with nothing more than a tree or a hedgerow for protection. Robin and Little John were accustomed to such primitive sleeping arrangements, but it was a lowly setting for a knight, and Robin could not help but be glad that the worthy gentleman was able to ride up to the bishop's grand residence upon his elegant mount with some measure of dignity intact.

"Well now," Little John muttered upon setting eyes on the ostentatious palace for the first time, "it does not seem that the Bishop of Hereford is in great need of additional property."

"No, indeed." Sir Richard's tone was grim. "I believe today's meeting will be nothing more than a test of the Bishop of Hereford's ability to show mercy."

"As a man of the cloth, he seems strangely lacking in that particular virtue," Robin said.

"Along with several others," Little John grumbled. "If you are able to wring the slightest concession out of him, we shall consider it a fight well fought. If not, we will be happy to see the Sheriff of Nottingham's coins used for so just a cause."

"I have yet to truly believe we shall obtain our goal," Sir Richard said, "but you are the very best of men to have supported me so completely."

"Stand tall and believe in the seemingly impossible, good knight," Little John said, tugging his hood lower over his forehead so that nothing more than his chin was visible. "That is the charge given to all friends of Robin Hood and his Merry Men."

Following his companion's lead, Robin adjusted his hood. Little John was right. They had experienced countless miracles in the past. This encounter with the Bishop of Hereford certainly had the potential to qualify as one. Was it too much to ask for yet another? One that would help him overcome the chasm that had suddenly opened between him and Marian?

Little John and Sir Richard had conversed freely as they'd traveled. For the most part, Robin had chosen to remain silent. His thoughts had been far from the long road or the greedy bishop at the end of it; they had been centered almost exclusively upon Marian. Something had changed in her attitude toward him. He had wondered if it was so when he'd gone for the rabbits. He had become sure of it when he'd bid her farewell. But no amount of pondering had given him the answers he sought. He hoped it had nothing to do with her past, because he was beginning to realize how desperately he wished her to be part of his future.

"The porter has spotted us." Little John's warning whisper brought Robin's musing to an abrupt end.

"I imagine the bishop is expecting you, Sir Richard," he said. "Tell the porter your men will be accompanying you inside."

"Very well." Sir Richard's posture spoke of the strain he was under, but his expression remained calm, his voice authoritative. "Let us be about this foul business."

The elderly porter shuffled forward. "Who goes there?"

"Sir Richard of the Lea," the knight said. "The bishop is expecting me."

"Aye, sir." He stood aside to allow them entry. "The stable's to yer right."

"I thank you, but I have no need of the stables. My men and I shall not be here long."

The porter inclined his head. "Very good, sir."

Urging his horse forward, Sir Richard led them across the cobblestoned courtyard to the palace's main doors. He dismounted, and Robin tied the horse's reins to a nearby post.

"Little John and I shall remain at the threshold to the great hall when you enter," Robin said. "Should the need arise, it will enable us to facilitate a rapid exit."

"I am as anxious to quit this place as you are," Sir Richard admitted.

"Then let us be about our business," Little John said. "Though I would wager that when all is said and done, the Bishop of Hereford will desire our departure more than anyone."

Sir Richard knocked on the door. A manservant, who must have been forewarned of their arrival, immediately answered and ushered them inside without asking Sir Richard's identity. He led them directly up a flight of stairs to another set of wide doors. He knocked once before pushing open the door and stepping aside so the men could enter.

Sir Richard walked directly into the center of the large room. Robin and Little John took their positions on either side of the entrance, and while the eyes of all the other occupants were fixed upon the knight, Robin perused the room.

Stone pillars sat on a smoothed flagstone floor and reached up to a cross-vaulted ceiling. Tapestries hung on the walls. A fire burned in a large fireplace, and a long table covered in a white cloth was piled with baskets of bread and trenchers full of meat and fruit. Goblets of mead were placed before each of the three men seated at the table.

Dressed in blue silk with a velvet hat trimmed with gold, the Bishop of Hereford sat at the head of the table. A chain of gold hung around his neck, and a falcon perched upon the back of his throne-like chair. The gaunt man dressed in black, seated at the bish-op's left, was a stranger to Robin. But the gentleman wearing a purple velvet and fur-lined tunic at the bishop's right was all too familiar.

Robin heard Little John's angry hiss and knew his friend had raised his head high enough to catch sight of the Sheriff of Notting-ham.

"You have come, Sir Richard!" The bishop could scarcely con-tain his gloating.

"It is the appointed day, and I am a gentleman of my word," Sir Richard said.

"Just so." He gestured toward his guests. "As you see, I have a worthy doctor of law and a second witness here to assist us in today's proceedings." The Bishop of Hereford raised a haughty eyebrow. "Have you brought my money?"

In accordance with the plan Sir Richard, Robin, and Little John had hatched, the knight fell to one knee. "Alas," he said, "I have come here with not one penny in my purse." He bowed his head in suppli-cation. "I come to plead for mercy."

"I am not completely without feeling, Sir Richard. It gives me no pleasure to reduce your wife to homelessness and her husband to pov-erty." Greed filled the bishop's eyes even as he glibly feigned concern. "Unfortunately, I cannot circumvent the law. Your day of reckoning has come, and with no money on the table, your land is forfeit." He turned to the man of law. "Is that not so, learned doctor?"

As though unaware that the bishop's question had been directed toward him, the insipid man of law studied his trencher silently.

The bishop's jaw tightened in obvious annoyance, and he turned to the sheriff. "What say you, good sheriff?"

"This is painful for all involved," the sheriff said piously. "Never-theless, it would seem to me that Sir Richard cannot escape his debt. None of us is exempt from the law after all."

Robin battled his outrage as Little John muffled a derisive snort. The Sheriff of Nottingham made his own laws. And each of them was drawn up to benefit him alone.

Unaware of his disbelieving and angered audience, the sheriff stroked his beard thoughtfully. "Mayhap it would serve to illuminate your goodness and generosity if you eased Sir Richard of a portion of his debt."

The look in the Bishop of Hereford's eyes turned from greedy to calculating. He undoubtedly believed that since the knight was penniless, a show of godly kindness was no risk whatsoever. A token offer of mercy, however, would be something he could spread abroad as further confirmation of his worthiness.

"Well said, Sheriff." The bishop smiled soullessly. "Three hundred pounds, Sir Richard. If you can produce that amount, I shall give you quittance of your debt."

Still on his knees, Sir Richard raised his head to face the bishop. "You know full well that three hundred pounds is no easier for me to pay than four hundred. Will you grant me but twelve additional months to plant crops and bring in a harvest?"

"The law is fixed," the bishop said, his temporary show of patience gone. "You shall have not one day more. Pay now or release your lands to me and be gone from my hall."

It was time. Robin raised his head just enough to watch Sir Richard come to his feet.

The knight's chainmail rustled, and he set his hand on the hilt of his sword. "You false, lying priest!" His voice rang with indignation and fury. "Have you so little courtesy that you would make a knight of the realm kneel before you? Or have him come in to your feast and offer him no food or drink?"

The Bishop of Hereford's face turned puce. Beside him, the man of law's gaze had yet to leave his trencher. The sheriff was staring at Sir Richard with mouth agape. Sir Richard extended his arm. Robin stepped forward and handed him a leather purse.

Instantly, the sheriff's mouth snapped shut. He stared at the purse that had once hung around his own waist, and his eyes narrowed. Rising, he placed both hands on the table, leaned forward, and glared at Robin. "Remove your hood."

Sir Richard stiffened. "Remember your place, Sheriff! These are my men, and you have no jurisdiction over them." He signaled Robin back to the doorway. "Bishop, I would have you recall that you promised me quittance for three hundred pounds." He loosened the leather laces around the pouch and poured the coins inside onto the table. They rained down, scattering along the white cloth in a trail of shining gold pieces. "Not one farthing more will you receive from me. As these witnesses can attest, I have paid my debt, and there is nothing more to be said between us." He turned on his heel and marched to the door. "Come, men," he said, speaking to Robin and Little John. "It is long past time to quit this vile place."

Robin and Little John needed no persuading. Withdrawing from the great hall, they descended the stairs and crossed to the outer door with brisk strides. The servant who had greeted them was gone. Little John heaved open the door. Exiting quickly, they hurried to Sir Richard's horse. The knight mounted while Robin untied the straps.

"That unscrupulous sheriff may be on to us," Little John muttered.

"Aye." Robin tossed Sir Richard the reins. "And there's no accounting for what he will do next."

"Guards!" The sheriff's voice reached them through the partially open door. The sound of rapid footsteps on the flagstones followed his shout.

"I hope you men are capable of moving swiftly," Sir Richard said. "It looks like we may be in for a chase."

Sir Richard urged his horse through the palace gates. Little John ran at his left. Robin did the same at his right, but he knew full well that to outrun guards on horseback would be impossible, especially if they stayed on the road. Their only hope of escaping the sheriff's men was to outwit them.

"We likely have only the length of time it takes the stableboys to saddle the guards' mounts before they're after us," Little John said, breathing heavily as he kept up with the trotting horse.

Robin managed a brief nod, his attention on their surroundings. Unless his memory failed him, when they'd come this way, the thoroughfare they'd been traveling had been joined by another. And unlike the pasture they were currently passing, the area at the roads' convergence had been wooded.

"The fork in the road, Sir Richard," he said, breathlessly. "How much farther?"

Raising himself slightly in his saddle, Sir Richard looked over the stone wall at his left. "I see where the two thoroughfares meet," he said. "I would wager it's another furlong, mayhap two from here."

"We must reach that spot before the guards are upon us," Robin said.

Behind them, the clatter of hooves on the cobblestoned yard forewarned of the guards' rapid progress. Impatient shouts filled the air. And then the sheriff's furious voice cut through the rest.

"I am surrounded by incompetents! Saddle these horses this instant!"

They turned a corner, and the voices became muted. Robin's lungs burned, and his legs screamed for relief. He ignored them. It was not often that he pushed his body this hard, but he was not of a mind to make this chase easy for the Sheriff of Nottingham. Little John must have been feeling similarly because though he was panting heavily, he had yet to slow his pace.

"There," Sir Richard said. "The trees are up ahead."

"Praise the Lord," Little John wheezed.

"Take the north road, Sir Richard," Robin said. "If anyone follows, your horse will outrun them."

"What of you?"

"Little John and I will hide in the trees. We are well used to doing that. When the danger is past, we shall go east."

"I cannot leave you here alone and undefended."

Little John managed a throaty chuckle. "Your gallantry is noted, Sir Richard, but in this instance, it is unnecessary."

They reached the fork in the road at last. Robin stopped running. Resting his hand on the trunk of an ash tree whose branches overhung the narrow thoroughfare, he willed his pulse to slow. Beside him, Little John set his hands on his knees, battling to steady his breathing.

"Go, Sir Richard," Robin insisted. "Now. Before they catch sight of you. If they hear your mount's hooves on the north road, they will likely follow, which will enable us to go east unhindered."

Sir Richard's expression was awash with irresolution. He turned his head. The sound of horse hooves was louder now.

"They are almost upon us." Little John moved into the copse. "Farewell, Sir Richard."

The decision was made. There was no time for further argument.

Sir Richard turned his mount toward the northern route. "I am forever indebted to you for what you have done."

"Not so," Robin said. "I have full faith that you shall repay that debt tenfold. But more importantly, the men of Sherwood can now claim a new and worthy friend."

"Of that, you may be sure." Already the cloak of despair that had hung so heavily upon the knight's shoulders had lifted. He raised his hand. "Godspeed, Robin Hood and Little John. I shall see you again 'ere long." Leaning forward, he tapped his heels to his horse's sides.

His mount responded straightway, and startled by the horse's sudden movement, a crow took off from its place on the stone wall. With a harsh cry, it sailed away, just ahead of the galloping horse.

CHAPTER 25

"This way," Little John hissed.

Pushing past a bramble bush, Robin hurried after him. The grove of trees was small but dense. Little John crouched in a slight hollow behind the largest bramble bush. He slid his bow off his shoulder and nocked an arrow, his gaze on the small sliver of road between the gnarled branches. Robin pressed himself against the trunk of an oak tree, offered a quick, silent prayer that there would be sufficient undergrowth to conceal them, and prepared his own bow.

The guards had reached them. Robin could hear the horses' snorts above the clatter of hooves.

"Which way?" one of the guards yelled.

"Divide!" the sheriff ordered. "You three go north. The rest of you, follow me. If Robin Hood is returning to Sherwood Forest, he will be on the road that goes east."

"What would you have us do if we find them?" It was the same guard. He must be a captain.

"What do you think?" The sheriff spat the words. "Capture them."

"But, Sir Richard—"

"I want nothing to do with Sir Richard!" the sheriff snapped. "Bring me the other two."

"Yes, my lord sheriff."

Hardly daring to move, Robin eyed the road Sir Richard had taken. Though he was surrounded by branches and shrubs, he could just make out the stone wall that marked the thoroughfare. There was no sign of the knight, and Robin was willing to guess that he was well away by now. Robin's concern was not for Sir Richard. Rather, he wondered how he and Little John could make their way back to camp if the sheriff and three of his men were actively traversing the very route they needed to take. Avoiding the road would hardly aid them if their only alternative was crossing pastures where they would be clearly visible. And there was far too much open land between Hereford and Sherwood Forest.

The chink of bridle buckles blended with the clopping of hooves. The men were moving. Robin glanced at Little John. His friend raised a questioning eyebrow. *What now?* This tangled copse may have served them well as a temporary hiding spot, but its thorny bushes and limited size made it a poor choice for a long stay.

Robin's gaze shifted to the north road again. Less than a furlong away, a large pine tree stood against the stone wall. It was alone except for the vast number of crows perched upon its upper limbs. Some of them cawed occasionally, as if wishing to remind all those in the vicinity of their presence. Fearless, belligerent, and mean. Robin had no fondness for crows, but he would gladly make use of them if they aided his cause. And he had a surprisingly clear shot of their perch.

Silently, he raised his bow and aimed for the top of the pine tree. One bird had voiced its irritation when Sir Richard had left. Was it possible that the sheriff and his men would equate a flock of startled birds with a disturbance caused by more than one rider? If the birds rose to the air in fright, would they make enough din to capture the attention of the sheriff and his men?

With no time for further contemplation, Robin aimed and released his arrow. The distance was long, but his arrow was true, and any sound it may have made entering the tree trunk was lost in the instant and raucous cawing of the crows. The birds took to the air in an angry black cloud.

"Something on the north road has upset the crows," the guard said warily.

Robin caught a flash of purple through the branches as the sheriff wheeled his mount around to face north.

"This way," the sheriff barked. "All of you. If Sir Richard and the outlaws he calls his men are the cause of the commotion, we shall be upon them momentarily."

The clatter of rapid hooves had barely receded before Robin and Little John burst forth from the small grove and started down the opposite road at a run.

"How long?" Little John asked between breaths.

"Five minutes," Robin replied, pushing past the pain in his calves. "A little more if they continue farther than the tree before some of them turn back."

It wasn't enough time to reach the nearest village and lose themselves among people and buildings.

"The barn." Little John pointed to a small stone farmhouse with an adjoining barn situated at the base of the nearby hillside. "If we are fortunate, most of the animals will be in the pasture."

An isolated building was not ideal, but it was an improvement over a briar patch. And it took them away from the road. Robin clambered over the stone wall and tore across the meadow that separated them from the farmhouse. Aware of Little John pounding the ground behind him, Robin kept his sights on his destination. The door facing the road likely led into the portion of the building where the farmer and his family dwelt. It would be safer for all concerned if no one knew he and Little John were in the vicinity, so they would make directly for the door on the other side of the building and pray that they could come and go with no one the wiser.

Crossing the small yard at a run, they rounded the building and staggered to a halt opposite a wide wooden door. With no one in sight, Robin lifted the latch and stepped inside. The small room smelled of straw and manure. A plow horse standing in one of three narrow stalls raised its head and eyed them curiously. Thankfully, it appeared to be the only other occupant of the barn. Hay was stacked against the opposite wall along with a couple of wooden pails, a pitchfork, a shovel, and a scythe.

Little John followed him in and tilted his head toward the tools. "Worthy weapons should the need arise."

"True." Robin studied the modest space. Wooden beams ran across the roof. A skein of rope hung from a hook at the end of the nearest one. A trough of water, a threadbare, dirty blanket, and an unlit lantern sat beside the door and were the only other objects to be seen. "Let us hope that the farmer and his animals do not return until we are gone from here."

"Agreed." Little John moved over to the small window and pushed open the shutters a fraction. "It is possible to see the road from here."

"And?" Robin moved to stand beside him.

"Horsemen are coming."

"How many?"

"Four," Little John said.

"The sheriff has reverted to his original plan. But we do not know if he intends to search buildings along the way or simply follow the road."

With mounting tension, they waited.

"They are continuing toward Worcester with no sign of slowing," Little John said.

Robin allowed himself a measure of relief. "After they pass by on their return to the bishop's palace, we shall make our way back to Sherwood. Until then, we simply watch and wait."

"And talk."

"Talk?" Robin offered him a surprised look. "I had thought you would wish to rest. I can take the first shift at the window; you may lie in the hay."

"I will claim that temporary comfort soon enough," Little John said. "But now, regardless of our current malodorous and somewhat perilous situation, I wish to speak with you."

Robin's puzzlement deepened. Few would deny that their situation was precarious. This was most definitely not the optimal time for a conversation. "Why?"

"It should be obvious."

"I fear that I can summon no reason that is remotely obvious."

Little John sighed. "Then it is as I suspected. You are a numskull."

"I beg your pardon."

"You are a numskull."

Robin glared at Little John. "Would you care to elaborate?"

"If I had the details, I surely would."

"What details?" Robin demanded. "You are speaking in riddles."

"What did you say or do to Marian to cause her to all but ignore you when we left?"

"You want to speak of Marian now? Whilst we are running for our lives?"

"We are not currently running," Little John said. "Indeed, a helpful discussion will pass the time nicely."

Robin shook his head. "I have nothing to say."

"If you have not been thinking on her this entire journey, I shall eat my hat."

Though Robin wished he could deny it, he could not. "It does not matter how much I have thought on her or on her recent change in behavior; I am unable to answer your question."

Little John raised his eyebrows. "It is as I thought, then. You are in need of my help."

"Whatever gives you that idea?"

"You have been so caught up in your own thoughts that for five days and nights, you scarcely spoke more than two words at a time to either me or Sir Richard," he said. "Any fellow who cannot recognize the mistake he made after pondering it for that long needs assistance."

Robin had hoped Little John had not noticed. He should have known better. "What would you have me tell you?"

"When did you notice the change in Maid Marian's disposition?"

"At the end of our time together in the grove."

"And what had you been doing there?"

Robin kept his eyes fixed on the gap in the shutters. "I encouraged her to face her fears and take up a bow."

"And how did she fare?"

Robin experienced a familiar albeit nonsensical spark of pride at Marian's success in using her new weapon for the first time. "Remarkably well."

"Was she happy when that first arrow was spent, or did it cause her further distress?" Little John asked with startling perception.

"I believe it pleased her to know that she had overcome so large a hurdle."

"Hmm." Little John ran his hand across the back of his neck. "There is something else, then." He paused. "Exactly how did you express your pleasure at her success?"

Robin had no desire to share anything more with his friend. It was time to move on from this line of questioning. "When we leave here, I believe we should stop to eat at the next inn that we come upon."

Employing his typical obstinacy, Little John disregarded Robin's blatant change of subject. "What happened when you kissed her?"

Robin frowned. "I said nothing about kissing Marian."

"You had no need to," Little John said smugly. "But you have yet to answer my question."

"You shall be waiting a long time."

"Not if you sincerely wish to know what is ailing Marian."

Robin looked away, his desire for some small portion of privacy battling his desperation to understand what had happened between him and Marian. For several minutes, he maintained an awkward silence. But then his desperation won out. "She returned my kiss," he said.

"The saints be praised for that," Little John said. "And what happened afterward?"

"I apologized."

With an aghast expression, Little John rubbed his hands over both his ears. "Please repeat that. I must have misheard."

"I apologized," Robin said.

Little John slapped his forehead with his palm. "I was wrong. To call you a numbskull is wholly insufficient for an error of this magnitude."

Robin felt his hackles rise. "You would call me out for being a gentleman? Marian's emotions were raw. I had no right to take advantage of that."

"That may be, but I have no doubt she maintained complete control of her senses," Little John argued. "Marian is made of sterner stuff than you know. She did not waver for one moment when we asked for her assistance with your rescue, even though her role was the most challenging of all."

"I am fully aware of her courage. She has shown it in more ways than you know."

"Well then"—Little John threw his hands in the air—"whatever possessed you to apologize for kissing her?"

"Is that so wrong?"

"It is the very worst thing you could have done."

Clinging to his rapidly diminishing convictions, Robin raised his chin. "Or else the most noble."

Little John eyed him incredulously. "Unbelievable. After five days and five nights, you have yet to see this from Marian's perspective."

"Pray, enlighten me," Robin said, more irritated than he cared to admit.

"By allowing you to kiss her, Marian lowered her guard. By returning your kiss, she expressed a desire to further what promised to be a singular and wondrous development in your relationship. But at its conclusion, instead of offering her reassurance that she had interpreted your actions correctly, you told her that you were sorry the kiss had occurred."

As the truth behind Little John's insight entered Robin's heart, a rock the size of a boulder took up residence in his stomach. Marian's stumbling retreat following his apology finally made sense. As difficult as it was to accept, Little John was surely correct. This was the only possible explanation for her immediate withdrawal. Which meant that, like it or not, Robin truly was the greatest of numbskulls and fools.

He ran shaky fingers through his hair. Now that he saw his mistake, he was frantic to undo it. "Heaven help me, Little John. Will she ever offer me a chance to explain myself?"

Little John shot him an astonished look. "Well, that took far less persuasion than I had anticipated."

"I shall allow you three minutes to soak in your own brilliance," Robin said. "But that is all. After that, I expect your humble assistance."

Little John's astonishment quickly turned to laughter. "I guessed as much, but this simply proves it. You, my fine fellow, have fallen completely in love with Maid Marian."

His friend's observation settled upon Robin with a veracity that could not be denied. There was so much he had yet to learn about Marian—but he wished to know everything. There were so many things he already admired and loved in her, and he instinctively knew he would find more. It was a stunning and somewhat frightening realization, yet it brought with it new hope.

"I believe my feelings for her began all those weeks ago at the market," he admitted.

Little John slapped his hand upon Robin's shoulder. "I would agree, and if I were you, I would tell her as much as soon as we return."

"And if she refuses to believe me?"

"Then you shall have to demonstrate the depth of your feelings in a deeply personal and fully repentant way." Little John's eyes shone with mirth. "Do you require my assistance with that also?"

Robin ignored him. It was a hard-earned show of discipline, but it would be his only chance for peace for the remainder of their journey. "Make use of the hay to catch up on sleep," he said. "Depending upon which one comes first, I shall wake you within the hour or when the sheriff and his men return."

"I cannot decide if I wish that to be soon to shorten the agony of waiting or a considerable time from now so that we may both sleep."

"Soon," Robin said forcibly. "If the sheriff passes this farmhouse with no thought of examining it, he is more dim-witted than I supposed. But I shall accept his carelessness gratefully and will happily put as many furlongs as possible between us before morning."

"What of that inn you mentioned so recently?" Little John said.

"If we travel quickly, we should reach one soon after dawn."

Little John issued a disapproving snort. "I had thought you knew of one nearby."

"I would argue that safety is of more importance than convenience at present," Robin said. "Besides, the farther we travel tonight, the shorter the distance we shall have ahead of us." And the sooner they would reach Sherwood Forest.

The words remained unspoken, but to his credit, Little John moved away from the window, slid his bow from his shoulder, and dropped onto the hay. He stretched out and set his arm across his eyes. "I shall take advantage of a few minutes' peace to dream of our next hot meal."

Robin took Little John's place at the window. He did not ask for clarification, but he thought it likely that his friend was anticipating Marian's stew rather than anything a local inn might produce.

— · · ✳ · · —

The sun was lowering in the sky, and Little John was enjoying his second nap when Robin finally spotted the sheriff and his men returning. The sheriff sat stiffly upon his mount, his face forward. And no matter the distance that separated them, Robin recognized the man's habitual scowl and simmering fury. It was likely that his men had already been the recipients of a tongue lashing. Their solemn expressions and weary postures suggested that they were well aware of their failure. But when one of them turned in his saddle to study the farmhouse and then urged his horse forward to speak with the sheriff, Robin tensed. Mayhap not every man had given up hope of finding the outlaws.

The guard pointed to the farmhouse, and the sheriff studied it for a moment. Then, shouting an order to his men, he steered his mount off the road and onto the track that led to the unpretentious building.

Robin abandoned the window and was at Little John's side in an instant. "Little John." He shook his friend's shoulder.

With a start, Little John bolted into a sitting position. "How soon will they be upon us?"

"One minute at most."

In an instant, Little John was on his feet and reaching for his bow. "Are they riding together still?"

"Aye." Robin returned to the window. "If they are foolish enough to limit their search to the farmer's dwelling space, we may yet escape without detection. But if they come to the barn, we shall be forced to take them on."

"Two against four," Little John said. "Not the best odds, and yet, we have known worse."

The men were dismounting in the yard. They were close enough now that Robin could hear the sheriff's brusque voice issuing orders.

"Wilmott! Come with me! You two, check the barn!"

"It appears that it will be two against two," Robin said, reaching for the old horse blanket.

"Good." Little John slid his bow onto his shoulder and took up the shovel. "Better odds by far."

"Aye. As long as we prevent the men who enter the barn from alerting the others to our presence."

Sometime earlier, Robin had seen a young child and a woman—presumably the girl's mother—exit the farmhouse only to return a little while later with eggs in a basket. They'd gone back inside, and he'd heard their muted voices through the door that led from the barn into the farmhouse's living quarters. There'd been no sign of the farmer. He was likely working out in the fields still. His wife would undoubtedly feel obligated to allow the sheriff and his man into their home. But how long would the sheriff linger there?

"So, we disable those sent to the barn before they sound an alarm." Little John pressed himself against the wall beside the door and tightened his grip on the shovel. "Should be easy enough."

"Even if we best them straightway, keeping them quiet will be the greatest challenge." Pulling his knife from his belt, Robin pierced the worn fabric of the blanket and cut off a strip.

Little John eyed him knowingly. "It is just as well that filthy rags are as efficacious as clean ones when one wishes to silence an unwelcome visitor."

"Aye."

Men's voices sounded, drawing nearer.

"I'll take the first one," Little John murmured. "You take the second."

Robin tore a second strip off the blanket and stuffed the two pieces under his belt. The door latch lifted. He darted behind the nearest stall and nocked his arrow.

A gust of fresh air blew in. Heavy, hesitant steps followed. Robin held perfectly still.

"Looks like one old 'orse is all that's in 'ere," a man said.

"Ya'd best check the stalls," another responded.

"You do it," the first one said. "I've 'ad me fill of walkin' through muck on this fool's errand."

"Stop yer moanin'. The sooner we've checked the stalls, the sooner we can be gone from 'ere."

Footsteps—this time more purposeful—moved toward Robin. Then the door thudded closed.

"Oy!" one of the guards cried out in alarm.

Guessing it had been Little John who'd shut the door, Robin stepped out from behind the stall's short wall, his bow ready. The two guards had swung around to face Little John, but his friend appeared unperturbed. Holding the shovel the way he would have grasped a quarterstaff, Little John swung at the first guard's legs. With a mangled cry, the guard went down.

The second guard lunged forward, his sword flashing. Little John swiveled and parried with the shovel, forcing the guard into the shadowy recesses of the barn. The felled guard struggled back onto his feet, preparing to go after them.

"Don't move!" Robin warned.

The hobbling man turned, took one look at the arrow aimed directly at his chest, and dropped his sword. It clattered to the ground. Robin moved closer and kicked the weapon out of the way. Grunts and thuds echoed behind him.

"Sit," Robin ordered. "Utter a word, and I release the arrow."

The guard dropped to the floor as if his quaking knees were glad of the excuse.

"Little John?" Robin spoke softly.

Something fell over—a bucket, most likely—and the horse whinnied nervously.

Little John uttered a low curse. "Can you not fight like a man?"

"Little John," Robin repeated, not daring to divert his gaze or his aim from the man before him. "I believe it would be in our best interest if you finished your contest forthwith."

"Hear that, you good-for-nothing fellow?" Little John growled. "We must needs cut our time together short."

"Then you'd best surrender," the guard panted.

The ring of his sword hitting the shovel's metal blade filled the barn, and the guard at Robin's feet flinched. Robin's jaw tightened. If the battling men made much more noise, the sheriff would end his inspection of the farmer's house and turn his attention to the barn.

"Make haste, Little John!" Robin said.

There was another loud thud, followed by a moan, and then Little John bounded into Robin's circle of vision and reached for the rope hanging from the crossbeam.

"I shall have his hands bound momentarily," he said, pulling his knife from his belt and slicing off a portion of the rope.

"Very well," Robin said. "And when you've done the same with this fellow, take the fabric from my tunic and tie it around their mouths."

Little John hurried away, and without relaxing his vigil over the quivering guard at his feet, Robin strained to make out the voices on the other side of the stone wall. The sheriff's impatience permeated his angry words, but he was yet within the farmhouse. Unfortunately, since it would take very little time to search the humble dwelling, that would likely not be the case much longer.

Thankfully, Little John had both guards trussed and gagged in short order. Finally able to shoulder his bow, Robin drew a few coins from his purse to cover the cost of a new blanket and rope and tossed them onto the old blanket remnants before joining Little John at the door.

"It was good of the sheriff and his men to leave us their horses," Little John said, carefully lifting the latch.

Robin stifled a grin. After all these years, it should come as no surprise that Little John's thoughts mirrored his own.

They paused to listen. The creak of another set of hinges reached them.

"The sheriff is leaving the farmhouse!" Robin warned. "Go now. Claim one horse for yourself and take the reins of another."

He caught the flash of Little John's teeth one second before his friend took off across the open yard. Robin bolted after him.

"There!" The sheriff's furious voice reached them from the farmhouse door. "Catch them!"

Footsteps pounded across the yard, but Robin and Little John had gained the waiting horses. Leaping into the saddle of the nearest mount, Robin reached for the straps of the one standing beside it. Little John was already astride a large black destrier and was making for the road, with the sheriff's stallion cantering alongside his mount.

"Gah!" Robin touched his heels to his horse's sides, and the well-trained animal instantly sprang forward. "Fear not, Sheriff," Robin called. "You have only to travel as far as the nearest village on foot. We shall leave your horses with the blacksmith there." And then, without bothering to turn back, Robin lowered himself in the saddle and chased after Little John.

CHAPTER 26

Mariah slid the wooden paddle Will had made for her into the opening of the rustic oven and rotated the closest loaf of bread half a turn before doing the same for the three lined up beside it.

"No nasty bread for you this time, Lady Kluck," she muttered. "Third time's a charm, and I'm determined to conquer this skill."

After two failed attempts that had ended in loaves with burnt crusts and doughy interiors, Mariah had decided her only recourse was to stay beside the oven and watch the loaves cook. If medieval bakers throughout the centuries could manage to make edible bread this way, she could too. After all, she was the sous-chef who had mastered making a perfect Baked Alaska in an air fryer.

She shifted one of the loaves again. Already, she had discovered the importance of rotating the position of the bread frequently.

Ellen appeared around the corner with a bucket of goat milk in hand. "Mercy, M-Marian. The forest has never s-smelled so good."

"It's certainly an improvement over the burnt aroma that has been so prevalent over the last couple of days."

Ellen laughed. "And it l-likely explains the steady stream of men who have p-passed by here. They have a p-personal interest in your success."

"Ah, that would explain it," Mariah said. "I wondered why they weren't gathering around the pot of pottage. Are you managing that all right?"

Unwilling to leave the bread to cook unwatched, Mariah had placed Ellen in charge of the pottage.

"Aye." Ellen set down the pail of milk. "I added the thyme j-just as you said, and when David stopped b-by, I allowed him a small taste." Her cheeks pinked slightly. "He declared it the b-best pottage ever and offered to w-watch over it while I did the milking."

Mariah smiled. David o' Doncaster was developing a growing tendency for showing up wherever Ellen was located. And it hadn't escaped Mariah's notice that when rain had forced everyone to gather in the cave rather than the clearing the last two evenings, he and Ellen had chosen to sit together in a quieter spot at the rear of the cave. Mariah had caught the protective older-brother look that Will had tossed their way on more than one occasion, but he hadn't seemed unduly worried. For her part, Mariah was thrilled that Ellen was developing friendships—and maybe the hope of something more—among the men of Sherwood.

Pushing aside the dull ache that seemed to have taken up permanent residence in her heart since Robin had left, Mariah checked the bread again. The loaves were turning golden brown. Not much longer, and they should be cooked through.

"Please give David my thanks for his help—that is, as long as he plans to stir the pot rather than repeatedly sample."

"I told h-him that one spoonful was his first and last until everyone gathers for their meal." Ellen picked up the pail, preparing to take it into the cold cave used for food storage. "And I t-trust him."

The ache in Mariah's heart intensified. Over the last eleven days, she'd had plenty of time to ponder on her experience in the grove with Robin, and she'd come to realize that though her confidence in reading his nonverbal cues had taken a beating, her trust in him remained. As long as she protected her heart, she knew she was safe with Robin, and she missed him horribly.

She'd spent most of the evenings he'd been gone sitting in the clearing beside Friar Tuck. The kind-hearted cleric had regaled her with stories about the arrival of each of the Merry Men in Sherwood Forest. The tales had helped her come to know the individuals better, and they had also increased her appreciation for the unity found among the diverse group of men and a strengthened admiration for Robin's leadership abilities.

"Do you think I can trust all the men to do nothing but sniff at the bread if I take it out and leave it to cool on the slab?" Mariah asked.

"It will t-test them sorely," Ellen replied, humor shining in her eyes. "But I d-daresay they each know that anyone who r-risks breaking off a piece would be p-pummeled at every wrestling match for at l-least a month."

Mariah laughed. Wrestling matches and quarterstaff battles were regular forms of entertainment in the clearing. She far preferred the evenings when Allan a Dale sang or the men participated in impromptu archery competitions, but she recognized the need for those who were less skilled with the bow to have their turn in the spotlight. Thankfully, no one had suggested that she participate in the archery competitions since the first time. She desperately hoped that when it happened—for she knew it would eventually—she would be ready.

"Do you plan to return to the pottage when you've put away the milk?" Mariah asked.

"Aye. I t-told David I would relieve him of his stirring d-duty as soon as this chore was completed."

It was likely that David would stick around, which meant Ellen would have all the company she needed.

"If you don't mind, I might take a walk while the bread cools?"

"Aye, you do that," Ellen said cheerfully. "There's still t-time afore the men gather to eat."

She started up the steps to the cave's entrance, and Mariah turned her attention to carefully drawing the artisan loaves of bread out of the oven. The paddle Will had crafted was not unlike a future-day pizza peel, and by using a long-handled wooden spoon, Mariah was able to push the loaves onto the paddle and then slide them off onto the stone slab David had set beside the oven. Once they were positioned in a tidy row, she checked underneath each one. Golden brown but not burnt. And when a tap on their upper crusts produced the desired hollow sound, Mariah couldn't prevent a wide smile from forming. She wouldn't know for sure until she cut into the loaves and tasted them, but from all outward appearances, she'd baked four perfect wholewheat loaves.

Reaching into the pocket of her apron, she withdrew a square of linen and carefully covered the bread. The cloth should be enough to protect the bread from flies and hungry men but would allow the remaining heat and steam in the bread to escape. That done, she ran up the steps to the cave.

Ellen was on her way out. They exchanged smiles but didn't stop to talk any longer, and by the time Mariah reached her pallet, her friend's footsteps had faded to nothing. Wasting no time, Mariah picked up her bow and slid it over her shoulder. She attached the quiver to her waist with her apron strings, and then hurried out of the cave.

The trail to the grove was completely familiar now. Mariah had made this walk at least once a day since Robin had left. On her first visit there alone, she'd forcibly blocked out all thoughts of the earth-shattering kiss they'd shared and had sat on the pondering rock, reliving her experience shooting an arrow with Robin's arms around her. She had borrowed from his strength, but she couldn't do that forever. She'd known that first day that she needed to stand before the oak tree with bow and arrow in hand and aim for the gnarly knot all by herself. The second day, she'd brought along the equipment Robin had given her. Her shots had been shaky, and her aim had been abysmal. But she'd crossed a seemingly insurmountable barrier. And every day from then on, her ability had improved, and her love of the sport had steadily come flowing back.

The rain they'd experienced the last couple of days had left the ground wet and muddy. Water droplets clung to some of the leaves, and as she passed, low-lying bushes dripped moisture onto her skirt and sleeves. For about the millionth time, she wondered how Robin and Little John were faring. Robin had suggested that inclement weather may slow their journey. She hoped that was why there had been no sign of them after ten days. She couldn't countenance the alternative.

She'd watched for any sign of concern in Friar Tuck when they'd spoken about the missing men the night before, but he'd seemed blissfully sure that they would make their way back as soon as their circumstances allowed. He'd been far more worried about Will's report that the Sheriff of Nottingham had set guards to keep watch over the comings and goings at the White Stag Inn.

Mariah would be feeling far more reassured about Robin and Little John's safety if they'd received a text message or had access to a Find My Friends app. But those luxuries were lost to her now, and she was starting to realize that those living in this earlier time period were forced to rely far more on patience and faith than their future counterparts. Those particular virtues would take work to cultivate, but she wanted more of both in her life.

The gurgle of the stream welcomed her into the grove. Grateful that Robin had shared this special place with her, she walked over to the pondering rock, brushed away the damp leaves lying on its surface, and sat. For a moment, she simply soaked in the peace and beauty of the spot. She was not sure how breathing the air here had the power to diminish her worries and calm her fears, but she felt it every time she came.

Leaving her seat, she walked across the grove to the old oak tree that usually served as her target. A few days ago, she'd hung a piece of fabric on the trunk. On it, she'd drawn concentric circles with a piece of charcoal. The bull's-eye in the center was black. It was the closest she'd come to creating the kind of target she was accustomed to, and it had worked perfectly. After smoothing down the wet fabric, she walked back toward the trees on the opposite side of the grove, turned, and readied her bow.

The breeze picked up, dancing through the branches above her head. Mariah waited. When the rattle of leaves ceased, she drew back her bowstring and released the arrow. It sailed through the air, landing in the darkened center of the fabric with a satisfying thud. Mariah smiled and reached for another arrow in the quiver. All being well, it would not be long before she was ready to participate in Sherwood Forest's archery contests.

Robin had not been mistaken. The smell of freshly baked bread was growing stronger and stronger the closer he and Little John drew to their camp.

"Tell me the scent of hot bread is not a cruel trick my nose is playing on me after smelling nothing but mud and wet vegetation for days," Little John moaned. "I believe my stomach has taken to eating my liver for want of any real food."

"If your nose is playing tricks, then mine is doing the same," Robin said. "However, methinks it more likely that during our absence, David finished the oven, and Marian is using it."

"By all the saints, if Marian has learned to make bread in that excuse for an oven—" Little John broke off and gave Robin a pointed look. "Mark my words, Robin, if you do not take that remarkable maiden to wife, I shall do it myself."

Robin likely should have laughed, but he could not bring himself to do it. Now that he was minutes away from setting eyes on Marian again, an unfamiliar nervousness had taken hold of him. He needed to speak with her straightway, but their conversation required more privacy than the cave or clearing afforded. Would she agree to walk with him?

Male voices reached him from the direction of the clearing. It would not be long before all the men gathered for their evening meal. They would expect a full report on his and Little John's undertaking in Hereford, and whereas their enthusiastic response over the success of the endeavor would once have excited him, it now seemed unimportant. He was far more anxious about the response he would receive when he approached Marian. He took a steadying breath. If his time away had made her even more resolute in her determination to maintain a barrier between them, he would merely have to break it down. One painful rock at a time.

They reached the entrance to the cave and found no one there. Little John made directly for the stone slab beside the oven and lifted a corner of the linen cloth covering.

"You are hereby forgiven for urging me to walk faster every step of the way from Hereford," Little John said. "To arrive in time to eat this bread fresh from the oven is worth the aching legs and feet."

Robin chuckled. "You'd best step away before you are tempted beyond what you can bear."

With a groan, Little John dropped the cloth. "I daresay I needed that warning."

"I daresay you did," Will agreed, entering the clearing with a welcoming smile. "I am right glad to see you both returned. Though I confess, coming upon Little John standing so close to that freshly baked bread was cause for concern."

"Justly so," Little John said. "I have not eaten a good meal in days."

Ignoring Little John's typical complaint, Robin studied Will more closely. His friend's pleasure at seeing them again was clear, but there was another emotion hovering just beneath the surface. Something that portended less agreeable news and instantly ignited Robin's unease.

"Was all well in Sherwood during our absence?" he asked.

"Aye," Will replied. "David bested Thomas in a wrestling match, and Thomas took the loss poorly, but an extra serving of Marian's pottage soothed his ruffled feathers fast enough. Her meals have been the source of such praise that I suspect Allan will compose a ballad about them ere long."

Robin's relief that whatever was causing the furrow across Will's brow had nothing to do with Marian was immediate, but he was unwilling to disregard his impression that something was amiss.

"I am glad for the men," he said, "But I should like to know what it is that has caused the lines of worry on your forehead."

Will gave him a startled look. "It seems that I must work harder to hide my emotions."

"Not at all. I would much rather have a forthright conversation with my men than be left guessing." His recent dialogue with Little John was clear proof of that truth. "So out with it."

"The sheriff is up to something," Will said.

Little John grunted. "He is always up to something."

"Aye. But usually, his activities are centered upon capturing Robin or exacting more money from poor citizens. This time, he is setting traps for those in town who are loyal to the men of Sherwood."

Robin's jaw tightened. Will was right. This was a new and concerning turn of events. "How so?"

"He returned to town three days ago. Within hours, he'd set men to watching the comings and goings at the White Stag, Much's mill, Bertram the Baker's shop, and certain market stalls. Mistress Talitha managed to get one message out, warning us to stay away until the sheriff assigns his men elsewhere."

"Most certainly," Robin agreed. "But the fact that he has singled out those in town who have aided us in the past is disturbing. How did the sheriff learn of our connection with those people?"

"Someone must have inadvertently let something slip," Will said.

"Or purposely spoken out." Little John frowned. "I imagine the sheriff would pay well for such information."

"Either way, we can learn little more until the sheriff becomes disillusioned with this devious approach and calls off his guards,"

Robin said. "If our presence in town endangers more than ourselves, we must bide our time."

Will nodded. "As soon as Mistress Talitha's message reached us, Friar Tuck told the men the same. No one has left the forest since then."

"We shall be doubly glad of our food storage if this latest threat lingers," Little John said.

"Aye." Robin glanced at the entrance to the cave. An hour ago, conducting an inventory of their supplies had not entered his mind. Now it was something he intended to do first thing on the morrow.

"Little John! Robin! You are b-back!" Ellen appeared on the path that led to the clearing and greeted them with pleasure.

"We are," Little John said, smothering the concern on his face with a smile. "And just in time for dinner."

She laughed. "The m-men will be right glad to have you j-join them. They are g-gathering in the clearing even now."

"Is Marian also there?" Robin asked.

Ellen shook her head. "She took a walk after the b-bread came out of the oven. But I expect her b-back shortly."

A walk in the forest. Robin needed to consult with Friar Tuck about the news Will had shared, but if he could meet up with Marian before she returned, this might be the very opportunity he had been seeking to speak with her alone.

"Do you know the direction she took?"

Ellen pointed down the trail he and Little John had just traveled. "She goes that w-way every day."

Every day. That sounded as though she were set upon a specific destination. Somewhere like the pondering-rock grove.

"I shall go that way to meet her," he said. "If either of us is delayed, have the men start eating without us. I feel sure that Friar Tuck would help serve the meal."

"Of course," Ellen said. "We shall m-manage very well."

She turned to gather the bread and set the loaves in the basket she carried.

"I hope you are significantly delayed," Little John said, keeping his voice low.

Robin set his hand on his friend's shoulder. "I assume that is merely because you wish to claim my portion of bread."

Little John inclined his head. "Well, there is that too."

Robin managed a faint smile, and then, offering up a silent prayer that he had guessed correctly, he started down the path that led to the grove at a run.

He heard the distinctive thwack of an arrow penetrating a tree before he saw Marian. Not wanting to startle her, he slowed his steps and approached cautiously. She was standing with her back to him, her beautiful hair flowing loose, and a bow in hand. She bent her head to withdraw another arrow from the quiver at her waist, and his gaze shifted to the target she had created on the distant oak. Half a dozen arrows hung suspended in the tree trunk, all tightly packed inside the target's small, dark center.

His smile was instant. She had been practicing. And if the location of today's arrows was any indication, she had developed a feel for her new bow and reclaimed her skill. Slipping his own bow off his shoulder, Robin reached for an arrow. Nocking it swiftly, he stepped to his left until he had a clear shot of the tree. Then he raised his bow and waited. Marian adjusted her stance, drew back her bowstring, aimed, and shot. As expected, the arrow hit the center of the target. Two heartbeats later, Robin's arrow landed beside it.

Marian gasped and swung around. "Robin!" For one fleeting moment, her face illuminated with pleasure, but then a polite mask doused the light. "When did you get back?"

"Just now," he said. "We were led home by the aroma of your freshly baked bread."

"The bread!" With a stricken expression, she glanced at the lengthening shadows tracing the grass. "I lost track of the time. The men will be wanting their meal." She ran toward the tree and began pulling her arrows free.

Robin joined her. He removed his arrow and then claimed the last of hers. Handing them to her, he caught the slight tremble of her fingers. He tightened his jaw. His presence was causing her distress. She would not have shot so cleanly unless her hand had been completely steady moments ago.

"There is no need for you to rush. Ellen and Friar Tuck will take care of serving the men. I told them to start without us."

Her head shot up. "Why would you do that?"

"Because I need to speak with you. To offer you yet another apology."

She took two steps back. "No. That is not necessary. You have already apologized enough."

"Please, Marian," he begged. "If you offer me nothing more, please grant me a moment of your time to hear me out."

"If this is about our kiss, nothing more needs to be said. You can forget about it. Act like it never happened. We're both adults and can move forward with no hard feelings."

"I cannot do that," he said.

He recognized the shock in her eyes.

"You cannot move forward without hard feelings?"

"No," he said. "I cannot forget about it or act like it never happened."

She opened her mouth as if to speak and then closed it again.

"Marian, that kiss—our kiss—was unlike anything I have ever experienced before. I will never forget the way it made me feel. The way you make me feel." He ran his fingers through his hair. "No matter what occurs between us after this, that matchless experience will remain with me forever."

"But you said—" She swallowed. "Even if the memory remains with you, I understand that you regret kissing me, and I'll not let it happen again."

There it was. Little John had been right. Relief that his friend had correctly identified the miscommunication mingled with sorrow for the needless pain his words had caused.

"No, my sweet Marian. My apology was motivated by my worry that you would think I had taken advantage of your fragile condition. I had all but forced you to face a deep fear, to relive a traumatic event, and then I took you in my arms. I offered you little means of escape had you wished one."

She was staring at him. "You thought I felt trapped?"

"Did you?"

"Robin." Her voice was barely above a whisper. "I could not have shot that first arrow without your arms around me. You offered me strength when I needed it most. That is the very opposite of taking advantage of me."

"That truly is what you believe?"

"Yes."

Hardly daring to hope that she would allow it, he reached for her hand. Her fingers curved around his. They were no longer trembling.

"Please permit me to do what I set out to do when I came in search of you—to apologize once more. Not for kissing you but for expressing my concerns so poorly. And for causing us both to suffer so unnecessarily."

She studied him with a puzzled expression. "If your earlier apology really meant nothing more than what you've just told me, why did you suffer afterward?"

"Because our connection was gone, and I did not know why. After you left the grove that day, you showed more interest in speaking to Friar Tuck and Little John than you did to me." He smiled ruefully. "It would have been easier to feel grateful that you were developing deeper friendships amongst my band of men had it not seemed that those friendships had taken the place of the one we had shared."

"I think perhaps I owe you an apology too." She hung her head. "I should not have ignored you the way I did, even if I did it partially for the sake of another Marian."

Robin placed the forefinger of his free hand beneath her chin and gently raised it. He would need time to prove to her that there was no other Marian in his life, but this day was for mending things with the woman standing before him. "I believe it is my turn to say, no more apologies."

She gave him a watery smile. "What now, then?"

"Now I tell you that you have had a special place in my heart since the day I kissed you in the marketplace."

Her eyes widened. "But you didn't even know me then."

"No, but I wished to. And that desire only grew stronger after you came to warn me of the sheriff's dastardly plan to trick the butcher out of his meager payment." He could go on to tell her of his search for her and his feelings when he recognized her at the archery tournament, but he thought those confessions would be better suited for a later date. "I wish to know all about you, Marian. The world you came from and your place in it, your likes and dislikes, your joys and fears. Everything that makes you the woman you are today."

"That would take a huge number of conversations," she said.

"That is my hope."

She smiled. "Will you tell me more about the real Robin Hood too?"

"Anything you wish to know." He paused. "Except perhaps the details surrounding the times Little John has bested me in quarter-staff matches or when Friar Tuck has reprimanded me for neglecting to say long enough prayers."

She laughed. It was a beautiful, happy sound, and Robin's heart lifted. They had much yet to learn about each other, but he looked forward to every minute of that journey. His gaze traced her beautiful face and settled on her lips.

"Marian," he said quietly. "May I kiss you?"

"With no apologies?"

"None whatsoever."

"Then, yes," she said, drawing her fingers free from his so that she could rest her hands against his chest. "I would like that very much."

He wrapped his arms around her waist, and as he drew her close, he was struck with the startling realization that Robin Hood, the infamous outlaw of Sherwood Forest, was about to embark upon the greatest adventure of his lifetime. The thought filled him with unmeasurable joy, and as he lowered his lips to Marian's and the sparks that flew between them became a burning flame, he made a silent pledge that he would do all in his power to prove himself worthy of the trust this extraordinary woman had placed in him.

CHAPTER 27

Mariah poured the basting liquid over the deer carcass and turned the handle on the large spit that hung above the fire. The flames sizzled as the juices dripped off the cooking meat. This would probably be the last time the men would feast on venison until spring. Keeping them all from going hungry would be more challenging in the winter, especially with their food storage prematurely depleted.

The sheriff's men had maintained their vigils over those believed to have assisted Robin and his men far longer than anyone in Sherwood Forest could have anticipated. But the outlaws' commitment to stay clear of the town had had its desired effect. There had been no illegitimate arrests among the shopkeepers, market-stall operators, or tavern owners. Even Much the Miller, who had risked dropping off a sack of flour on his way to Owthorpe a fortnight ago, remained a free man. Perhaps the sheriff had recognized that if he threw all those who furnished Robin and his men with food into the dungeon, he would also be cutting off his own food supply.

Mariah worried about their decreasing stores, but Robin had repeatedly reassured her that they would have sufficient for their needs. She guessed that he and his closest men meant to slip into Nottingham under cover of darkness sometime soon. And though she knew that they would do everything possible to avoid implicating any of the townspeople as collaborators, she feared that Robin's desire to restock their food supply would cause him to risk his own recapture.

The lack of light notwithstanding, she was quite sure the sheriff's guards were as vigilant during the night as they were during the day.

It had been almost three months since Mariah had fled Nottingham to begin her life in Sherwood Forest. In many respects, it felt like a lifetime ago. But it was not nearly so distant a memory as was her life in twenty-first-century London. Sometimes as she was going about her work, making meals for the men of Sherwood, hanging herbs to dry for the winter, and inventorying the food supplies in the rear cave, she would think about her job at Ricardo's and marvel at how different and yet equally fulfilling it was to prepare food for those living in both centuries.

She still thought of her father often, hoping he would one day be reconciled to her unexplained disappearance. She wished she could tell both her father and Patrick at the London Archery Club that she was safe and happy, using her archery skills every day, and very much in love with the only man she knew who could shoot an arrow with more accuracy than she.

She smiled at the memory of their contest in the grove earlier this morning. When her arrow had hit the very center of the mark they'd placed on the beech tree, she'd thought she'd finally bested Robin. But then he'd taken his shot, and his arrow had split hers in two. She should have been indignant that he'd destroyed a perfectly good arrow, but it was hard to be cross when he was the one who supplied her with replacements, especially when he'd celebrated his win with a long and perfectly wonderful kiss.

The grove that Robin had introduced her to on her very first day in the forest continued to be their private safe haven. Unless Robin was away, they visited it together almost every day. His pondering rock had become their conversation rock, and over the days and weeks that had passed, Mariah had answered his many questions about twenty-first-century life. He considered the medical advances, personal conveniences, and future methods of transportation to be fascinating. Other things, such as computers and microwaves and mobile phones were almost more than he could comprehend.

For his part, Robin had shown her how to find peace in the simplicity of life in the forest. He'd also taught her innumerable medieval life skills, including how to light a fire with flint, how to identify edible plants, and how to use the stars to navigate her way home.

It was bewildering, really, that she could feel such a strong sense of home for a series of caves and an open clearing in the middle of a vast forest. But the sensation was too real to deny. And on the few occasions that she'd accompanied Robin and his men to other areas of the forest on hunting expeditions, she was always grateful to return to this sanctuary afterward.

Of course, the familial relationships she enjoyed with Ellen and the Merry Men only enhanced the feeling of homecoming. She had gone from being an often-lonely only child to someone who could claim a devoted younger sister and over two dozen brothers who were both fiercely loyal and typically tormenting. And though Little John's teasing occasionally bordered on irritating, a single warning look from Robin was usually enough to cause him to redirect his mischief-making toward Allan a Dale or Friar Tuck.

Mariah smiled to herself. Fortunately for Little John, he was wise enough to refrain from teasing Ellen. Will may have allowed some friendly quips, but David o' Doncaster was far too protective of the young woman to put up with any nonsense. It wouldn't surprise Mariah at all if David turned that general protectiveness into something more official and personal very soon. She hoped he would, and if the happiness Ellen exhibited whenever she was with the gentle giant of a man was any indication, Ellen did too.

As though Mariah's thoughts had summoned her, Ellen appeared in the clearing and hurried toward her. "I've s-stoked the fire in the oven," Ellen said. "The l-loaves have risen nicely, so they can g-go in to bake anytime."

"Wonderful. Thank you, Ellen." Mariah ran her arm across her forehead. She would be glad to step away from the roasting meat for a few minutes. "I shall be there shortly."

Ellen surveyed the empty clearing. "The men m-must have gone farther af-field today. It's unusual that they're not b-back by now."

"I think most of them went for more firewood," Mariah said. There had been frost on the ground the last few mornings that had delivered a new sense of urgency to their preparations. The men had been gathering fuel just as the women had been keeping watch over the food supply.

"They'll c-come home hungry, then," Ellen said.

Mariah smiled. "When do they not?"

"Do you smell that roasting venison, men?" Little John's voice reached them from beyond the line of trees. "That is my payment for carrying this wretched log on my shoulder all this time. By all the saints, I believe it has gained twenty stones in weight over the last furlong."

Ellen's humor-filled eyes met Mariah's as Little John staggered into the clearing hauling a log that was almost as long as he was tall. Behind him, Robin and David were bearing up the two ends of a second log. They were followed by a dozen more men, each loaded down with wood. One after the other, they crossed to the far side of the clearing, where two axes marked the spot where today's haul would be chopped into firewood.

With a mighty groan, Little John dropped his load. "Marian!" he called, brushing his hands off on his sap-covered tunic. "I shall be ready to eat the moment you say the word."

"One hour more, Little John," she called back. "Which is just enough time for you to go to the stream to clean yourself more thoroughly."

She heard Robin's chuckle over Little John's groan and the thud of wood dropping to the ground. With a smile, she basted the meat one more time and had just set down the bowl and brush so she could check on the readiness of the oven when Robin came up behind her and slid his arms around her waist.

"Are you dirty too?" she asked, leaning her head back so that she could see his face.

His lips twitched. "I missed you."

"I'm very glad," she said, "but that's not what I asked."

"Not nearly as dirty as Little John," he said. He dropped a soft kiss on her forehead. "And today's haul was worth a little soil on our hands and clothes. It will keep us in fuel for some time."

It was good news, but Mariah could not help but feel a pang of misgiving over what was ahead. Surviving a winter in the forest felt much more daunting than being here during the warm summer months. "Will we manage, Robin?"

"Aye, my love. The men and I have done it many times before. We will likely spend more time in the cave than you are accustomed to, but it will be warm enough, and, I give you my word, we shall not go hungry." He smiled gently. "In truth, if you are beside me, I can think of nowhere else I would rather be."

"I have come to love the forest too," she admitted. "Even if it doesn't have flushing toilets."

He raised an eyebrow. "If you could but remember exactly how they function, we might set David o' Doncaster to work on creating one of those contrivances."

"I'll think about it," she said. "But I know almost nothing about plumbing."

He kissed her again, this time claiming her lips and lingering there for a few blissful moments. "At least we have running water," he murmured. "Even if its temperature is either cold or frigid."

Fighting back laughter, she turned to fully face him, pulled a leaf from his dark hair, and pushed him away. "Go join your men," she said. "I want nothing more to do with you until you are clean."

— · ✳ · —

Robin had just taken his place beside Marian, a trencher of food in his hand, when Friar Tuck entered the clearing followed by eight men dressed in similar brown robes to the one the jovial friar habitually wore.

"See here, friends," Friar Tuck called. "I have brought eight brothers to share our meal." He jingled a small purse hanging from his belt. "They offered me fifty pounds for the opportunity to dine with the men of renown in Sherwood Forest."

Robin rose, eyeing the friars curiously. It was far more likely that the coins had come into Friar Tuck's possession through skillful persuasion than as a generous offering, but those who were truly devoted to the work of the church rarely carried so much money on their persons.

"You are most welcome," Robin said. "We have just now sat down to eat; please join us."

Each friar stood with head bowed, their long hoods draped low over their faces, but the one at the head of the group turned toward Robin. "We are most grateful. This appears to be a fine feast."

Vaguely aware that Marian had left her place beside him to help Ellen fill extra goblets with mead, he nodded. "Aye. You have chosen the day of your visit well. It is not often that we dine upon roast venison. We shall be reliant upon smoked and salted meats 'ere long."

"You are not above poaching the king's deer, then?"

Robin folded his arms. If this friar wished to be made welcome, it would behoove him to refrain from calling his hosts to repentance. "We take only what is needful for our survival. And as we spend our time doing the king's work, it would seem to be fair compensation."

The friar gestured toward the sheepskin rugs on the ground. "If we may, we shall sit beside you so that we may converse whilst we eat. I am anxious to hear what manner of royal duties you perform."

It appeared that the friar had taken Robin's words more literally than Robin had intended them to be taken. But if the clerics wished to see the men of Sherwood's efforts to relieve the poor as a royal duty, so much the better.

"Of course," he said. "Be seated. All of you. Maid Marian and Maid Ellen are seeing to your drinks already, and I daresay Friar Tuck will return shortly with meat and bread."

"You have our thanks." The friar who had spoken lowered himself to the ground, and his companions followed suit.

Marian and Ellen handed them each a goblet, and when Marian had reclaimed her place on the sheepskin, Robin sat between her and the talkative friar.

"Pray, feel free to remove your cowls so that you may eat and drink more freely," he said.

"A worthy suggestion," the friar replied, "but we have vowed not to show our faces for twenty-four hours."

"Ah. Well, far be it from me to cause you to break your vows." Robin took up his bread again. "I would surmise that we have not seen brethren of your order before this. Where do you hail from? And what brings you to Sherwood Forest?"

"We are of the Order of the Black Friar and journeyed here by way of Oxford. The cleric who met us on the road and *suggested* that we pay for a meal in the forest had us leave our horses tied to some trees just beyond this clearing."

Robin knew the spot. They used it often for those who visited on horseback.

"Your mounts will be safe enough there."

Friar Tuck handed the men trenchers overflowing with succulent venison and Marian's fresh bread, and for several minutes, they ate in silence.

"I am impressed by the number of men you have gathered here," the friar said at last. "King Richard himself would be glad of such bodyguards."

"There is not a man here who would not give his life for King Richard," Robin said proudly. "They are as loyal as they are true."

"So you say, but I fail to see how they demonstrate such fidelity when each one of them unlawfully dwell upon King Richard's land and eat his game."

"And yet they are placed in this untenable position as a direct result of King Richard's poor decisions."

There was a moment of complete silence.

"You speak your mind plainly, Robin Hood."

"I do. And though it may be hard for you to separate personal godly devotion from the need to care for His children, I would urge you to consider what King Richard has done. His pilgrimage, though motivated by noble desires, removed him from the very people who needed him most. His unfortunate capture further exacerbated the problem. This country is overset by greedy men who are driven by naught but their own ambition. With nothing more than vague rumors of the king's release reaching England, there is no end in sight for those who have suffered for so long." He shrugged. "And so this band of supposed outlaws does what it can to assist the helpless. We offer little enough, but a few coins or sufficient food to feed hungry mouths for a day or two is more than they would have without our aid."

"You make an interesting case." The friar studied the mead in his goblet. "I assume you would include Prince John amongst those who show such avarice?"

"Prince John, the Sheriff of Nottingham, the Bishop of Hereford—"

The friar's head shot up only to quickly drop again.

"You are surprised by that last name?" Robin asked. "You must not have had any interaction with the supposed man of the cloth, for he does nothing to hide his love of the finer things of the world or his disdain for those beneath his exalted station."

"I am sorry to hear it."

"Aye. But such is the unfortunate state of affairs in England at present."

"I pray there will be a change for the better very soon," the friar said.

"As do we all." Robin raised his goblet. "Here's to good King Richard and his swift return. May his enemies be confounded."

All around the clearing, the men raised their goblets and cheered. "To good King Richard!"

The men's enthusiasm brought a cheerier tone to the gathering, and it was not long before laughter interspersed with the various conversations around the large oak tree. The friars became absorbed in finishing their meal, and Robin had a moment to speak with Marian.

"How do you fancy your chances with the bow this evening?" he asked.

She gave him a knowing look. "Is Little John threatening to beat you in a quarterstaff competition?"

"Your ability to discern my thoughts is disconcerting."

She laughed. "Your thoughts or your concerns?"

"Both." He lowered his voice. "Save me from humiliation at Little John's hands."

Humor shone in her eyes, but she feigned a serious expression. "You would rather be humiliated at mine?"

"Most certainly. You display unparalleled skill; Little John uses brute force and doles out bruises."

It was at least partially true. Should he agree to a match with Little John, Robin's body would ache for days afterward, but everyone in Sherwood Forest acknowledged that the large man's dexterity with the quarterstaff could not be equaled.

"Very well," Marian said. "If the men desire an archery competition, I shall participate. But be warned, I shall not let you win."

Robin chuckled and turned to speak to the friar at his other side. "Are you of a mind to stay for some entertainment? I can promise you a fine show of archery."

The friar's head tilted slightly as though he were considering the offer. "Though we have come from afar, word of your skill with the bow has reached us. I believe we would be fortunate to see a demonstration."

"Then it shall be done," Robin said. "Though, in truth, by the contest's end, methinks you will be more amazed by the skills of another in our midst."

CHAPTER 28

Mariah waited for the men's cheers to subside and then raised her bow. She and Robin were the only ones left in the contest. The leafy garland Friar Tuck had hung for a target on the distant beech tree had one arrow piercing its very center. Robin's arrow. If she were to claim victory, she would need to do what he had done to her in the past—split his arrow clean in two.

She eyed the target once more before shifting her aim a hair-breadth to the right. Silence fell over the clearing. She took a breath and released the bowstring. Her smile was instant. The arrow was true. She knew it without having to watch its steady course. It seemed that Robin did too. He crossed the distance between them in three short steps. Lifting her off her feet, he swung her in a wide circle to the sound of his splintering arrow.

"You did it!" His exultant voice was barely audible above the approving roar of the other men. "You are the best archer in all of Sherwood!"

Mariah laughed. "Not at all. That title fully belongs to you. I had an advantage this evening because your arms were tired."

Loud clapping in addition to the cheering interrupted whatever else Robin may have said. He set her back on the ground, and they both turned their attention to the friars. They had come to their feet, and the one who had spoken to Robin during their meal approached.

"I am twice amazed," he said. "Robin Hood, the acclaim you have garnered for your marksmanship was not exaggerated. And,

Maid Marian, I believe you could outshoot every one of the king's guards."

"Thank you, Friar. That is very kind."

"It is nothing but the truth." He inclined his head politely, and as he did so, Mariah heard a strange rustle. It was an unfamiliar sound, yet it stirred a memory. A memory that felt important.

"You have entertained us well." The friar raised his arm to point to the remnants of deer carcass. "And fed us even better." There was an edge to his voice now that hadn't been there before, and as he lowered his arm once more, the rustle came again.

Remembrance came surging back. She'd been in the corridor on her first night at Nottingham Castle, searching for the door that would take her back to McQuivey's Costume Shop, and the castle guard had found her. As he'd walked toward her, she'd heard the rustle of his chainmail. She'd identified it immediately because she'd seen it glistening in the candlelight. This time, she could see nothing, but she was almost positive it was the same noise. But that made no sense. Why would a friar be wearing chainmail?

She'd barely formed the unspoken question when another memory flitted through her mind: Errol Flynn portraying Robin Hood on the big screen, leaping from the branch of a tree to stop a group of abbots riding through Sherwood Forest, unaware that the abbots were, in fact, King Richard and his men.

Suddenly, her heart was beating too fast. Was it possible that that classic film was actually based on fact? Over the last few months, she'd learned how much future stories and movies had distorted Robin's real life. But they had contained sufficient grains of truth for her new life and relationships here to feel uncannily familiar. Was Errol Flynn's encounter with King Richard patterned after what had really happened? If the friar were truly King Richard, it would explain his displeasure over their serving him the king's venison. And it put Robin in serious jeopardy.

She had to speak to Robin. Now. Before he said anything more to the supposed friar that he might later regret.

"Robin." She reached for his hand. "May I speak with you for a minute?"

From beyond the barrier of trees, a horse nickered nervously. A twig cracked. And then another. Robin tensed, his attention shifting from Mariah to the clearing's entrance as Much the Miller stumbled into view and fell to his knees with his arms tied behind his back.

With a shout of alarm, the men sitting closest to the trussed newcomer scrambled to their feet.

"Much!" Little John reached him first. "What is this all about?"

Much's agonized eyes scanned the men until they settled on Robin. "Forgive me, Robin. When the sheriff learned that I'd delivered flour to the forest, 'e 'ad my wife and children thrown in the castle dungeon. The only way 'e'd grant their release was if I led 'im to your camp."

Mariah scarcely had time to register what his words meant before leaves all around the glade trembled, and the sheriff and a dozen of his guards burst through the trees, swords in hand.

"Take them!" the sheriff bellowed, his face alight with triumph.

The men of Sherwood reacted as one. Robin's bow was off his shoulder in an instant. The other outlaws seized whatever weapons they could lay their hands on, ready and willing to enter the fray, no matter the cost.

"Seek shelter, friars," Robin shouted, nocking an arrow and letting it fly.

A guard bearing down on Will Scarlet screamed, his leg buckling as Robin's arrow entered his thigh. Will pounced upon him, claiming the guard's blade before rushing to assist David o' Doncaster, who was fending off two guards with a stout stick.

"Go to the cave, Marian!" Robin urged, nocking another arrow. "Find Ellen and take her with you!" He released the arrow and then took off running.

Shouts, thuds, and the clash of steel filled the air, and for two heartbeats, shock kept Mariah's feet rooted to the ground. Then tearing her gaze from the horrific scene in the clearing, she unshouldered her bow and reached for an arrow. But her quiver was empty. Racing to the spot where she'd eaten her meal, she slid her bow beneath the sheepskin and grabbed the knife lying beside the wooden trencher. Without any arrows, she could not hope to take on a guard, but she could assist another who might.

Clasping the knife tightly, she darted between the dueling men until she reached Much. He had managed to pull himself upright and was furiously tugging at the ropes that bound his wrists.

She ran up behind him and clasped his arm. "Stop moving! I have a knife."

Much froze, and Mariah set the blade on the rope. Her first slice severed a few fibers, but the rope was so thick that her efforts scarcely made a difference. With her heart pounding, she attempted to block out the surrounding chaos and began sawing. More fibers gave way.

"Make 'aste, Maid Marian," Much muttered.

Gritting her teeth, Mariah pressed down harder on the blade and pulled it toward her.

The last of the rope severed, and Much yanked his right hand loose. "Praise the 'eavens!" He pivoted. Rope still hung from his left wrist, but his arms were free. "Give me the knife," he begged. "I must enter the fight." She handed it to him. "Bless you, Maid Marian," he said, and then he raced across the clearing to aid Friar Tuck.

Mariah frantically scoured the once-peaceful clearing that was now a battlefield. Where was Ellen? And the friars? If they were truly who she thought they were, would they take cover, as Robin had suggested? Or would they join the conflict?

Several yards away, Little John released a powerful roar, and as the giant of a man knocked one of the guards to the ground with his quarterstaff, Mariah caught sight of Robin. His bow was now slung across his shoulder, and he held a knife in his hand. His back was to her, his attention on the two guards advancing on him with drawn swords. He began circling slowly to the left. The guards adjusted, approaching steadily. Mariah's breath caught. Surely Robin could not take on two men at once.

She took an instinctive step toward him before rational thought took over. Without her bow, she was powerless to help him, and if she distracted Robin in any way, it could prove fatal. Forcing herself to breathe, she watched as the guard on Robin's right lunged at him. Robin darted left, but the other guard must have anticipated his move. He thrust his right arm forward, the tip of his sword directed at Robin's chest. Robin leaped back a pace, pivoted, and swung out his leg. The guard at his right tripped, and Robin pounced, wrestling for control of the man's sword. But before Robin could take possession of the weapon, the second guard was upon him.

In horror, Mariah watched the second guard raise his arm, preparing to thrust his blade into Robin's back. "Robin!" she screamed.

Robin spun around and seized his assailant's wrist. The guard cried out in pain, his weapon wavering. But the first guard had regained his footing. He turned on Robin, and holding his sword firmly in both hands, the man swung hard and fast. He had a clear target, but before his blade hit its mark, it was knocked off course by a stout stick. Mariah gasped, hardly able to believe her eyes as David o' Doncaster appeared at Robin's side.

Taking advantage of his larger frame, David pushed the guard backward, his stick and the guard's sword trapped between them. Robin launched himself at the remaining guard. The man stumbled back a few paces before falling to the ground with Robin on top of him. They rolled, and the guard's blade flashed as he raised it once again.

"No!" The word escaped Mariah's lips in an agonized whisper, but before she could utter anything more, Robin drew one knee up and heaved the guard over his body.

The guard's head hit the ground with a thump. Robin leaped to his feet, and while the guard was still regaining his wits, Robin seized his sword, darted around another skirmish, and disappeared from sight.

Mariah pressed her hand to her mouth, staring at the guard who was slowly rising from the ground. He had almost killed Robin. She'd watched it happen and would likely see it again in her nightmares. She swallowed. For now, Robin was safe. But if David had not come when he had . . . She lowered her trembling hand. She could not go there. Not while the battle was far from over.

There was no sign of the guard David had been fighting, but David was already wielding his stick against another of the sheriff's men. Mariah searched the area for Ellen, finally spotting her standing at the edge of the clearing, her devastated expression a reflection of Mariah's churning emotions.

"Ellen!" Mariah started toward her but made it only two steps before a gloved hand caught her arm and wrenched her backward.

"One captive in exchange for another," the Sheriff of Nottingham hissed. "I believe that is only fair."

Mariah met his hate-filled eyes and could barely repress a shudder. If there had ever been any hint of goodness in this man, it had been stamped out by his overarching quest for vengeance, power, and wealth. Fear churned in her stomach, but so too did anger.

"You are despicable!" she cried.

Baring his yellowed teeth, he dragged her toward a nearby tree, then standing with his back to the trunk, he pulled her up against him and pressed the tip of his dagger to her throat. "Call me what you will, Maid Marian," he growled. "You are the one who shall seal Robin Hood's demise." He raised his voice and called out across the clearing, "Surrender, Robin Hood, or Maid Marian dies!"

Immediately, the fighting came to an uneasy halt. The only sounds were the faint moans of the wounded and the ragged breaths of those who had been fighting for their lives only moments before.

Robin stepped out from behind Alan a Dale. His bow was in his hands once more, his arrow nocked and ready. "Release her, or you shall suffer the consequences, my lord sheriff!"

"Forgive me if I do not believe you," the sheriff sneered. "Methinks that capturing this maiden has given me the upper hand."

"Taxing the good citizens of Nottingham until they have no food to feed their children, consigning innocents to the cesspool you call the dungeon, and hanging those who remain loyal to King Richard is no longer enough to satisfy your evil designs, then?" Robin asked. "You wish to add the killing of blameless young maidens to your vast list of misdeeds as well?"

"This woman is far from blameless," the sheriff spat. "She is one of yours and assisted in your escape from the gallows. That is crime enough for her to hang."

The sheriff's threat should have been sufficient to send ice through Mariah's veins. Instead, she experienced an unexpected surge of courage. She could not tell whether it was because Robin had yet to lower his bow or because Little John was surreptitiously weaving his way around the dazed men toward her or because the sheriff considered her to be one of Robin's band. She only knew that she refused to wilt beneath the sheriff's contemptuous threats. Lifting her chin, she turned her gaze to the cluster of friars standing beside the fire. Were they listening? Could they discern the sheriff's dark heart beneath his costly clothing?

"Where I am from," Mariah said loudly, "no one has the authority to put a person to death."

The sheriff tightened his hold on her, and his knife shifted. She held completely still.

"Then you shall rue the day you left that place," he said. "In Nottingham, I am the law, and I answer to nobody."

"Not even the king?" she asked.

The sheriff snorted. "England's king cares nothing about what occurs here!"

"Long live King Richard!" Friar Tuck shouted.

All around her, Robin's men raised their fists, repeating the words in a resounding chorus. It was exactly the distraction they'd needed. Across the distance that separated them, Mariah met Robin's eyes and caught his subtle nod. In one swift movement, she raised her foot and ground her heel into the sheriff's soft shoe. He grunted in pain, dropped his gaze, and shifted his weight to the left. Robin's arrow sailed past Mariah's shoulder, catching the edge of the sheriff's cloak and pinning him to the tree.

The sheriff gave a furious shout, and swinging Mariah around, he lowered his knife long enough to tug himself free.

Little John was ready. He stepped forward, and with one powerful swing of his quarterstaff, he hit the sheriff soundly across the back. The vile man swayed, and Mariah broke out of his grasp right before his legs crumpled.

"Little John!" Much hurried to the outlaw's side, a length of the rope that had been used to bind his own wrists in his hand. "Take this," he said. "It seems only fittin' to use it on 'im."

"Indeed, it does," Little John said, deftly wrapping the rope around the sheriff's arms.

Mariah swiveled. All around them, the sheriff's men were standing statuesque, their expressions a mixture of shock and panic. The one closest to Will Scarlet roused himself and raised his sword, but an arrow landed at his feet before he could do anything more.

"If you value your lives, you will all drop your weapons." Robin's commanding voice cut through the clearing, his readied bow pointed toward the largest group of guards. Thuds and the clatter of falling metal followed. "Ensure that every guard is disarmed, men, and then relocate them to the old oak. Friar Tuck, if you and Ellen would be good enough to fetch some rope, I would be most grateful. I believe we will be in need of a fair amount."

On shaking limbs, Mariah started toward Robin. Out of the corner of her eye, she saw the friars approaching from the other direction.

Her initial fears came surging back. Picking up her skirts, she managed an unsteady run.

Robin saw her coming. "Marian!" Lowering his bow to the ground, he gathered her in his arms and held her tightly. "I thank the heavens that you are safe! Did he hurt you?"

"No." Though she desperately wanted to stay in his embrace, she pulled back. "But there is something else." Until they confirmed the friars' true identities, no one in Sherwood was out of danger. Especially Robin. She looked over his shoulder. The lead friar was almost upon them. "I need to speak with you most urgently."

His brow furrowed. "You can say whatever you wish."

"Not here." She reached for his hand just as the friars joined them.

Robin gave her a puzzled look but curved his fingers around hers willingly. "I beg your pardon, friar." He offered the one who had sat beside him at dinner an apologetic look. "Had I any indication that our time together would be interrupted by a violent confrontation, I would have sent you on your way rather than have you witness it. I pray that neither you nor your brothers were injured."

"We are well enough," the friar said.

"I am relieved to hear it." Robin inclined his head. "If you would excuse me, Maid Marian needs a moment of my time, but I shall return to speak with you directly."

Mariah could not see the man's face beneath his hood, but she sensed a stiffening. Perhaps he wasn't used to being dismissed. More concerned than ever that her theory had validity, she attempted to maintain an unhurried pace as she led Robin away from the robed men.

"What is so urgent that it cannot wait until we have the sheriff and his men away from here?" Robin asked.

"The friars." The words tumbled out. "I . . . I think the talkative one may be King Richard. And the others—the ones who haven't said much—they're probably his knights."

Robin stared at her. "After what we have so recently endured, I am twice amazed that you would jest about so serious a matter."

"I wish I were." Her grasp on his hand tightened. "Something like this happened in one of the films I saw about Robin Hood."

Lines formed along his forehead. "The moving, talking pictures you told me about?"

"Yes. The king and his men came to the forest disguised as abbots."

"Why would they do that?"

"To get a clearer understanding of what had been happening in Sherwood Forest while the king was gone."

Robin's gaze shifted to the remains of the roasted venison near the fire, and his face blanched. "I pray you are mistaken."

"It's possible." Her voice caught. "But I think I heard the rattle of chainmail beneath his robe."

"The horses!"

"What about the horses?"

"Friars are known to travel on foot or, at best, by mule. I have yet to encounter one with the means to own a horse. And yet each of these men arrived upon one." He ran his hand across his face. "Merciful heavens, what have I done?"

"Nothing," she said desperately.

"Notwithstanding causing the death of a royal forester all those years ago, I poached the king's deer," he reminded her. "Feeding it to the monarch while expounding volubly upon his failings—not to mention capturing his sheriff in front of his very eyes—all but seals my fate."

"The villain tied up beneath the old oak is not *his* sheriff. The current Sheriff of Nottingham cares nothing for King Richard." She glanced over her shoulder. "I may be wrong. They might just be friars."

"But more likely, you are right, and we are in the presence of royalty." Robin turned to look at the men whose long brown cowls hid their faces from view. "I believe it is time to discover the truth."

With stoic calm, he led her back toward the gathered men. One member of the group murmured something to the friar who had spoken to Robin earlier, causing that friar to turn to watch their approach.

Releasing Marian's hand, Robin dropped to one knee and bowed his head. "I humbly beg your forgiveness, Sire."

A second hush fell over the clearing. And then the man standing before Robin pulled back his hood. His golden-colored hair and beard were partially covered by a chainmail coif, but his regal bearing was unmistakable.

Awareness and recognition rippled through the watching men, immediately followed by gasps of wonder. In unison, every person still standing lowered onto one knee. Mariah knelt beside Robin, watching dazedly as the other men who had posed as friars revealed themselves. Beneath their brown robes, they each wore a hauberk topped with a white surcoat decorated with a red cross. As one, the knights drew their swords.

Mariah took an unsteady breath as the enormity of this moment washed over her. She was in the presence of Richard the Lionheart and those who had accompanied him on his crusades.

"What would you have me forgive you of, Robin Hood?" the king asked, his tone grim. "The death of a forester, the poaching of my deer, the trespassing on my land, the repeated robberies that have plagued those traveling through Sherwood Forest, the seizure of the sheriff and his men, or the stark criticism you meted out so freely during our recent meal?"

Two of the knights stepped closer, the tips of their swords hovering inches from Robin's chest. Helpless to do anything to save him, the Merry Men watched with stunned expressions. Mariah caught the flicker of pain in Robin's eyes as King Richard reviewed the condemning list, but Robin did not flinch beneath the monarch's reproving gaze or the knights' threatening presence.

"Though I can deny none of those things," Robin said, "I kneel before you as a loyal and devoted subject whose intent has been to relieve the suffering of others and defend the rightful king's claim to the throne."

A muscle twitched in King Richard's jaw. "Noble sentiments indeed, and yet I cannot ignore the very laws that govern our land over one man's claim of moral decency."

"Then permit me to take the blame and suffer the punishment for the misdeeds attributed to the band of men in Sherwood Forest," Robin said. "And allow my men to go free."

Mariah's chest tightened. This was all wrong. King Richard was supposed to exonerate Robin Hood. That was how every version of the legend ended. Wasn't there something she could do or say to sway the king? He had been given a front-row seat to the Sheriff of Nottingham's perfidy. She scanned the Merry Men's stricken faces and then turned her attention to the knights. One of the knights was moving. He strode past his companions and dropped to one knee beside Robin.

"Your Majesty," he said. "If I may be so bold, I would ask that you look kindly upon this outlaw."

The king frowned. "You are a beloved knight, Sir Henry, but in this instance, your plea is misplaced."

"Sire, I recently learned that my father, Sir Richard of the Lea—whose welfare is as dear to me as my own—owes his life, honor, and everything he holds dear to this Robin Hood." He hesitated as if girding his courage. "As one who has stepped between you and death on multiple occasions in Palestine, I beg of you to consider pardoning this man. Though he may be considered an outlaw to many, he has been a beacon of hope for others and the means of rescuing one of your most worthy knights from the clutches of evil men."

The shock on Robin's face gave way to gratitude. Mariah swallowed the lump in her throat. Sir Henry had done what no one but Sir Richard of the Lea himself could have attempted. Clasping her hands, she waited, silently praying that the king would listen to his brave knight.

"You would have me pardon the most renowned outlaws in England, Sir Henry?"

"Aye, Sire. For I am assured that there is much good to be had amongst them, and in an England rife with traitors, they have already proved themselves true to your cause."

King Richard raised his head, his gaze flitting to the bound sheriff and his guards before following the circle of men kneeling deferentially around him. Finally, he directed his attention back to the two men at his feet.

"Arise, Sir Henry," he said. "Your love for your king and your father does you great credit." He waited until the knight was on his feet. "Robin Hood, notwithstanding your lawless past, can I take you at your word that you and your men will serve me unquestioningly from this day forth?"

"I pledge my life upon it, Sire."

"Then rise a free man. And your fair maiden and men the same."

Tears pricked Marian's eyes as Robin helped her to her feet amid the jubilant cheers of his men. His face shone with elation, but before he could say a word, the king raised his hand. Silence immediately fell over them again.

"Though you are pardoned, I cannot permit this band of men to continue to roam the forest as it has done in the past. Your leader has pledged you to my service, and so I would ask that those of you who are of a mind to employ your skills with the bow in the defense of your king return with me to London as members of my guard. Those who wish to remain in Nottinghamshire shall do so as royal foresters, sworn to be law-abiding caretakers of my forest.

"My men and I shall stay in Nottingham until the morrow, whereupon those who choose to join my guard will leave with us." His expression became grave. "I shall be grateful for assistance as I root out dishonorable guards and mete out swift punishments on a certain sheriff and bishop who appear to have chosen corruption and avarice over loyalty and watch care."

Mariah looked at Robin. Would he choose to go with the king? He was, by far, the best archer among the Merry Men, and he deserved the recognition he would receive as a member of the royal guard. But if her experience at the tournament in Nottingham were any indication, no matter how well she used the bow, she would not be welcome in the king's entourage.

At the close of the king's announcement, a second cheer rang out, and soon, the clearing was filled with spirited conversations.

"You have my deepest gratitude, Sire," Robin said.

"Sir Henry's reminder was well taken, and coming as it did on the heels of the sheriff's condemning diatribe, it was wise counsel. Much has changed in England since I have been gone—including allegiances. I must surround myself with those whom I can trust." He eyed Robin speculatively. "Which will you choose, Robin Hood? To ride alongside your king or to protect his land?"

"If I may serve my king in either situation, I shall remain in Nottinghamshire," Robin said. "For though the one will likely offer great adventures, the other allows me to have Maid Marian at my side."

"Robin," Mariah gasped. "Are you sure that is what you want?"

Robin nodded. "More sure than I have ever been."

King Richard raised an amused eyebrow. "I must say, you have taken your defeat at this young lady's hands remarkably well."

"In truth, Sire, she can best me in most things, and I have come to love her more than life itself." He met Mariah's eyes. "And now that I am a free man, I pray that someday soon, she will agree to be my bride."

"What say you to that, Maid Marian?" the king asked.

Mariah reached for Robin's hand, struggling to find her voice over her brimming emotions. Over the last few months, there had been more than one occasion when she'd almost lost him. And having already tasted of that agony, she had no need to question her heart again. "I say yes."

King Richard laughed. It was the first time he'd shown real pleasure since he'd arrived, and the simple act seemed to lift years and the
weight of the throne off his shoulders. "In truth," he said, "mayhap
there should be a wedding before this band of brothers disperses."

Robin tightened his grip on Mariah's hand. "Will you marry me,
Marian? First thing in the morn so that Ellen and the Merry Men
may celebrate with us?"

A wedding in Sherwood Forest, surrounded by friends and loved
ones. It was exactly what she would have chosen.

"Can we have the ceremony in the grove?" she asked.

The warmth of his smile filled her heart to overflowing. "I cannot conceive of a better place."

Mariah entered the grove as the faint light of dawn was just beginning to dispel the shadows of night. She wrapped her cloak more
closely around herself, the nip in the air warning of colder weather
on its way. Above her head, a bird sang in the ash tree, its trill barely
audible above the babble of the stream. The leaves on the trees were
starting to turn from their various shades of green to yellow, orange,
and brown. A light dusting of them coated the mossy grass, adding
a slight crunch to her footsteps.

She had craved the peace found in the grove. If only for a few
minutes. Today was to be her wedding day, and though she had been
grateful for the enthusiasm and excitement that had filled the cave
last evening, she needed a short time to ponder quietly before her life
changed once again.

Her thoughts turned to her former life in London. The mental images of the places where she'd spent almost all her time—her
one-bedroom flat, the kitchen at Ricardo's, and the Tube ride between
them—were beginning to fade. They were so far removed from her
present reality that they'd taken on a dreamlike quality. She closed her
eyes, picturing her father as she'd last seen him, waving goodbye to

her before leaving to return to his new home in Portugal. She couldn't deny an ache of regret that he would not be here to see her get married. But more than that, she wished that he could know of the happiness she'd found here with Robin.

A twig cracked. Mariah opened her eyes and turned to follow the sound. Someone was coming. Someone wearing a green dress covered in enormous pink flowers.

Mariah's mouth went dry. "Mrs. McQuivey?"

"Ah, there you are dear." The white-haired lady, dressed just as she had been all those months ago, cut through a small gap between two beech trees. "I've found another dress for you to try on."

"I . . . I don't understand. How did you get here?"

"The same way as you, dear." She stepped forward and eyed the brown cloak that covered the white smock and green kirtle Mariah had first donned in the woman's costume shop. "Would you like to go back to the changing room to try on something else?"

To leave Sherwood Forest? Leave Robin?

Mariah knew a moment of panic. "Do I have to?"

"Of course not. If you are happy with your selection, there's no need to make a change."

"I don't have to return . . . ever? I can stay here, in this place and time?"

"Yes, dear. If that is what you want."

Relief caught at Mariah's throat, and in that moment, she knew with certainty that she was exactly where she was supposed to be. "I'd really like to stick with what I have now," she said.

Mrs. McQuivey's hazel eyes twinkled behind her pink-framed glasses. "It does my heart good to know that you're pleased. Sometimes, we don't realize what it is we need until we've found it."

Like love. And a place that truly felt like home.

"Thank you for helping me," Mariah said.

The older lady smiled. "Well, if you're happy, I shall go back to the shop."

"Will I see you again?"

"Not unless you require another outfit." She glanced at the gown draped over her arm. "I think maybe I'll leave this one with you. You can try it on at your leisure. It's the same size and time period as the one you're wearing, but it's a little fancier." She handed the costume to Mariah, who immediately ran her fingers across the light-blue kirtle's embroidered flowers.

"It's lovely."

Mrs. McQuivey gave a contented sigh. "Isn't it? And I'd say it's just the thing for a medieval wedding."

Mariah's fingers stilled. Mrs. McQuivey obviously knew a lot more than she was letting on.

"Before you go," Mariah said, "would you tell me what you can about Maid Marian?"

"Ah." The older lady's eyes were twinkling again. "Robin Hood's one true love."

"So, she was a real person?"

"Oh, I'm sure of it. Interestingly, she didn't appear in any of the original legends, and no one seems to know exactly who she was. She's been portrayed as a Norman noblewoman, a ward of Prince John, and a Saxon who knew Robin from childhood. Some historians claim she lived in Sherwood Forest and was an even more skilled archer than Robin himself."

Mariah smiled. It was as though she'd been handed the last piece of a puzzle. "I think I like that last version best," she said.

"Yes. It's rather nice to think that Robin had a wife who was his equal in that way."

The sound of footsteps in the dry leaves reached them, and Mrs. McQuivey stepped away. "I'd best be going."

"Wait!" Mariah said, a new and unforeseen possibility suddenly striking her. "Before you go, may I ask one more thing of you?"

Mrs. McQuivey paused, and Mariah took it as acceptance.

"If my father or Patrick from the London Archery Club ever come looking for me, would you tell them that I'm well and happy? Let them know that I've found the place where I belong."

"But of course."

Mariah's heart warmed at her willingness. "Thank you, Mrs. Mc-Quivey. For everything."

"It has been my pleasure, dear." The older lady smiled and raised her hand in farewell. "May your new life be filled with much joy, Maid Marian," she added, and then she disappeared between the trees.

Mariah was still staring at the empty gap when Robin walked into the grove.

"I thought I might find you here," he said, but his feet slowed as he approached, and a hint of concern entered his voice. "Are you well, Marian?"

"Yes." She took a deep breath and turned to face him. "So well. And so happy. Mrs. McQuivey was here."

"Mrs. McQuivey?" Robin's gaze darted from the fabric in Mariah's hands to the trees lining the grove. "The one from the shop in London?"

"Yes."

His concern was now visible in his eyes. "Why did she come?"

"She asked if I wished to go back."

"I . . . I see," he said. "And what did you say to that?"

Mariah gently set the kirtle on the ground and closed the short distance between them. She raised her arms and threaded them around his neck. "I thanked her for gifting me the life I was always meant to have in Sherwood Forest and for bringing me a new kirtle for my wedding."

His hands came around Mariah, drawing her closer. "Truly?"

She laughed softly. "Truly. And just before she left, I discovered something else." She met his eyes. "I am the Maid Marian in the Robin Hood legends."

He smiled. "I have known that for a very long time."

"You have?"

"Aye. When we first came to this grove, you told me that Maid Marian was my one true love." He trailed a line of soft kisses up her neck. "That meant it had to be you."

"Oh," she breathed.

He chuckled softly. "Happiest of wedding days, my darling. I love you more than you will ever know."

"And I love you, Robin."

His lips, now hovering close to hers, turned upward. "Ah, Maid Marian," he whispered. "Though I hardly deserve it, I knew that too."

AUTHOR'S NOTE

Robin Hood and Maid Marian are characters who have captured the attention and affection of people across the centuries. In recent history, countless books and movies have been created featuring these characters, and though each version of the story is slightly different, it wasn't until I began my research for this book that I came to realize how much the legends have changed over the centuries.

No one knows for certain if there was ever one particular man named Robin Hood. The title may have been given to several men—particularly outlaws—over the years. One of the oldest references to Robin Hood is found in a 1226 court register from Yorkshire, England, and the first known mention of him in English verse is found in *The Vision of Piers Plowman*, written by William Langland in the latter half of the fourteenth century.

Composed in the fifteenth century, *Robin Hood and the Monk* is one of the oldest known written ballads that mentions Robin Hood and is also the first one set in Sherwood Forest near Nottingham. Later ballads from this century show him as exacting vengeance on villains and aiding the downtrodden.

In the sixteenth century, the stories of Robin Hood were absorbed into May Day celebrations. The legends became less violent, and it became popular among the nobility to dress up as Robin Hood for the festivities. By the next century, Robin Hood had gone from being a yeoman to an aristocrat, and his experiences in

Sherwood Forest were intrinsically connected to him living there during the reign of Richard the Lionheart.

The legends of Robin Hood experienced a resurgence in the nineteenth century, after Walter Scott put his own spin on the character in his novel *Ivanhoe*, and Howard Pyle re-created some of the older legends in his book *The Merry Adventures of Robin Hood*.

For this book, I chose to use the legends recounted by Howard Pyle as my primary source. As in Pyle's book, the Robin in *The Maid of Sherwood Forest* is a yeoman, and the story he tells Mariah about how he became an outlaw comes from the old, traditional tales. Other anecdotes, such as Robin's dressing up as a butcher and giving away his meat for a kiss, the archery tournament, the rescue of Sir Richard of the Lea, and the arrival of King Richard and his knights disguised as friars, are all based on ancient stories.

During this time period, people would have spoken Middle English, and the discrepancy between the English spoken by Mariah and the English spoken by those living in twelfth-century Nottinghamshire would have been far greater than I have portrayed it. Like most novelists and filmmakers before me, however, I chose to minimize the differences in favor of readability.

In *The Maid of Sherwood Forest*, King Richard returns to England in October 1193. He actually returned in February 1194, following a long incarceration in Europe. It probably took him a few weeks to travel as far north as Nottingham, but Prince John's attempts to usurp the throne during Richard's absence made it imperative that Richard travel the country straightaway to assess the loyalty of those in positions of power.

Marian (or Marion, as her name is sometimes spelled) did not appear in the earlier versions of the Robin Hood stories. Even though the priory church of Little Dunmow in Essex boasts an alabaster tomb dedicated to Maid Marian, her identity is still uncertain. Most historians believe her character is based on Matilda Fitzwalter, the daughter of Robert, Baron Fitzwalter, but she has been portrayed in a variety of roles—from a wealthy, beautiful ward of the Crown to a female outlaw whose skills with the bow and sword rival Robin's.

Knowing that Marian's true identity remains a mystery made this time-slip adventure all the more fun to write. After all, if historians have yet to agree on the beautiful young lady's identity, who's to say that she couldn't have arrived in Nottingham from a far-distant place or time?

ACKNOWLEDGMENTS

When it comes time for me to write an acknowledgment for a novel, I'm always struck by how very many people play a vital part in that book's creation. Most of those people receive very little recognition for their efforts—other than a brief mention in the back of a book—but I hope they know how much I appreciate them.

A huge thank-you to all those at Shadow Mountain who have had a part in the publication of *The Maid of Sherwood Forest*. I'm especially grateful for my editor, Samantha Millburn. Not only is she incredibly skilled, but she's also a constant source of good advice and encouragement. Thank you, Heidi Gordon and Callie Hansen, for all you do behind the scenes. I'm glad we now have a story for your title, Heidi. Thanks also to Halle Ballingham for designing such a beautiful cover, and to Amy Parker, Tasha Bradford, and the rest of the marketing team for being marketing wonders and unfailingly supportive.

I'm so thankful for Marilee Merrell, who was the first person to read this manuscript and has championed it all the way to release day. I'm also grateful to Gabrielle Meyer and Michelle Griep, who gave of their precious time to read early versions of this book. The writing community is remarkable, and I'm so grateful to be part of it. The friendships I've formed with authors and readers alike are some of my greatest treasures.

I could not write without the unqualified support of my husband and family members. I am eternally grateful to each of them. And I am especially grateful to my Heavenly Father, who has blessed me with the opportunity to share stories with others and who lifts and guides me on the days when writing is hard.

BOOK CLUB QUESTIONS

1. *The Maid of Sherwood Forest* takes place in both modern-day London and medieval Nottingham. How does the author contrast these two time periods?

2. Mariah has to rely on her resourcefulness to adapt to life in an unfamiliar time. What were some of the ways she used her ingenuity to survive? Were there any moments when you thought her actions might be too risky?

3. Mariah is torn between her modern identity and a new life in medieval times. How does this inner conflict shape her actions and decisions, particularly when it comes to her relationship with Robin Hood?

4. What does "home" mean to Mariah, and how does her concept of home evolve as the novel progresses?

5. Trust and betrayal are recurring themes in the book. How do betrayal and loyalty play out in the story? Discuss the moments when characters had to make difficult choices about who to trust and how those choices affected the plot.

6. How did the author balance the historical aspects of Robin Hood's legend with the fictional addition of Mariah and her time travel? Did you think the historical elements were well researched and integrated into the story?

7. Love is a central theme in this book. How does Mariah and Robin's relationship highlight the importance of sacrifice in relationships? Are there any moments where one character has to sacrifice something important for the other?

8. If you were suddenly transported to a completely different time and place, what skills or knowledge do you think would help you survive? How would you adapt to a world that's drastically different from your own?

9. Robin Hood and his band of outlaws are key figures in the book. How does the portrayal of Robin Hood's outlaw band differ from other versions of the tale you might know? What does the author do to make these familiar characters feel fresh and compelling?

10. Archery is an important skill in the book. How do Mariah's skills change the dynamics within the story? How does her proficiency with the bow impact her relationship with Robin Hood and his men?

11. Mariah's modern values sometimes clash with the medieval values she's surrounded by. How do you think such principles as justice, punishment, forgiveness, and inclusion differ between the two time periods? How do these clashes influence Mariah's decisions?

12. Which of the secondary characters in this book did you find the most compelling and why? How important are they to the story as a whole?

13. What do you think Mariah most needed to learn through her time-travel experience? How did she learn it? In what ways was she a stronger character at the end of the book than she was at its beginning?

14. How does humor play a role in this book? Does the author's use of humor endear you to any character in particular? If so, which one and how?

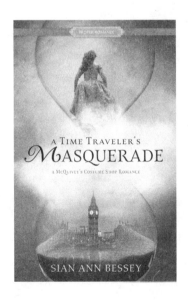

ABOUT THE AUTHOR

SIAN ANN BESSEY was born in Cambridge, England, and was raised on the island of Anglesey in North Wales. She moved to the US to attend university and earned a bachelor's degree in communications with a minor in English.

An award-winning *USA Today* bestselling author, Sian writes historical romance and romantic suspense, along with children's books. She is a RONE Award runner-up and a Foreword Reviews Book of the Year finalist.

She and her husband live in southeast Idaho, where she enjoys reading, cooking, and spending time with her grandchildren. She also loves to travel, and though she doesn't have the opportunity to speak Welsh very often anymore, *Llanfairpwllgwyngyllgogerychwyrndrobwllllantysiliogogogoch* still rolls off her tongue.

She loves hearing from readers! Visit her website at www.sianannbessey.com, or follow her on Facebook (@sianannbessey) and Instagram (@sian_bessey).